"1914"

"1914"

JOHN OXENHAM

WILDSDE PRESS

Originally published in 1916.
Published by Wildside Press, LLC.
Visit us online at wildsidepress.com

CHAPTER I

THE early morning of July 25th, 1914, was not at all such as the date might reasonably have led one to expect. It was gray and overcast, with heavy dew lying white on the grass and a quite unseasonable rawness in the air.

The clock on the mantelpiece of the morning-room in The Red House, Willstead, was striking six, in the sonorous Westminster chimes, which were so startlingly inconsistent with its size, as Mr John Dare drew the bolts of the French window and stepped out on to his back lawn.

He had shot the bolts heavily and thoughtfully the night before, long after all the rest had gone up to bed, though he noticed, when he went up himself, that Noel's light still gleamed under his door. His peremptory tap and 'Get to bed, boy!' had produced an instant eclipse, and he determined to speak to him about it in the morning.

He had never believed in reading in bed himself. Bed was a place in which to sleep and recuperate. If it had been a case of midnight oil and the absorption of study now—all well and good. But Noel's attitude towards life in general and towards study in particular permitted no such illusion.

And it was still heavily and thoughtfully that Mr Dare drew back the bolts and stepped out into the gray morning. Not that he knew definitely that this twenty-fifth of July was a day big with the fate of empires and nations, and of the world at large,—simply that he had not slept well; and bed, when you cannot sleep, is the least restful place in the world.

As a rule he slept very soundly and woke refreshed, but for many nights now his burdened brain had neglected its chances, and had chased, and been chased by, shadowy phantoms,—possibilities, doubts, even fears, —which sober daylight scoffed at, but which, nevertheless, seemed to lurk in his pillow and swarm out for his undoing the moment he laid his tired head upon it.

Out here in the fresh of the morning,—which ought by rights to have been full of sunshine and beauty, the cream of a summer day,—he could, as a rule, shake off the shadows and get a fresh grip on realities and himself.

But the very weather was depressing. The year seemed already on the wane. There were fallen leaves on the lawn. The summer flowers were despondent. There was a touch of red in the Virginia creeper which covered the house. The roses wore a downcast look. The hollyhocks and sweet-peas showed signs of decrepitude. It seemed already Autumn, and the chill damp air made one think of coming Winter.

And the unseasonal atmospheric conditions were remarkably akin to his personal feelings.

For days he had had a sense of impending trouble in business matters, all the more irritating because so ill-defined and impalpable. Troubles that one could tackle in the open one faced as a matter of course, and got the better of as a matter of business. But this 'something coming and no knowing what' was very upsetting, and his brows knitted perplexedly as he paced to and fro, from the arch that led to the kitchen-garden to the arch that led to the front path, up which in due course Smith's boy would come whistling with the world's news and possibly something that might cast a light on his shadows.

Mr Dare's business was that of an import and export merchant, chiefly with the Continent, and his offices were in St Mary Axe. He had old connections all over Europe and was affiliated with the Paris firm of Leroux and Cie, Charles Leroux having married his sister.

As a rule his affairs ran full and smooth, with no more than the to-be-expected little surface ruffles. But for some weeks past he had been acutely conscious of a disturbance in the commercial barometer, and so far he had failed to make out what it portended.

Politically, both at home and abroad, matters seemed much as usual, always full of menacing possibilities, to which, however, since nothing came of them, one had grown somewhat calloused.

The Irish brew indeed looked as if it might possibly boil over. That gun-running business was not at all to his mind. But he was inclined to think there was a good deal of bluff about it all. And the suffragettes were ramping about and making fools of themselves in their customary senseless fashion, and doing all the damage they possibly could to their own cause and to the nation at large.

The only trouble of late on the Continent had been the murder of the Archduke Ferdinand and his wife about a month before. And that seemed to be working itself off in acrimonious snappings and yappings by the Austrian and Servian papers. Austria would in due course undoubtedly claim such guarantees of future good behaviour on the part of her troublesome little neighbour as the circumstances, when fully investigated, should call for. The tone of the note she had sent, calling on Servia no longer to permit the brewing of trouble within her borders, was somewhat brusque no doubt but not unnaturally so. And Servia, weary with her late struggles, would, of course, comply and there the matter would end.

It was unthinkable that the general peace should suffer from such a cause when it had survived the great flare-up in the Balkans the year before. Austria would not dare to go too far since she must first consult Germany, and the Kaiser, it was well known, desired nothing better than to maintain the peace which he had kept so resolutely for five-and-twenty years. If it had been that hot-head, the Crown Prince, now— But fortunately for the world the reins were in cooler hands.

Then again the Money Market here showed no more disturbance than was to be expected under such unsettled conditions, and the Bank-rate remained at three per cent. The Berlin and Vienna Bourses were somewhat unsettled. But there were always adventurous spirits abroad ready to take advantage of any little disturbance and reap nefarious harvests.

Anyway he could see no adequate connection between any of these things and the sudden stoppage of his deliveries of beet-sugar from Germany and Austria, and the unusual lapsus in correspondence and remittances from both those countries,—which matters were causing him endless worry and anxiety.

His brother-in-law, Leroux, in Paris, had hinted at no gathering clouds, as he certainly would have done had any been perceptible. And the sensitive pulse of international affairs on the Bourse there would have perceived them instantly if they had existed. The very fact that M. Poincaré, the President, was away in Russia was proof positive that the sky was clear.

The only actual hint of anything at all out of the common was in that last letter from his eldest girl, Lois, who had been studying at the Conservatorium in Leipsic for the last two years.

She had written, about a week before,—"What is brewing? There is a spirit of suppressed excitement abroad here, but I cannot learn what it means. They tell me it is the usual preparation for the Autumn manœuvres. It may be so, but all the time I have been here I have never seen anything quite like it. If they were preparing for war I could understand it, but that is of course out of the question, since the Kaiser's heart is set on peace, as everyone knows."

There was not much in that in itself, though Lois was an unusually level-headed girl and not likely to lay stress on imaginary things. But that, and the evasiveness, when it was not silence, of his German correspondents, and the non-arrival of his contracted-for supplies of beet-sugar, had set his mind running on possibilities from which it recoiled but could not shake itself entirely free.

5

Presently, as he paced the well-defined track he had by this time made across the dewy lawn, he heard the rattle of the kitchen grate as heavy-handed Sarah lit the fire, and the gush of homely smoke from the chimney had in it a suggestion of breakfast that put some of his shadows to flight. Sarah and breakfast were substantial every-day facts before which the blue devils born of broken sleep temporarily withdrew.

Then from behind Honor's wide-open window and drawn curtains he heard her cheerful humming as she dressed. And then her curtains were switched aside with a strenuous rattle, and at sight of him she stuck out her head with a saucy,

"Hello, Mr Father! Got the hump? What a beast of a day! I say,—you *are* wearing a hole in that carpet. Doesn't look much of a day for a tennis tournament, does it? Rotten! I just wish I had the making of this country's weather; anyone who wished might make her—"

Smith's boy's exuberant whistle sounded in the front garden, and Honor chimed in, "Good-bye, Piccadilly!"—as her father hastened to the gate to get his paper.

Smith's boy was just preparing to fold and hurl it at the porch—a thing he had been strictly forbidden to do, since on wet and windy days it resulted in an unreadable rag retrieved from various corners of the garden instead of a reputable news-sheet. At the unexpected appearance of Mr Dare in the archway, his merry pipe broke off short at the farewell to Leicester Square, and Honor's clear voice round the corner carried them triumphantly to the conclusion that it was "a long long way to Tipperary," without obbligato accompaniment. The boy grinned, and producing a less-folded paper from his sheaf, retired in good order through the further gate, and piped himself bravely up the Oakdene path next door, while Mr Dare shook the paper inside out and stood searching for anything that might in any way bear upon his puzzle.

His anxious eye leaped at once to the summary of foreign news, and his lips tightened.

"The Austrian Minister has been instructed to leave Belgrade unless the Servian Government complies with the Austrian demand by 6 p.m. this evening."

An ultimatum!... Bad!... Dangerous things, ultimatums!

"It is stated that Russia has decided to intervene on behalf of Servia."

"H'm! If Russia,—then France! If France,—then Germany and Italy!... And how shall we stand? It is incredible," and he turned hastily for hope of relief to the columns of the paper, and read in a leader headed "*Europe and th Crisis*,"—"All who have the general peace at heart must hope that Austria has not spoken her last word in the note to Servia, to which she requires a reply to-night. If she has we stand upon the edge of war, and of a war fraught with dangers that are incalculable to all the Great Powers."

Then the front door opened and his wife came out into the porch.

"Breakfast's ready, father," she said briskly. "Any news?"

She was a very comely woman of fifty or so, without a gray hair yet and of an unusually pleasing and cheerful countenance. The girls got their good looks from her, the boys took more after their father.

"Any light on matters?" asked Mrs Dare hopefully again, as he came slowly along the path towards her. And then, at sight of his face, "Whatever is it, John?"

He had made it a rule to leave ordinary business worries behind him in town where they properly belonged. But matters of moment he frequently discussed with his wife and had found her aloof point of view and clear common-sense of great assistance at times. His late disturbance of mind had been very patent to her, but, beyond the simple facts, he had been able to satisfy her no more than himself.

"Very grave news, I'm afraid," he said soberly. "Austria and Servia look like coming to blows."

"Oh?" said Mrs Dare, in a tone which implied no more than interested surprise. "I should have thought Servia had had enough fighting to last her for some time to come."

"I've no doubt she has. It's Austria driving at her. Russia will probably step in, and so Germany, Italy, France, and maybe ourselves—"

"John!"—very much on the alert now.—"It is not possible."

"I'm afraid it's even probable, my dear. And if it comes it will mean disaster to a great many people."

"What about Lois? Will she be safe out there?"

"We must consider that. I've hardly got round to her yet. Let us make sure of one more comfortable breakfast anyway," he said, with an attempt at lightness which he was far from feeling, and as they went together to the breakfast-room, Honor came dancing down the stairs.

"Hello, Dad! Did they give extra prizes for early rising at your school?" she asked merrily, and ran on without waiting for an answer, —"And did you choke that boy who was whistling 'Tipperary'? I had to finish without accompaniment and he was doing it fine. He has a musical soul. It was Jimmy Snaggs. He's in my class at Sunday School. You should hear him sing."

"You tell him again from me that if he can't deliver papers properly he'd better find some other walk in life," said Mr Dare, as he chipped an egg and proceeded with his breakfast.

"It looks all right," said Honor, picking up the paper. "Let's see the cricket. Old No's aching to hear. Hm—hm—hm—Kent beat Middlesex at

Maidstone,—Blythe and Woolley's fine bowling,—Surrey leads for championship. That's all right. Hello, what's all this?—'Servia challenged. King Peter's appeal to the Tsar. Grave decisions impending. The risk to Europe.' I—*say*! Is there going to be another war? How ripping!"

"Honor!" said her mother reprovingly.

"Well, I don't mean that, of course. But a war does make lively papers, doesn't it? I'm sick of Ireland and suffragettes."

"If this war comes you'll be sicker of it than of anything you ever experienced, before it's over, my dear," said Mr Dare gravely.

"Why?—Austria and Servia?"

"And Russia and Germany and France and Italy and possibly England."

"My Goodness! You don't mean it, Dad?" and she eyed him keenly. "I believe you're just—er—pulling my leg, as old No would say?" and she plunged again into the paper.

"Bitter fact, I fear, my dear."

"How about Lois? Will she be in the thick of it?" she asked, raising her head for a moment to stare meditatively at him, with the larger part of her mind still busy with the news.

"We were just thinking of her. I'm inclined to wire her to come home at once."

Then Noel strolled in with a nonchalant, "Morning everybody!... Say, Nor! What about the cricket? You promised—"

"Cricket's off, my son," said Honor, reading on. "It's war and a case of fighting for our lives maybe."

"Oh, come off!"—then, noticing the serious faces of the elders,—"Not really? Who with?"

"Everybody," said Honor. "—Armageddon!"

He went round to her and pored eagerly over the paper with his head alongside hers. They were twins and closely knit by many little similarities of thought and taste and feeling.

"Well!... I'll—be—bowled!" as he gradually assimilated the news. "Do you really think it'll come to a general scrap?"—to his father.

"Those who have better means of judging than I have evidently fear it, my boy. I shall learn more in the City no doubt," and he hurried on with his breakfast.

The front-door bell shrilled sharply.

"Post!" said Honor. "Must be something big," and dashed away to get it. She never could wait for the maid's leisurely progress when letters were in question, and she and the postman were on the best of terms. He always grinned when she came whirling to the door.

"Why—Colonel!" they heard her surprised greeting. "And Ray! You *are* early birds. I thought you were the post. What worms are you after now? Is it the War?"—as she ushered them into the drawing-room.

"Bull's-eye first shot," said a stentorian voice. "Has your father gone yet, Honor?"

"Just finishing his breakfast, Colonel. I'll tell him," and as she turned to go, her father came in.

"How are you, Colonel?" said Mr Dare. "Good morning, Ray! What are our prospects of keeping out of it, do you think?"

"None," said the Colonel gravely. "It's 'The Day' they've been getting ready for all these years, and that we've been expecting—some of us, and unable to get ready for because you others thought differently. But we want a word or two with Mrs Dare too. Will you beg her to favour us, Honor, my dear?" and Honor sped to summon her mother to the conference.

"We must apologise for calling at such an hour, Mrs Dare," said the Colonel, as they shook hands, "But the matter admits of no delay. Ray here wants your permission to go out and bring Lois home. We think she is in danger out there."

"You know how things are between us, dear Mrs Dare," broke in Ray impulsively. "We have never really said anything definite, but we understand one another. And if it's going to be a general scrap all round, as Uncle Tony is certain it is, then the sooner she is clear of it the better. I've never been easy in my mind about her since that little beast von Helse brought her over last year."

At which a reminiscent smile flickered briefly in the corners of Mrs Dare's lips and made Ray think acutely of Lois, who had just that same way of savouring life's humours.

"I was thinking of wiring for her to come home, as soon as I got to town," said Mr Dare.

"If my views are correct," said the Colonel weightily, "and I fear you'll find them so, travelling, over there, will be no easy matter. The moment mobilisation is ordered—and the possibility is that it's going on now for all they are worth,—everything will be under martial law,—all the railways in the hands of the military, all traffic disorganised,—possibly the frontiers closed. Everything chock-a-block, in fact. It may be no easy job to get her safely out even now. But if anyone can do it, in the circumstances, I'll back Ray. He's glib at German and knows his way about, and where Lois is concerned—"

"It is very good of you, Ray,"—began Mrs Dare, warmly.

"Not a bit. It's good of you to trust her to me. I can start in an hour, and I'll bring her back safe or know the reason why. Thank you so much!" and he gripped her hand and then suddenly bent forward and kissed her on the

9

cheek. "I'm nearly packed,"—at which Mrs Dare's smile flickered again. —"I'll cut away and finish. I must catch the ten o'clock from Victoria, and bar accidents I'll be in Leipsic to-morrow morning. You might perhaps give me just a little note for her, saying you approve my coming," and he hurried away to finish his preparations.

Honor and Noel heard him going and sped out after him, all agog to know what it was all about.

"Here! What's up among all you elderly people?" cried Noel.

"No time to talk, old man. They'll tell you all about it," Ray called over his shoulder and disappeared through the front gate.

"Well!—I'm blowed! Old Ray's got a move on him. What's he up to, I wonder."

"I'll tell you, No. He's going after Lois—"

"After Lois? Why—what's wrong with Lo?"

"Don't you see? If there's going to be war over there she might get stuck and not be able to get home for years—"

"Oh—years! It'll all be over in a month. Wars now-a-days don't run into time. It's too expensive, my child."

"Well, anyway, old Lo will be a good deal better safe at home than in the thick of it. And I guess that's what Ray and the Colonel think."

"I'd no idea they'd got that far. Of course I knew he was sweet on her. You could see that when that von Helse chap was here, and old Ray used to look as if he'd like to chew him up."

"I knew all about it."

"Of course. Girls always talk about these things."

"She never said a word. But I knew all the same."

"Kind of instinct, I suppose."

Here the elders came out of the drawing-room, preceded, as the door opened, by the Colonel's emphatic pronouncement,

"—Inevitable, my dear sir. We cannot possibly escape being drawn in. Their plans are certain to be based on getting in through Belgium and Luxembourg. We've been prepared for that for many years past. And if they touch Belgium the fat's in the fire, for we're bound to stop it—if we can. If some of us had had our way we'd be in a better position to do it than we are. Anyhow we'll have to do our best. We'd have done better if you others had had less faith in German bunkum. Noel, my boy," as Noel saluted, "We shall probably want you before we're through."

"You think it'll be a tough business, sir?"

"Tough? It'll be hell, my boy, before the slate's all clean again. And that won't be till the Kaiser and all his gang are wiped off it for ever."

"I thought it would be all over in a month or two."

"A year or two may be more like it. Germany is one big fighting-machine, and till it's smashed there'll be no peace in the world."

"Think they'll get over here, sir?" chirped Honor expectantly.

"They'll try, if we leave them a chance. Thank God,—and Winston Churchill—we're ready for them there. That man's looked ahead and he's probably saved England."

"Good old Winston!"

"If you're off, Dare, I'll walk along with you. I must call at the Bank. It won't do for Ray to run out of funds over there. Good-bye, Mrs Dare! Bring you good news in a day or two. Ta-ta, Honor!"

"You'll let me stand my share—" began Mr Dare, as they walked along together.

"Tut, man! You'll need all your spare cash before we're through and I've plenty lying idle."

"You really think it may be a long business?"

"I don't see how it can be anything else. Have you had no warnings of its coming from any of your correspondents?"

"We told you of Lois's letter. We've had nothing more than that—except delay in goods coming through—and in remittances."

"Exactly! Railways too busy carrying men and horses; and business men preferring to keep their money in their own hands. I tell you they've been working up to this for years, only waiting for the psychological moment."

"And why is this the psychological moment? The Servian affair hardly seems worth all the pother—"

"Do you remember a man named Humbert attacking the French War Minister in the Senate, about a fortnight ago, on the subject of their army,—no boots, no ammunition, no guns worth firing, no forts, and so on?"

"I remember something about it. I remember it struck me as a rather foolish display of joints in the armour—"

"And Petersburg was all upside down, the other day, with out-of-work riots. Crowds, one hundred thousand strong, slaughtering the police, even while Poincaré was visiting the Tsar. You remember that?"

"Yes."

"And at home here, matters in Ireland looked like coming to a head. In fact it looked like civil war."

"I never believed it would come to anything of the kind, as you know."

"But to that exceedingly clever busy-body, the Kaiser,—at least, he thinks he's exceedingly clever. It's possible to be too clever.—Well, here were his three principal enemies all tied up in knots. What better chance would he ever get?"

"H'm! All the same he seems doing his best to smooth things over."

"Bunkum, my boy!—all bunkum! He may try to save his face to the world at large, but I bet you they're quietly mobilising over there as fast as they know how to, and that's faster than we dream of. And the moment they're ready they'll burst out like a flood and sweep everything before them—unless we can dam it, damn 'em! Perhaps you'll look in this evening and tell me how the City feels about it," and at the door of the Bank they parted, and Mr Dare went on to his train in anything but a comfortable frame of mind.

CHAPTER II

THEY had been neighbours now for close on ten years and close friends for nine and a half of them.

Noel and Honor were mischievous young things of eight when the Dares took The Red House, and in their adventurous prowlings they very soon made the acquaintance of Miss Victoria Luard, aged nine and also of an adventurous disposition, who lived at Oakdene, the big white house next door with black oak beams all over its forehead,—"like Brahmin marks only the other way,"—as Honor said, which gave it a surprised, wide-awake, lifted-eyebrows look.

From the youngsters the acquaintance spread to the elder members of the two families, and grew speedily into very warm friendship, in spite of the fact that the Dares were all sturdy Liberals, and the Luards, as a family, staunch Conservatives.

Colonel Luard, V.C., C.B.—Sir Anthony indeed, but he always insisted on the Colonel, since, as he said, "That was my own doing, sir, but the other—da-ash it!—I'd nothing to do with that. It was in the family and my turn came."

He was small made, and of late inclined to stoutness which he strove manfully to subdue, and he wore a close little muzzle of a moustache, gray, almost white now, and slight side-whiskers in the style of the late highly-esteemed Prince Consort. But though his moustache and whiskers and hair and eyebrows all showed unmistakable signs of his seventy-eight years, his little figure—except in front—was as straight as ever. He was as full of fire and go as a shrapnel shell, and his voice, on occasion, was as much out of proportion to his size as was that of the clock with the deep Westminster chimes on the breakfast-room mantelpiece at The Red House.

He looked a bare sixty-five, but as a youngster he had been through the Crimean campaign and the Indian Mutiny, and in the latter gained the coveted cross "For Valour" by exploding a charge at a rebel fort-gate which had already cost a score of lives and still blocked Britain's righteous vengeance.

He had been on the Abyssinian Expedition and in the Zulu War, and had returned from the latter so punctured with assegai wounds that he vowed he looked like nothing but a da-asht pin-cushion. Then he came into the title, and a very comfortable income, through the death of an uncle, who had made money in the banking business and received his baronetcy as reward for party-services; and after one more campaign—up Nile with Wolseley after Gordon—the Colonel retired on his honors and left the field to younger men.

He found his brother, Geoff, just married and vicar of Iver Magnus, went to stop with him for a time, and stopped on—a very acceptable addition to the vicar's household. When the children came, who so acceptable, and in every way so adequate, a godfather as the Colonel? And, with the very comfortable expectations incorporated in him, how resist his vehement choice of names,—extraordinary as they seemed to the hopeful father and mother?

And so he had the eldest girl christened Alma, after his first engagement; and the boy who came next he named Raglan, after his first esteemed commander; and the next girl he was actually going to call Balaclava; but there Mrs. Vicar struck, and nearly wept herself into a fever, until they compounded on Victoria, after Her Majesty.

When Vic was five, and Ray ten, and Alma twelve, their father and mother both died in an heroic attempt at combating an epidemic of typhoid, and Uncle Tony shook off the dust and smells of Iver Magnus, bought Oakdene at Willstead, and set up his establishment there, with little Miss Mitten, the sister of his special chum Major Mitten—who had been pin-cushioned by the Zulus at the same time as himself only more so—as vice-reine.

Miss Mitten was sixty-seven if she was a day, but never admitted it even at census-time. She was an eminently early-Victorian little lady, had taught in a very select ladies' school, and had written several perfectly harmless little books, which at the time had obtained some slight vogue but had long since been forgotten by every one except the 'eminent authoress' herself, as some small newspaper had once unforgettably dubbed her.

She was as small and neat as the Colonel himself, and in spite of the ample living at Oakdene her slim little figure never showed any signs of even comfortable rotundity. She was in fact sparely made, and the later fat years had never succeeded in making good the deficiencies of the many preceding lean ones. She wore the neatest of little gray curls at the side of her head, and, year in year out, they never varied by so much as one single hair.

She was very gentle, a much better housekeeper than might have been expected, and was partial to the black silk dresses and black silk open-work mittens of the days of long ago. The youngsters called her Auntie Mitt., and the Colonel they called Uncle Tony. She alone of all their world invariably addressed the Colonel as 'Sir Anthony,' and in her case only he raised no objection, since he saw that she thereby obtained some peculiar little inward satisfaction.

Alma, the eldest girl, was, in this year of grace 1914, twenty-six, though you would never have thought it to look at her. She was a tall handsome girl, dark, as were all the Luards, and three years before this, had suddenly shaken off the frivolities of life and gone in for nursing, with an ardour and steady persistence which had surprised her family and greatly pleased the Colonel, whose still-keen, dark eyes twinkled understandingly and approvingly.

Raglan—Ray to all his friends—was twenty-four, two inches taller than Alma, broad of shoulder and deep of chest,—he had pulled stroke in his College eight, and his clean-shaven face, with its firm mouth and jaw and level brows, was good to look upon. He was studying the honourable profession of the law and intended to reach the Woolsack or know the reason why. Partly as a sop to the martial spirit of Uncle Tony, and also because he had deemed it a duty—though he speedily found it a pleasure also —he had joined the Territorials and was at this time a first lieutenant in the London Scottish, and a very fine figure he made in the kilt and sporran.

Victoria, who so narrowly escaped being Balaclava, was nineteen and the political heretic of the family. She was an ardent Home-Ruler, a Suffragist, a Land-Reformer, played an almost faultless game at tennis, could give the Colonel 30 at billiards and beat him 100 up with ten to spare; and held a ten handicap on the links. She was in fact very advanced, very full of energy and good spirits, and frankly set on getting out of life every enjoyable thrill it could be made to yield.

Their close intimacy with the Dares had been of no little benefit to all three of them. Accustomed from their earliest years to the atmosphere of an ample income, they had never experienced any necessity for self-denial, self-restraint, or any of the little dove-coloured virtues which add at times an unexpected charm to less luxurious lives.

They found that charm among the Dares and profited by it. To their surprise, as they grew old enough to understand it, they found their own easy lives narrower in many respects than their neighbours', although obviously Uncle Tony's open purse was as much wider and deeper than Mr Dare's as Oakdene, with its well-tended lawns and beds and shrubberies and orchard and kitchen-gardens, was larger than The Red House and its trifling acre. And yet, as children, they had always had better times on the other side of the hedge, when they had made a hole large enough to crawl through; and Christmas revels and Halloweens in The Red House were things to look back upon even yet.

Perhaps it was Mrs Dare that made all the difference. Auntie Mitt was a little dear and all that, and Uncle Tony was an old dear and as good as gold. But there was something about Mrs Dare which gave a different feeling to The Red House and everything about it; and Alma very soon arrived at the meaning of it, and expressed it, succinctly if exaggeratedly, when she said to Lois one day,

"Lo, I'd give Auntie Mitt and Uncle Tony ten times over for half your mother."

And Mrs Dare, understanding very clearly, had mothered them all alike so far as was possible. And her warm heart was large enough to take in the additional three without any loss, but rather gain, to her own four, and with benefit to the three which only the years were to prove.

The Luard youngsters, in short, had lived in circumstances so wide and easy that they had become somewhat self-centred, somewhat aloof from life less well-placed, somewhat careless of others so long as their own enjoyment of life was full and to their taste.

Auntie Mitt was not blind to it. In her precise little way she took upon herself—with justifiable misgiving that nothing would come of it—to point out to them that they were in danger of falling into the sin of selfishness. And, as she expected, her gentle remonstrances fell from them like water off lively little ducks' backs.

Uncle Tony considered them the finest children in the world, would not hear a word against them, and spoiled them to his heart's content and their distinct detriment.

Their association with the Dares saved them no doubt from the worst results of Uncle Tony's mistaken kindness, but even Mrs Dare could not make angels of them any more than she could of her own four. She could only do her best by them all and leave them to work out their own salvation in their own various ways.

Connal Dare, the eldest of her own tribe, had been in the medical profession since the age of eight, when the game of his heart had been to make the other three lie down on the floor, covered up with tidies and shawls, while he inspected their tongues, and timed their pulses by a toy-watch which only went when he wound it, which he could not do while holding a patient's pulse. As he invariably prescribed liquorice-water, carefully compounded in a bottle with much shaking beforehand, and acid drops, the others suffered his ministrations with equanimity so long as his medicaments lasted, but grew convalescent with revolting alacrity the moment the supply failed.

Since then, true to his instinct, he had worked hard, and forced his way up in spite of all that might have hindered.

His father would have liked him with him in the business in St Mary Axe, but, perceiving the lad's bent, raised no objection, on the understanding that, as far as possible, he made his own way. And this Connal had succeeded in doing.

He was a sturdy, fair-haired, blue-eyed fellow, several inches shorter than Ray Luard but fully his match both in boxing and wrestling, as proved in many a bout before an admiring audience of five—and sometimes six, for the Colonel liked nothing better than to see them at it and bombard them both impartially with advice and encouragement.

Connal had overcome all obstacles to the attainment of his chosen career in similar fashion; had taken scholarship after scholarship; and all the degrees his age permitted, and had even paid some of his examination fees by joining the Army Medical Corps, which provided him not only with cash, but also with a most enjoyable yearly holiday in camp and a certain amount of practice in his profession.

He had, however, long since decided that general practice would not satisfy him. He would specialise, and he chose as his field the still comparatively obscure department of the brain. There were fewer skilled workers in it than in most of the others. In fact it was looked somewhat askance at by the more pushing pioneers in research. It offered therefore more chances and he was most profoundly interested in his work in all its mysterious heights and depths.

At the moment he was the hard-worked Third Medical at Birch Grove Asylum, up on the Surrey Downs, and whenever he could run over to Willstead for half a day his mother eyed him anxiously for signs of undue depression or disturbed mentality, and was always completely reassured by his clear bright eyes, and his merry laugh, and the gusto with which he spoke of his work and its future possibilities.

With the approval and assistance of his good friend Dr Rhenius, who had attended to all the mortal ills of the Dares and Luards since they came to live in Willstead, he was working with all his heart along certain definite and well-considered lines, which included prospective courses of study at Munich and Paris. In preparation for these he was very busy with French and German, and for health's sake had become an ardent golfer. His endless quaint stories of the idiosyncrasies of his patients showed a well-balanced humorous outlook on the most depressing phase of human life, and as a rule satisfied even his mother as to the health and well-being of his own brain.

It was just about the time that he settled on his own special course in life, and accepted the junior appointment at Birch Grove, that Alma Luard surprised her family by deciding that life ought to mean more than tennis and picnics and parties, and became a probationer at St Barnabas's.

Lois, who came next, had a very genuine talent for music, and a voice which was a joy to all who heard it. For the perfecting of these she had now been two years at the Conservatorium at Leipsic and had lived, during that time, with Frau von Helse, widow of Major von Helse, who died in Togoland in 1890. Frau von Helse had two children,—Luise, who was also studying music, and Ludwig, lieutenant in the army. It was Ludwig's obvious admiration for Lois, the previous summer,—when he had escorted her and his sister to Willstead for a fortnight's visit to London in return for Frau von Helse's great kindness to Lois during her stay in Leipsic—that had fanned into sudden flame the long-glowing spark of Ray Luard's love for her.

Honor was Vic's great chum and admirer. When Honor began going to St Paul's School, Vic insisted on going also, and the experience had done her a world of good. Even Alma had been known to express regret that she had not had her chances. An exceedingly high-class and expensive boarding-school at Eastbourne had been her lot. An establishment in every respect after Auntie Mitt's precise little heart, but comparison of Vic's wider, if more democratic, experiences with her own eminently lady-like ones always roused in Alma feelings of vain and envious regret.

Noel had been at St Paul's also, and on the whole had managed to have a pretty good time. He was no student, however. The playing fields and Cadet corps always appealed to him more strongly than the class-rooms. He was now having a short holiday before tackling, with such grace as might be found possible when the time came, the loathsome mysteries of St Mary Axe.

There was nothing else for it. He had shown absolutely no inclination or aptitude for any special walk in life. His father's hope was that, under his own eye, he might in time develop into a business-man and relieve him of some portion of his at times over-taxing work.

By dint of strenuous labours Mr Dare had, in the course of years, worked up a profitable business in foreign imports and exports, but, like most businesses, it had its ups and downs, and it would be a great relief to be able to leave some of the details to one whom he knew he could trust, as he could Noel. He had had—or at all events had had the chance of—a good sound education. His father could only hope that he had taken more advantage of it than he had ever permitted to show. And experience would come with time.

CHAPTER III

W HEN the taxi, for which Ray had 'phoned, came rushing up, they all met again at the front gate to give him their various God-speeds on his gallant errand.

Mrs Dare handed him the note she had hastily penned to Lois, with a warm, "We are very grateful to you, Ray, for your thought of her. Bring her safe home to us."

The Colonel handed him a small buff paper bag which chinked, saying, "If you haven't enough there, my boy, you will let me know. God bless you both!"

Vic said enviously, "Just wish I was going! Wouldn't it be ripping, Nor, to be stranded out there and have someone come out from England to rescue you?"

"Ripping! Let's try it! Where could we get to?"

"Little girls are better at home," said Noel, with his golf-clubs slung over his shoulder so that not a moment of this last precious holiday should be missed. "Good-luck, old man! If you get into any boggle wire for me and I'll come and get you out of the mud. Jawohl! Hein! Nicht wahr!"

"I shall hope to find you all in the best of health about Tuesday or Wednesday," said Ray, with a final wave of the hand, and the taxi whirled away round the corner.

"See you two later," cried Noel, as he swung away towards the links. "I'll feed up yonder and meet you at the courts at three."

The girls sauntered away, arm in arm, up the Oakdene path, to talk it all over. The Colonel wrung Mrs Dare's hand again, and said, with warm feeling that subdued his voice to some extent, "We will congratulate one another again, ma'am. Nothing could have pleased me better. Lois is one of the sweetest girls I've ever met, and Ray will do us all credit."

"He's a fine boy. I'm sure they will be very happy. I am thankful it has fallen out so. I was a little afraid, at times, last summer—"

"You mean that spick-and-span, cut-and-dried, starched and stuck-up German dandy? Pooh, ma'am! I knew better than that myself."

"He was a good-looking lad, you know, and his music was quite exceptional."

"Always strikes me as rather namby-pamby in a man. But—a word in your ear, ma'am!"—in a portentous whisper induced by the discharge of his feelings,—"D'you know, I wouldn't be a bit surprised if we came on another link in the chain before long."

"Another link?" echoed Mrs Dare, and stared at him in great surprise.

"Yes," with a twinkle of beaming eyes. "What do *you* suppose made my eldest girl take to that nursing business? You know she'd no need to—"

"You mean Con?"

"Why, of course! Who else? I've a great belief in Con. He'll go far before he's through. And I know Alma. And it's only in the light of Con that I can explain her."

"You're just an incorrigible old match-maker," laughed Mrs Dare, more amused than convinced.

"When you're out of the game yourself there's nothing like watching the young ones at it. If it had been my luck now to meet yourself before Dare came along—"

"You'd have found me in my cradle," she laughed again, as she went up the path towards the front door.

"No,—in short frocks," said the Colonel emphatically. "But I'd have waited all right."

It was a standing joke among them that the Colonel had fallen in love with his neighbour's wife, and he confessed to it like a man, to John Dare's very face.

"Duty calls," said Mrs Dare. "I've got two rooms to turn out this morning, because my charlady couldn't come yesterday. And there she is going in at the back gate. Good-bye, Colonel! I'm half hoping Con may come over to-day. It's three weeks since he was here and he sometimes manages it on a Saturday. I'll send you word if he comes and perhaps you'll come round for a cup of tea."

"I will. And bring Alma with me," he twinkled.

"Is she to be here? I didn't know."

"Neither do I, but they generally manage to hit on the same day somehow. Curious, isn't it?" and he lifted his hat and marched away, chuckling to himself like a plump little turkey-cock.

CHAPTER IV

CON'S visits were like those of the angels, unexpected, generally unannounced, and always very welcome. The one curious thing about them was, as the Colonel had said, that, as often as not, they coincided in most extraordinary fashion with the whirling home-calls of Alma Luard. And whenever it happened so, the Colonel chuckled himself nearly into a fit in private, and in public preserved his innocent unconsciousness with difficulty.

Mrs Dare went off to superintend the operations of her charlady, whose attention to corners and little details in general was subject to lapses unless the eye of the mistress was within easy range. And as Mrs Skirrow worked best under a sense of personal injury Mrs Dare became of necessity the recipient of all her conjugal woes and endless stories of filial ingratitude.

She had a husband,—an old soldier in every sense of the word,—who was cursed with a constitutional objection to authority and work of any kind, and two sons who took after their father. One or the other stumbled into a place now and again and lost it immediately, and Mrs Skirrow slaved night and day to keep them from any deeper depths than half-a-crown a day and her food was able to save them from.

"Is ut true, mum, that we'll mebbe be having another war?" asked Mrs Skirrow as she flopped and scrubbed.

"I hope not, Mrs Skirrow, but there's said to be the possibility of it. We must hope we'll be able to keep out of it. War is very terrible."

"'Tes that, mum, but there's a good side to ut too. Mebbe ut'd give chance o' someth'n to do to some as don't do much otherwise. If ut took my three off and made men of 'em or dead uns ut'd be a change anyway."

"You'd find you'd miss them."

"I would that," said Mrs Skirrow emphatically, and added presently, "And be glad to.... I done my best to stir 'em up, but ut's in their bones. Mebbe if they was in th' army they'd manage to put some ginger into 'em."

21

"It might do them good, as you say. But you might never see them again, you know."

"I seen enough of 'em this last two years to last me. 'Taint reasonable for one woman to have to work herself to the bone for three grown men that can't get work 'cause they don't want to."

"It is not. I think it absolutely shameful of them."

"Not that they quarrel at all," said Mrs Skirrow, instantly resentful of anyone blaming her inepts but herself. "I'm bound to say that for 'em. They're good-tempered about it, but that don't keep 'em in clo'es, to say noth'n of boots. I suppose, mum, you ain't got an old pair of ..." and Mrs Skirrow's lamentations resolved themselves into the usual formula.

It was close upon tea-time when Con came striding up the path, with a searching eye on the next-door grounds.

"And what do you think of the war, mother?" he asked briskly, with his face all alight, as soon as their greetings were over, and he had satisfied himself as to the welfare of the rest of the family, and expressed his entire satisfaction with the news about Lois and Ray.

"You mean this Austrian business? It's very disturbing but I hope we won't be drawn into it, my boy."

"I expect we shall, you know. Pretty certain, it seems to me. And if we are I'm pretty sure to get the call...."

"I had not thought of that, Con," and her hands dropped into her lap for a moment and she sat gazing at him. "That brings it close home. I pray it may not come to that."

"Well, you see, I've had the cash, and the goods have got to be delivered—"

"Of course. But—"

"And if it comes to a scrap they'll need every medical they can get. What does Rhenius say about it all?"

"He's away,—in Italy, I think."

"I remember. He wrote me he was hoping to get off, if he could find a locum who wouldn't poison you all in his absence. Well, anyway, I'm getting my kit packed—"

"That's business, my boy," pealed the Colonel's hearty voice, as he came in with a telegram in his hand. "I saw you turn in and I'd already been invited to drink a cup of tea with you. Alma can't get off,"—he said, in a matter-of-fact way, showing the telegram.

"Oh?—did you expect her, sir?" with an assumption of surprise to cover his disappointment.

"I did, my boy, when I heard from your mother that she thought you might come to-day. Did you?"

"Medicals and nurses are not their own masters," said Con non-committally. "Do you really think we'll be into it, sir?"

"I do, Con. I don't see how we can possibly keep out. It's a most da—yes, damnably inevitable sequence, it seems to me. Austria goes for Servia. Russia won't stand it. In that case Germany is bound to help Austria. France will help Russia. Exactly how we stand pledged to help France and Russia no one knows, I imagine, except the Foreign Secretary. But everyone knows that the German war-plan contemplates getting at France through Belgium. And if they try that, the fat's in the fire and we've got to stop them or go under."

"That's exactly how they're looking at it at our place, and all the R.A.M.C. men are getting their things together in readiness for the call."

"It'll be a tough business," said the Colonel weightily, but with the light of battle in his eye. "But we've got to go through with it ... right to the bitter end."

"Have you any doubts about the end, sir?"

"None, my lad. But the end is a mighty long way off and it'll be a hot red road that leads to it, unless I'm very much mistaken. They've been preparing for this for years, you see. It had to come, and some of us saw it. Da-asht pity we didn't all see it! We'd have been readier for it than we are. Lord Roberts was right. Every man in Great Britain and Ireland ought to have been in training for it."

"Conscription again, Colonel!" said Mrs Dare. "And you still think England would stand it?"

"Not conscription, my dear madam,—Universal Service,—a very different thing and not liable to the defects of conscription. France broke down through her faulty conscription in 1870. Germany won on her universal service. And, da-ash it! we ought to have had it here ever since. But you others thought we were all screaming Jingoes and mad on military matters because that was our profession. Now, maybe, it's too late."

"Still, you say you don't believe they can beat us, sir?" said Con earnestly.

"Not in the long run. No, I don't, my boy. But can you begin to imagine what a long run will mean in these times? I've seen war and I know what it meant up to twenty years ago. But—if I know anything about it—that was child's-play to what this will be. Those—da-asht Germans are so infernally clever—and you must remember they've been working for this and nothing but this for the last twenty years, while we've been playing football and cricket, and squabbling over the House of Lords and Home Rule. Da-ash it! If our side had kept in I believe we'd have been readier."

"I doubt it, sir," said Con, with the laugh in the corners of his eyes. "You'd have been fighting for your lives all the time, whereas we at all events have done something—Old Age Pensions, and National Insurance, and so on," at which the Colonel snorted like a war-horse scenting battle.

"And how is the work going, Con?" asked Mrs Dare, as a lead to less bellicose subjects.

"Oh, all right. About same as usual. We got a new old chap in the other day and he's taken a curious fancy to my grin. He stops me every time we meet, and says, 'Doctor, do smile for me!' and he's such an old comic that I just roar, and then he roars too, and we're as happy as can be."

"He's no fool," said the Colonel. For Con's grin was very contagious. The corners of his eyes had a way of wrinkling up when the humorous aspect of things appealed to him, his eyes almost disappeared, and then his face creased up all over and the laugh broke out. And as a rule it made one laugh just to watch him.

"But we had two rather nasty things, last week," he said, sobering up. "Two of the old chaps were set to clean up an out-house, and one of them came out after a bit and sat down in the sun with his back against the wall, humming the 'Old Hundredth,' they say. One of the attendants asked him what he was doing there, and he said old Jim was tired and was lying down inside. And when they went in they found old Jim lying down with his head beaten in and as dead as a door-nail."

"Good Lord!" said the Colonel. "And what did you do to the other?"

"What could we do? He was quite unconscious of having done anything wrong. He'll be kept under observation of course. But the other matter was worse still, in one way. A table-knife disappeared one day from the scullery and couldn't be found anywhere. And for a week we all went with our heads over both shoulders at once, and the feel of that knife slicing in between our shoulder-blades at any moment. I tell you, that was jolly uncomfortable."

"And did you find it?" asked Mrs Dare anxiously.

"Yes, we hunted and hunted till we discovered it inside the back of a picture frame, and we were mighty glad to get it, I can tell you."

"Gad!" said the Colonel, with extreme energy. "I'd sooner be at the front any day. It's a safer job than yours, my boy."

"I suppose there are possibilities of getting hurt even there, sir," and Con's creases wrinkled up.

"Oh, you can get hurt all right enough, but it's not knives between your shoulder-blades."

"Assegais," suggested Mrs Dare, who knew his record.

"Assegais are deucedly uncomfortable, but that was fair fighting—"

Then Mr Dare walked in, very much later than usual for a Saturday. And, though he greeted them cheerfully, his face was very grave, to his wife's anxious eyes.

"I waited a bit to see if any further news came along," he said quietly.

"And how are they feeling about things?" asked the Colonel.

"Nervous. In fact, gloomy. Everybody admits that it seems incredible, but there's a general fear that we may be drawn in, in spite of all Sir Edward Grey's efforts."

"We shall," said the Colonel emphatically. "I feel it in my bones. Germany is very wide awake. She's been crouching for a spring any time this several years, and here are England, France, and Russia tied up with internal troubles. It's her day without a doubt. Take my advice and make your preparations, my friend. When it comes it'll come all in a heap. I only wish we were readier for it, and I wish to God they'd have the common-sense to put Kitchener in charge of the Army. He's the man for the job, and what earthly use is he in Egypt when Germany may be at our throats any day? Asquith can't be expected to understand all the ins and outs of the machine."

"Yes, it's too much to expect of him. And as to Kitchener, I quite agree. He's the right man for the job."

"Exchange upset? Money tight?"

"Slump all round. Consols down one and a half. Bank rate three still, but expected to jump any day. In fact things are about as sick as they can be."

"We're in for a very bad time, I'm afraid," said the Colonel gravely. And the shadow of the future lay upon them all.

When, presently, the Colonel got up to go, Mrs Dare and Con went with him to the front door, and Con went on down the path with him.

"May I speak to you about Alma, Colonel?" Con began, before they reached the gate.

"Yes, my boy, you may. But I know what you want to say."

"You've seen it, sir? You know how we feel then. And you don't object?"

"On the contrary, my boy. I'm very glad you have both chosen so wisely."

"That's mighty good of you, sir. I would have spoken to you before but I wanted to see my way a little more clearly. And now I can. Sir James Jamieson of Harley Street,—he's the biggest man we have in mental diseases, you know,—well, he saw some scraps of mine in the 'Lancet' and asked me to call on him. He's a fine man, and he wants me to go to him as soon as my courses are finished,—Munich and Paris and the rest. He's getting on in years, you see, and he was good enough to say that, from what he had heard of me, he believed I was the man to carry on his work when his time came to go. It's immense, you know."

"Capital! I always knew you'd go far, Con. My only fear was lest the—er—atmosphere of your special line should in time affect your own mind and spirits. But so far it seems to have had no ill effect. Your spirits are above par, and I've just had an excellent proof of your judgment,"—at which Con laughed joyously.

"When you're really keen on a thing it doesn't upset you, no matter how unpleasant it may be. And this work is anything but unpleasant to me. It's packed with interest. There's so much we don't know yet. And there's heaps of quaint humour in it, if you look out for it."

"Well, keep yourself fit, my boy, and I don't think your brain will suffer. *Mens sana*, you know."

"I see to that. I get a couple of hours on the links every day and I never play with a medical,—get quite outside it all, you know. Then I may speak to Alma, Colonel? She knows, of course, but we've never said very much."

"Yes, my lad,—whenever you can catch her. She's an elusive creature these days."

"I'll catch her all right," said Con, all abeam.

The other young people had just returned from their tournament and were discussing points over the tea-cups.

"Hello! Here's old Con," shouted Noel, and they all jumped up and gave him merry welcome. Vic inquired earnestly after the state of his brain; and satisfied on that head, they poured out their own latest news.

"Vic and I won," chortled Honor. "6-5, 6-4, against No and Gregor McLean."

"Oh well," explained Noel. "If you'd been round the links in the morning you wouldn't have been half so nimble on your pins."

"Bit heavy, I suppose?" said the Colonel.

"Heavy wasn't the word for it, sir, and a beastly gusty wind that upset all one's calculations. However, I licked old Greg into a cocked hat and he's no end of a nib with the sticks; so that's one to me. Pick up any lunch scores as you came along, Con?"

"Sorry, old man! I didn't. I was thinking of other things," and the Colonel nodded weightily, and said,

"In a week from now we'll all have other things to think about, I'm afraid."

CHAPTER V

RAY LUARD'S quest was one in which the soul of any man might well rejoice. He was flying, like a knight of old,—though as to ways and means in very much better case,—to the rescue of his lady-love from possibilities of trouble. More than that he did not look for, and possible difficulties and delays weighed little with him.

He reached Flushing about seven in the evening after a gusty passage which did not trouble him, and was at Cologne in the early hours of the morning. But after that his progress was slow and subject to constant, exasperating, and inexplicable delays.

He had secured a berth in the sleeper and took fullest advantage of it. But all night long, as he slept the troubled sleep of the sleeping-car, he was dully conscious of long intervals when the metronomic nimble of the wheels died away, and the unusual silence was broken only by the creaking complaints of the carriage-fittings and the long-drawn snores and sharper snorts and grunts of his companions in travel.

The train was crowded and every bunk was occupied. The occupant of the one above him was so violently stertorous that Ray feared he was in for a fit, and did his best to save him from it by energetic thumps from below. But the only result was a momentary pause of surprise in the strangling solo up above and the immediate resumption of it with renewed vigour, and Ray gave it up, and drew the bed clothes over his ears, and left him to his fate.

In the morning the noisy one turned out to be an immensely fat German who rolled about the car as if it and the world outside belonged to him,—the repulsively over-bearing kind of person whose very look seemed to intimate that no one but himself and his like had any right to cumber the earth. And just the kind of person that Ray Luard loathed and abominated beyond words.

Ray's disgust of him, and all his kind and all their doings, showed unmistakably in his face, and the fat one became aware of it and took offence. He dropped ponderously into the seat alongside Ray so that he filled three-quarters of it, and proceeded to stare at him in most offensive fashion. His little yellow pig-like eyes, almost lost in the greasy fat rolls of his face, travelled suspiciously over his neighbour from head to foot as though searching for something to settle on.

Ray knew the look and its meaning. Had he been back at Heidelberg he would forthwith have demanded of the starer when and where it was his pleasure they should meet to fight it out. But this mountain of fat was long past his Mensur days, and Ray was doubtful how to tackle him.

He did perhaps the best thing under the circumstances,—turned his back on him and looked out of the window.

But the fat one was not satisfied to let matters rest so. He loosed a wheezy laugh and said, "Ach, zo! Ein Engländer!" with another wheezy little laugh of extremest scorn.

"And what of that, Fat-Pig?" rapped out Ray, in German equal to his own, and the shot took the fat one in the wind.

"Fat-Pig! Fat-Pig! Gott im Himmel, you call me Fat-Pig?"

He rose, bellowing with fury, and was about to drop himself bodily on Ray, when others who had watched the proceedings—a Bavarian whose foot he had trampled on without apology ten minutes before, and a Saxon upon whose newspapers he had also plumped down and pulped into illegibility—jumped up and laid hands on him and dragged him back.

"So you are! So you are!" they shouted. "The Englishman has doubtless paid his fare and is entitled to the whole of a seat without insult or annoyance."

"They ought to charge you double and then carry you in the baggage-van," said the Saxon.

"You should try to remember you're not yet in Prussia—you!" growled the Bavarian, jerking the mountainous one down into an empty seat.

"Ja!—Mein Gott, if I had you all in Prussia I'd show you who's who," and he wagged his dewlaps at them with menacing malevolence.

"A damned English spy, if I have any eyes," he wheezed.

"No more a spy than you're a gentleman," retorted Ray.

"Enough! Enough, mein Herr! Let him be! He's just a Prussian and they're all like that,—blown out with their own conceit till they've no decent manners left," said the Bavarian.

"That is so," said the Saxon, and they removed themselves with Ray out of sight and sound of the swollen one.

The other two were quite friendly, and through their smoke endeavoured to arrive at an understanding of Ray,—how he came to speak German so well,—what his business in life was,—where he was going, and why? And, as he had nothing to conceal and felt resentful still of the fat man's insinuations, he told them frankly what he was there for.

Their reserve and soberness over the political outlook impressed him greatly. He felt more than justified in the decision he had taken as to Lois.

He did his best, without being too intrusive, to get at their view of the future, and they at his. But it was all too pregnant with awful possibilities, and too obscure and critically in the balance, for very free speech. From their manner, however, he gathered that, while they personally desired no interruption of the present prosperous state of affairs, they doubted if the dispute between Austria and Servia could be localised, and feared that if Russia supported Servia the fat would be in the fire.

"For me, I do not like Prussia and her insolent ways," said the Bavarian. "Yon stout one is typical of her. But if she goes, we have to follow—unfortunately, whether we approve or not. We are all bound up together, you see, and there you are."

And all their discursive chats throughout the day went very little deeper than that.

It was a very wearisome journey. Time after time they were shunted into sidings while long and heavy trains rolled past. And when Ray commented on it with a surprised,

"Well!—for a quick through train this is about as poor a specimen as I've ever tumbled on,"—their only comment, as they gazed gloomily out of the window, was, "The traffic is disorganised for the moment."

The stations they passed through were packed with people, and the military element seemed more in evidence even than usual.

It was close on five o'clock in the afternoon before they arrived in Leipsic. The Bavarian had left them at Cassel. The Saxon, as he bade Ray adieu, said quietly,

"You may find things more difficult still if you try to return this way, Herr. If you take my advice you will strike down South into Tirol and Switzerland, and meanwhile say as little as possible to anyone," and with a meaning nod he was gone.

Ray went along to the Hauffe, secured a room, had a much-needed bath and dinner, and then set off at once for Frau Helse's house in Sebastian Bach Strasse.

The plump Saxon maid informed him that Fräulein Dare was out, that Frau Helse was out, that Fräulein Luise was out;—they were in fact all at a concert at the Conservatorium; and the Herr Lieutenant, he was with his regiment. So Ray left his card with the name of his hotel scribbled on it, and Mrs Dare's letter, and promised to return in the morning.

Then, after a stroll about the unusually thronged streets, he returned to his hotel and looked up trains for Switzerland.

CHAPTER VI

KNOWING how anxious Lois would be for a fuller understanding of his coming, Ray set off for Frau Helse's house the moment he had finished breakfast next morning.

Lois had obviously been on tenterhooks till he came. He was hardly ushered into the stiff, sombre drawing-room, when the door flew open and she came hastily in.

"Oh, Ray!"—and he caught her in his arms and kissed her.

"There is nothing wrong at home?—Mother?—Father?—" she asked quickly, her anxiety accepting the unusual warmth of his greeting as somehow appropriate to the circumstances. "Is it only what Mother says, or—"

"Just exactly what Mother says, my child, and quite enough too. Everybody is perfectly well. Our only anxiety is on your account."

"And you really think there is going to be trouble?"

"Uncle Tony is certain we're in for a general European war,—in fact for Armageddon foretold of the prophets. And the mere chance of it is more than enough to make us want you home."

She could still hardly quite take it all in. She stood gazing at him in amazement.

"And you?—you really think it, Ray?"

"Nothing's impossible in these times, and I'm not going to run any risks where you're concerned. How soon can you be ready?"

"I'll finish my packing at once. I started early this morning, though I was not at all sure what it all meant."

"One moment, Lois," he said meaningly. "You can trust these people, I suppose?"

"Frau Helse? Oh yes. They're as nice as can be."

"Very well then. Pack just your choicest possessions into a small bag that I can carry, and everything else into your trunk. We'll leave the trunk in Frau Helse's care and take the other with us."

"But why not take the trunk also?" she asked in surprise.

30

"If matters are as I think, from what I've seen, they're mobilising here for all they are worth, and the lighter we travel the better. Our train could hardly get through coming. Going back will be worse. Indeed I've already had it hinted to me that our safest way will be to strike right down south into Switzerland."

"Into Switzerland?"

"Yes, if things develop rapidly, as they probably will, all the traffic here will go to pieces—all in the hands of the military, you know. And you know enough of Germany to know what that means."

She nodded thoughtfully, and said, "There's been something going on below-ground for some time past. I was sure of it. They said it was manœuvres, but it looks as if it was a good deal more. I can be all ready in an hour. Will you see Frau Helse?"

"Perhaps I'd better, so that she may see I'm at all events respectable to look at. Then I'll go to the station and see if the trains are running all right. You've told her, I suppose."

"Yes, I showed her Mother's letter. But she was decidedly shocked at the idea of my going off alone with any man who wasn't at least a cousin."

"Oh—cousin! She'll be more shocked before she sees the end of it all, maybe."

So Lois went away and brought in Frau Helse and Luise, and introduced Ray to them. They had been mightily surprised at Fräulein Lois's news, and Frau Helse—when the two girls had gone off to finish the packing—let it be seen that she was distinctly doubtful as to the perfect propriety of allowing her to go off with this good-looking young Engländer, who was not in any way related to her. However, in the face of Mrs Dare's letter she could scarcely raise any objection, and Ray got away as soon as he could, promising to be back in an hour.

He had decided to take the friendly Saxon's advice and make for Switzerland. He reasoned the matter out thus,—Austria and Servia were practically at war. Though no formal declaration had yet been made, the Austrian Legation had left Belgrade. Russia would almost certainly help Servia. Germany would help Austria. France would help Russia. Without doubt Germany would endeavour to strike at France quickly and heavily. She could only do that down south. So all the railway lines leading thither would be taken over by the military, and ordinary travellers—and still more especially foreigners—would meet with less consideration even than usual.

So he enquired for trains for Munich, intending to get from there into Tirol, and so into neutral Switzerland. Since the first clash of arms would undoubtedly come far away to the south on the Servian frontier, it was reasonable to expect that this remote corner of Austria would still be comparatively free and open to traffic.

There was a train at ten o'clock and another at half-past twelve. He decided on the earlier one, paid his bill at the hotel, and drove off to Frau Helse's to secure his prize.

Lois was waiting for him, all dressed for the journey, and the slightness of her travelling equipment evoked his surprised eulogiums.

As they were making for the station, with just comfortable time to get their tickets, they passed on the sidewalk a man of unforgettable proportions.

There was no possibility of mistaking him, but Ray had no desire for his further acquaintance and permitted no sign of recognition to escape him. The stout one, however, turned ponderously and looked after them, and then said a word or two to a policeman.

Ray had got their tickets, and had despatched a telegram—which never reached him—to Uncle Tony, saying they were just starting for home via Munich and Switzerland; and they were waiting impatiently for the doors of the Wartesaal to be opened to let them through to their train, when a couple of police-officers came pushing through the throng to Ray and abruptly requested him to follow them.

He was taken aback, but knew his Germany and its unpleasant little ways too well to make trouble.

"Follow you? Certainly! But why?"

But they were not there to answer questions, only to carry out orders.

"Come!" they gruffly insisted, and Ray gave his arm to Lois and went.

They were put into a carriage and driven away to Police Head-Quarters, and after a long wait were ushered into the presence of a high official, who looked worried and overworked.

"Who and what are you? And what are you doing here?" he asked brusquely.

Ray supplied him with the desired information.

"Your passport?"

"I have none, Herr Head-of-Police,"—he had no idea what his questioner's standing might be, but knew that in addressing officials in Germany you can hardly aim too high. "I left London at almost a moment's notice on Saturday morning, to bring this lady home to her mother. I did not know a passport was necessary."

"We have definite information that you are a spy."

"From the fat gentleman who insulted me in the train yesterday, I presume," said Ray, with a smile. "He tried to sit on me and then called me names, and I called him Fat-Pig. He had already annoyed everyone in the carriage, and they all sided against him and told him what they thought of him. I am no more a spy than he is, mein Herr.... Stay—here is my return ticket to London dated, as you see, Saturday. My fiancée has been studying

32

in Leipsic here for the last two years. She lived with Frau Helse, 119 Sebastian Bach Strasse. Have you your mother's letter with you, Lois?"—and she got it out and handed it to the official.

He read it carefully and seemed to weigh each word and seek between the lines for hidden treason.

"And why is Fräulein Dare leaving so hurriedly?"

"Her mother wished her at home and we judged there might possibly be difficulties for a girl travelling alone."

"Why?"

"When there are rumours of war in the air, mein Herr, one's best place is in one's own country. That was how we looked at it."

"But the war—if it comes to anything—is far enough from here," and he eyed Ray keenly, as though to penetrate his whole mind on the matter.

"May it remain so!" said Ray earnestly. "But when a fire starts one never knows for certain how far it will spread."

"And you were going to Munich,—towards the danger in fact."

"Yes, we were going by Innsbruck and Tirol into Switzerland and so home. The traffic on the direct lines seems disorganised. The booking-clerk refused me a ticket via Cologne."

"I shall have to keep you awhile till I have made some further enquiries. If they are satisfactory you will be allowed to proceed. If not—"

"Herr Head-of-Police," pleaded Lois, in her best German, which was very good indeed, and in her prettiest manner, which was irresistible, "It is too ridiculous. Herr Luard is a student of law in London. He is the nephew of Sir Anthony Luard, who lives next door to us at home, and we are fiancés. That is why he came for me. He is no more a spy than I am. And Frau Helse will tell you all about me. Fräulein Luise and Ludwig were across at our home in London last year."

He nodded somewhat less officially. "I know Frau Helse, and doubtless it is all as you say, Fräulein. But we have to be careful in these days. I trust your detention will not be prolonged."

He touched a bell and they were ushered into an adjoining room and left alone.

"Looks as if my assistance was not of much use to you, my dear," laughed Ray. "I wish I'd smashed Fat-Pig's ugly old head in. It would at all events have put him hors-de-combat for a day or two and would have been a great satisfaction to my feelings as well."

"Then I should never have seen you at all," said Lois. "It will be all right, I'm sure. Frau Helse will satisfy him. I'm glad he knows her."

And an hour later they were released without a word of apology. But it was enough for them to be free, and they made their way back to the station in good enough spirits.

The delay, however, had lost them both the earlier and the later trains, and the time-tables showed that the next one for the south would land them at a place called Schwandorf at four o'clock in the morning, with the remote possibility of reaching Munich six hours later. There was a fast through train a little after midnight, which, barring accidents or delays, would get them there a couple of hours earlier, but after their late experience, and with the chance of running across their fat friend again, and perhaps becoming further victims to his pig-headed venom, Ray thought it best to get out of Leipsic as early as possible, even at cost of a weary night journey in a train that stopped at every station. Every station would at all events be that much between them and Pig-Head.

So they had their mid-day meal in the Station restaurant, and dallied over it as long as possible, and spent the rest of their time in the waiting-room, so that the authorities should have no possible pretext for suspicion.

They were perfectly happy, however, in one another's company and the new relationship which Ray's coming had jewelled into accepted family fact. Ray told her all he could think of about home-doings, and was keen to learn the smallest details of her life in Leipsic, and so there was no lack of talk between them and the time did not seem long.

Streams of people passed through the station, mostly men, and mostly in uniform. Ray saw without seeming to notice, and was confirmed in the view that great and grave events were brewing.

Their train was an hour late in starting, and, by reason of many stoppages and much side-tracking to allow other heavily-laden trains to pass, was more than two hours late in reaching Schwandorf.

It was a deadly wearisome journey,—the carriages packed beyond reason, everyone somewhat on edge with anxiety and excitement, senseless disputations and bickerings, jokes that lacked humour but led to noisy quarrelling, no rest for mind or body. They were glad to turn out into the chill morning air at Schwandorf, only to find the express already gone and none but slow trains till the 1 p.m. express which would, if it kept faith, land them in Munich about four in the afternoon.

They had breakfast and then propped themselves into corners in the waiting-room and endeavoured to make up for the loss of their night's rest.

The express was not quite so crowded, but even it was frequent captive to the sidings, and as their fellow-travellers regarded them with polite but unmistakable suspicion they deemed it wise to keep silence, and so found the journey very monotonous. And everywhere, from such glimpses of the country and stations as their middle seats afforded them, they got the impression of unusual activities and endless uniforms.

"Is it always like this?" whispered Ray into Lois's ear one time, and she shook her head.

It was after five o'clock when they at last drew into Munich, and as they stood in the carriage to let other eager travellers descend, Lois plucked Ray warningly by the arm, and he saw, rolling along the platform, the Ponderous One who had already got them into trouble in Leipsic.

"Hang the Fat-Pig!" he murmured. "Is there no getting away from him? What a Thing to be haunted by!"

They peered out of the window till they saw him roll through the barrier, and only then ventured to descend and make for the restaurant. For to be delivered over to the police as suspects here, where they knew no one, might involve them in endless trouble and delay. The one thing they desired now, above food or even sleep, was to set foot in a country where English folk were not looked upon as suspicious outcasts.

"Can you go on?" asked Ray. "I'm sure you're dead tired, but—"

"Oh, let us get on," she replied, with a touch of the all-prevailing anxious strain in her voice. "Anything to get out of this horrid country. They make me feel like a leper."

There was a train marked to leave at 5.30 which had not yet started, and without waiting to get anything to eat, though their last meal had been early breakfast at Schwandorf, they climbed into a carriage, thankful at all events at thought of leaving their gross bête-noir behind in Munich.

It was close on 11 p.m. when they reached Innsbruck, and Ray led her straight across to the Tirolerhof, engaged two rooms, boldly registered their names as Raglan and Lois Luard, and ordered supper,—anything they had ready, and they fell upon it with a sixteen-hours' appetite.

"For the time being," said Ray, with reference to the name he had conferred upon her, when the sharpest edge of their hunger was blunted, "We are brother and sister to the obnoxious outside public. If you don't want to be a sister to me you shall tell me so in private. It strikes me, my dear, that we may possibly not get home quite as quickly as they will be expecting over there."

"If you hadn't come it looks as though I would never have got home at all. Oh, I *am* so glad you came, Ray. What does it all mean, do you think?"

"Mighty trouble all round, I fear. They are evidently mobilising here at top pressure. That means an attack on France. And what that may mean to us I can't quite foresee.... We may have to get home through Italy.... But— Heavens and Earth!—Italy will be into it too. She's bound to go in with Germany and Austria.... Do you know what *I* think, my child?"

"No, what? Anything to the point?"

"Seems to me we may be bottled up here—that is in Switzerland, if we ever succeed in getting there—for the rest of our lives. What do you say to getting married as soon as we do get there—if ever, Miss—er—Luard,— and so regularising the position?" and he looked whimsically at her.

"We'll wait and see, as Mr. Asquith says," she smiled. "If we really do get bottled up it may have to come to that."

"H'm! And I was hoping you'd jump at the chance!"

"It's rather sudden, you see, and a bit overwhelming. We've only been really engaged since yesterday morning...."

"Oh ho! That so? But you knew all about it. Now didn't you?"

"A girl can never really know quite all about it, you know, until she is asked. She may know her own side of the matter—"

"As you did."

"And she may have every confidence in—er—the other side—"

"As you had."

"But—"

"But me no buts, my child! I consider my idea an eminently sensible one. You think it over.... And consider all the advantages!—no fuss, no wedding-breakfast, no hideous publicity. Just a quiet wedding and right into the blissfullest honeymoon that ever was. Heavenly!"

"Well, I'll think it over, and we'll see how we go on. What time do we start in the morning?"

"There's a train at 9.45, but it only goes as far as Feldkirch. And there's a fast train at 1.15 which should land us in Zurich some time after 8."

"Let us take the 1.15, then we can have a good rest. I'm awfully tired."

"One-fifteen it is. And you don't need to get up till ten,—eleven, if you like," and he escorted her upstairs to her room.

"Do brothers and sisters kiss at your house?" he whispered at the door. "They don't at ours."

"Nor at ours," and she put up her face to be kissed.

Innsbruck was as yet fairly quiet. The garrison had gone and had been replaced by men of the reserve; most of the visitors had taken fright and fled; a few bewildered—or phlegmatic—English and Americans were left, but the empty streets and the anxious and preoccupied looks of the women gave the pleasant little town an unusual and dreary aspect, and our travellers were glad to be en route for a land less likely to be disturbed by alarms and excursions and all the fears of war.

CHAPTER VII

WHEN Lois came down next morning she found Ray on the front doorstep, deep in conversation with an elderly gentleman of most impressive appearance. He was tall and straight, and had white hair and beard and moustache, a very kindly face, and extremely polished manners. When he spoke, an occasional very slight nasal intonation, which none but a well-trained ear would have detected, suggested the United States—most likely Boston, she thought, since it reminded her of a Boston girl with whom she had been friendly at the Conservatorium.

Ray unblushingly introduced her as his sister, and said,

"Our friend here is advising me to change our route, Lois."

"Oh—why?" she asked, looking up a little anxiously into the pleasant, interested face.

"Because, my dear young lady, I got through from Bâle myself only late last night, and not without difficulty. The situation is becoming worse every hour. Austria declared war against Servia yesterday. What that may lead to no man knows,—unless, perhaps, the Kaiser and his advisers. And even they are not absolutely omniscient. It may all peter out as it has done before, but I am bound to say that this time I fear Germany means business, and if she does it will mean very grim and ghastly business indeed. Mobilisation is going on quietly and quickly, everywhere, even in Switzerland. The clash will come on the French frontier if it comes at all, and I believe it to be inevitable. The Swiss fear for their neutrality, and their fears are justifiable. If it suits Germany's book she will trample across Swiss or any other territory that happens to be in her way."

"But—it is too amazing. Why should Germany break out like this?"

"Simply because she thinks her time is ripe. Some of us have been expecting this war for years past. Now it is upon us."

"And how do you think we ought to go?"

"I was just telling your brother that any attempt to get through on any of the direct routes is quite out of the question. Every carriage and truck on every line is packed with soldiers. Your best way, I think, will be to get across country. Make for the Rhone Valley and get down to Montreux or Geneva, and wait there till things settle down somewhat, when you will be able no doubt to get across France and so home."

"It means footing it, Lois. How does it strike you?" said Ray.

She knitted her brows prettily while she considered the matter. It was certainly all very disturbing.

"And are you going across country also?" she asked the American gentleman.

"No. I'm going back to my home in Meran. I have lived there for the last five years, and my wife is there. I had to run over to London on some business, and I'm glad to have got back in time. Another day and it might have been impossible."

"And how long will it take to walk from here to the Rhone Valley?"

"You can still get a train to Landeck. Then strike right up the Lower Engadine Valley,— Stay! I'll show you on the map," and he turned to the one on the wall. "Now,—see!—you go first to Landeck. Then follow up the Inn to Süss. Then strike across by the Flüela Pass to Davos, and then by the Strela Pass to Chur. Then by Ilanz and Disentis to the Gothard. There are no difficulties. The roads are good. It will be an exceedingly fine walk."

"What about our bags?" asked Lois.

"Get a couple of rucksacs. Pack in as much as you can carry, and the rest.... You could have them forwarded from here. But I should be very doubtful if they'd ever reach you in the present state of matters.... Would you care to leave them in my charge? I will take them to my house and send them on as soon as things settle down."

And he pulled out his pocket-book and handed Ray his card—Charles D. Lockhart. Schloss Rothstein. Meran.

"I came across a very fine book on Tirol by a Mr Lockhart not long since—" began Ray.

"Quite right! I have written much on Tirol. Since I made my home here I have grown very fond of both the country and the people. I fervently hope we shall have no more than back-wash of the war here. But there's no telling. Once the spark is in the stubble the flames may spread wide."

"We are greatly indebted to you, Mr Lockhart," said Ray, "and since you are so good we will take advantage of your very kind offer. That is—if you can get all you will want till we get to Montreux into a rucksac, Lois."

"I'll manage all right."

So they all had breakfast together, and much talk of the gigantic possibilities the near future might hold if it came to a universal war. Then, under their new friend's experienced guidance, they made a quick round of the

38

shops, bought rucksacs, alpenstocks, a Loden cloak each, and had their boots nailed in Swiss fashion.

By the time they had packed their rucksacs and repacked their bags it was time for Mr Lockhart to catch his train for Botzen and Meran, and they accompanied him to the station and said good-bye to him and their property.

And when the train had disappeared they looked at one another and burst out laughing.

"I'm sure it's quite all right," laughed Lois, "But it does feel odd to send off all one's belongings like that with a man one never set eyes on till an hour ago."

"It's quite all right, my dear. I'd trust that old fellow with all I have—even with you. He's a fine old boy, and we've got to thank him for putting us on to a gorgeous trip. Nothing like padding it for seeing the country!"

And an hour later they had turned their backs on Landeck and the snow peaks of the Lechtaler Alps, and were footing it gaily up the right bank of the roaring Inn, with the northern spurs of the Oetztaler towering up in front of them beyond the dark mouth of the Kaunser-Tal.

It was a gray day and none too warm, but excellent weather for walking, and there was in them an exuberant spirit of relief at having shaken off the trammels of ordinary life and left behind, for the time being at all events, the gathering war-clouds and ominous preparations. If it had rained in torrents they would still have been perfectly happy, for that which was within them was proof against outside assault of any kind whatsoever.

It was a lonely walk, and so the more delightful to them. They desired no company but their own. Beyond an occasional man of the hills hastening towards Landeck, with sober face, coat slung by its arms at his back, and jaunty cock-feathered hat on the back of his head, they did not meet a soul till they came to Ladis.

As a rule these hurrying ones passed them with a preoccupied 'Grüss Gott!' and a hungry look which craved news but grudged the time.

One stopped for a moment and asked anxiously, "Is it true, then, Herr? Is it war?"

And Ray answered him, "With Servia, yes! How much more no man knows."

"War is the devil," said the man soberly, and hurried on.

They talked cheerfully,—of the folks at home and all the recent happenings there,—dived into happy reminiscence of their own feelings towards one another, and how and when and where these had begun to crystallise into the radiant certainty of mutual love,—and more than once, in the solitude of the little mountain sanctuaries where they stopped at times for a rest, Ray caught her to him and kissed her passionately in the overflowing fulness of his heart.

It was the most entrancing walk Lois had ever had, and the glow in her face and the star-shine in her eyes told their own tale.

They crossed the river where the road wound away into Kaunser-Tal, and again by the bridge at Prutz, and six o'clock found them within sight of the castle of Siegmundsried, with the pretty little village of Ried below.

"We'll stop the night there," said Ray. "We've done about ten miles and all uphill, and that's quite enough for a first day. How are the feet?"

"First rate. I feel as if I could go on for ever."

"If you went on for ever you'd wish you hadn't next day. We've got a long way to go and there's no great hurry,—unless you feel as if you'd like to get it over and done with."

"Oh, but I don't. I'd like it to last for ever and ever."

"Mr and Mrs Wandering Jew," laughed Ray. "What would your mother say?"

"She would say, 'She'll be all right since she's with Ray.'"

"See what it is to have a good character," and they turned into the 'Post' and demanded rooms and supper.

Next day they walked on, first on one side of the river, then on the other, loitering on every bridge to watch the gray water roaring among the worn gray rocks below.

They ate their lunch on the terrace of the little inn at Stuben, looking across at Pfunds lying in the mouth of the valley opposite. And when they came to the Cajetan Bridge, instead of crossing it with the high-road, Ray kept to the old path along the left bank, through the narrow Finstermünz Pass, and made straight for Martinsbruck, and so avoided the long bends and steep zig-zags leading to and from Nauders in the mouth of the Stillebach Valley.

It was rough walking, but he explained,

"It cuts off a lot, you see, and when we cross that bridge at Martinsbruck we're in Switzerland."

"That sounds like getting near home," said Lois.

"It's a neutral country anyway, and maybe we'll get news there of what's really happening. But it's a good long way from home. I believe you're tired of tramping already."

"Am I? Do I look it?"

"You do not. But you look as though a kiss would encourage you—to say nothing of me."...

The tops and sides of the mountains had been wreathed with smoke-coloured clouds all day. It was only as they drew near to Martinsbruck that the evening sun struggled out, and they saw a peak here and there soaring up above the clouds and all aglow with crimson fire,—a wonderful and up-lifting vision.

"The Delectable Mountains," murmured Lois, at this her first sight of the alpen-glüh.

"Our Promised Land lies the other way," said Ray, "But we'll carry our own glory-fire with us."

They stood watching till the red glow faded swiftly up the summits of the cloud-borne peaks and left them chill and ghostly, and Lois heaved a sigh of regret.

"Wait!" said Ray, with his hand on her arm; and in a minute or two the cold white mountain-tops flushed all soft rose-pink, so exquisitely sweet and tender that Lois caught her breath and laid her hand in his, as though she must fain share so exquisite a joy with him.

"How lovely!" she whispered, profoundly moved by the sight and the warm grip of his hand, through which his heart seemed to beat up into hers. "The sun's last warm good-night kiss! Oh, if they could only be like that al-ways!"

"Then we would not enjoy them half as much. Don't watch it fade," and they turned and went. "We will always remember it at its best.... Life is to be like that with you and me, right on and on and on for ever. It is a good omen. And here,"—as they crossed the bridge—"we are in Switzerland, and this little Post Hotel will serve us excellently."

Those solitary suppers in the common-rooms of the little wayside inns were things to remember. Not so much for the quality of the viands and the wine, though they never had a fault to find with either, but because of the cheerful goodfellowship and delightful camaraderie they engendered. And there was without doubt a subtle crown of joy to it all, in the feeling that here they were doing something out of the common, something that would possibly administer some slight shock to the nerves of Mrs Grundy if she had been aware of it.

Their procedure, however, was not so unusual as they in their inno-cence imagined.

As they sat over their meal that night in the Post at Martinsbruck, there came in two later arrivals who presently joined them at table,—a strapping young fellow of five-and-twenty and a very pretty girl of a year or two less, with large blue eyes and abundant fair hair coiled in great plaits round her head, and they were soon all chatting together on the friendliest of terms.

These two were tramping also and had come up that day from Süss.

"A good walk that, mein Herr, for little feet!" said the young man, looking proudly at his companion. "Thirty-eight kilomètres, I make it, per-haps a trifle more."

"Twenty-four miles!" said Ray. "Yes, that's a good long stretch. Twenty miles,—say thirty, thirty-two kilomètres—is our longest. But then we're only just beginning."

"And we are just ending," sighed the girl. "He has to go to the army. Do you think it will be a bad war, mein Herr?" she asked anxiously.

"All war is bad, mein Frau," began Ray.

"Fräulein," she corrected him with a little smile. "I am Anna Santner. He is Karl Stecher. We are of Innsbruck."

"And in another month—in September—she is to be Frau Stecher," said Karl with a broader smile. "We are taking a portion of our honeymoon in advance. To see how we get on together, you understand. It is not unusual with us—"

"And I am sure you have got on very well together," said Lois, with her prettiest smile.

"Oh, yes. You see, we love one another very much," said Anna. "But now—! What do you think of it, mein Herr?"

"We can all only hope it will not be as bad as some people fear, Fräulein. But, at best, it is bad."

"Yes, war is bad," said the young fellow, with gloomy vehemence. "It is devil's play from beginning to end. Still, those Serbs had no right to shoot our Archduke, you know, and they deserve a whipping."

"Possibly. But the danger is that it may spread. If Russia takes umbrage, then Germany will join in, and Italy and France."

"And your country? What will you do?" asked Stecher.

"I do not know. We certainly don't want war, but if it comes to a general struggle we may be in it too. It is horrible to think of. In these days— all Europe at one another's throats! It is almost inconceivable."

"Du meine Güte!" said Anna, clasping her hands tightly together. "It is too terrible. What will happen to me if you get killed, my Karl?" and she could hardly see him for the tears that filled her large blue eyes.

"I don't feel a bit like getting killed, my little one, I assure you."

"That won't stop those horrid bullets, all the same."

"Ach, my Nanna, don't weep for me before it begins anyway! Let us talk of something else.... And you, Herr and Frau?—Fräulein?—you are married?—yes?—no?—or have you this same pleasant custom with you?"

"Like you," said Ray, "we are to be married very soon, and we are having our honeymoon in advance. You see, the Fräulein was in Leipsic, studying, when we heard this ill rumour of war. And her mother gave me permission to go and bring her home. And as they are mobilising in Germany—"

"Ah—they are mobilising?" jerked Stecher with a nod.

"We were advised to get back through Switzerland, and here we are."

"We also were in Switzerland," sighed Anna, reminiscently.

"You came over Flüela?" asked Ray. "How's the walking there? That's how we are going."

"It is a good enough road," said Stecher, "but you will need a full day from this end. It is all up hill, you see, and pretty stiff. You must get as far as Süss to-morrow night and start early next day. We stayed at the Flüela. It is quite good and not dear. And you can rest and eat at the Hospice under the Weisshorn. Oh, it is all quite easy. I wish we were going that way too."

"Ach Gott—yes!" sighed Fräulein Anna. And Lois's heart was sore for her, for her future and Karl's was bound to contain possibilities of sorrow and misfortune, and she would have liked everyone to be as happy as she was herself.

And next morning, in the strong fellow-feeling of somewhat similar circumstances, they shook hands and parted almost like old friends,—none of them knowing to what they were going.

The four-and-twenty uphill miles from Martinsbruck to Süss were somewhat of a tax on Lois. They were on the road soon after seven, however, as Karl and Anna also had to be off early, and with occasional halts they made Schuls before mid-day, had a good dinner there and a long rest on the terrace of the hotel, with all the noble peaks, from Piz Lad opposite Martinsbruck to Piz Nuna opposite Süss, spread wide before them. They were at Ardetz in time for an early cup of tea and another rest, and reached Süss before sunset.

But long as the way was they enjoyed every rough step of it. For one thing it was a brighter day of mixed cloud and sunshine, which wrought most wonderful atmospheric effects on the soaring peaks and sweeping mountain-sides. Their road wound along the flanks of the Silvretta. Below them the Inn foamed white among its gray boulders. Innumerable valleys, each with its thread of rushing white water, debouched on either side and gave them wonderful peeps at the monarchs behind—the Oetztalers, the Ortlers, and the Silvrettas. Running water was everywhere—gray glacier streams and sparkling falls, and every here and there, on spurs of hills and vantage points, were the grim ruins of castles that had played their parts in the days of the Grey Leaguers and the Ten Droitures.

But all this delectable outward circumstance was no more than exquisite setting for that which was within them, and each of these reacted on the other. Never had they found such charm in their surroundings before. Never before had surroundings so charming had such effect upon their spirits and feelings.

They went along hand in hand at times like country lovers, and more than once their hearts broke into song as spontaneous as the lark's, from simple joy of living.

Lois's voice, in the full rounded beauty of its two years' careful cultivation at the Conservatorium, was a revelation to Ray and thrilled him to the depths.

"My dear," he said deeply, one time, "You have a gift of the gods. It would be a sin against humanity to deprive the world of it."

"Oh, you will let me sing even after we are married."

"Let you!... Am I a traitor to my kind? Let you, indeed! You will lift men's souls with that voice. The world has need of you, my child, and what am I to say it nay?"

"You're the world to me. I'm glad it pleases you."

And maybe the menacing war-cloud, which could not be entirely excluded from their minds, but served to brighten their radiant enjoyment of that perfect day. Stars shine brightest in a winter-black sky.

CHAPTER VIII

THEY took the road very early again next morning, and turning their backs on the ruined castle of Süss and the triple peaks of Piz Mezdi, climbed steadily up past the long snow-galleries till they came to the mouth of the dreary Grialetsch Valley, with ragged Piz Vadret at its head; and there, with their backs against the road-mender's hut, they sat for a long half-hour's rest and the chance of passing a few words, for the road had claimed their breath as they climbed.

It was all so lonely, so peaceful, so aloof from the storm and stress of life, and so altogether delightful, that it was only now and again that the appalling reason for their being there obtruded itself upon them. And whenever it did so it came with something of a shock.

They had in themselves endless gardens of delight to ramble through, and it was, "—Do you remember that day at ——, Ray?" and "—I tell you, old girl, you gave me some rotten quarters-of-an-hour while that stuck-up little ramrod of a lieutenant was buzzing about you!"—and so on and so on, —every recollection rosy now with the joy of complete understanding, though at the time one and another had been anything but joyful.

The old road-mender came trudging up from his work while they still sat there. He nodded benevolently with something of a twinkle in his eye, as though he could still recall similar times of his own, and gave them a cordial "Grüss Gott!"

"We're doing our best to hold your house up for you," said Ray.

"So I see, Herr and Fräulein, and it is quite at your service. Everybody puts their backs against it after climbing from below. You are from Süss this morning?"

"From Süss this morning, and yesterday from Martinsbruck, and the day before that from Ried, and the day before that from Innsbruck," said Ray.

"It is a long walk. But when one is young— I also have been to Innsbruck. It is a great city. But there are too many people. They fall over one another in the streets. I like my mountains better and just one or two people a day. Thanks, Herr!"—at Ray's offer of a cigar—"With permission I will smoke it later. I am going to eat now," and he put it carefully away into his waistcoat pocket and got out bread and cheese from his little house, and sat and ate and talked.

"I had a Herr and a Fräulein here, yesterday," he said reminiscently. "No, it was the day before—"

"We met them at Martinsbruck."

"They were hastening home in fear of some war. But I did not clearly make out what it was all about. Is there going to be war, Herr?"

"I'm afraid it looks rather like it. That is why we are hastening home also."

"But what is it all about, Herr? And why, in the name of God, do men want to fight in these times?"

"Ah! Now that is a big question, my friend, and it would take a lot of answering. But, so far as we know at present, it is only Austria that wants to fight. You heard of the Archduke and his wife being shot, down in Bosnia?"

"I heard of that. I was sorry. I have had them here. They sat with their backs against the house just as you are doing. They seemed nice enough people. He gave me five kroner for sitting against my house—"

"Ah!—he was an archduke and rolling in money."

"I did not mean it that way, Herr. I do not want anything for people sitting against my house. It is a pleasure to me to have a word with them. There are not too many, you see."

"It is not like Innsbruck where they fall over one another in the streets," smiled Lois.

"No, it is not like Innsbruck, Fräulein, and I am glad of that. But why should their being shot make the rest want to fight?"

"That is only the pretext," said Ray. "Austria wants to stretch herself down south. In fact, I suppose, what she really wants is to get to the sea, and Servia lies in her way."

"If all men lived among the mountains they would learn a great many things you never learn down below there. I think one is nearer God up here, Herr and Fräulein."

"I'm sure of it," said Lois.

"But even the mountains have heard the sound of fighting," said Ray, to draw him on.

"If the men from below wanted to take our rights from us we would fight again of course. But they are not likely to come up here, are they, Herr?"

"Not up here, I should say. The trouble is, you see, that if Austria attacks Servia, Russia will probably intervene, and then Germany will come

46

in, and so France, and possibly Great Britain. We hope not, but one can never tell."

"Herrgott! That sounds bad," and the rough hand and big clasp-knife, which had been mechanically feeding the slow-munching jaws, stopped in mid-air and he sat staring at them. "Servians I do not know," he said presently. "Russians I have had here, and Frenchmen, and Austrians, and many English, and all those I have found good. But Germans, of whom I have had still more, I do not like.... And yet I hardly know why," he mused. "Their manners are not good, it is true; but it is something more than that. Well, I don't know—it is just that I do not like them and perhaps they perceive it."

"It is a very general feeling," said Ray.

"Is it now? Well, that is strange, but it shows it is they who are somehow in the wrong."

"They don't think so," laughed Ray, as he drew Lois to her feet by both hands. "We must be jogging on or we won't reach Davos to-night."

The old man firmly but politely declined Ray's offer of a mark, saying, "I thank you, Herr, but there is no need. It has been a great pleasure to talk with you and the Fräulein," and, not to tarnish so bright and unusual a trait, Ray did not press the matter, but offered him instead another cigar which was accepted at once as between man and man, and they all shook hands and parted.

They crossed the river and threaded their way through a rock-strewn valley, and up and on, with the Weisshorn towering white on the right and the Schwarzhorn on the left. Then they passed two little lakes, the one on the right clear as crystal, the one on the left greenish-white and opaque, which Ray told her was glacier-water while the other was probably fed by hidden springs.

They had lunch and another long rest at the Hospice, and then began the easy ten-mile stretch to Davos, through long stretches of pine-woods, dropping with the stream till it joined the Landwasser at Davos-Dorf, where they took the omnibus for Davos-Platz.

"We'll go to the Grand," said Ray,—"clothes or no clothes. We're sure to find English people there and we'll learn what's going on in the world outside."

So to the Grand, and sumptuous rooms and meals, though the very trim young gentleman in the office and the pompous head-waiter did look somewhat superciliously at their lack in the matter of wedding-garments.

But breeding tells where uttermost perfection in attire without it makes no headway at all, and by the time dinner was over they were on the best of terms with their nearest neighbours, who were delighted to find someone who had had no news of the world's doings for several days and were therefore eager and receptive listeners. And afterwards they sat in the lounge while a Canon, and a Doctor, and a Barrister, and a Colonel on the retired list,—who knew Uncle Tony very well by repute and asked Ray at once if he were related to Sir Anthony Luard as soon as he heard his name,—and several of their wives and daughters, fed them volubly with fairy-tales and fictions, some of which had some small substratum of fact, but mostly they were snowball legends which had grown out of all knowledge as they passed from mouth to mouth.

Their latest English papers were three days old. Swiss and German papers they had as late as July 30, but the news in them was for the most part vague and unsatisfying to souls that craved simple actual fact as to what was going on behind the veiled frontiers. Local letters were arriving, but none from England since July 28.

Lois and Ray sat and listened but got little from all the talk that went on. The general opinion—to which the Colonel stoutly refused to conform —was that things looked decidedly unpleasant but that, somehow or other, Great Britain would manage not to be drawn into any such awful mess as a European war. Sir Edward Grey had handled the Balkan affair admirably, and though they were all on the opposite side in politics, they one and all,— not excepting even the Colonel—acknowledged that he was the very best possible man for his difficult and delicate post.

The Colonel however dogmatically prophesied war all round.

"We can no more get out of it," he said warmly, "than we can any of us get home for some months to come."

"Do you really think we can't get home?" asked Lois anxiously.

"Think—my dear young lady?—I'm as sure of it as I am that I'm sitting here and expect to be still sitting here, or somewhere in this neighbourhood, two months hence. You see,"—and he proceeded to prove, beyond any possibility of doubt, that—granted the general war he was so certain of —every outlet—north, east, west, and south,—would be already blocked by the urgencies of mobilisation, and that until all the troops of the various nations were massed along the frontiers traffic across the denuded countries behind would be out of the question.

"Martial law everywhere," said he, "and thank God we're not in Germany!"

"There won't be any difficulty in getting about in Switzerland, I suppose," said Ray.

"Not on your own two feet. The diligences may stop any day. They'll want every horse they can lay hands on. They're sure to mobilise at once, just as they did in 1870. Every man they have will be on the frontiers yonder, from Schaffhausen to Basel, and round the corner towards Pontarlier, and again in all the passes leading from Italy. It's curious how they fear and detest the Italians. I met a young fellow the other day who went across to Tripoli solely to get a whack at the Italians, and got a bullet through the calf which he insisted on showing me. You see," he said to Ray, "we can't possibly keep out of it, for the simple reason that Germany will certainly try to get at France through Belgium—"

"That's just what Uncle Tony says."

"Of course. Every military man who has studied the question knows that is their game. Russia is slow, and Germany's plan is to smash France into little bits right away, then go for Russia, and then of course for us. Oh, it's all been mapped out to the last haystack for years, I warrant you, while we've been swallowing their bunkum and persuading ourselves they are really very decent quiet people something like ourselves, who only want to be let alone to go their own gentle way."

"And what's your idea of the prospects all round, Colonel?"

But at that the Colonel shook his head. "Germany is the principal factor in the case and I don't know her well enough to express an opinion. If she's really as strong and well-organised as she thinks she is, and as most people believe, it will be a red-hot business. Austria I don't think much of from what I've seen. Italy I do not know well. But I'm sure they're not hankering for the expense of a big war. France is better than some folks think. Adversity has taught her something."

"And England?" asked Ray, as the oracle lapsed into silence.

"England is, as usual, not ready. And besides she is not anxious for continental adventure. If England had hearkened to some of us old croakers —Jingoes and firebrands and scaremongers, we've been called,—she would be a decisive factor in the game. As it is—"

"Oh come! What about our fleet, Colonel?" said the Canon, whose eldest boy was second lieutenant on the "Audacious," and his youngest a middy on the "Queen Mary."

"Our fleet's all right, thanks to Churchill. But you can't utilise a fleet, say at Belfort or Nancy or on the borders of Belgium."

"What about Belgium?" asked Ray. "Has she any fight in her?"

"I have never imagined so. If old Leopold were alive the Germans would have a walk-over and the old boy's coffers would be fuller than ever. This new man—of whom I know very little—may be of a different kidney. But what can he do against Germany? She would simply roll over him if he tried to stand up for his rights. It would be sheer madness on his part."

"Divine madness!" said the Canon musingly. "Such things at times effect wonders beyond the understanding of man."

"And with England and France to back her up, and Russia piling in on the other side—" said Ray.

"There you are," said the Colonel, "—practically a European war."

49

Mrs Canon had meanwhile been quietly and unobtrusively, but none the less pertinaciously, affording Lois opportunities of explaining the exact nature of her relationship to Ray. And two vivacious Misses Canon, with their sympathies already openly given to the victim, eagerly awaited developments.

But Lois saw no reason for any beating about the bush. She explained the matter in full, acknowledging somewhat of irregularity in their proceedings but smilingly suggesting that if the war gave no one grounds for greater complaint they would all be very well off.

"How ripping!" said the younger girl, with dancing eyes.

"Katharine, my *dear*!" said her mother reprovingly.

"Absolutely and perfectly delectable!" asserted her sister, quite unabashed by the maternal disapproval. "I just wish——"

"Madeleine!"

And Madeleine's envious desires remained locked in the secrecy of her maiden heart until she and Katharine went upstairs to bed that night. But she and her sister could not make enough of Lois for the rest of the evening, and their eyes rested on her caressingly and longingly as though by much looking they might possibly absorb some of her obvious happiness.

"It must be delightful beyond words," whispered Katharine.

"It is," beamed Lois.

"Just like a honeymoon, only more so," sighed Madeleine rapturously. "Just all that."

"And you were at the Conservatorium at Leipsic!" said Katharine.

"I had nearly completed my two years there. It was a very jolly time. I enjoyed it every bit."

"Do come and sing something for us. There's a music-room over there and quite a decent piano."

"I don't mind. I love singing," and they slipped quietly away to the music-room and shut themselves in.

But no doors made by man could contain the full rounded sweetness of that fresh young voice, and presently the handle was quietly turned from the outside and the door pushed noiselessly open so that the multitude beyond might share in the enjoyment of it.

She had no music with her, of course, and what lay about—the jetsam of the years—did not appeal to her. So she played and sang some of the old Scotch songs dear to her mother, and they went right home to the hearts of some of her listeners as perhaps the more stately productions of the greater masters would not have done.

Between times, on the expectant silence of the hall, there would trickle from the inner sanctuary a subdued murmur of talk and now and again a ripple of laughter, and then the chords would sound again and the full sweet voice would peal out gloriously, and hearts swelled large in sympathy with it.

She wound up with "Home, Sweet Home!" and before some of her listeners had finished using their handkerchiefs in various furtive and surreptitious ways, she was pealing out "God save the King!" like a trumpet-call, and "By Gad, sir! It went!"—as the Colonel said afterwards.

"My dear!" said the Canon, as he thanked her very warmly for the pleasure she had given them. "You have a God-given gift. You can touch the hearts of men and lift them to higher things. That is a wonderful power for good."

"I love singing," said Lois simply.

"Or you could not sing like that," said the Canon. "Your joyous young heart is in your voice."

As the following day was Sunday, and their next march would take them once more into the wilds—over the Strela and by Schanfiggthal to Chur and then up Rheinthal to Andermatt,—they decided to take a rest-day where they were, in the hope that further news from the outside world might arrive before Monday morning.

Nothing came, however, except the Berne newspapers, which hinted at mobilisation in Russia, and told of the murder of M. Jaurès in Paris. Even these scraps of news, however, afforded the Colonel ground for ample comment, and that of the gloomiest character, on the general outlook.

"Jaurès," he said, "was a great leader and he worked hard for a better understanding between France and Germany. His removal, at this crisis and in this fashion, seems to point to a fanatical revulsion of feeling against his ideas. That means that the tinder is ready for the match. If Russia is mobilising, Germany will follow suit, if she has not done so already. The fat may be in the fire at any moment. For all we know the fire may have broken out now, even while we sit here discussing it." Which made them all unusually thoughtful.

And as a matter of fact, with good reason. For Germany had declared war on Russia at 7.30 the previous night.

"Which way were you thinking of going?" the Colonel asked Ray, over their cigars in the lounge that night.

"First to Chur. Then up the valley to Andermatt, over the Furka, and down the Rhone Valley to Montreux."

"That's your best way. The East and North of France will certainly be closed. You may eventually get through by the Midi. But you'll probably have to wait even for that. It'll be a terrible upsetting all round. And I wish to God we could keep out of it, because we're not ready. But we can't. I'm as certain of that as that I'm sitting here."

"It'll be an awful business if it comes to a general scrap," said Ray.

"Yes. I've seen fighting in several parts of the world and it's grim business at best, but this will beat anything we've ever imagined, if I know anything about it. Germany is just a huge fighting-machine, and she'll fight like the devil. If Russia is in, France is in, and that almost certainly means we're in too. How do you stand yourself, Mr. Luard?"

"I'm in the London Scottish,—lieutenant. Do you think they'll want us?"

"Pretty sure to,—sooner or later,—every man that's available. How long have you had?"

"Four years."

"You should know your business fairly well. I think you'll have to reckon on a call. You'll go if needed?"

"Of course."

Which brought the possibilities very close home and made Ray Luard a very thoughtful man that night.

Next day they bade their friends good-bye, such of them as were up at so early an hour. And the Colonel and Katharine and Madeleine walked with them through the freshness of the morning by the winding forest-paths up Schatzalp, and were loth to part with them even on the top.

The Colonel, indeed,—whose youth lay away back amid the mists of antiquity, and whose years had discovered to him the existence of a heart that pumped on up-gradients, and a certain stiffness in the legs which filled him with wrath,—called them to many a halt to view the scenery. His hearty good-will was so obvious, however, that they complied with his necessities and accommodated their pace to his without regret; and the girls buzzed about Lois with outspoken envy of her happy lot, and vehemently regretted that they could not go and do likewise in every particular.

At the restaurant on top they drank a parting cup of coffee together, and then Ray and Lois set their faces towards the long ascent of the Strela, and the others stood and waved to them till they were out of sight.

"Do you know what the old boy was saying, Lois?" Ray broke out as soon as they were quite alone.

"No. What?"

"He's quite certain that England will have to go into the scrap, and that she'll need every man she can put into the fighting-line. And I'm one of them, you see."

"Oh!—Ray!" and she stopped in her tracks, and stood gazing at him with sudden woe in her face.

"It brings it close home to one, doesn't it, dear?" he said quietly, pressing her arm tight to his heart. "I've been thinking about it all night. It will be hard on us, but if the call comes I must go."

"Yes ..." she said, slowly and reluctantly; sense of duty prevailing, with obvious difficulty, over her heart's desire. "You must go.... But, oh,—it will be hard to let you go ... just when we've come to know one another, and life is at its brightest.... Oh, my dear! Suppose...."

"We won't suppose anything of the kind," he said cheerfully. "Life is not long enough at its longest to waste one minute of it on forebodings. But I named this, dear, because it seems to me that it settles for us the question I raised the other day. Unless you say no, we'll get married as soon as we get to Montreux."

"Yes!" she said simply, and the matter was settled.

And, in the feeling of still warmer and closer companionship that thereby came upon them, they climbed on up the Strela, and down the steep zig-zags on the other side to the Haupter Alp, and down and down past Schmitten and Dörfli, first this side of the river, then the other, till they came to the Schanfiggthal and Langwies, where they stopped for lunch and a long rest.

It was as they were coming down the hillside to Castiel that Lois had a quaint experience which Ray laughingly hoped would teach her a lesson.

They came suddenly on an immense herd of goats, whose bells they had heard tinkling far away below them for half an hour or more. Captivated by the graceful activities of a black and white kid, which sprang up a high rock at the side of the road and posed there like a little Rodin, with its glassy eyes fixed vaguely on them, Lois produced a biscuit from her pocket and proffered it to the youngster. He sniffed doubtfully, nibbled eagerly, and leaped down for more. And in an instant she was the centre of a writhing mass of goats, who pushed and reared themselves against her and would take no denial.

At first she laughed and pushed them off with her hands. Then it got beyond a joke. She gave them all she had, but they wanted more. Like the Danes and Ethelred, payment to go only drew them in larger numbers. Ray did his best to drag them back and get her clear, but they pushed and struggled and reared, with weirdest determination in their strange eyes and curving horns, till Lois grew somewhat startled.

"Stupid beasts! Don't you understand? You've had it all," and she shook her empty hands in their stolid straining faces. They pushed all the harder. She grew frightened, especially when she saw the futility of Ray's efforts.

It was his angry shouts, as he laid about on their bony ribs and backs with his alpenstock, that at last drew a small boy in velveteens and a slouch hat round the corner, and at a shrill whistle from him the beasts came to their senses and left their victim hot and dishevelled and very much put out.

"Why don't you keep your ugly beasts in order?" shouted Ray.

"Grüss Gott!" said the small boy with a vacant grin, and with stones and blows sent his flock jangling down into the lower woods.

"That's the most forcible argument I've ever come across against promiscuous charity," laughed Ray, as Lois shook herself clear of the sense and smell of them and did up her hair.

"The hideous beasts! Their stony eyes and stupid faces were awful,—a perfect nightmare! I shall dream of them for ages."

They stopped that night at Chur, and Lois duly dreamed of a never-ending struggle with multitudinous stony-eyed goats, and had a fairly bad night of it.

She seemed, indeed, so unrefreshed in the morning that Ray decided to make an easy day's work by taking train to Ilanz, and the diligence, if it was still running, for such further distance as it would take them.

And so it was half-past six in the evening when they reached Ruēras, where the diligence stopped for the night and they perforce stopped also. The accommodation was somewhat primitive, but the freedom of the simple life condoned everything. They ate well and slept well, and started off next morning in the best of spirits, with no cloud upon their horizon but the nebulous possibilities of the unknown future; and quite unconscious of the fact that, at eleven o'clock the night before, the mightiest die in the world's history had been cast. Great Britain had declared war on Germany.

They crossed a brook and a torrent, and in a deep ravine below the fragment of a ruined castle, Ray pointed out to her the little stream which he told her was the Baby Rhine in its cradle.

"It's always interesting to get back right to the beginning of a thing which in the end becomes a very big thing. We know what the Rhine is at its best and there's where it begins."

"I shall never forget it," said Lois, hanging on to his arm.

"And if the old Colonel is right, away over yonder it will soon be running red," said Ray thoughtfully.

"We'll try and not think about it till we have to.... But whatever comes, Ray, life has been very good to us."

"Yes, thank God! We have tasted the joy of it, whatever follows."

And away over yonder, the German hordes had, days ago, surged over the Rhine, and now they had burst into Belgium and were hammering at Liége, and the Meuse was running red and pouring its flood into the Rhine on its way to the sea.

They climbed steadily, with wonderful views over Rheintal and up into Vorder Rheintal, crossed the summit of Pass da Tiarms, and came down again to the old high-road at the eastern end of the gloomy little Oberalp-See.

"There lies the highway to happiness," said Ray, pointing away in front where, in the dim distance, a white thread of a road wound along a lofty mountain-side. "That's the Furka. Once we're over that we're in the Rhone Valley and almost at Montreux," and he pressed her arm tight again as a reminder of all that Montreux would mean for them.

They took the short cut down to Andermatt, got shaken almost to pieces with its stony steepness, and went to the Bellevue to recuperate with a well-earned lunch, and in hopes of getting some recent news from the outside world. But the Berne papers had not yet arrived and the foreign ones were many days old, and a chat with the manager furnished only disquieting war-like rumours, gathered by him from the officers of the big artillery-camp who sometimes came into the hotel for a meal or a smoke.

Ray was obviously restless under this lack of news, and Lois was quick to perceive and understand it.

"Let us get on," she said.

"Can you? Sure you're not done up?"

"Not a bit of it. It is delightful rambling along like this, but I've always the feeling that dreadful things may be going on outside, and if they are, the sooner we know the better."

"Yes. It's the not knowing that's so worrying. It's like wandering about in a fog with collisions and smashes going on all about one and no chance of seeing what's up. I'd sooner know the worst than nothing at all. I wanted to stop at the jolly little Golden Lion at Hospenthal. I stopped three days there once and I've always wanted to go back. But if we can get as far as Realp it will shorten to-morrow's walk over the Furka. The hotels at Gletsch are only for millionaires, not for tramps like us."

So they started off, determined to push along to Realp, or even to Tiefenbach if they could manage it, but Fate had arranged for them to stop at Hospenthal after all.

While they sat at lunch the sky darkened. The rain began before they had gone half a mile, and it came down in such sheets that Ray considered the advisability of turning back. But Lois would not hear of it, so with their Loden cloaks outside their rucksacs, they plodded on up the stony road which very soon became a river, while the mountain tops all round took on new white coats of snow.

"We'll have a rough time on the Furka to-morrow," said Ray. "I know what it's like in snow."

"I think I'd sooner have snow than cataracts like this. Will these cloaks keep the wet out?"

"They will, my child. The wetter they get outside, the less gets through."

"Then it's all right. We'll stop at your little hotel as soon as we come to it and get dry stockings on."

"And a jolly big fire and a first-rate supper. We'll be as cosy as cats."

"Who are all these men in front?"

"Weary ploughmen plodding their homeward way. But they look to me like Italian navvies—about the unpleasantest class of person you can meet in Switzerland. The rain's too much for them, I suppose, so they're knocking off for the day."

"Here's another lot coming the other way."

"Switzers these, by the look of them."

The two bands of about a score each passed one another some distance ahead of them, just about where the road forked, and one part struck up to the left towards the stony desolations and frowning peaks of the Gothard.

"Hello!" cried Ray. "What on earth are they up to?"

For the dark clump of men now nearest them, the Switzers,—halted suddenly, and turned, and then, as though moved by one spring, these made a dash at the others and flung themselves on them with shouts and blows till they broke and fled up the stony way.

"Well, well!" said Ray, watching keenly. "That's a little bit of racial feeling right under our noses, unless I'm mistaken. Symptomatic of the times. The Colonel said there was no love lost between them, and here's the proof of it. War's in the air, my child."

The Switzers having chased their opponents well up the stony road came swinging along now with cheerful faces and martial tread.

"What was it?" asked Ray as they came up.

"Just a swarm of Italian rats, Herr," said one jovially, while the rest gathered round grinning delightedly, and one or two wiped away smears of blood from their faces.

"They're mobilising for the war, over there, you see, and we're mobilising for the war, over here; and one of them showed his teeth at us as he passed, so we gave them a lesson in manners."

"But you will have no war here."

"Please God, no, Herr! But we've got to be ready, and if anyone sets foot on Swiss soil so much the worse for him. Those rascals would like to try it, we know, but if they do we'll treat them as we did this little lot and kick them back into their own country. We do not like them," and he spat disdainfully and all the others did the same.

"You are not thinking of going up Gothard way, Herr?" asked another meaningly.

"No, we stop at Hospenthal for the night, since it's raining so, and cross the Furka to-morrow."

"I wouldn't like to cross the Gothard within arm's length of that lot all by myself," said a third. "They may be good men but they don't look it. Have you any news of the war, Herr? Is France in it?"

"We've no news for days past. We're hoping to get some over yonder. But I'm afraid there's little hope of France keeping out."

"It'll be a big blaze," said the leader. "What about you, Herr, in England? Will you be in it too?"

"I'm very much afraid so. We're hurrying home as quick as we can."

"Well, for me, I hope Germany will get her head broken. Frenchmen I like, and Englishmen and Americans still better. But Italians I do not like, and Germans still less. They are too big for their clothes, and they are pigs to have any dealings with," and the others said "So!" and "Jawohl!"

"Well—grüss Gott, Herr and Frau! And may we all live to see better times!" and with a rumble of "grüss Gotts!" they went on their way, and Ray and Lois plodded on towards Hospenthal and a big fire and dry stockings and such defiance of the rigours of the road and the weather as a warm welcome could supply.

It was with a sigh of relief that Lois hastily felt over her rucksac, as the smiling maid drew off her dripping cloak, and found it sound and dry; and in spite of her soddened feet and streaming face and draggled hair the sight of a roaring fire in a room on the right induced a sense of coming comfort.

"You are wet, madame?—no?—not inside? That is goot. You will change your feet, and then hot tea, and all will be well,"—she had the cheerfullest face Lois had seen for months and she spoke English charmingly.

"That's the ticket, Freda," said Ray joyously. "The hottest tea you can make and a dash of cognac in it, and poke up that fire still more if you can do it without setting the place ablaze."

"Ach!"—and then, running at him with outstretched hands. "Why it is the Herr who stopped with us two years ago, and I did not for the moment know him. And this is madame? And you will stop the night? Yes?—in such weather?"

"Oh, we'll stop the night all right. Wild horses could not drag us away from that fire such a day as this."

"I will show you to your room and the tea will be ready by the time you come down. This way, madame—iff you please!"

"Steady on, Freda! Two rooms—iff you please."

"So?" in a tone of vast surprise, with a touch of disappointment in it.

"Mademoiselle is to become my wife as soon as we reach Montreux. I have been to deliver her from the hands of the Philistines—the Germans, I mean. She was in Leipsic—"

"Ach—those verdomte Germans! They are always making trouble. Then two rooms. This way, mademoiselle, iff you please!"

Hail and rain thrashed wildly on the window-panes as Lois refitted herself, but a quarter of an hour later, when they came down the stair together, and entered the cosy room whose dark wood panelling reflected the dancing flames all round, there was their tea-table drawn up close to the blazing hearth with two easy chairs alongside, and she felt a sense of home-iness greater than she had enjoyed during the last two years.

At a table not far away a burly, broad-backed man was busily writing letters with a big cigar in his mouth.

At sight of them he jumped up in vast surprise and came at them.

"Why—Ray Luard!—and Miss Lois?... Now what in the name of—what is it?—Mrs Ghrundy—are you two wandering round here for?"

"Hello? Why!—if it isn't Dr Rhenius! How are you, sir? We're as right as trivets—whatever they are, though we *hve* walked from Ruēras to-day."

"Ah—you come from Ruēras? And before that?"

"Lois was in Leipsic, as you know. Mrs Dare sent me to fetch her home. We couldn't get direct so we came round. What news have you? We've heard nothing but rumours for days. Let's have tea, Lois. I'm sure you're only half warmed yet. Have a cup of tea, Doctor?"

"I thank you, no. But I will smoke—if I may," with an appealing look at Lois.

"Oh do, please! I like it."

"Well now—where are *you* from, Doctor, and what's the latest facts?" asked Ray, as he laced his hot tea with cognac and insisted on doing the same with Lois's in spite of her protesting hand. "It's good for her under these circumstances. Now isn't it, Doctor?"

"I do not prescribe stimulants as a rule, as you know," said Dr Rhenius weightily. "But to anyone who has been out in that"—as the hail dashed against the windows again—"a moderate dose is undoubtedly indicated."

"That's better," said Ray, passing up his cup again. "Now, sir,—where are we?"

"At war," said the Doctor gravely. "Great Britain declared war against Germany last night."

"That's bad," said Ray, and he and Lois both sat staring aghast at the massive face lit up by the dancing flames.

They had known Dr Rhenius for ten years or more. He was established in Willstead before any of them came there. He had a good practice and private means of his own, and was generally esteemed and trusted. He was a bachelor, of five-and-forty or so, and in spite of his German-sounding name claimed Polish descent. His father, Casimir Rienkiwicz, had, he had told them, fled from Russian domination in Warsaw to the freedom of London, where his son was born. The father had adopted the less cumbrous name of Rhenius, and prospered in business. The son studied medicine in Edinburgh, in London, in Munich and in Paris, spoke German, French, and English with equal fluency, kept in close touch with the most advanced medical thought of all three countries, and employed their latest curative discoveries while his English confrères were still sniffing suspiciously at their outer wrappers.

The one thing that ever disturbed his equanimity was to be referred to as a German. At times the younger folk with humorous malice would drop an innocent, "Of course, you Germans," etc. etc., when the Doctor would lose his placidity and repudiate the innuendo with scorn and indignation. Victoria Luard was especially good at baiting him and enjoyed his outbursts to the full.

Such spare time as his patients allowed him he devoted to research into the subject of mental diseases. Whereby he and Connal Dare had become great friends. He had encouraged Con in the choice of his special line, and had helped him freely out of his own well-filled stores of knowledge and experience. When they met, which was rarely now, they went at it hammer and tongs, and in the intervals corresponded vigorously concerning any unusual cases Con came across, and the newest methods of treating them, and the results.

"Yes," said Dr Rhenius soberly. "It looks like being a general flare up, and that will mean—it will mean more than any of us can imagine."

"Where did you hear it?" asked Ray. "We have been aching for some definite word of what was going on, but no one seemed to know anything and no letters or papers were coming through."

"I was at Piora, near Airolo. The news came there this morning, and I packed up and started at once for home. I came through the tunnel to Göschenen, booked a seat in the diligence for to-morrow morning, and walked on here, because I know this little place of old and always enjoy it. It may be the last time some of us will enjoy it for a long time to come."

"You think it will be a long business, Doctor?" asked Lois anxiously.

He shook his big head discouragingly. "War is full of surprises, my dear. It is the very last thing I would care to prophesy about."

"Italy will go in with Germany and Austria, of course," said Ray.

The Doctor's big moustache crinkled up as he compressed his lips. "Eventually, one would suppose so. But, truly, I could discover no enthusiasm, or even inclination, for warlike adventure in the few with whom I had the opportunity of conversing. They are still suffering from Tripoli, down there, you see.... Where are you making for?"

"Two big M's, Doctor. Montreux and Marriage. We're going to get married as soon as we get there."

"So!"

"You see it's hardly right and proper—as you suggested just now—to be gadding about in this fashion together. So we're going to regularise the situation at the first possible moment."

"I will chaperone you with pleasure."

"Thanks awfully! But we'd sooner get married. We wouldn't like to be a burden on anyone."

"And how do you go?"

"We've walked mostly so far—all the way from Landeck, except one spell from Chur to Ruēras. We like it."

"If you take my advice you will get them to telephone for seats in the diligence and come along with me. It will not be walking weather for some days now. And the Furka in snow is a tough job. We get to Brigue to-morrow evening and to Montreux next day. They are mobilising here but the trains are still running. I wired to ask."

"I think we will. Lois is a splendid walker, but if it's going to be like this the sooner we're at Montreux the better," and he went at once and got Freda to telephone to Göschenen for seats in the diligence for the following morning.

She came in presently with the information that every seat was booked both for the morning and afternoon service.

"And for the following day?" he asked.

"Two coupé-seats only are left, Herr."

"Book them for us at once, Freda, and we will either stop here or walk on up the Furka and take our places when the diligence catches us up."

"Jawohl, Herr!"

"I must get on," said the Doctor, "or I would joyfully wait with you here."

"Oh, we wouldn't think of it. How about getting on from Montreux?"

The Doctor nodded musingly. "There one will have to be guided by circumstances. I shall go on to Geneva and endeavour to make my way through France. But it may not be an easy matter. Everything will be under military law and mere civilians will not be of much account just now. You may have to wait there for a time till the first rush to the frontiers is over."

"We expected that. That's why we're going to get married as soon as we get there."

"I will tell them all about it at home, if I succeed in getting there. They will be very suspicious of foreigners in France. They may lock me up. You have no passports, I suppose."

"Not a scrap between us. I've never carried one in my life."

"This has taken us all unawares. But I always carry one. It is useful at times, in procuring one's registered letters and so on.... And money?—you have plenty?"

"Enough to go on with. If we don't turn up you might ask Uncle Tony to send us some more—to Poste Restante, Montreux," and the Doctor methodically made a note of it.

They talked much of matters connected with the coming war, all through supper and afterwards. They had the hotel to themselves. Freda told them that up to three days ago they were full; then, at once, everyone fled at news of the possibility of war.

But, except as to the broad facts of the case, the Doctor was very noncommittal, and thinking over all their discursive talk afterwards, Ray found himself very little the wiser for it all. His own opinions he could remember expressing very fully and freely. But, though the Doctor had discoursed weightily at times on various points, Ray could not recall anything of any great importance that he had said or any new light that he had cast upon the complex situation. The matter visibly weighed upon him and even cast its shadow on him.

They saw him for a few minutes next morning, and then the diligence rolled up and he was gone.

It was a bleak day, cold slush under foot and a wind that held in it the chill of the snow-peaks. They delighted Freda by deciding to wait there for the diligence next morning, and enjoyed the warmth within the more for the cold without.

CHAPTER IX

AT home, meanwhile, they were living in a whirl of conflicting rumours, fears, hopes, which changed their faces with every edition of the papers, but possessed one lowest common denominator in an intense and ever-increasing anxiety.

Mr Dare wore a very grave face in these days; and as his wife understood—to some extent at all events—the difficulties he had to wrestle with in consequence of the total cessation of business with the Continent, she found it no easy matter to keep as cheerful a heart as she would have wished, but bravely did her best that way.

One quick glance at her husband's face, when he came in of a night, told her more than all the papers, and the news was never encouraging.

Every evening, the Colonel, possessed of a firm belief in the efficacy of the commercial barometer as an index of the political outlook, came in to gather John Dare's latest observations of it. And he too could tell with one glance at John Dare's face how things were going.

When Mr Dare was late, as often happened, he generally found the Colonel sitting there waiting for him and doing his best meanwhile to cheer Mrs Dare. But, try as they all might, their cheerfulness was of a gray autumnal character which foresaw wintry weather before any hope of Spring.

From the mere business point of view the fact of Great Britain being dragged into the mêlée could not make matters very much worse for Mr Dare than they were. But that dreadful possibility entailed others of so intimate a character that it was impossible to close one's eyes to them.

"I wish those two were safely home," said Mrs Dare, busy with her sewing one evening, as the Colonel, in Mr Dare's easy chair, sat waiting with her for its proper occupant's arrival.

"I'm sure you needn't worry about them, dear Mrs Dare," said the Colonel emphatically. "Ray knows his way about and they'll be perfectly all right. We may get a wire from them at any moment saying they'll be here in an hour."

"I'm surprised we've had no word of any kind since Ray left."

"I expect things are all upside down all over the Continent. We'll hear from them all right in time."

Then Mr Dare came in and they saw by his face that the City barometer was still at stormy.

"Rumours galore," was his report, "and mostly disturbing. Sir Edward Grey is doing everything in his power for peace, but the general feeling is that the Kaiser means war, and the City is preparing for it. Bank-rate is up to 4. It may be 8 to-morrow. Consols down to 70. Everything is in suspense. No business doing."

"And what do they say as to our being dragged in?" asked the Colonel anxiously.

"General idea is that only a miracle can keep us out, and that miracles aren't common."

"Any talk of mobilising?—fleet and army?"

"No orders yet, as far as one can learn, but there is little doubt word has been sent round to be ready. I saw Guards marching through this morning. In fact there is an undoubted sense of war in the air."

"And how do they feel as to our preparedness, if it comes to that?"

At which Mr Dare shook his head. "Not a doubt as to our readiness at sea. But on land—" he shrugged discomfortingly, "Well, the general feeling is that what we have is good, but so small as to be of very little account among the huge masses that may be engaged over there. They say there may be ten million men fighting—"

"How awful!" said Mrs Dare. "Ten millions! And all with relatives of one kind or another! Just think of the aftermath—the suffering and misery! I am not a violent person, but, truly, there is no ill I could not wish for the men who bring such a horror about."

"They'll suffer!" said the Colonel.

"We too," said Mr Dare soberly. "And here is how it comes home to us. If we're drawn in there will be an urgent call for more men—"

"Quite right!" said the Colonel. "If you'd listened to advice we'd have had 'em ready. Now we shall have to do the best we can with what we can get."

"The Territorials will be mobilised—"

"But they are surely for home defence," said Mrs Dare.

"They will be needed at the front. Presumably the choice will be given them."

"And they'll go," said the Colonel. "They're not half as bad as some folks have been trying to make out, and this will buck them up to top notch."

"That means your Ray will be in it."

"He wouldn't be my Ray unless he was, sir."

"And our Noel. He's been at us for days past for permission to join," said Mrs Dare without enthusiasm.

"He'll go London Scottish with Ray of course. Good lad!"

"He was up seeing about it to-day," said Mr Dare. "And he's hoping he can get into the Second Battalion if they form one. He's put down his name for it anyway and I suppose he'll have to go. I never knew him so keen on anything in his life before."

"Good lad!—The right sort! Does honour to his parents."

"And Con is expecting to be called up," said Mrs Dare.

"And I bet you Alma will want to be in it. Our two families are doing their duty. Da-ash it! If all the others would come up to the scratch as well there'd be no lack of fighting-men."

"And suppose they none of them come back," said Mrs Dare forebodingly.

"One never supposes such things, ma'am. If they go, they go to the duty God has called them to. And if they never come back they'll have done their best for their King and their country, and that is the noblest thing any man or woman can do."

"I know, Colonel, but ... all the same, it would be very sore to lose them."

"It would be sorer still for Germany to ride rough-shod over England. They're great fighters, and if it comes it'll be hot work. Thank God, they're not barbarians, however, and they'll fight decently and respect the rules of the game."

But even in that thought Mrs Dare found but little comfort, and try as she might she could not attain to the Colonel's altruistic heights of patriotism.

"It is different," she said to herself. "After all, his two are not bone of his bone and flesh of his flesh, and that makes all the difference in the world."

"Where are they all to-night?" asked Mr Dare. For the thought that before very long partings might come unconsciously distilled within him a curious little desire to know they were still within reach. "Noel came up to have lunch with me and to tell me about the London Scottish. I understood he was coming straight home."

"He came and told me about it," said Mrs Dare. "It has given him a new zest in life. He was on the links all afternoon, and then he insisted on taking the girls into town to 'When Knights were Bold.'"

"H'm!" said Mr Dare. "I must be out of touch with eighteen and a half. I can't say I feel like the theatre myself."

"Young blood runs red," said the Colonel. "The jump in it that makes him want to go to the theatre will help him through tight places later on."

"Do you think it will be a long business, Colonel?" asked Mrs Dare, in pursuance of her own thoughts.

"Hard to say, ma'am. Personally I should be inclined to say not. The expense of all those men in the field will be so enormous,—to say nothing of the upsetting of business and life generally. One or two tremendous battles and it may be over. War is full of surprises. One side or the other may crumple up unexpectedly and cry 'enough.' On the other hand it is not easy to think of Germany doing that, after all her bumptiousness. And I'd hate to think of France and Russia giving in. Auntie Mitt is hard at work knitting winter socks and comforters, and Balaclava helmets."

"Goodness me! Does she think it will last as long as that?"

"She says she remembers hearing they were badly wanted in the Crimea,—which was a fact. I've been hinting to her that she probably remembers making them at that time, and, being a good Conservative, instinct impels her to do as she did then."

"Too bad!" smiled Mrs Dare. "She could hardly have knitted for the Crimea."

"I'm not so sure of that. She's frightfully close and touchy about her age. She's wonderfully well-preserved, and she's a good little soul, but I do enjoy chaffing her. It's a pleasure to see the prim and extremely lady-like way in which she takes it. She always makes me feel like a little boy at school again. You've no definite word from Con yet?"

"He's all ready packed to start at a moment's notice, and is quite sure he will have to go. Nothing more than that. It's all very disturbing to one's peace of mind."

"Not half as disturbing, ma'am, as if the Germans got across here. Let us be thankful that if there is to be fighting it'll be on the other side of the water. Business is quite at a standstill, I suppose, Dare?"

"Mine is, and most other people's. If the mere threat of war curdles things up like this it's hard to imagine what they'll be like if it actually comes."

"It'll be a case of everybody helping everybody else," said the Colonel, gallantly and meaningly, and on that note jumped up to go. "I must run along and see how Auntie Mitt's getting on with those Balaclava helmets!" he said, and shook hands with them warmly, and went.

CHAPTER X

THE unsettled state of international politics affected the younger folk much as it did their elders, only in a different way and to a less extent.

It produced in them an excitement and effervescence of spirits which left no room for broodings or forebodings. They closed their eyes to the grimmer possibilities and saw only the picturesque and dramatic and thrilling.

They were all most keenly interested in every move in the mighty game, and somewhat impatient of the slow development of the intricate situation. The number of evening papers that found their way into both houses was astonishing, and extremely wasteful.

Their local weekly paper arranged for a telephonic news-service with a London paper, and posted in its windows irregular bulletins, the more startling the better. Whoever went into the village was expected to bring back the latest rumours. Mrs Dare, when she went, was content to carry the items of any importance in her mind. The Colonel, and Noel, and Honor, and Victoria Luard invariably bought latest editions as well, sometimes of half-a-dozen different papers, in the hope that one or other would contain something illuminating which had escaped the rest. And in the anxious search for that illuminating item they read the same news over and over again in all the papers, till, as Noel said, they "got fairly fed up with chewing the same bit till there was no taste in it." Yet the exercise seemed only to leave them the hungrier for more startling later editions. They all, in fact, had a pretty severe attack of news-fever, and it grew worse with every day that passed and with all the thin and unsatisfying pabulum it fed upon.

Noel and the girls and young Gregor MacLean spent much time on the links. There was no talk of going away for holidays this year, not at all events while things were in their present unsettled condition.

The Luards had planned to spend September in Switzerland, at Saas-Fée and Zermatt. Noel and Honor were to have gone with them, and Mr and

Mrs Dare had intended making a round of visits in Scotland.

Connal Dare and Alma Luard, if they could get off at the same time, had been going to friends on Dartmoor not far from Postbridge. As for Miss Mitten, she never would hear a word about going away. No place was as comfortable as home, she averred,—she had everything there that she wanted, so why should she make a change which could only be for the worse?

But all plans had had to be given up, and the younger folk consoled themselves with much golf and tennis, and flung themselves into these things with the gusto of players whose time might be short.

But, among them all, bad as things looked, there was still—except in the mind of the Colonel, and perhaps also of Mr Dare,—a strong undercurrent of feeling that so incredible a catastrophe as a general European war, in this year of grace 1914, was impossible. Things had looked threatening before, time and again, and the clouds had rolled by without breaking. The men at the head of affairs, Mr Asquith and Sir Edward Grey, were eminently safe and experienced, and pre-eminently set on peace. It was all mighty interesting, thrilling indeed at times, though the thrills of the evening were not seldom found to have been wasted when they eagerly scanned the more sedate morning papers. But it would—they could not but believe—all end in smoke, as it had so often done before.

And so the younger folk got all the thrills the papers could afford them, and all the enjoyment out of life that was to be had under the circumstances; and no one, from their merry talk and laughter, would have imagined that just across the water issues so tremendous for the future of the world were surely and quickly coming to grips.

Gregor MacLean lived with his widowed mother at White Lodge, on the other side of Willstead Common. He was an only son, but, through the good Scotch common-sense of his parents, had escaped the usual penalty of only sons. He was in fact a genuinely good fellow, somewhat reserved and unexpressive of his feelings, and in no way spoiled either by his mother's delight in him or the good-sized shoes he had stepped into at his father's death.

He was on the Stock Exchange, in his late father's firm, Dymoke and MacLean, of Draper's Gardens. But the Stock Exchange was for the time being dead, and as Gregor said he saved in every way,—money, gray matter, and nervous energy—by stopping at home, he stopped at home and enjoyed himself,—gauging the pulse of affairs by the price of Consols and the Bank-rate in the evening and morning papers, and laying in stores of health on the links, while yet there was time, against the demands the future might make upon him.

The firm of Dymoke and MacLean was of long-standing and high repute. It had a solid old connection which at the best of times did little in the way of speculation, and never dreamed of realising when things were at their worst. It did, occasionally, when the bottom had fallen out of things generally, confer ponderously with the heads of the firm and empower them to buy for it good old reliable stock which the less fortunate had had to jettison, and sometimes it invested on a large scale, as provision for younger sons and unmarried daughters. And so the business was an eminently safe one and satisfactorily profitable, and old John Dymoke could sit comfortably in his big swing-chair in his office in Draper's Gardens, no matter what wild storms swept the Street outside, and young Gregor could spend his days on the links with perfect equanimity, though the virus of possible war had thrown the Exchanges of the world into convulsions such as they had not known for generations.

Mr Dymoke played neither golf nor tennis. He loved Draper's Gardens and the society of his old cronies of the Exchange. Gregor MacLean took great interest both in golf and tennis and in the play of Miss Honor Dare, and looked upon Draper's Gardens as one of the necessities of a comfortable existence but not as a place to spend more time in than was absolutely imperative.

And that is how he came to be spending profitable days on the links while his less-pleasantly-situated fellows were worrying themselves gray over the slowly unfolding developments of international politics.

Between him and Honor there existed an entente cordiale which Gregor hoped in time to consolidate into a more comprehensive alliance. Honor understood him very well,—far better than he understood her, and she was not averse to an eventual acquiescence with his hopes and views as to her future. But in the meantime—partly no doubt as the result of her close intimacy with Victoria Luard—she was in no hurry to surrender her entire freedom of action even for what most girls would have considered the higher estate of an affiance with Gregor MacLean.

She liked him better than any of the other young men to whom her pretty face and comradely ways proved so great an attraction. He was, as she not infrequently told him, if anything too well endowed with this world's goods. So well that no incentive to arduous work was left him.

To which he would reply that you couldn't judge of a fellow entirely by his form at tennis or his handicap on the links. She should see him on 'Change, wrestling with beasts at Ephesus, and carrying fortunes on his bare head.

At which Honor's merry laugh would ring out and set him to soul-searching for means of approving himself to her in larger and loftier ways.

Between Noel Dare and Vic also there existed a distinct feeling of something more than friendliness, which was not without its humorous aspects both to themselves and their families.

They had known one another intimately for ten years. At the beginning, when they were both about of an age—between eight and nine—Noel had genially bullied her and Honor to his heart's content, ordered them about, pulled their pig-tails when he pleased, and called them kids, and they had accepted his masterfulness as quite in the natural order of things.

By the time they reached fourteen they were on a level, and Noel found his powers of command over them gone. He might order, but they only laughed and went their own way.

And now, at nineteen, their positions were reversed. Victoria had developed into a young woman of advanced and very decided views, with aims in life and immense energy in carrying them out. And Noel felt himself little more than a schoolboy in her presence.

As to touching her hair!—it would have been a desecration! He never dreamed of it,—not of actually doing it anyway. It was something even to touch her hand. And he sombrely said to himself at times that she was getting beyond him. And he doubted within himself, whether even the most assiduous devotion to St Mary Axe could ever place him in the position he aspired to regarding her.

They all four came clattering into the hall at Oakdene one afternoon, after a splodgy round of the links, damp and bedraggled and thirsting for tea. Auntie Mitt had it served in next to no time, and between little sips at her own cup sat busily knitting and listening to their wonderful flow of spirits, which found vent in a jargon that was still utterly unintelligible to her, in spite of the amount of it to which in her time she had listened.

But by the time they had finished their third cups they had fought the battle all through again, had explained away all their failures to the entire satisfaction of those chiefly concerned, had replumed themselves on their more outstanding successes, and then, as the boys lit their cigarettes with sighs of satisfaction, their minds came down again to mundane affairs.

"Where's Uncle Tony, Auntie Mitt?" asked Victoria.

"Sir Anthony is just coming up the drive, my dear," said Auntie Mitt, with a glance out of the window. "He went down to the village to see if there was any news," and Uncle Tony came in, paper in hand.

"Ah-ha!" said he, "Mudlarks!..."

"And as merry, sir," said Gregor. "Damp but undaunted"....

"Dirty but not dispirited," said Honor briskly.

"Defeated but defiant," said Vic. "Your turn, No."

"Oh, dash!" said Noel, who was not over-good at that kind of mental gymnastics.

"My copyright!—since Victoria-who-should-by-rights-have-been-Bala-clava won't allow me to say damn," said the Colonel.

"Of course I won't,—with Auntie Mitt, sitting there listening with all her ears—"

"I heard it not infrequently before you were thought of, my dear," said Auntie Mitt, with her little bird-like uplook and smile. "It was, I think, much more commonly used even in the best society than it is now. I believe even the Duke himself"....

"Ah—he needed me to keep him in order. I wonder you didn't do it yourself, Auntie Mitt."

"Oh,—my dear!"

"Any news, sir?" asked Gregor.

"Bank-rate 8 per cent—"

"Deuter-on-omy!"

"And the Stock Exchange closed till further notice."

"Gee-willikins! Things are shaping badly then, sir!"

"Very badly, I fear. Russia and Germany are practically at war, though no formal declaration has yet been made, I believe."

"And how do we stand now, sir?" asked Noel eagerly.

"On the brink, my boy. Sir Edward Grey is still working his hardest for peace. But, personally, I should say the chances are of the smallest."

"I wonder where Lois and Ray have managed to get to," said Honor anxiously.

"You trust Ray, my dear. They'll be all right. I just called in to reassure your mother. I knew her first thought would be for them when she heard the news."

"But surely we ought to have heard from them before this—"

"Not under the circumstances. Nothing would pass into or out of Germany the moment they began to mobilise,—no letters, no telegrams, certainly no foreigners. But they would start at the latest on Monday. This is Friday. They ought certainly to be well on their way by this time. But, you see, they may have had to take some roundabout route,—perhaps off the beaten track. We shall hear from them all right in time. They don't cause me the slightest anxiety."

"Think of closing the Exchange! ... and eight per cent! That shows what the big pots think of things anyway," said Gregor, beating a soft tattoo on the floor with his heels in his amazement. "Shows I was right in stopping away too! Sight better here than mouching about down there! I wonder when they'll open shop again."

"If we're right into it—as we shall be," said the Colonel, with conviction, "it's impossible to say how things will go on. We've never had such a crisis before, you see, and I don't suppose any living man can foresee just how things will work out. Money will be very tight, I expect. Provisions may go up beyond anything we've ever known. That will depend on the fleet. If we can hold the seas—"

"Why, of course we can, sir. What's our fleet for?" said Gregor.

"They have some ships too, I believe."

"They have, and we'll give them beans if they'll give us half a chance," said Noel.

"It might be wise to lay in a stock of provisions," suggested Miss Mitten. "I remember during the—I mean, hearing—that food went to extraordinary prices during the Crimean War."

"Go it, Auntie Mitt! We'll go up to the Army and Navy to-morrow and clear them out," laughed Vic. "This really sounds like war times."

"You'd better load us up too, while you're at it, Vic," said Honor, "or maybe we'll be sitting by the roadside crying for a crust."

"Wait a moment, you giddy young people," said Uncle Tony, nodding his gray head sagely at them. "Let us look at this matter for a moment. Suppose everybody acts on that idea. What is going to be the result?"

"The bulls will clear the market and outsiders will go short," said Gregor.

"Exactly! And the outsiders would be in the proportion of a hundred—perhaps a thousand—to one. I've no doubt some—perhaps even many—will do as Auntie Mitt proposes. It will naturally suggest itself to the provident housekeeper,"—with a conciliatory little bow to the already conscience-stricken little lady,—"but the effect will be bad all round. It will drive up prices unnecessarily. It will deplete stocks. It will emphasise the gap between the rich and the poor. Carried to extremes it might well lead to riot and revolution, for starving men stick at nothing."—Miss Mitten clasped her thin little black-mittened hands as though she saw them coming and begged for mercy, and her face was woe-begone. "Indeed, in such a case, I would hold a man justified in storming any house which had provisioned itself in such a way—"

Miss Mitten unclasped her hands and waved them at him in gentle deprecation, saying almost with a sob, "I am sorry, Sir Anthony. I stand rebuked. The matter had not presented itself to me in that light. But I assure you I was thinking of you all rather than of myself, or indeed of anybody else. I was in the wrong. I see it."

"You never thought of yourself before anybody else in all your life, my dear," said the Colonel gallantly. "We know you were thinking only of us. But all the same, as you see, it would be an unpatriotic thing to do and we will set our faces against it. If prices go up—as they will—we'll pay 'em. If supplies run short we'll do the best we can. We can always fall back on porridge,"—which was Miss Mitten's particular detestation.

"It is said to be very sustaining," she said meekly, at which he choked violently through politely endeavouring to swallow a chuckle.

"How'll we be off for men, sir?" asked Noel.

"Short as the dev—the deuce, my boy. Have you heard from your London Scottish yet?"

"Not yet, sir. There's hopes of a Second Battalion, but it's not decided yet. I shall go up again to-morrow—"

"I'll go with you," said Gregor, with sudden decision.

"And we'll sit on their door-step till they make up their minds and take us on. Golf and tennis are off, my children,"—with a nod at the girls. "It's pipes and sporrans and skean-dhus now, and 'Up with the Bonnets of Bonnie Dundee!'"

"Good lads! When the need is known they'll all come flocking up. The trouble is that you can't make even volunteers into fighting-men without training. We ought to have had you all at it years ago. Then we'd be ready now."

"We'll do our best, and pick it all up as fast as we can. It'll be better business than footling about the links anyway," said Noel.

"Rather!" said Gregor.

And the girls took no umbrage at that, but they seemed a trifle quieter than usual.

CHAPTER XI

DR CONNAL DARE was striding along the passage leading to the general room when he met old Jackson.

He and old Jackson met in that passage every morning, and always the same thing occurred.

Old Jackson, with the fatigues of another night of hideous dreams still heavy upon him, awaited Con's coming with anxious face. As soon as he saw him in the distance his dull face lightened with a look of expectancy. And at sight of him Con's face began to crinkle up amusedly at the corners of the eyes.

"Doctor! Won't you smile for me?" the old man asked, as they drew near one another, and Con set his broad shoulders to the wall and laughed out in spite of himself and the regularity of the proceeding.

The weary old eyes gazed up at him intently, and the woe-begone old face lost some of its over-carefulness. A twisted grin flickered over it, as if in spite of itself, and then he said, "Thank you, Doctor! Sight o' you does me a sight o' good," and shambled off re-inspirited, while Con, with the crinkles still in the corners of his eyes, continued his rounds.

But, though he had laughed as usual for old Jackson's benefit, and though the remains of the laugh lingered in the corners of his eyes, he was feeling graver than he ever remembered feeling in his life before. For he had just been reading, over his breakfast, the momentous news that Great Britain, having received no reply to her ultimatum respecting the neutrality of Belgium, had declared war on Germany. And that was enough to make any man grave indeed.

He was on his way back from the women's hospital wards, where he had two or three cases which were causing him some anxiety, when one of the attendants caught sight of him and came hurrying up.

"I've just taken a letter to your room, sir. Special, I think. I didn't know where you were."

"Thank you, Barton! I'll go along and get it," and he knew what that letter was likely to be.

And it was. A long official envelope with O.H.M.S. in peremptorily solid black letters above the address 'Dr Connal Dare, R.A.M.C.'

He ripped it open and found himself no more Dr Dare of Birch Grove Asylum but Dr and Lieutenant Dare of the Royal Army Medical Corps, under orders to report himself within twenty-four hours at Medical Head-Quarters in London.

He read the orders quietly, and stood for a moment considering them and himself, and the whole matter aloofly. His eyes wandered thoughtfully round the room—over his books, his few pictures and photographs of the home-folks. It was quite within the possibilities that he might never see any of these things again. War was full of mischances, even in the non-combatant arm.

He was all ready, kit packed, notes of his cases carefully written out. He added a word or two to these and swung away to see the Chief, his mind hard at work on another matter.

Two hours later, all very spick and span in his uniform, he had deposited his baggage in the Luggage-Office at London Bridge, had invaded St. Barnabas's and interviewed the Matron, and had masterfully talked her into breaking the rules, or at all events straining them to such a point that the desire of his heart could creep through.

He had been one of her favoured boys when he was there and they were on very friendly terms, and, as he explained to her with extreme earnestness, it was, after all, only a technical breach and—it was war-time. He tried to prove that they were all under martial law but she only smiled at him. He might be. She was not.

Still, she was willing to admit that circumstances—such as a general European War—altered cases. She had been young herself and she understood fully how he felt. As a matter of duty she put it to him to consider whether it was the best thing to do, and he proved to her, with his most irresistible smile, that it was. And finally she sent an attendant to find Nurse Luard.

Alma came in in a few minutes and became a radiant illumination at sight of Con in his uniform—a radiance of sparkling eyes and tell-tale cheeks.

"I was expecting you," she said happily.

"You are to arrange your work on somebody else's shoulders and come out with me for the afternoon, Alma. Matron is not quite sure if it is wisdom or foolishness—"

"We will prove it to be wisdom. I'll be ready in ten minutes. Will you wait?"—as she sailed away.

"I'll wait ten minutes," grinned Con.

"When do you expect to go?" asked the Matron.

"As soon as the men go. And the sooner they get across the better. We ought to be in Belgium now. The Germans are hammering away at Liége, and I doubt if the Belgians singlehanded can do much. They never struck one as particularly martial."

"Well, I hope you'll come through it safely. It would be a terrible thing for you both if ..." and she nodded gravely.

"No good forecasting troubles. The worst ones don't come as a rule, and it's no good thinking about them. We're under the Red Cross, and they fight straight and respect it."

"Shells and bullets are no respecters of persons, and in war one never knows what may happen."

"Anyway it will be a mighty satisfaction to know that we belong to one another."

"We must hope you are doing the right thing. It's a very natural thing, I acknowledge."

"And the natural thing is the right thing as a rule, now isn't it?"

"Sometimes,"—and Alma came in, her dark eyes dancing and her face still flushed with the thought of the great adventure on which they were bound.

The Matron shook hands with them both very warmly, and wished them 'God-speed!' very heartily, and then they were gliding away in a taxi to Doctors' Commons, and from there to the nearest Registrar's Office, and they came out of it a few minutes later man and wife.

"We'll have a little wedding-feast at the Savoy under the guise of lunch," said Con gaily. "I had breakfast at eight. And then we'll taxi all the way home. I can't possibly permit you to mingle with ordinary people in ordinary trains yet. Besides, I want to kiss you all the way down, and there's nothing like a closed taxi—"

"Dear, dear! What experience you seem to have had!"

"Not a quarter enough, as you'll see, Mrs Dare. Here we are! Now we'll get a table in the balcony and watch old Father Thames rolling down to the sea."

"The tide is coming in," said Alma, as she drew off her gloves.

"Good omen! The rising tide!—and here's the sun to add his blessing,"—as the watery gray clouds up above parted and let a gleam of sunshine through.

They had the most memorable little lunch of their lives there,—with the turgid yellow-gray flood brimming below them, dotted here and there with a great creeping water-beetle of a black barge;—and the gray and black spans of the bridges, up-stream and down, looming in and out of the picture in the wavering sunlight;—and the yellow trams spinning to and fro like shuttles through the gray web of life;—and the tall chimneys and the shot tower on the opposite bank, with the ragged wharves at their feet;—and the Embankment gardens and trees and sauntering mid-day crowds, all just as usual and manifesting no undue concern about anything.

"And we're actually at war with Germany at last," said Con, as they sat looking down on it all.

"I'm glad we're taking it so quietly," said Alma. "We mean business."

Their very polite waiter attended punctiliously to all their wants, acknowledging all orders with a grave inclination of the head and never once opening his mouth. He might have been dumb for any evidence they had to the contrary. Between courses he hovered about watchfully, seemed interested in Con's uniform, and distinctly appreciative of Alma's nurse's costume and general appearance. Even Con's very generous tip he only acknowledged with a final silent bow.

When Alma commented on such refinement of taciturnity, Con suggested that he was possibly a German looking forward without enjoyment to a change of occupation which would be less to his taste.

They had a delightful run out to Willstead, and Con made best use of his opportunities, having taken care to seat his wife directly behind the driver.

All too quickly they were there, taking Mrs Dare Senior's breath away by the magnitude of their announcement.

"Mother—my wife!" was Con's little way of breaking the news. "I have to leave to-morrow morning so we decided to get married to-day."

"Well!" gasped his mother, and then took Alma to her heart and kissed her warmly.

"He never could have made a better choice, dear," she said. "But it is very sudden.... I hope it is wisely done."

"We think it is, mother," said Alma joyously. "Whatever happens we have this, and it has made us very happy."

"Have you seen the Colonel?"

"Not yet," said Con. "Mothers come before Uncles. We'll go along presently and make him jump. Auntie Mitt will probably have a fit."

"Have you had any lunch,—or did this great business make you forget it?"

"We had our wedding breakfast at one o'clock in the balcony of the Savoy," said Alma. "It was delightful."

"Then you're ready for a cup of tea," and she rang the bell and ordered it in as quickly as it could be got ready.

"But won't this mean your giving up your post, Alma?" asked Mrs Dare thoughtfully, as soon as she had time to look at the matter all round.

"Not at present. Matron had to be told of course. But Con is one of her old favourites, and she is to say nothing about it for a time. You see, if the war amounts to anything and goes on long, they are sure to be called on for nurses to go to the front and they'll be short-handed—"

"And they couldn't afford to dispense with the best nurse they've got, on a mere technicality," said Con. "And as soon as it's all over I'm to join old Jamieson in Harley Street, and we'll set up housekeeping—probably with him. He's got room enough for four families in that big house of his."

"Well, well!" said Mrs Dare, and said no more, but her mother's heart prayed fervently that no whiff of the war-cloud might dim the bright and hopeful outlook of these eager young lives.

They chatted quietly over their tea, of Lois and Ray, and of Noel and young MacLean and their war-like cravings, and of Vic and Honor, and all the other little family matters in which they were all interested.

"I'd love to see those boys in kilts," said Alma.

"They don't know yet if there will be a Second Battalion," said Mrs Dare. "But if they don't get into the London Scottish they'll join something else. They are quite set on going."

"It's only natural," said Con.

"All the same I can't help hoping they may not have to go to the front."

At which Con shook his head. "I'm afraid you must not count on that, mother dear. One never knows what may happen in war, of course. But everyone who knows says the Germans are mighty fighters, and they've been preparing for this for many years. In fact some folks seem to think their big war-machine may even be too perfect,—so very perfect that if anything goes wrong with any part of it it will all tumble to pieces."

"I wish it would and smother that wretched Kaiser in the ruins," said Alma heartily.

"I don't think it likely. They are very wonderful folks. In organization, and scientific attainment generally, they have made us all sit up and they beat us still. There is just one thing in this matter in which we have the advantage over them."

"Ships? Guns?" queried Alma.

"No,—greater than either,—the simple fact that we're in the right and they are utterly in the wrong. And that, you'll find, will tell in the long run. They are forcing on this war to serve their own selfish ends; and we, thank God, have no axe of our own to grind in the matter. We're out to make an end of wars, if that is possible."

"That is worth fighting for," said his mother heartily.

"Ay! Worth dying for if necessary.... It will be very hot work, I expect.... But we've got to win,—or go under. And that is unthinkable. But the cost may be heavy."

"Our thoughts ... and our prayers will be with you all the time, my boy.... May God grant us all a safe deliverance!" said Mrs Dare fervently.

"And that will help to buck us all up," said Con cheerfully. "But we mustn't get morbid. Suppose we go over and break the good news to the Colonel and Auntie Mitt, Mrs Connal Dare!"

"I'm ready. Do it gently, Con. Remember they are older than we are."

"Good news never hurts. Come on!"

Noel and Gregor MacLean, while anxiously awaiting news from Head-quarters as to the possible formation of a Reserve Battalion, were preparing themselves for the chance by developing their skill in musketry at the private shooting-school on the heath not far away. They went up every day and spent many pounds at the targets and then at clay pigeons, and in addition set themselves rigorous route-marches of ten and fifteen miles to get themselves and their feet into good condition. And each night they came home thick with mud and hungry as hunters, and well-satisfied that they were doing everything in their power to fit themselves for the real thing when the hoped-for call should come.

So Vic and Honor were thrown more than ever upon their own congenial companionship.

They were inseparable, and the days not being long enough for adequate expression of their feelings, they generally spent the nights together also. And Mrs Dare and Auntie Mitt were growing accustomed to the sudden announcements,—"Vic's sleeping with me to-night, Mother," and,—"Auntie Mitt, Honor's going to sleep here to-night,"—and the older folk made no objection, since it pleased the girls and alternately brightened each house in turn. The times were somewhat out of joint and anything that tended towards mitigation of circumstances was to be made the most of.

And so, when Con and Alma walked into Oakdene, they found the family party still lingering over their tea-cups in the hall;—Miss Mitten's knitting-needles going like clock-work, the Colonel expatiating on the monstrous perfidy of Germany in attacking Belgium, the girls nibbling their final cakes and listening somewhat abstractedly, wondering no doubt what those boys were doing to-day, and feeling that life—and certainly golf—without them was distinctly thin and flavourless.

"Ah—ha!" said Con magniloquently, "Here are the tribes assembled together. Colonel!"—with a punctilious military salute,—"Auntie Mitt!—and you two little girls!—we have come to gather your views on the subject of marriage. A worthy subject! Don't all speak at once."

"It is usually accounted an honourable estate," said the Colonel, beaming on them, while Miss Mitten peered up, bird-like, but knitted on for dear life, and the girls looked anticipative.

"We thank you!" said Con with a comprehensive bow. "Then you will permit me to introduce to you—Mrs Connal Dare,"—at which, as he swung Alma gracefully forward by the hand, they all sprang to fullest life as though pricked by an electric shock.

"Well—I'm da-asht!"

"Alma! My *dear*!"

"Con!—Is it true?"

"Oh, you dear, horribly mean things!"—

"To do us out of it all like that!"

"Horrid of them, but awfully jolly all the same!"

"You see," said Con,—when Alma had kissed them all round, and he had insisted on one also, to the immense gratification of the girls,—"This is war-time, and I am off to-morrow, and from my earliest youth I have been taught never to put off till to-morrow what I could do to-day. And so,—well!"—with a wave of the hand towards Alma,—"There it is!... We knew we had your approval, sir. We knew Auntie Mitt would graciously accept the fait accompli. And we hoped from the bottom of our hearts that Vic and Honor would in time forgive us and receive us back into their favour. And —we're very happy over it."

There was no possible doubt about that, and the Colonel, who was the only one who had any right to take exception to the matter, was far too good a sportsman to cast any shadow of a shadow upon their happiness. He had witnessed very many similar cases, and most of them had turned out very happily—when they had had the chance. It was that possibility only that added a touch of solemnity to his benediction,—

"Well, well! You've certainly given us a most delightful surprise, you two. War, as I know by experience, is a mighty crystalliser of the emotions, and essentially a promoter of prompt decisions. God grant you all happiness, my dears!" and he kissed Alma as if she had been his very daughter, and wrung Con's hand warmly.

"You look well in khaki, my boy," he said, with his eyes still glistening.

"And feel well, sir. I am, I think, a man of peace, but the uniform makes one feel distinctly soldierly, and if I find it absolutely necessary to knock out a German or two I believe I could do it."

"What with?" asked Vic, fingering his empty scabbard.

"Oh, with my fists if needs be. But I'm for binding not for wounding. It would only be under a sense of the sternest necessity that I should give that German a daud on the neb."

"I think I shall be a nurse," said Honor. "You do look spiffing, Alma."

"Too late for this war, my child. 'It's a long long way to Tipperary,' and this is to be the last war. Still there's always plenty to do even in peace-times."

"Will you be going out too, Al?" asked Vic.

"I don't know yet. There's sure to be a call for nurses. Wouldn't it be delightful to go out and meet Con there?" and her face was radiant at the thought.

Mrs Dare had made them promise to come back for dinner, so that Mr Dare might have the chance of seeing them also. When, in due course, they went across they found him just in from the City, and Con was struck with the change these last ten days had made in him.

He made, indeed, for their benefit a brave assumption of cheerfulness and gave them very hearty greeting, but pretended to be scandalised at their escapade, and expressed the hope that the Colonel had done his duty and told them what he thought about them.

They reassured him on that point and enquired for the latest news.

"Things are moving fast," he said soberly. "John Burns and Lord Morley leave the Cabinet. Government takes over all the railways. Jellicoe is to command the Fleet, French the Army, and Kitchener is to be Minister of War."

"That's good. He'll stand no nonsense anyway."

"The Germans are attacking Liége furiously. Everyone is amazed that the Belgians can stand up against them for a day. But every hour they can hold them is gain to us and France. We are both taken unawares, you see. And the fact of their tremendous onslaught shows that they were all ready, —more than ready. What the upshot of it all will be it's hard to say. Germany is a very big nut to crack."

"And how are business matters, father?" asked Con quietly, between themselves.

"Bad, Con. And likely to be worse. There is to be a big issue of paper, —ten-shilling and one-pound notes, and Lloyd George appeals very earnestly to people not to draw gold from the banks. He is doing all he can. But business is at a standstill, and as to getting in any money from the Continent—! That's all gone, I'm afraid."

"I've got a few hundreds saved. Would that be any use, sir?"

"You're a married man now and your wife must be your first consideration," said his father with a grave smile, which, however, conveyed to Con his appreciation of his desire to help. "And your uncle-in-law has very generously offered me assistance if I need it. At present I don't. If things come to the worst I may perhaps make some arrangement with him. You see it's a case of the devil and the deep sea. On the one hand contracts made which I'm expected to fill, and, on the other, total stoppage of the wherewithal to fill them. And again goods I've paid for here and shipped, and no payment forthcoming for them from Germany and Austria."

"There must be many in the same position. Won't a state of war bar all unpleasantness?"

"It's hard to say. We've had no experience of such a state of things, you see. No doubt there will have to be give and take all round and some working arrangement come to. I think there's a general disposition that way. But it's very trying business," he said wearily.

"I'm sure it is, sir. I wish I could be of some help."

"You have your own work cut out for you, my boy, and fine work. It will be a trial to you to leave now. But I suppose you considered all that."

"We did, sir. It is trying to have to part so soon, but it will be a help to us both to feel that we belong to one another whatever comes."

"I hope to God you'll come through all right, Con. For all our sakes take every care you can, and don't run into any unnecessary dangers."

"Trust me for that, sir."

Then the Colonel and the girls came across "for coffee and smokes, and to see how Mrs Con was bearing up," as Vic said, and they all fell to talk about the war and the future, and on the Colonel's part to the extraction of the latest news from the City.

"I hope you are not upset by these young people's precipitancy," said Mrs Dare quietly to the Colonel, under cover of the general talk beyond.

"On the contrary, my dear—, let me see, what *is* the exact relationship between us now? My niece, who is my daughter as it were, is now your daughter also. And your boy is my nephew-in-law. What does that make me to you?"

"I give it up," smiled Mrs Dare. "We will remain the best of friends."

"This makes us even closer than that. However, as I was saying, I'm entirely and absolutely pleased with them. They've done the natural thing under the circumstances. I've seen the same thing happen many times before, and it generally turns out well. There are always risks in war, of course—"

"And as to that we can only leave them in God's hands, and hope for the best."

"Amen to that, best of friends! My girl has at all events shown wisdom in her choice of a mother. We will hope ... and—er—pray"—he added, with a touch of the naïve shyness of a man who was in the habit of keeping his inmost feelings very strictly to himself,—"for their welfare and happiness."

"Yes.... The times are very trying and will probably be more so, but I'm inclined to think they may be the means of bringing out all that is best in us all."

"War does that ... as something of a set-off for the darker side of it. For it also brings out the worst unfortunately."

"Here are the boys," said Mrs Dare, jumping up at the sound of heavy boots on the path outside. "They generally come in together and they're always hungry. I'm the commissariat," and she hastened away to see to their provisioning.

"Hel-lo!" cried Noel, in a pair of old riding-breeches and puttees, at sight of the assembly, while Gregor, similarly apparelled, looked eagerly over his shoulder in hopes of an approving spark in Honor's eye. "Quick, Mac!—salute, ye spalpeen, or ye'll be shot at dawn. Here's a blooming little Horficer!" and they both drew themselves up and saluted Con in smartest possible military style.

"Why," prattled Noel. "I'm blowed if it isn't just old Con,—and Alma! So you two have managed to hit the same day this time."

"Yes, we've managed it for once, No," said Con. "How are you, Mac? Allow me to introduce you to my wife," with a proprietorial wave towards Alma.

"No!—really?" jerked Noel.

"Really and truly," laughed Alma. "I hope it isn't objectionable to you in any way."

"Lord, no! Quite the other way. If there's two things I admire about old Con they're his uniform and his jolly old cheek. Think of him going and getting you to marry him right away like that."

"He's off to-morrow morning, you see, so I thought it best to make sure of him."

"He's really going? I wish we were."

"How do things stand with you now, Mac?" asked Con. "Any nearer bull's-eye?"

"There's rumours of a possible Second Battalion being formed, but nothing definite. We've put our names down, and meanwhile we're getting ourselves into good shape. If they don't buck up and do something soon we shall try elsewhere. But we'd sooner be London Scottish than anything else."

"You see, the girls there think we'd look so well in kilts," broke in Noel.

"What on earth gave you any such impression as that, my child?" asked Honor.

"Oh, we can see it in your eyes."

"Ah,—little boys see what they want to see sometimes."

"When we can. Can't always, can we, Mac?"

"Come along, you hungry ones," called Mrs Dare from the doorway, and they sped away for a very necessary wash before eating.

Alma's short leave expired at ten o'clock, and as Con had promised to return her safely to the hospital by that hour, they had to set off in such time as would allow a margin for contingencies.

Their good-byes were outwardly cheerful enough, and as exuberant as high and hopeful spirits could make them. But, below all the surface confidence and fortitude, not one of their hearts but was saying to itself—"This is the beginning of partings," and was asking itself—"Shall we ever all meet again?" And the necessity for smothering, as far as might be, the chill possibilities evoked by these importunate voices, made the younger folk but the more outwardly determined on most valiant gaiety.

"Meet you across there, maybe, old man," said Noel.

"I'll be on the look-out for you. Do my best for you in case of need."

"Do be careful not to lose one another on the way home," begged Vic, with an assumption of anxiety. "You are very young, you see, and naturally somewhat entêtés at the moment."

"I'm inclined to think we really ought to go with them," said Honor. "They may wander away hand-in-hand, and never be heard of again. Get your hat, Vic, and we'll go."

"Right-o!" said Noel. "We're on. We'll go along too to take care of you."

"Then we'll stop at home," said Honor resignedly. "We couldn't think of taking you out again after your hard day's play."

"To say nothing of the fact that your southern extremities are inches thick with mud," said Vic. "Everybody we met would think we'd taken to walking out with the gardener's boys—"

"Or the young butcherlings. Yes, we're sorry, dears,"—to Con and Alma, "but under the circumstances I'm afraid you'll have to find your way by yourselves."

"We'll manage somehow," said Con, and in their good-byes to the older folk there were suspiciously shining eyes and lingering hand-grips and convulsive kissings which told their own tales.

"The beginning of partings!"... "Shall we ever all meet again?" ... and hearts were heavy though faces smiled.

"God bless you both and keep you from all harm!" was Mrs. Dare's last word, and with that in their hearts they ran across to say good-bye to Auntie Mitt, who said exactly the same words and made no assumption of anything but gloomiest forebodings as to the future.

As to the Colonel, when they had actually gone, he blew his nose like a trumpet-blast, till his moustache bristled white against the dark-redness of his face, and he turned back into the room with a fervent,—"Damn the Kaiser and all his works!... I trust you will excuse me, best of friends!"

"I will excuse you," said Mrs Dare. "It is terrible for one man to have such power for ill in his hands."

CHAPTER XII

AT the station Con got another taxi.

"We could not stand the train to-night," he said, as they swept down into the high-road, and he slipped an arm round her and drew her close and kissed her. "This will be our last little spell together for some time probably.... You've not felt any qualms or regrets yet?"

"Do I feel as if I had?" and she nestled the closer inside his protecting arm. "I shall never feel anything but glad, Con, ... whatever comes. We belong to one another and nothing can take that from us.... But you will be very careful, dear, for my sake, won't you?"

"I will, dear. Be sure of that.... For the rest, we are in God's hands and we must just leave it at that."

They did not talk very much. It was enough to feel one another so close in body and closer still in heart,—enough to lie back in the shadow, with arms and hands interwoven, while the taxi whirled in and out of the lamp-lights, and Alma's face, sweet and strong in the restraint she was imposing on herself, swam up out of the darkness like a beautiful cameo growing under the unseen touch of a master-hand,—dim ... clear ... perfect, to his hungry eyes, as the face of an angel in its confident hope and trust ... then in a moment it was gone, and all he had was the feel of her as he watched for the first glimmer of her face again in the darkness.

They did not talk much, because there was so much to say—so little need to say it—so much that could never be put into words. Silence and nearness sufficed them,—the silence of overfull hearts, the nearness of souls about to part,—perhaps, as each well knew, for ever.

"Wife!" said Con one time, drawing her still closer, though that had seemed impossible.

"My husband!" murmured Alma, and drew his head down with her arm and kissed him passionately.

An unforgettable ride, and all too soon at an end.

Con stopped the cab a hundred yards this side of the hospital, and they walked slowly on towards the great gateway.

It was still one minute to ten as they stopped there in its shadow. There was little traffic at that time of night and few passers-by.

He took her face gently between his hands and held it before him. He could not see it but he knew the pure sweet eyes were looking straight up into his.

A big clock in the distance boomed the first stroke of ten. Their time was up. He kissed her fervently, a kiss for each stroke, and she kissed him back.

"May God in His great mercy have us both in His keeping!" he said, hoarse with the depth of his feeling.

"Dear ... He will!"

He turned and pressed the button of the bell. The door opened and, with one more look, full of confident hope, she was gone—and in tears before the door closed, but that he did not know.

With that last sweet sight of her—to him the fairest vision of Faith and Hope and Love Incarnate that ever was or could be—he turned and walked away along the dark empty street, slowly and heavily, and felt his life for the moment as dark and empty as the street.

CHAPTER XIII

WHEN Lois Dare and Ray Luard came downstairs on the morning of August 7, they found the dark-panelled little salon of the 'Golden Lion' as cheerfully bright as a blazing fire and a pale sunbeam could make it; and outside, the upper alps of Urseren Thal were swathed with long wreaths of mist, above which the white tops of the Spitzberge shone like silver in the sunshine.

Freda came hastening in with the coffee and milk and a distressed face on their account.

"But it is too bad for you," she burst out. "They have just sent us word on the telephone that there will be no diligence to-day, nor any more at all. All the horses are wanted for the war,—ach!—the cursed war! It will be the ruin of us all."

"That's all right, Freda," said Lois cheerfully. "Don't worry about it on our account. We'll manage quite well."

"We walked here, you see," said Ray. "And we'll just walk on over the Furka and down the valley till we get to Montreux—if there are no trains running."

"But, mon Dieu, what a walk! To Montreux! It will take you weeks!"

"Not a bit. We get along quicker than that. So get our bill made out,—that's a good girl, and we'll start as soon as we've finished breakfast."

"Shall I put you up some lunch, monsieur and mademoiselle?"

"No," said Ray, after a moment's thought. "We'll have a proper lunch and a good rest at the Furkablick,—or the Belvédère, if we can get that far, and then get on to Oberwald. I don't want to stop at Gletsch," at which Freda smiled knowingly.

She added four different kinds of cheese to their menu, buzzed about them to see that they laid in adequate supplies of honey and blaeberry jam, and finally brought them a bill which surprised them by its modesty and provided Ray with a pocketful of change out of a five-pound note.

From the length of time Freda took to bring back the change he opined that she had had some difficulty in obtaining it. But how much he never knew.

For Madame of the hotel had, for the first time in her life, looked dubiously at an English five-pound note.

"But, Freda," she said, "Will that be all right if England is beaten in the war, as they say she will be?"

"She won't," said Freda oracularly. "And in any case an English five-pound note is always good."

"I don't know. It always has been, but—"

"I will change it myself then. I have no fear of England being beaten by any pigs of Germans. It's enough to make you sick just to hear them eat," and she took the note and climbed up to her own small room, and opened her box, and got out the other box in which she kept her savings, and came back with the change in her hands, much of it in five-franc pieces.

"Là!" she chirped triumphantly. "There then is madame's money, and here is monsieur's change. I would not have them think we doubt them,—no, not for five francs," and she went off with the receipted bill and the change on a plate.

"Freda," said Ray, as he added a lordly remembrance for herself, "I'd like to stop here for a month."

"Well—why not? Monsieur and mademoiselle will be very welcome indeed," and Freda's beam was a thing to remember.

"Duty calls, my child. We're going to Montreux to get married, you know, and then we want to get home as soon as circumstances will permit. Any news this morning?"

"By the telephone they say there is terrible fighting in Belgium. The poor little country! I was there for a year, in Bruxelles. They are such nice quiet people, but not great fighters, I would think. And the Germans—they are strong. Oh, it is terrible to think of."

Half an hour later, while the sun was still wrestling with the mist-wreaths, they were climbing the long straight road to Realp. Turning off there by the second bridge, they took the old road in order to avoid the endless zig-zags of the new one, and following the telegraph posts they mounted rapidly towards the little Galenstock Hotel.

On the Ebneten Alp, below the hotel, they sat down on a glacier-scored boulder for a last look over the Urseren-Thal and a rest before tackling the Furka. It was a wonderful sight—the wide green sweep of the valley right to the great white barracks at Andermatt and the zig-zags of the Oberalp-road beyond;—on the one side, the sprawling green and gray limbs of Spitzberge, still dappled with mist-wreaths but shining like frosted silver up above;—on the other side Piz Lucendro, with the Wyttenwasser-Thal and glacier below it;—and the upward road which led to the Furka was all white with snow.

It made the walking more difficult, but the air was crisp and clear up there and the very fact of walking on snow was exhilarating. In places it was over their shoe-tops and the drifts by the road side, when they plunged their poles into them, were many feet deep.

Far away below them in the Garschen-Thal they could see the cuttings and bridges for the new railway from Brigue to Disentis and Ilanz, but there was no work going on. The men had all gone to the front, and the unnatural offence of their blastings and delvings was for the time being suspended, though the scars and wounds of their previous efforts remained in painful evidence.

Presently they walked up into a mist-wreath and had the novel experience of plodding along an invisible road smothered in close-packed glimmering whiteness. The sun outside was evidently shining brilliantly on the thick bank of mist, but, so far, its rays failed to disperse it and penetrated only in a weird luminous diffusion, which had a most curious effect on the senses.

It made Lois's head spin till she reeled dizzily along and at last clung to Ray's arm for safety.

"I believe I'm drunk," she laughed mazedly. "Have we had anything stronger than coffee this morning?"

"Not that I remember," laughed Ray, in the same high-strung way. "Unless you slipped into one of the hotels we passed unbeknown to me. It's queer, isn't it? I feel absolutely light-headed. In fact I think the top front of my head is coming off. Hel-lo! Who's this now?"

This was a burly overcoated sentry, who loomed suddenly large in front of them and courteously informed them that they must keep to the lower road as this one led only to the barracks. So they stumbled back till they came on the main road again, and feeling their way by the granite posts, set up along the side of the road to keep the diligence from tumbling over into the valley, they came at last to the Furkablick Hotel, and were glad to grope into the hall and warm themselves at the blazing stove.

"We can't possibly go on if it keeps like this," said Ray. "It's neither safe nor wholesome. We can see nothing and might find ourselves walking over the edge into the valley."

"Suppose we have lunch and a good rest, and perhaps it will draw off. How far is it to the place we were to stop for the night?"

"It's about six miles to the Gletsch,—a bit less by the short cuts, and four miles or so on to Oberwald."

"Say three hours. We can give it a couple of hours to clear off, or even more if necessary."

So they fared sumptuously, and both fell fast asleep in big arm chairs near the stove in the salon afterwards, and when Ray yawned and woke it was close on three o'clock, and the sun had won and the mountains all round were shining white against the clear deep blue.

There was no one else in the salon. There seemed, in fact, no one else in the hotel except a few officers who kept to the smoking-room. So he kissed Lois awake, and in five minutes they were footing it gaily up the Furka road, with the Bernese giants towering in front and dwarfing all the lesser wonders closer at hand.

"That must be Finsteraarhorn," said Ray, pointing to the highest and sharpest peak. "And that one further on is probably Jungfrau, but I know her better from the other side."

Then they passed the fortifications and turned a corner, and the great Rhone glacier lay below them, dappled here and there, where the sun got into the hollows, with the most wonderful flecks of fairy colour—tenderly vivid and lucently diaphanous blues and greens so magically blended that Lois caught her breath at the sight.

"How beautiful! How beautiful!" she murmured. "It is a dream-colour, but I never dreamed anything half so lovely."

He could hardly get her along. She wanted to stop at every second step to gloat on some fresh wonder. But they came at last, by slow degrees, to the point, just below the Belvédère, where sturdy pedestrians can drop from the main road into the valley and so avoid the tedious winding-ways.

"We'll get down here, if you think you can manage it," said Ray. "Then we can get right up to the glacier-foot where the Rhone comes out. It's worth seeing, but it's a bit of a scramble down unless they've improved the path."

"I'll manage it all right if you'll go first and show me the way."

So they started on that somewhat precarious descent, and had gone but a little way when Ray began to be sorry he had not stuck to the solider footing of the road.

For the apology of a path had in places disappeared entirely under the attrition of the wet season and many heavy boots. Whole lumps of it had slipped away and left gaps and slides down which a rough-clad Switzer might flounder with possible impunity, but which suggested serious possibilities to the ordinary traveller.

He had gone on hoping it would improve, but it did not. Instead it grew worse. But if falling down such awkward slides was no easy matter, reclimbing them to gain the high road was next to impossible.

They bumped and slipped and floundered downwards as best they could.

"I'm truly sorry," he said, as he helped her down one specially awkward place. "It was nothing like this last time I came."

"It's all right," she laughed. "It's fun—all in the day's work. Don't tumble right out of sight if you can help it."

And then he did. A lump of rock to which he had trusted his foot came squawking out of the wet bank, and he and it went down together a good half-dozen yards.

He brought up with his rucksac over his head and turned at once to see to her safety.

"All right," he shouted. "No bones broken. But I don't advise you to try it. Strike to the right and try and find a better place. Throw me down your rucksac and cloak, then you'll be free-er."

She dropped them down to him, with a startled look on her face, and he scrambled round, as well as he could so laden, to meet her round the corner. But she had to make quite a long détour before she came at last on another and less precarious path and was at last able to join him.

"Sure you weren't hurt?" she asked anxiously.

"Quite sure. Bit scraped, that's all. I suppose it's the rains that have boggled the path so. Now, if we keep on round here we'll be able to get right up to the ice-cave where the stream comes out. Here's the rain on again. Better put that cloak on," and they scrambled on over the rough detritus from the glacier and the hillsides till they reached the ice-foot, and stood looking into the weird blue-green hollow out of which the gray glacier water came rushing as though in haste to find a more congenial atmosphere.

"It's the most wonderful colour I've ever seen," she said, drinking it in with wide appreciative eyes. "It hardly looks real and earthly. It looks as though a breath would make it vanish. I suppose if we got inside there it would simply be all white."

But just then, in sullen warning, a solid lump of overhanging ice came down with a crash, and a volley of stones came shooting at them mixed with its splinters, and they turned and went on their way down the stony valley.

The rain ceased again just as they arrived at the big hotel, and as Ray swung off his cloak and shook it, Lois laughed and said,

"When we get to Oberwald you must hand me over your trousers and I'll stitch them up."

"Why?—what?—" and he clapped his hands to his hips to feel the damage, while Lois still stood laughing at the rents and tears which his cloak had so far hidden.

"I should keep my cloak on if I were you," she suggested, and then asked quickly, "Why—Ray? What is it? Are you more hurt than you thought?"—for the look on his face was one of concern if not of actual consternation.

"I am," he jerked, with a pinch on his face, and then he felt hastily in his other pockets and the tension slackened somewhat. "But it's not in my person,—only in my pocket. Would you mind kicking me, dear? Here,— we'll go round the corner," and he stepped back the way they had come. "And—would you also mind telling me what money you have in your pocket or your rucksac."

"Not very much, I'm afraid. Two or three pounds, I think. Why?"

"Because," he said, displaying the catastrophe. "That stupid slip of mine has busted my hip-pocket and all our money's gone. All except the change out of this morning's five-pounder. With that and yours we can get to Montreux all right, and I can wire from there to Uncle Tony, but it's confoundedly stupid,—"

"Couldn't we find it if we went back?"

"I'm going to try, but you'll stop here and have some tea to pass the time."

"Oh no, I won't. It's share and share alike. Aren't we almost man and wife? Come along! We'll have a hunt for our money anyway," and she led the way back towards the glacier.

They searched for an hour, but looking for a flat leather purse in that stony land was like searching for the proverbial needle in the haystack. They found the exact spot where Ray took his sudden slide, but search below it discovered nothing. They followed step by step the way he had taken till he met Lois and then, as well as they could, the path they had taken to the ice-foot. But there was no sign of the purse and he came to the conclusion that his pocket was probably torn by the slide and the purse fell out of it later on,—anywhere down the two-mile stretch of stony valley between them and the hotel.

They paced it with meticulous care, searching cautiously, but found nothing, and at last gave it up and went on,—soberly as regards Ray, amusedly as regards Lois, who persisted in looking only at the humorous side of the matter.

"We'll walk all the way," she laughed, "and pick out the cheapest-looking hotels, and you'll have to haggle like a German about terms."

"I'm awfully sick of myself for being such an ass," he said gloomily. "It's hateful to be short of cash in a strange land. I often used to run it pretty close. I remember once reaching home from this very place with only a halfpenny in my pocket. I remember I wanted a cup of tea on the train, more than I'd ever wanted one before, and I had to go without."

"Had you lost your purse then also?" asked Lois mischievously.

"No,—just stopped longer than I'd planned and ran it a bit too fine."

They plodded into Oberwald just before dark, and stumped heavily up the steep wooden steps that led from the stony road to the door of the little Furka Hotel, fairly tired out with the day's walk, which their diversion in search of Ray's purse had extended, he reckoned, to close on five-and-twenty miles, and he proceeded to haggle with the depressed-looking land-lady like any German of them all.

She was glad enough to have them, however, even on their own terms, and gave them a quite sufficient supper, in which three different kinds of sausage, and veal in several guises, figured principally; and her bed-rooms, if somewhat meagrely furnished, were at all events clean. And they went up early to bed, tired with their long tramp and still tireder,—as Ray expressed it, concerning himself—of playing the fool with his money and throwing it about for some wiser man to pick up.

The landlady knew nothing about the war, except that the diligences had stopped running because the horses were wanted, and most of the men had gone—to Thun, or Berne, she was not quite sure where, but it was all because of the talk of war, and she did not hold with any of it,—stopping business and upsetting everybody and everything.

Oberwald, they decided, could not at the best of times be a very inspiring place. Under the shadow of the war-cloud it was dismal. They had early breakfast on the wooden platform outside the front door, while the deserted village below and about them roused itself, lazily and obviously against the grain, to its day's work.

But Ray was obviously not up to his usual standard, even though Lois had borrowed needle and thread from the landlady and had patched up his rents with deft fingers and visible enjoyment at being of service to him.

"You're not letting that old purse worry you, are you?" she had asked, as they sat over their coffee and cheese and honey on the wooden platform.

"Not at the loss of it, though the stupidity of losing anything always annoys me. It's the possible consequences I'm thinking of. It came on me all in a heap in the night that it's just possible we may have difficulty in communicating with them at home if things are really bad. I wish to goodness we could get some definite news. I wanted very much to take you up the Eggishorn—it's just close here, and it seems a shame to pass right under it without going up. You don't really know what a glacier's like till you've seen the Aletsch. But...."

"I think we'd better go right on. We can come back some other time and see all these things. Suppose they shouldn't have got your telegram from Leipsic! They'll be getting frightfully anxious about us. Let us get on as quickly as possible."

"I'm afraid there's nothing else for it," he said regretfully. "Let's see now—it would take us at least four days to walk down the valley to Montreux.... How much money did you say you have with you?"

"I've got three pounds, five shillings. I'll get it for you."

"No. Better keep it safe. I might lose it, you know. Well, four days' tramping at the lowest possible rate means at least forty francs. It will pay us to take the train from Brigue. There's a quick train about mid-day, I remember ... that is, if it's still running. They may have taken the trains off also. It comes from Milan, you see, through the Simplon."

"Third class?"

"Rather. I've come home by it more than once, and it's generally packed with Italians, who are not the pleasantest of travelling companions. But needs must when you're such a fool as to lose your purse,—and they're probably all being kept at home just now anyway. We had a tough day yesterday, so to-day we'll just jog along to Fiesch. That's another place I wanted you to stop at. Most fascinating country, all the hillsides covered with little irrigation channels about a foot wide, and the natives spend most of their time turning them on and off. That's where you strike up for the Eggishorn ... and the Märjelen See ... and then there's Binn.... It's a mighty pity to pass them all ..." and he rattled the few coins in his pocket thoughtfully.

But—"Needs must!" said Lois firmly, anxious to get into touch with the outer world again and especially with the folks at home.

"Wait a bit!" said Ray thoughtfully, and got down the map from its peg in the hall, and began figuring with his pencil on the back of the bill the landlady had just brought him, which came to 9.50 francs for the two of them. "Just ... you ... wait ... a bit ... my child!" and he measured and figured away with immense energy and growing enjoyment.

"We can do it all right," he burst out at last. "See here!—We've got 160 francs left after settling up here. We'll get Madame here to put us up the usual trampers' lunch,—that's one franc each. We'll walk on to Fiesch and then up to the little Firnegarten Inn—small but clean—on the Fiescher Alp, and stop the night there. That'll be, say, 10 francs. It would cost us more down below. To-morrow we'll make an early start and climb up to the Märjelen See and the Eggishorn, taking our lunch with us again. Then we'll come down by the big hotel,—we can only afford to look at the outside of it this time,—and walk along the ridge to Rieder Alp. It's wonderful,—worth coming all the way from England for,—that and the Aletsch. Stop the night at Rieder Alp. That will be say 12 francs, if I haggle well. And next day we'll walk down to Brigue and Oberried and Bitsch and the Massa, and get the mid-day train there for Montreux,—"

"If it's running."

"If not we'll just toddle on."

"But can we afford it?"

"Including fares and all it will come to just about as much as four days' tramping along the road. And two days up aloft here are worth forty days on that road. The road's fine but it's not to be compared with the bridle path along Rieder-Alp."

He was so obviously set on it that, in spite of her anxiety to get on, she had not the heart to raise any objection, and five minutes later they were on the road, with the dew-drenched green slopes above and below them shimmering like diamond-dust in the early sunshine, and Ray's spirits at their highest again at this getting the better of the misfortune that would have done them out of the best bit of the journey.

As to the fact that they would arrive in Montreux with only 120 francs between them, that did not trouble him in the slightest now that they were going up aloft.

"I'll wire Uncle Tony the very first thing when we get there. It'll be quite all right, you'll see, my child. 'The year's at the Spring—'"

"Ninth of August!"

"That's nothing. It's our year I'm talking of, and it's only a week or so after New Year's Day.... 'The day's at the morn. Morning's at seven;'—"

"Nearer eight,"—with a glance at her wrist-watch.

"'The hillside's dew-pearled,'—"

"Undoubtedly,"—with a comprehensive wave of the hand uphill and down.

"'The lark's on the wing;'—"

"Maybe—somewhere."

"'The snail's on the thorn; God's in His Heaven; All's right with the world!'"

"With your and my little world. But, oh, I wonder what's going on outside there, Ray! It's terrible to think of war at any time, even though we none of us really know what it means. But for all the Great Powers to be flying at one another's throats,—and England too! I can't realise it."

"Don't try, child. Rhenius may have caught some flying nightmare by the tail. I haven't much faith in Italian newspapers. Anyway we'll make the most of these few days of grace and be thankful for them.... You see, if things really are as bad as he said, we may be stuck for some time in Switzerland, and an extra day up here in heaven will make no difference in the end and is all to the good now. Learn to gather your roses while you may, my child," and his determined enjoyment carried the day.

They made Fiesch about noon, and Ray marched her right through the little town to the house he had stopped at more than once—the cosy-looking little Hotel des Alpes, near where the rushing Fieschbach flung its gray waters into those of the Rhone.

They knew him there and were much hurt that he had not come to stop with them again, and were greatly interested in Lois. He had to explain matters very fully before they were pacified sufficiently to permit him to have a bottle of Asti, with a small table and two chairs outside in the sunshine, and the mistress and the two comely maids hung about them all the time they ate their Oberwald lunch of bread and sausage and cheese and biscuits, and insisted on supplementing it with apples and pears and grapes, grumbling good-humouredly at him and chattering and giving such news as they had.

"You'd do much better to stop with us. Firnegarten cannot keep very much of a table up there, you know. Most people go right on to the Jungfrau Hotel for the night—"

"I know. But we're pauper-tramps, you see, till we get to Montreux, and we have to look twice at every sou. You see, I was fool enough to lose my purse up at Gletsch there—"

"Ach! To lose your purse! That was foolishness. But if you had come to us we would have helped you."

"It's awfully good of you, and we're going to come back here as soon as ever we can. There's heaps of things I want to show mademoiselle,— Binn, and the Fiescher Glacier, and Ernen—oh, heaps. But now we've got to get on. We're going to get married as soon as we reach Montreux, but I couldn't bear to stump along the road down here when Aletsch and the Rieder-Alp called me. Mademoiselle is not at all sure we're doing the right thing in not going straight on."

"You will never regret it, mademoiselle," they assured her.

"Though, of course, when one is hurrying along to get married,—" interjected one of the girls thoughtfully.

"The Great Aletsch is a thing to see before one dies,—" continued Madame.

"Or even before one gets married, when you have to pass right under it," said Ray. "And the Märjelen—"

"Ach—the poor Märjelen! It is gone. It got a hole in it somewhere and all the water has run out, and so now there is nothing to see."

"So! But the Aletsch is still there?"

"Och, yes! The Aletsch can never run away through a hole. There it is and there it will remain till the world comes to an end."

"And the war? What news have you?"

"They are fighting terribly over there, it seems,—at some place called Liége. But we do not hear very much since the diligence stopped. And all our visitors went away at once. We were quite full and not one has come since. War is bad for everybody. For me, I cannot understand what people want to fight for. It will not come into Switzerland, do you think, monsieur?"

"I shouldn't think so, but when war once starts you never know where it will stop. And I've no doubt Germany would be only too glad to get hold of Switzerland if she got half a chance."

"Ach—those Germans! No, I do not like them. Whenever I see one come in here I say to myself, 'Another trouble-maker!' They are never satisfied, and they want everything—except to pay proper prices. No, I do not like them. If they all get killed in the fighting I shall not care one bit."

Their leave-taking could hardly have been warmer if Madame had been jingling in her hand a whole month's pension fees instead of the price of a modest bottle of Asti, and presently they were slowly and steadily climbing the steep and stony path to Firnegarten.

The maid in charge there was sister to one of those down below, and she also remembered Ray. She was much astonished at their intention of stopping the night there, and laughed merrily when Ray proceeded to hammer her price down to his level and then explained why he was, for once, acting like a German.

She made them very comfortable, however, in a simple way, and obviously enjoyed their company. They went early to bed, and were well on their way up the Fiescher Alp soon after seven next morning.

It was close on noon before they struggled up the tumbled débris of the top, and sank down on a flat rock, with that great glory of the Aletsch glacier sweeping down in front of them, from the great snow-basins of Jungfrau and Finsteraarhorn, till it curled out of sight behind the green ridges of Rieder-Alp away down below them on the left.

"The Chariots of the Lord!" came involuntarily to Lois's lips as she sat gazing on it, and her eyes followed the strange dark parallel lines which ran throughout its length and looked exactly like gigantic wheel-tracks. "What makes them?"

"The continuous slow downward movement of the ice, I believe. It picks off earth and stones from the sidewalls and gradually throws them into exact lines like that. Curious, isn't it? I remember it struck me in just the same way the first time I saw it."

It was long before she could be got to look at anything else.

"I can't help expecting it all the time to do something," she explained.

"I know. But it never does. See!—that's Jungfrau over there, and that one is Finsteraarhorn. And round this other side you can see the Matterhorn and Mont Blanc. Those big white lumps are the Mischabels."

In time he got her to start on her lunch, though she asserted that it felt like eating in church,—desecration.

"I'm glad you insisted on coming," she said softly. "It is a sight one could never forget," and he was radiant.

"And to think," she said again, presently, "that over yonder the guns are booming and men are doing everything they know to kill one another! Isn't it dreadful to think of—in face of this great silent wonder which takes one's thoughts right up to God?"

"It's simply brutal.... I just hope whoever's to blame for bringing it about will get whipped out of existence."

He could hardly drag her away. She vowed she could never weary of that most wonderful sight, and was certain it would begin to move if they only waited long enough. And so it was a very tired but very well-satisfied pair that dropped into the first chairs they came to in the homely little Riederalp Hotel, with barely enough energy left to arrange terms on the German plan.

Next morning they came down the steep wooded ways by Oberried and Bitsch and the Massa gorge, and reached Brigue exactly fifteen minutes before a train started for Montreux.

The run down the Rhone Valley and up to Montreux was full of enjoyment, tempered only by their doubts as to being able to get any further than that.

Ray pointed out to her all the things he knew,—the new Lötschberg line away up on the opposite mountain-side,—the openings of Nicolai Thal, leading to Zermatt and Saas Fée,—the Val d'Anniviers leading to Zinal, and the Val d'Herens to Arolla, and promised to take her to them all when the times got re-jointed. Then they were at Martigny, and presently the flat delta and the upper end of the lake came into sight, and Chillon, and they were at Montreux.

Ray enquired at once from the station-master as to trains for Paris.

"Paris, mon Dieu?" jerked that much harassed official. "Ask again in a fortnight's time, monsieur, and perhaps we shall know something then!" and Ray made at once for the Post Office and wrote out a telegram to Uncle Tony,—"Just arrived here. Both well. Lost purse. Send cash Poste Restante."

The young man behind the official window looked at the address and said in excellent English, "We can send it from here, but we cannot make sure it will ever get there. You see it must go through France or Germany, and they are fighting and everything is disarranged.... It is very awkward," as they looked at one another in dismay.

"Very awkward!" said Ray. "Please do your best. Are letters coming through?"

"Not from England for some days. Doubtless in time matters will arrange themselves."

In time, doubtless! But the one thing about which there was no doubt whatever was the fact that they were in a strange land, cut off from communication with their own, and that the sum total of their united funds amounted to something under five pounds,—and there was no saying when they could procure more.

CHAPTER XIV

ALMA at St Barnabas's, and Mrs Dare at The Red House each received a brief note from Con, from Southampton, saying he was leaving immediately but was not permitted to say more.

He seemed in the best of spirits and said he had plenty to do. After that the vail of war fell between him and them, and to them was left the harder task of possessing their souls in hope, with such patient endurance as they could draw from higher hidden sources. Both, however,—Alma in her crowded ward, and Mrs Dare in the less strenuous and so the more meditative sphere of home,—went about their daily tasks with tranquil faces which permitted no sign to show of the fears that might be in them. It was their quiet part in the crisis to give of their best and suffer in silence, as it was the part of the millions of other women similarly circumstanced.

Mr Dare had perhaps the heaviest burden to bear at this time, and in spite of his attempts at cheerfulness the weight of it was apparent in him. His business at a deadlock, valued customers urgently claiming the fulfilment of contracts, the goods they wanted hermetically sealed within the flaming borders of Germany and Austria, accounts for goods sent to those countries falling due, and no money forthcoming from abroad to meet them. No wonder he looked harassed and aged, and at times grew somewhat irritable under the strain.

What his wife was to him in those days none but he knew,—not even Mrs Dare herself in full. In her own quiet fashion she would at times draw him gently on to unburden himself to her in a way that would have been impossible to anyone else, and her great good sense would seek out the hopeful possibilities and tone down the asperities of life. And when things were past speaking about she would show, by her silent sympathy and brave face, that she understood but still had faith in the future.

But for an unusually alert and active business man to find himself, without warning, plunged suddenly into a perfect morass of difficulties, for which no blame attached to anyone save to the blind precipitancy of unto-

ward circumstance;—to find himself helplessly idle where his days had always been briskly over-full,—it was enough to drive any man off his balance, and in some cases it did.

He went down to St Mary Axe each morning and stopped there all day
in gloomy exasperation. He explained his situation to irritated clamourers
for goods till he grew sick of explaining. He was grateful when release
came at night; and in the night he lay awake at times and hugged to himself
the few precious hours which still intervened before he must shoulder his
burden again. Sunday he looked forward to, all the week long, as a dies non
when business matters ceased perforce from troubling and his weary soul
could take its rest. He longed for weeks of Sundays. At times, in his utter
weariness, the thought of the final unbroken rest made infinite appeal to
him.

The complete lack of any word from Lois and Ray added not a little to
their anxieties. The Colonel, indeed, never would admit any possibility of
mischance in the matter.

"Don't you worry, Mrs Mother," he would adjure her. "They're having
the time of their lives somewhere or other, I'll wager you a sovereign."

"If they're shut up in Germany it may be a very unpleasant time," argued Mrs Dare.

"But they're not. Ray's no fool and he got out of that trap instanter. Of
that I'm certain. Where to I can't, of course, say. Tirol seems nearest, from
the map—"

"That's Austria," said Mrs Dare quietly.

"Well then, Switzerland—Russia—Italy—anywhere,—I don't know.
But if he's still in Germany he's a much bigger fool than I ever thought
him. They're all right. Don't you worry!"—which was all most excellent in
intention but did not bring to the anxious mother-heart the comfort that one
word from the missing ones would have done.

But the Colonel was too busy to waste time and energy in worrying,
and, besides, he was not given that way. Immediately on the declaration of
war, he had donned his uniform and gone down to Whitehall and tendered
his services in any capacity whatever. His bluff, antique enthusiasm over-
came even the natural repugnance of War-Office messengers to further the
wishes of any but their own immediate chiefs, and he succeeded in seeing
Lord Kitchener, whom he had not met since they toiled up Nile together in
quest of Gordon.

The quiet, level-eyed man, who had gone so far and high since those
days, gave him cordial greeting and expressed the hope that the younger
generation would exhibit equal public spirit, in which case this belated cre-
ation of a sufficient fighting force would prosper to the extent of his wishes,
which he acknowledged were great, though not more than the dire necessi-

ties of the case called for. He tactfully switched the Colonel's enthusiasm on to the recruiting branch line, and the fiery little warrior had since then been devoting himself, heart and soul, to the business of presenting Kitchener's Army to the youth of Willstead and neighbourhood as the one and only legitimate outlet for its duty to its King and Country.

With his V.C. and his Crimean and Mutiny and African medals, he made a brave show on a platform, and his fervid exhortations persuaded many from the outer back rows to the plain deal tables where the recruiting forms awaited them.

He toured the neighbouring villages in a motor car, and until the muddle-headed mismanagement by the authorities of the earlier comers cast somewhat of a chill on their waiting fellows, the Colonel was a great success.

Noel and Gregor MacLean were still impatiently hanging on for the War Office to decide whether or not the London Scottish were to be permitted to form a Second Battalion. And Noel, with the impetuosity of youth, grew so restive under the strain at times that he stoutly urged Gregor to enrol with him in one of the regiments of Kitchener's army.

"Man!" he would growl, after the usual ineffectual visit to Headquarters. "We're going to get left. It'll all be over and done with before we get a look in. Let's join the Hussars!"

"I'm for the London Scottish, my boy, if it's at all possible. They say they'll know in a week or two for certain, and we can wait all right. I know such a lot of the fellows there and I'd sooner be among friends. It makes a mighty difference and they're all good chaps in the Scottish. Besides I've a natural yearning for the kilt. If they shut down on us, then we'll sign on wherever you like."

"Hang it, man! The fun'll all be over."

"Don't you believe it, my son. K of K isn't raking in all these men just to amuse himself. He's the squarest-headed chap we've got, and those eyes of his see a long long way past Tipperary, you bet. We're up against a jolly tough job and he knows it.... Anyway we'll be fitter than most when they do take us on. I bet you there aren't many recruits can down ten out of twelve clays at two hundred yards."

This was Noel's top score so far. He was rather proud of it and judicious reference to it always had a soothing effect on his feelings. So they strenuously kept up their training, walking all the way in and back whenever they went up to Buckingham Gate for news, and spending much time and money at the shooting-grounds.

The girls missed them, of course, but consoled themselves as best they could with one another. They did a round of the links each day for health's sake, but felt the lack of Noel's outspoken jibes and Gregor's curt criticisms and all the subtle excitation and enjoyment of the former times, and learned that golf for duty and golf for pleasure are greens of very different qualities.

Still they would not have had it otherwise. The boys were doing their duty as it appeared to them, and it was their portion to miss them and get along as best they could without them. For their sakes they heartily wished Headquarters would make up its mind what it was going to do, and get them settled down to actual work and disciplined courses.

For this waiting on and on, with no definite certainty as to the outcome, was wearing on Noel's temper, and bits of it got out on the loose at home at times and disturbed the atmosphere somewhat.

Like most boys of his age, when things went his way he was as pleasant as could be. And they so generally had gone his way that when they did not he resented it and let people know it. Like nine boys out of every ten, whose chief concern in life had so far been themselves and their own troubles and enjoyments, there was a streak of natural selfishness in him, any implication of which he would have hotly resented. He could be generous enough of his superfluities, but so far had had to make no call on himself for the higher virtues of self-denial or self-restraint. In short he was just an ordinary boy merging into man, very full of himself and his own concerns and enjoyments, and at times a little careless of others.

This odd new friendliness which had sprung up of late between himself and Victoria Luard was all very much to the good. It came in between him and himself and made him feel ready, and even anxious, to do great things for her, and to consider her feelings even before his own. But, at the same time, his feeling of personal discrepancy with regard to her, drove him in the rebound to occasional little displays of bearishness and boyish arrogance, the springs of which Victoria understood perfectly and was vastly amused at.

Gregor MacLean, with the advantages of his extra five years and much shoulder-rubbing with his fellows, had grown out of these youthful discordances, and he sometimes took Noel humorously to task for his little lapses, and Noel would take more from him in that way than from anyone else.

Honor of course, in sisterly fashion, saw his faults and did not pass them over in silence. Still, she also generally did it in humorous fashion which left no more than a momentary sting even if it did not produce much result.

Miss Mitten knitted untiringly. Victoria gravely asserted to Mrs Dare and Honor, when they had dropped in for tea one afternoon, that, so assured was Auntie Mitt that the outcome of the war depended entirely on the number of body-belts and mufflers she could complete in a given time, that she went on knitting all night long in her sleep. And Auntie Mitt, in no way offended, though somewhat scandalised at such public mention of her in the privacy of her bed, only smiled and knitted harder than ever.

"The cold weather will be coming soon," she said gently, "and it's cold work fighting in the trenches.".

"But, my dear Auntie Mitt, they don't fight in trenches nowadays," said Vic.

"No?... They used to. I remember ... I remember hearing much of the discomforts of the trenches in the Crimean War from those who had taken part in it."

"Nowadays they fire shell at you from four or five miles away and you're dead before you know what's hit you," said Honor. "It's low kind of fighting to my mind."

"Or drop bombs on you from aeroplanes without a chance of hitting back," added Vic, "which is lower still."

"Well ... I don't myself agree with anything of that kind," said Auntie Mitt gently. "It certainly does not seem to me a very manly way of fighting."

"It isn't. But unfortunately it's the way that's in fashion," said Vic.

"It is very horrible," said Mrs Dare, busy with her knitting also and thinking of her two, one of whom would probably sooner or later be exposed to these barbarous novelties of civilised warfare. "But of course they respect the Red Cross men,"—in which case Con at all events might possibly return alive.

"Oh, they'll respect the Red Cross all right, Mrs Mother," said the Colonel, catching her last words as he strode in, with an early evening paper in his hand. "They're big fighters but they're civilised and they'll fight like Christians."

"What a horrible expression!" said Mrs Dare. "Fight like Christians!"

"Yes,—I apologise and withdraw. You are quite right, Mrs Mother," with an old-fashioned little bow towards her. "It was not happily expressed.... And yet Christians have to fight at times, and if ever fighting was justified it is now—on our side. We're fighting for Right and for the rights of everybody outside Germany. Never in the history of the world was there a more righteous war as far as we are concerned. And so we are fighting like—or if you prefer it—as Christians."

"Yes, I prefer it that way. It is my only consolation when I think of the boys. They are fighting for the Right."

"When they get to it," said Honor. "What's the latest, Colonel? Does Liége still stand where it did?"

"It stands marvellously—the forts that is. The Germans seem to have the town, but the forts are still alive and kicking. It's simply marvellous how those Belgians have suddenly transformed themselves into the pluckiest fighters the world has ever seen. Marvellous! No one ever believed they could hold Germany's millions for a day, and here they've kept them at bay for a whole fortnight and given France time to get herself in order. If the rest of the war goes the same way there can be no doubt as to how it will end."

"Doubt?" echoed Vic scornfully. "You don't mean to dare to say you've ever had any doubts as to how it would end, Uncle Tony?"

"There speaks Young England,—always cocksure of winning and inclined to despise the enemy. If you had seen as much of war as I have, my dear, you would be cocksure of nothing, except that you'd do your duty to the last gasp and would have to leave the rest to Providence. Germany is a tremendous fighting-machine. We have a tough job before us, but we're fighting for the Right and please God we'll win. It's good to see the new spirit the war is evoking everywhere. Great Britain and Ireland shoulder to shoulder, and India and all the colonies rushing to help. It's magnificent,—simply magnificent."

"Yes," said Mrs Dare quietly. "It is doing good in that way, and in matters at home also,—the matters which come home to the hearts of us women. We've just formed a committee for looking after the wives and children of the men who have to go to the front, and every single person I've seen about it is keen to help,—people in some cases who have hitherto shown no inclination for anything beyond their own concerns."

"There will be a good deal of distress one way and another, I fear," said the Colonel, nodding thoughtfully. "That is if things go on as they usually do."

"I'm inclined to hope they'll go better," said Mrs Dare. "Our men at the head of affairs are in closer touch with the needs of the people than yours ever have been,"—with a pacificatory little nod towards him. "I know you don't like Lloyd George, but you must acknowledge that he has handled the financial situation in a masterly way."

"I do acknowledge it. And I'll even go so far as to say that I don't believe our side would have handled the whole matter as well as it has been done. We might. Men rise to the occasion,—as yours have done. We might, —but I confess I don't at the moment see which of our men could have done what has had to be done as well as Sir Edward Grey, and Churchill and Lloyd George and Asquith."

"Hooray!" cried Honor. "You'll be on the right side yet, Colonel."

"I'm always on the side of right, anyway. What are you girls doing to help?"

"I'm going to knit body-belts and mufflers," said Honor lugubriously. "But I'm only a beginner and I'm shy of performing in public yet."

"And you, Victoria-who-ought-to-have-been-Balaclava?"

"Our Central Committee in town is considering how we can best help, and as soon as they decide I'm on to it. In the meantime, Honor is teaching me to knit body-belts and mufflers,—that is, she's passing on to me, the beginnings of her own little knowledge,—though I don't quite see the need of them. It'll all be over in a month, I expect."

"If it's all over in six months I shall be more than glad," said the Colonel weightily. "And there'll be plenty of cold days and nights before then. However, I'm glad you're all doing what you can. It'll do you all good."

CHAPTER XV

"Y US!" SAID Mrs Skirrow, with an emphasis that carried conviction. "It may seem a vi'lent utt'rance to you, mum, but, for me, I'm bound to say I'm right down glad o' this war. It's tuk my three off o' me hands, an' it's givin' me the time o' me life."

"Where have they got to?" asked Mrs Dare sympathetically.

"Jim and George, they're in Kitchener's lot at Colchester—the Hoozars, and me old man's back in th' Army Transport, an' if that don't mek him move his lazy bones I d'n know annything this side the other place that will. It tired him so last time he was in it, that he's bin resting ever since. But it's the thing he knows best, and when the call come he forgot his tiredness an' up an' went like a man. 'Damn that Keyzer!' he says,—you'll pardon me, mum, but them was his identical words,—'Damn that Keyzer!' he says. 'He is the limit,—walking over little Belgium with 'is 'obnails like that without so much as a by-your-leave or beg-pardon. He's got to be knocked out, he has, and I'm on to help jab him one in the eye. And you two boys,' he says, 'you're onto this job too, or I'll have the skin off of you both before you know where y'are. Yer King and yer country needs yer.' An' if you'll b'lieve me, mum, they went like lambs."

"And why did they go into the Hussars? Can they ride?"

"Divv—I mean, not a bit of it, mum. But they talked it over atween themselves, and Jim, he said, if it come to riding or walking, he'd sooner ride any day, an' the spurs made a man look a man. So they went up together and they was took on like a shot. An' I'm to get twelve-and-six a week now and mebbe more later on, they do say. I ain't got it yet, but it's a-comin' all right, an' then—"

"Well, I hope you'll save all you can, Mrs Skirrow. You never know what the future may bring, you know."

"That's true, mum. But I've worked harder than most for these three this many a year, and I'm inclined to think I'll mebbe tek a bit of a holiday and have a decent rest. How long d'you think it'll go on, mum?"

"I'm afraid no one can tell that, Mrs Skirrow. Colonel Luard says he will be glad if it's over in six months."

"Ah,—well,"—with a satisfied look on her face,—"that's a tidy spell. For me, if it was a year I d'n know as I'd mind. It'll keep a lot o' men out o' mischief."

"And put many out of life altogether, I'm afraid."

"Ay—well—mebbe! But there's always the pension to look forward to, an' they do say it's goin' to be bigger than ever it was before."

"Yes, I'm sure everybody feels that everything possible should be done for the men at the front and those they leave behind them."

"That's right, mum. 'Tain't such a bad old world after all. D'you hear about the Chilfers down the road, mum?"

"No. What about them?"

"A rare joke. Everybody's laughing at 'em. When yon first pinch come and it lukt 's if we might all be starvin' inside a week, Mr Chilfer he went up in his big motor to th' Stores, and he come back with it full,—'ams and sides o' bacon, all nicely done up, an' flour, an' cheeses, an' I d'n know what all. Lukt like a Carter Paterson at Christmas time, he did. An' now prices is down again he wants to get rid o' the stuff, an' nob'dy'll luk at it 'cos it's all goin' bad on 'is 'ands. And serve him jolly well right!—that's what I say."

"And I say the same. It was inconsiderate and selfish and decidedly unpatriotic. If everybody had done like that where would the rest of us have been?"

"That's it, mum. But it's them Chilfers all over. I'm glad to say they've tuk his car f'r the war, and they've tuk all the horses they could lay their hands on. That's rough on some. There's Gilling down our way. He runs a laundry. They stopped him in the street t'other day an' tuk his horse and left th' van and th' laundry he was delivering right there. It'll put a stop on him I'm thinking, and folks'll have to go dirty, unless th' big laundries pick up all the business."

"There will be discomforts in all directions, I'm afraid, Mrs Skirrow. But we're much better off than the poor people in Belgium who are being turned out in thousands and their homes burnt over their heads. It's dreadful work."

"'Tis that, mum. An' begging your pardon, I says like my old man, 'Damn that Keyzer, and put the stopper on 'im as quick as may be!'"

"One cannot help hoping he will suffer as he deserves."

"That's right, mum! Bet you I'd trounce 'im if I got half a chance. I'd twist his old neck like that, I would,"—and she wrung her wet floor-cloth into her pail with a vehemence that imperilled its further usefulness. "He's an old divvle, he is, an' th' young one's worse, they say. All the same, if they c'd do it so's none of 'em got killed, for me I wouldn't mind th' war going on for quite a goodish bit."

"And I would be thankful if it all ended to-morrow."

"Ah! 'twon't do that, mum," was Mrs Skirrow's safe prophecy.

Since Con's post-card saying they were expecting to leave within an hour or two, they had had no word from him, nor was any information as to the movements of the troops permitted in the papers. The rigid censorship dropped an impenetrable vail between the anxious hearts at home and the active operations abroad.

It was a time and an occasion for the exercise of unparalleled and implicit faith and hope and trust in the powers that held the ways, and still more in the Highest Power of all. And on all sides was manifested an extraordinary strengthening and quickening of those higher and deeper feelings which had become somewhat atrophied during the long fat years of peace. The nation and the Empire drew itself together, forgot the little family disputes which had enlivened its existence for so long, and stood shoulder to shoulder as never before. The waters were troubled and the sick were healed.

The Colonel, in the pursuit of his duties, was frequently at the War Office. He heard, there and at his club, many things of which he never spoke even to Mr and Mrs Dare in their intimate evening confabulations.

The full bleak blackness of the days of Mons and Maubeuge were known to him, and the peril of Le Cateau and Landrecies, and it was as much as he could do to keep the weight of these grave matters out of his face at times.

He saw the casualty lists as they were compiled at the office, long before they were issued, and groaned over them in general and in particular. Killed, wounded, missing,—many whom he had known, and more whose people he knew, were already gone. Who would be left when the full tale was told?—he asked himself gloomily,—when this was barely the beginning.

Then, one day, his anxious old finger, following the list down, name by name, stopped with a sudden stiffening on the name of "Dare, Lieut. C., R.A.M.C." under the head of "Missing," and he had to inflate his chest with a very deep breath and hold himself very tightly, before he could mechanically get through the rest of the list.

"Missing!"—Under all the ordinary circumstances of civilised warfare that would leave abundant ground for hope. But the appalling stories he had been hearing of late as to the newest German methods left only room for fear.

They were, on the most indisputable evidence, behaving worse than the worst of savages. Their barbarous cruelties were the result of a deliberate system of frightfulness and terrorism inspired by headquarters. They had shocked and wounded his soul till at times it had felt sick of humanity at large. But they filled him also with a most righteous anger which helped to brace him up again.

That a hitherto reputedly civilised nation could, of cold deliberation, do such things!—and exult in them!—Faugh! It was savages they were,—and worse than any savages he had ever come across!

And so he feared the worst for Con, and his heart was heavy for Con's wife and mother and father.

He went over to his club to think it over, but found too many friends there for his present humour. So he turned into St James's Park, and walked on and on, with his mind full of Con and Alma, past the Palace and the Duke's statue, and found himself in Hyde Park, where the London Scottish were drilling and manœuvering with a huge crowd looking on.

That made him think of Ray, and he wondered briefly where those two had got to. If Ray had been at home, as he ought to have been, he would have been among these stalwart kilties who looked fine and fit for anything. As soon as he got home he would take his place of course. And young Noel and Gregor MacLean,—he had heard that very day that reserve battalions were to be raised pretty generally. So they would be in it too. And that was all right. Duty called, and it was the part of the young to bear the burden and heat of this desperate life-struggle to the death.

But his heart gave a twinge, all the same, at the possibilities. Con was possibly gone. Suppose these others went too! It would leave a dreadful gap in their homes, and wounds in their hearts that would never heal. This was what war meant. God help them all!

He watched the brave swing of the boys in hodden gray for a time with approving eye, till they fell out to munch exiguous lunches on the grass, which reminded him that he was hungry himself, and he went off to feed thoughtfully all by himself at a quiet little restaurant in Jermyn Street.

Alma must be told at once. Sudden sight of the ominous news in the list when it was published would be very trying for her. He could break it gently and put a better face on it than, to his own mind, it actually bore. And then he must break it also to Mrs Dare and she would tell her husband and the others.

But he nodded his head gravely over the whole matter as he ate, and was full of bitterness and wrath as those stories he had been hearing of ghastly brutalities perpetrated by the Germans even on the wounded came surging up in his memory. He cursed them heartily, and prayed High Heaven to requite them in full for all.

But a couple of daintily-grilled cutlets, with crisp curly wafers of chip potatoes, and a nut of real old Stilton, and a pint of Burgundy, and a good cigar, induced a more hopeful state of mind.

There were black sheep in every army of course. With all our care we had never been able to eliminate them entirely from our own. And war was a terrible loosener of the passions. But a victorious army was perhaps less likely to indulge in vicious devilry than a beaten one. At least one might hope so. Unless, indeed, the Germans had all gone Berserk mad, as some were saying.

Con, busy with his wounded, had probably had to be left behind in the hurried retreat,—how hurried only those in the know really comprehended as yet. He was a non-combatant and there could be no possible reason for maltreating him. He was probably safe and sound in Germany by this time.... If only one had not heard all those devilish stories!... Even women and children! ... and the wounded!... God hold them to account for it all!

By the time his taxi set him down at the big gate of St Barnabas's, he was fairly himself again. He rang the bell and requested audience of the Matron.

"Bad news?" she asked, with an anxious look, as she shook hands with him.

"Might be worse—perhaps. He's in the list as 'missing.' And that may mean anything or not so much. I thought I'd better let her know before-hand. The list will be out in a day or two and...."

"I'll send for her," and she rang the bell and gave the order, supple-menting it after a second's hesitation with, "Tell Nurse Luard that her uncle has called to see her."

"It will prepare her for possible ill-news," she said, "and she will have time to pull herself together."

"Yes,—thank you! I am going to assume that it is not really very bad news, though to tell you the truth—"

"It leaves a loophole for hope, of course. But the Germans seem behav-ing very badly—"

"Damnably," jerked the Colonel.

"—If all the stories we hear are true."

"Must be some fire for all the smoke that's about," and then Alma came hastily in, her face white and set, her eyes painful in their anxious craving.

"Is he dead?" she asked quickly, and the Matron slipped quietly out.

"No, no, my dear!" said Uncle Tony, gripping her trembling hand firmly. "Nor, so far as we know, even wounded. But in the list I have just happened to see up yonder, his name is among the missing. And I did not want you to come on it suddenly in the paper, and think it worse than it is."

"Thank God!" she said quietly, with a sigh of relief, and drew her hand across her eyes as though wiping away a ghastly vision. "That is all you know?" she asked with a searching look. And if the Colonel had been breaking worse news by gentle steps he would have had a very bad time.

"That is all that is known by anyone, my dear. As soon as we hear more you shall know it. It may be that he will be safer as a prisoner, wherever he is, than if he were in the thick of it."

"He would sooner be in the thick of it," she said, with a decided shake of the head. "He will be terribly put out at being shelved so soon. I have put down my name for the next draft. I was hoping we might perhaps come across one another."

"One hundred to one against it, I should say. There will be so many hospitals and you might be sent anywhere."

"I'd have felt nearer him anyway. But if he's.... Where would they be likely to send him?"

"Away into some remote part of Germany, most likely. You think you'll go? If any further news comes you would get it quicker here than out there."

"They are needing all the help they can get. I think it is my duty to go, Uncle."

"Very well, my dear. Go, and God bless you! And bring you back safe to us. We shall miss you all. Noel and young MacLean will be in the London Scottish to-morrow, I expect. And Ray—"

"Any news of those two?"

"Not a word. I'm expecting a telegram any minute from Southampton or Folkestone or Newhaven, saying they've just got across and will be up in a couple of hours. And as soon as Ray gets back he'll join his battalion of course. We'll have no one left but the two girls."

"They'll keep you lively."

"We shall miss you all. But it wouldn't be in any of our thoughts to stand between any of you and what seems to you your duty."

"Things are not going well with us from all accounts. Are they really as bad as some of the papers seem to make out?"

"They have been too strong for us so far. They've simply rolled us back by weight of numbers. But they haven't rolled over us, and their losses must have been terrible. I have great faith in French and Kitchener. Safe men both. And the Frenchman, Joffre, seems a good steady sort too. No froth about him and France believes in him. The tide will turn, you'll see."

And presently he took his leave, bidding her keep her heart up and promising to send her instantly any further news he could get of Con. And then he went on home to break it gently to Con's mother also.

CHAPTER XVI

AS the Colonel marched up the platform in search of a suitable seat in the Willstead train, he spied his niece, Victoria, sitting in a corner, knitting—though not with the practised ease of the born knitter—for dear life, regardless of observation, and obviously full of thought.

"Hello, Uncle Tony!"—as he sat down beside her. "What's the latest from Head-Quarters? I've been up at a meeting of the Committee that is to look after Out-of-Work Girls. We're going to start them all knitting and sewing for the men at the front both on land and sea."

"Capital! And you're by way of setting them an example."

"I was just thinking some things out, and Auntie Mitt and Mrs Dare are quite right—"

"Of course they are."

"You can think a great deal better when your hands are employed."

"Personally, I—"

"Oh—you're only a man. You know nothing about it. Any news?"

"Yes. I've just been to see Alma,"—she stopped knitting and eyed him sharply,—"Con's name is in the list of missing—" she gave a sigh of relief and went on knitting furiously,—"It may be no more than that,—prisoner of war in Germany—"

"They're treating prisoners and wounded abominably," she said severely,—to hide the anxiety that was in her.

"There have been such cases reported. Let us hope they are the natural exaggerations of war. Anyway, till we hear more we can hope for the best, and to his people we must keep hopeful faces. His mother will naturally fear the worst. Do all you can to keep her spirits up and make no more of it than the facts warrant."

"I'll do my best. But ... I'll not be satisfied he's all right till we hear from himself. How long will it be—if he is all right?"

"It may be weeks, my dear. Things are in something of a mess over there, you see. Everything has gone so quickly. One hardly has time to breathe, and the Germans are too busy driving on to Paris to spare time for such little details as that. Anyway he's not among the dead or wounded—not officially so far—"

"It might mean either. We're falling back. Many of our dead and wounded must get left behind. I wish I could go out and help."

"Alma's going,—at least she's put down her name. But I hope she'll think better of it. She'll get news quicker here than out there. But you could do nothing without training, you know."

"To be sitting on Committees and talking,—and knitting, when our poor fellows are bleeding to death out there!" she said bitterly. "Why on earth didn't you insist on me learning nursing too? I could wash their hands and faces anyway."

"You'll find plenty to do at home, my dear. Only the fully qualified are any use out there. Presently,—ay already,—there are widows and orphans to look after, and your out-of-work girls, and the wives and children who are not yet widows and orphans but may be any day. Plenty to do at home for all of us. But, for the moment, we've got to quiet Mrs Dare's fears for Con."

"It would be too awful if—if the worst had come to him," she said, with a glistening in the eyes.

"It would be very sad for us all. But for him—my dear, a man can do no better than die at his post. If it should be so, be sure he died doing his duty. But we're not to think of him as gone. Con's one of the finest boys I know, and, please God, he's alive and well and will come back to us."

Mrs Dare and Honor had just suspended work and were sitting down to tea when they were shown in, and Mrs Dare rang for additional supplies as soon as she had greeted them.

"Well, Colonel? Any new news?" she asked cheerfully.

"Yes,—I came on purpose to tell you. I have just been to see Alma."

They both sat up at attention and eyed him anxiously, and he hurried on, "It is disquieting, but not necessarily more than that. Con's name is in the list of 'missing.' That means he has been captured and so may be out of further danger till the end of the war."

"Thank God, it is no worse!" said Mrs Dare, with a sigh of relief. And then, as her mind travelled quickly the possibilities, with a downward tendency natural under the circumstances, "Can we be sure it is no worse?"

"If he were known to be dead or wounded, it would be so reported. 'Missing' leaves us every ground for hope, Mrs Mother. And it is our bounden duty to hope for the best. And we will. A great many of our R.A.M.C.'s were captured at the same time. The retirement was very hurried, you see. They would be busy with their wounded. Probably they would not leave them. The Germans swept on, and there they were—behind the lines—prisoners."

"They have been behaving very brutally," said Mrs Dare depressedly.

"In cases—where they will probably claim to be justified, and even they are probably much exaggerated. Is it any good treading the stony ways before we actually come to them? There may be more than enough for us before we're through."

"You are right, my friend. I'm afraid I'm sadly lacking in faith. One gets somewhat disjangled with thinking overmuch about things."

"Mustn't think down," said the Colonel, shaking his finger reprovingly at her. "Think up! Half the ill things we fear never come to pass. Isn't that your experience now?"

"It is. But the times are out of joint, and—"

"And it's our business to put them in again, and we're going to do it."

"We're still falling back, I suppose," she said, uncheerfully, and he knew she was wondering if there would be any hope of news of Con if a change should come in that respect.

"Still retiring on Paris, and doing it uncommonly well too," he said, very much more cheerfully than he actually felt.

For the black Sunday of Mons still lay heavy on him, and he knew better than any of them the certain cost of those terrible rear-guard actions— from Cambrai-le Cateau to the Somme—Oise—Meuse, to Seine—Oise— Meuse, to Seine—Marne—Meuse, and he dreaded the thought of the tardy lists which would be hard to compile and harder still to read.

"You'll see we'll find the ground we're looking for soon," he said stoutly. "Then we'll right about face and maybe give them the lesson they're spoiling for. They are suffering terribly, as it is, but there seems no end to them. But, anyhow, Con will be all right in Germany by this time, and truly I don't think we need worry about him unduly."

"I'll try not to, but it is not easy,—hearing the things one does."

"If duty were easy it would lose half its virtue,"—and then the door flew open and Noel and Gregor MacLean stood in the opening, with their hands to their foreheads in most punctilious salute and broad grins of delight on their heated faces.

"London Scottish!" they said in unison.

"You're in?" cried the girls, jumping up.

"For King and Country! At your service," and they broke off and demanded tea,—much tea and all the cakes that were going.

The girls flew round ministeringly and buzzed about them full of questions and congratulations.

"And how soon do you get to work?" asked the Colonel.

"Medical inspection 9 a.m. to-morrow morning. But we're as fit as fiddles, so that's all right."

"And when will you get your kilts?" asked Honor.

"A-a-a-a-a-ah!" said Noel. "Now you're asking."

"Echo answers 'When?'" said Gregor. "From all accounts it may be months."

"O-o-o-oh!" remonstratively from the girls.

"But we want to see how you'll look in them," said Honor.

"You go right up to Head-Quarters, my child, and put it to them straight, and I shouldn't be a bit surprised if we got them by mid-day Monday," said Noel.

"'The kilt is but the guinea stamp, the man's the gowd for a' that,'" said Gregor with a grin, and a reddening under his tan at so unusual an outburst and an approving glance from Honor.

"Well, it's been worth waiting for," said the Colonel.

"I should say so. We'd sooner be full privates in the London Scottish than potty little lieutenants in anything else, wouldn't we, Greg, my boy?"

"Rather!"

"Do you know Con is missing?" said Honor.

"No?" unbelievingly from both of the boys. "Missing?"—and they stood staring from one to another with such startled looks that the Colonel thought well to interject a bluff, "He's probably tucked safely away in some remote corner of Germany by this time. But we shall hear in due course,"—and he accompanied it with so straight and meaning a look at the boys that they understood, and fell in with his intention.

"Poor old Con! How mad he'll be to be out of it," said Noel hastily. "Say, Greg, my boy, we've got to get out there as quick as ever we can. What a joke if we came across him—er—languishing in captivity and were the means of setting him free."

"Are the lists out then, sir?" asked Gregor.

"Not yet, my boy. I was up at Head-Quarters and they're compiling them as fast as they can. Pretty heavy, I'm afraid."

"Sure to be, sir. There's been some mighty tough work out there."

"The German lists will be ten times as heavy. That's one consolation," said Noel.

"No amount of German losses will compensate one mother for the loss of her son," said Mrs Dare soberly. "My heart is sore for all those German mothers too. It is terrible waste. And all so unnecessary too."

"Always bear in mind, Mrs Mother, that we did not want it," said the Colonel. "It was forced upon us, and we are fighting for freedom and the rights of the smaller peoples. It is an honour to fight in such a cause. It would be an honour to die for it."

"Hear, hear!" said Noel.

But when the Colonel took his leave, and the two boys lit their pipes and strolled along with him, Noel broke out impetuously, "Is there any more behind, sir, that you haven't told us? 'Missing' may mean anything."

"That is absolutely all that is known as yet, my boy. It may, as you say, mean anything. But until more is known we have every right to hope for the best. And for that reason I want you to take the brighter side of the possibility and do your best not to let your mother dwell on the other side. You understand?"

"I understand, sir," said Noel, very soberly.... "It would be awful if—if the worst had happened to him. Does Alma know?"

"I went and told her at once and minimised it as much as possible. But I've very little doubt they all understand what it may mean just as well as we do."

"They're behaving like perfect devils over there, from all accounts," said Gregor. "I can't understand it. I've known heaps of Germans, as nice folks as you'd wish to meet. And now—devils unloosed, and up to every dirty underhand trick imaginable. What do you make of it, sir?"

"War is a terrible unloosener of the worst that is in man, and there are black sheep in every army. And I've no doubt there's a great deal of exaggeration in the stories we hear."

"I'd like to stamp the whole darned lot out of existence like so many black beetles," said Noel hotly.

"I'm afraid they'll take a lot of stamping out," said the Colonel, as he turned and went through his own gate.

"By—Jing, Greg, I don't like it one little bit!" said Noel, as they linked arms and went on down the road to tell their own good news to Mrs MacLean.

"It may be as bad as we can't help fearing. But, as the Colonel says, it may not, and it's cheerfuller to look on the bright side. I can't imagine Con being killed."

"Neither can I, but they say we've lost about fifteen thousand already, and when you think of that it doesn't take much more thinking to think he may be one of them."

"That's not all killed, man. It's everything."

"I know, but it's been beastly hot work, and ... dash it, Greg, you know what I'm thinking of. They say they're sparing none and making a dead set at the Red Cross men."

And Gregor nodded gloomily.

"We'll say nothing to my mother about it at present," he said. "Maybe better word'll come in a day or two, and it's no good fashin' her unduly.

She'll be glad we've got in all right, because she knows we've been wanting it so much, but she'll feel it, you know, when we have to go."

"That'll not be for a good while yet. And anyway we're doing our duty to our country."

But this news about Con distinctly sobered their exuberance, and Mrs MacLean, as she congratulated them on the attainment of their wishes, thought what a fine sensible pair they were, and what a change the prospect of service was making in them already.

She was well over middle age, white-haired, and had the kindliest face and sweetest soft Scotch voice Noel knew, outside his own family. Gregor was her only child and her heart was wrapped up in him.

"I'm glad you're going to wear the kilt," she said gently. "When will you be getting them, do you think?"

"Oh, not for a while yet, I expect. First Battalion want everything they can get, you see. We're only in the nursery yet."

"You'll find it queer at first, but you'll soon get used to the bare knees," she smiled, to Noel.

"It's no worse than footer, you know. By Jove, Greg, my boy, we'll Condy them a bit to subdue their natural shiny whiteness. Then they won't startle people as we pass."

"All right. But we may as well wait till we get there,—unless you want to begin training them right away in the way they should go."

"And when do you start work?"

"Medical exam to-morrow morning, and then as soon as the top-knutties can lick themselves into shape."

And so they chattered on, very full of themselves and their new importance, and Mrs MacLean rejoiced in them,—but hoped fervently, nevertheless, that the war would be over before they would have to do any actual fighting.

CHAPTER XVII

I N the Post Office at Montreux, Ray and Lois, with startled looks, faced the fact that only a modest five pounds stood between them and poverty in a land which esteemed its visitors according to the size of their purses.

The quietly portentous statement of the young man behind the glass screen at the Post Office, as to the unlikelihood of their telegram ever reaching its destination, was well calculated to take away their breath. It left them floundering like incapable swimmers washed suddenly out of their depth.

Lois, having infinite faith in Ray, was the first to recover herself with a glimmer of amusement.

"We'll manage somehow," she said. "It's all part of the adventure."

Ray had had experience of shortage in foreign lands and knew how small was the sympathy it evoked. But it was assuredly not for him to emphasise the sorriness of their plight, which, he kept saying to himself, was all due to his own idiocy in losing his purse.

"Seems to me a cup of tea is indicated," he said. "Perhaps it will stimulate our jaded brains to see the way out," and he led her to the little tea-shop near the Kursaal.

They had it to themselves at the moment, and Mademoiselle in charge welcomed them with smiles as possible harbingers of a revival of business.

"Iff you please,—tea?" she asked, proud of her accomplishment.

"A good pot of tea and some of those cakes. How well you speak English!" said Ray.

"We haf many English, you see, and I wass in Bhry-tonn for one year. Yes, sank you, saire."

"Perhaps she could recommend us to some cheap pension," suggested Lois, as Mademoiselle tinkled among the tea-cups behind the screen. "She looks a sensible kind of girl and we can make her understand the position."

"Good idea!"—and when she came back with the tea and arranged it before them with an ingratiating, "Iff you please,"—he asked, "I wonder if you know of any pension, mademoiselle, where they take in stranded foreigners for nothing a day and feed them well?"

But that was altogether too cryptic for her.

"Please?" she asked, with a puzzled smile, scenting a joke but not fathoming it.

"We want to find a very cheap pension," explained Lois. "We are on our way home to England but have had the misfortune to lose our purse up there on the Rhone Glacier. And at the Post Office they tell us we may not be able to get any money sent from England for some time, because of the war."

"Ah—zis horreeble war! It is ruining us all. But yess, madame, I know a pension which is cheap. Pension Estèphe, opposite the Gare. It is not everything, but it is clean and it is honest, and it is cheap. I have myself stopped there once."

"Thank you. That is just what we want. We have telegraphed for more money, you see, but they cannot be sure it will ever get there, and we can't tell when we can get away."

"Ach! It is terreeble. There are many caught like that. Zis horreeble war! It will ruin everybody, yess!"

"What's the latest news about the war?" asked Ray.

"Mais, monsieur, we get little news. They are fighting all the time—oh, terreebly. But we do not know much about it. I do hope it will not come here. You do not think it will, monsieur?"

"We'll hope not, ma'm'selle. But if it suited the Germans to come I've no doubt they would, in spite of you."

"Ach, I do not like the Germans. No!"

"The feeling seems general. Well, we'll go along presently and look at the Pension Estèphe, and if we like it we shall come in and see you again, ma'm'selle."

"Iff you please, saire!"

Madame of the Pension Estèphe eyed them somewhat doubtfully at first. They were above her usual class of customer, and it took considerable explanation to make her understand why they wanted to stop with her, the exact relationship in which they at present stood to one another, and, more especially why they had no luggage but their rucksacs.

However, by dint of much talk, they came at last to terms. For a room each, and their meals, she would charge them seven francs per day for the two. If they got married and occupied only one room it would be a franc less. And she providently demanded a deposit of ten francs and that they should pay their bill each day.

"For," said she, without any beating about the bush, "you have no luggage, you see, and you might walk away and leave me nothing but your rucksacs which do not contain much."

Their rooms were alongside one another and their appointments were plain to the point of exiguity, but they were clean and the beds looked comfortable enough.

"From the mere point of economy it's obvious we must get married at once," laughed Ray, and Lois blushed but raised no objection.

"It'll have to be a pauper's wedding," he ran on, "And we'll have a wedding-tea at Ma'm'selle's shop and blow out one franc each on it. I wonder what it will cost to get married? If it's more than we save on the room in, say, a fortnight, we can't do it,"—at which Lois laughed enjoyably. —"There used to be a jolly old Scotch parson here. We'll look him up and put the case before him. Perhaps, in the circumstances, he'll do it for nothing—or at all events, give us credit till we reach home."

And, presently, they went along to the little church in the rue de la Gare and got the minister's address and went along to his house, but they found that he was away on holiday and so they had to deal with his locum.

He proved very pleasant and amiable, however, and when the whole matter had been explained to him he undertook to marry them as soon as they chose and free of charge.

"Then to-morrow, please," said Ray. "You see we save a franc a day by getting married, and when you've only got five pounds altogether it's something."

"If you get no reply to your telegram, you must see the Vice-Consul. He's Swiss, but a good chap. Some provision is to be made, I believe, for our stranded fellow-countrymen. There are a great many here in much the same position, and more coming in every day. It's making a lot of trouble, this wretched war."

"It'll make a lot more before it's finished, I'm afraid. If I were home I'd probably be in it myself—I'm in the London Scottish, you see,—"

"Ah?—You're a kiltie, are you?" with a sparkle in the eye.

"Been one four years, and I expect every man we can scrape will be needed before we're through. What are folks here thinking about it all, sir?"

"Not over well for us, I'm afraid,"—with a gloomy shake of the head. "The Germans are not liked here, as you may have found—"

"We haven't met one single person that has a good word to say for any one of them."

"Exactly! Their bumptiousness and lack of manners make them a byword. But all the same they are believed to be overwhelmingly strong and wonderfully organised. I should describe the general feeling as a fear that Germany may win. In which case it will be a bad thing for us here. We have one powerful factor in our favour, however."

"And what is that, sir?"

"We're in the right this time. We haven't always been, but this time we certainly are. And righteousness tells in the long run."

"I hope it will. I can't imagine England knocking under to Germany. It's unthinkable."

"The Right will win.... Meanwhile they are hammering away at poor little Belgium because she would not allow them free passage to Paris. And she's doing magnificently—"

"Belgium! Think of it! I'd no idea she had it in her. One has come to associate Belgium so with Congo atrocities and purely material things that anything heroic in her surprises one."

"Heroic is the word. She's holding the fort while Britain and France and Russia get ready. It may be that she is saving Europe from Pan-Germanism."

"Splendid! I take off my hat to her. Good thing old Leopold's not in the saddle! The new man must be a good sort."

"He must be.... Then to-morrow, Mr. Luard. Shall we say at eleven? And I hope, my dear,"—to Lois,—"it will make for your happiness."

"Oh, it will," she assured him. "And it is very very good of you."

When Ray and Lois came down to their dinner-supper, that first night, in the common-room of their unpretentious pension, they found a numerous company already busily at work, and were somewhat taken aback by their looks,—burly, moustached and bearded men in blouses and dungarees, with an odour and look of trains and engines about them;—loud of voice, disputatious indeed, and oblivious of manners.

Lois shrank a little at sight and sound of them. But their hostess directed them to a small table apart, covered with a red-and-white-check cover, over which she spread a table cloth and even provided them with napkins. For seats they had high stools without backs. "It feels like a music-lesson," whispered Lois,—and—"I hope it will be more satisfying," murmured Ray. "I'm hungry," and watched the black-a-vises critically out of the corners of his eyes. They toned down for a moment when the strangers entered, and passed remarks sotto voce between themselves, but in a minute or two were in full blast again.

"They look like brigands," murmured Lois. "They won't murder us in our beds, will they?"

"The fact of our being here will prove that we're not worth it, I should say."

"I shall barricade my door all the same ... if I can. There's not over-much to barricade with."

"They're probably quite decent fellows,—railway-men from the look of them, and they're generally a good sort."

And they proved entirely so and never gave them any trouble whatever, beyond the noise of their arguments, which was at all times tremendous and more than once looked like ending in blows.

Most of them drifted back to work when their meal was over. With the two or three who remained over their cigarettes, Ray got into conversation on the war and picked up some interesting bits of information.

Some of them had just, in the course of their work, come through from Italy, and the thing that was exercising them all at the moment was—what was Italy going to do? If she came in against France their opinion was that Germany would win. If Italy maintained neutrality, as some of them insisted was likely from what they saw and heard down there, then they thought the other side might have a chance, but it would be no easy job. They, also, were mightily impressed with the idea of Germany's strength and preparedness. But they liked her no better than anyone else. Most of their Italian fellows had already been recalled to the colours.

"It'll be a bad day for the world if she wins," said Ray.

And, "You're right, monsieur, without a doubt," was their unanimous verdict.

Lois duly barricaded her door with her alpenstock and only chair, but no murderous attempt was made on her, and she laughed at herself in the morning, and felt like apologising to the noisy, good-humoured crew.

Promptly at eleven o'clock, too joyous of heart to let themselves be troubled by their outward shabbiness, they walked into the little dark gray church on the road above the station and were quietly married, with the delightful assistance of the pastor's wife, who was immensely interested in their little romance. And afterwards he insisted on the newly-married pair joining them at their mid-day meal.

"It will be a very modest wedding-feast," he said. "But such as it is—"

"We can't afford to refuse such a noble offer," laughed Ray. "We were going to celebrate the great occasion by spending a whole franc each at the tea-shop near the Kursaal. We save two francs and enjoy your good company. It's great, and we are very much obliged to you."

"You would do as much for us if ever the occasion offered."

"Just give us the chance, sir, and you'll see."

Next day the kindly Scot accompanied him on a visit to the Vice-Consul, whom they found already being worried and badgered into desperation by the clamorous demands of their stranded fellow-countrymen and women, especially the latter. For every lady in distress seemed to think her own special plight the extremest limit in that direction, and each one claimed the individual attention of her country's representative and required him to send her home instantly, bag and baggage, and to ensure her safe arrival there.

It was obviously something of a relief to him to meet a man whose requirements were definite and modest and his methods business-like.

Ray briefly stated his case and asked if he could do anything towards getting a telegram through for him.

"My uncle, Sir Anthony Luard, will send me money instantly when he learns of our plight,—that is, if it is possible to do so," he said. "What do you think of the prospects?"

"At the moment—very doubtful. Later on things will settle down somewhat no doubt. I am trying to get through by way of the south. France and Germany are quite out of the question. What are your immediate needs, Mr Luard?"

"Very small. We are cutting our coat according to the cloth we have. Six francs a day pays our board and lodging,"—at which the Consul permitted himself a brief smile. "But we had to walk all the way from Innsbruck, you see, so we sent all our baggage to Meran with a Mr Lockhart, the man who writes about Tirol,"—the consul nodded—"And we really must buy some few things to go on with. Could I possibly draw on Sir Anthony through you for a small sum?"

"We'll manage it somehow. You see how I'm situated,"—with a wave of the hand towards the adjoining room full of clamorous applicants. "As far as I can I must do something for everybody. If I find you fifty francs a week at present, how will that do?"

"Splendidly, and I'm ever so grateful to you. I've had visions of us sleeping on a seat on the quai and eating grass."

"We'll hope it will not come to that for any of you," smiled the consul. "If the amount grows large enough to make a small draft I will get you to sign one. But I am hoping that some arrangement will be made before long for getting you all home through mid-France. All the fighting is likely to be on the frontiers for some time to come, I should say."

"And then in Germany we will hope."

"Germany is very strong," said the Vice-Consul cautiously. "One can't foresee what may happen."

And so their way was to that extent smoothed for them. Board and lodging were at all events assured, and if they were not everything that could be desired they might have been much worse, though truly they could not have been much cheaper. The food, if a little rough, was well-cooked and sufficient, and Monsieur and Madame of the Estèphe and their four comely daughters grew more and more friendly under the influence of prompt and regular payments, and did all they could for their comfort. And Ray and Lois testified their gratitude to Mademoiselle of the tea-shop by having a festive cup and a chat with her every day when their rambles had not led them too far afield.

Walking, since it cost nothing, was their one diversion. Fortunately they were both in good condition, and in spite of the heat they enjoyed their tramps immensely. Madame of the Pension met their wishes and provided them with portable lunches, which, if somewhat monotonous in their constitution, were undoubtedly satisfying, and she generally managed to amplify their evening meal to their entire contentment, and indeed showed herself not a little proud of the distinction such high-class guests conferred upon her establishment.

Their chief lack was news. English papers were beyond their pocket and almost unattainable, and the local ones contained but very one-sided and garbled statements of what was going on at the various fronts. Cook's offices were closed, so no news could be got there. The 'Feuille d'Avis' was indeed stuck up each day in the office-window in the Market-Place, and they went along every morning and read it for what it was worth. But it was only by applying to their friend the consul that they could get any actual facts, and those not of the most recent nor of the most vital. And he was so terribly overworked that they disliked troubling him.

At times, indeed, in sheer self-defence he locked his door and stuck up a notice saying that he was broken down and could see no one. Then the clamorous throng gnashed its teeth and leaned its elbows on his bell-push, and Lois and Ray were so ashamed of their fellows that they preferred getting along as best they could without news sooner than harass him further.

They managed to keep brooding at bay very enjoyably by exploring all their surroundings,—from Chillon—they could not afford to go inside,—to Vevey;—to the Rochers-de-Naye by Veytaux and Recourbes; and up to Les Avants and the Chauderon Gorge. Anywhere and everywhere attainable to pedestrians they went, with unbounded energy and immense satisfaction, and savoured the joy of life to the very fullest.

The restful beauty of the shimmering blue lake, and the uplifting glory of the peaks of the Valais and Vaudois and Savoy, viewed as they were through the glamour of their fulfilled love, wrought themselves into the very texture of their lives.

To Lois it was a time of rare enchantment, heightened and intensified —like the shining of stars in a blue-black sky—by the grim horror of the war-clouds beyond. It might all come to an end any day. The future might have in it unthinkable sorrows. But this at least was theirs, and the joyous memory of it would never fail them.

"Ray! I am so glad it has all happened just so;—as far as we are concerned, I mean. These days are my jewels. They will shine for me always and always, and I can never lose them. Oh I am glad, glad, glad to have lived them!"

"And what do you think I am, dear? Do you think there ever were two happier people on this earth?"

"Never! It is not possible."

They were perched in a little eyrie, high up the mountain-side near Crêt d'y Bau, shoulder to shoulder for the joyful feeling of one another, gazing out over the lake towards Geneva, eating the little wild raspberries of inexpressibly delicious flavour which they had gathered as they climbed.

"Whatever may come to us now we can bear it because we have had all this," she sighed contentedly. And asked presently, in a lower key,—"Do you think it is possible for people to be too happy, Ray? ... that we shall have to pay for it later on?"

"No, my dear, I don't. Why should we? We were meant to be happy. It's only folly or wickedness—either in ourselves or other people—that brings unhappiness ..."—and, stumbling along after the thread of his thought,—"and, it seems to me that if we keep ourselves up to the pitch of deserving happiness, whatever happens outside us cannot take it from us. Troubles may come. Not many folks get through life without them, and they don't turn out the best folks as a rule. But if we remain to one another what we are now, we shall be proof against them all and they won't hurt us.... In other words, my child, it is not outward circumstance that counts, but our own inner feelings."

"Yes! I'm feeling all that, and more and more every day.... If this horrid war goes on do you think you will really be called up? I thought the London Scottish and the rest were only for home-defence."

"I wish to goodness we knew just how things stand. If it's going to be a life-and-death struggle England must do her proper share. Compared with the armies over here ours is trifling,—in point of numbers, I mean. As far as it goes it's probably better than any of them. But it's very very small in comparison with their millions. And numbers tell. There may be a national call for volunteers. If it comes you wouldn't have me shirk it?"

"No ... but oh, I wish it might not come," and she pressed his arm closer against her heart.

The Kursaal concerts, costing at the lowest one franc each, were beyond them of course. So in the soft autumnal evenings they spent most of their time on the quais outside the gardens, sitting when a seat was obtainable, wandering along with the rest, leaning over the railings, with the dark lake stretching from under their feet away into the infinitude of night. There they could hear the music quite as well as the wealthier folk inside, and without a doubt enjoyed it more than any of them.

The sunsets were wonderful beyond words. The evening star hung like a jewel in the afterglow and twinkled at itself in the smooth mirror below. Then the summer lightning played fitfully over the further hills and set the lake, and the bayonets of the quai-patrol that guarded them from invasion, shimmering and gleaming, and looked so like menacing signals that their thoughts turned constantly to the fact that somewhere over there the world was dreadfully at war.

When it grew quite dark, parties of sober merry-makers would put off in small boats, each with its coloured lantern, and ply quietly to and fro, weaving their trailing reflections into patterns of extraordinary beauty, till the lake below looked like a great dark blue carpet shot through and through with wavering tracery of gleaming gold and all the colours of the rainbow. And it was all undoubtedly very charming and beautiful, but, to Lois, it was also all most strangely unreal and evanescent, as though at any moment, at the sound of bell or whistle, it might all vanish and give place to scenes less tranquil. For somewhere over there the world was at war and how far it might spread none could tell.

So the days ran on, and only now and again when it rained, and trips up aloft were out of the question, did they ever find them long.

Their chief lack still was news of what was actually happening over yonder behind the curtain. And this began to tell on Ray though he did his best at first to hide it. But Lois saw and understood.

Away across there in Belgium and the north of France, England might be feeling already the sore need of every man she could put into the field. His fellows might already be pressing to the front. And he was tied here by the leg.

He did his best not to show how he was feeling it, but there it was, and his thoughtful silences, and an occasional concentrated pinching of the brows which she had never seen in him before, told Lois the tale even before he spoke of it.

To her he was quiet thoughtfulness itself and the perfection of married lovers. For deep down in his heart was the knowledge that before very long the time for parting might come. It would be sore to leave her. It would wring his heart and hers. But he knew that if duty called she would not have him stop. He set himself to make sure, and surer still, that these brief days of married love should hold in their memory no smallest flaw, and he succeeded to the full.

He told her all that was in his heart concerning future possibilities, and they talked it all over quietly, soberly, lovingly, and were the stronger and richer in their love.

"Whatever comes, we have had this, and nothing can take it from us,—and the rest is in God's hands,"—was the end to which they always came and the strong rope to which they clung. And their love grew ever deeper and stronger for this trying of it.

CHAPTER XVIII

"ABSOLUTELY nothing further so far," said the Colonel, standing with his back to the fire in Mrs Dare's sitting-room, as she handed him a cup of tea. "All they can say is that quite a dozen of our R.A.M.C.'s of various grades have never turned up since Landrecies, and they believe they were all taken in a bunch. And that seems to me to improve the chances of Con's being all safe and sound. We shall hear from him before long, you'll see."

"It is sore waiting," said Mrs Dare.

"So many have not even the chance of doing that. The lists are again very heavy, I'm sorry to say."

"And we are still falling back?"

"Still retiring, but you'll see we'll stop before long,"—and then there came a ring at the bell, and presently the door opened and there stood in the doorway a burly figure whom neither of them recognised, and behind it the concerned face of the maid whose attempt at announcement had been forestalled.

The newcomer was tall and broad, and something about his face seemed familiar to both Mrs Dare and the Colonel, and yet they were sure they had never set eyes on it before. For it was most decidedly a face calculated to impress itself on the memory. To Mrs Dare it suggested the late Emperor of the French, but with more alert and wide-awake eyes. It made the Colonel think of Victor Emmanuel the First, of Italy.

"Well, well?" said the stranger, and then they knew him.

"Good heavens, Rhenius! What are you playing at? You gave me quite a shock. I took you for the ghost of Victor Emmanuel," jerked the Colonel half-angrily.

"And I thought you were Napoleon III come to life again," smiled Mrs Dare, as she poured him out a cup of tea.

"Ah-ha! So you accorded me promotion on both sides—"

"If you'd call it promotion?" growled the Colonel.

"Quite so. Very questionable. I have never greatly admired either of the gentlemen in question."

"And why on earth have you been playing such pranks with your face? Think it an improvement?"

"I was in Italy when the troubles broke out,—at Piora, near Airolo. Before I could get through, France was practically closed to any but Frenchmen. I wished to get home so I became a Frenchman for the time being—a Frenchman of the Second Empire, and me voici! But I came to bring you news."

"Of Con?" asked Mrs Dare eagerly.

"Of Con? No. What is wrong with my good friend Con?"

"He's reported missing," said the Colonel.

"Missing!"—with a pinch of the lips that jerked up the long moustache. "I am sorry. But that is better than either killed or wounded. He is at all events safe from harm."

"You really think so, Doctor?" asked Mrs Dare anxiously.

"Why, of course, my dear madame. As a prisoner of war he will be well-treated and out of harm's way."

"If one could only be sure of that," she sighed.

"What's your news then?" asked the Colonel brusquely, not having yet quite recovered from his umbrage at the Doctor's facial metamorphosis.

"Ah, yes—my news.... I came over Furka by way of Hospenthal, and there, at the Golden Lion, I met two of my young friends whom you know very well—"

"Lois and Ray?" and Mrs Dare dropped her knitting and stared up at him in anxious excitement.

"Yes—Lois and Ray—"

"I told you they'd strike down south and get out that way," said the Colonel triumphantly. "That's good. I forgive you your barbarisms, Doctor, —neat that, eh? And I'll take another cup of tea on the strength of it, Mrs Mother, if you please!"

"And they were quite all right?" asked Mrs Dare.

"Quite all right, and as happy as young people ought to be. They were hastening down to Montreux—"

"And why haven't they got here?" asked Mrs Dare.

"Well, you see, it was no easy matter even for me, and I had made up my mind to get through at any sacrifice," and he stroked, with a suggestion of regret, the remnant of the flowing beard that had had to go. "I made my way across country to St Nazaire and got across from there. But it was no easy matter, I assure you.—And, besides, they had plans of their own— great plans. They were hastening to Montreux to get married—"

"To get married?" echoed Mrs Dare, while the Colonel greeted the news with a shout of, "Well done, Ray! Da-ash it, that boy's got brains in him. I knew he had good taste," and he turned and grasped Mrs Dare's hands and shook them heartily.

"But why could they not wait till they got home?" asked Mrs Dare.

"Well—I think they felt it not quite proper to be wandering about together like that, you know. And there is no knowing how long they may be detained out there."

"Why didn't you bring them along with you?" asked the Colonel.

"I had booked a seat in the diligence to Brigue, and it proved to be the very last seat—and I fear the last diligence. The driver told me they would probably stop next day, as all the horses were wanted by the military at Thun. It may be weeks before you see them, and I'm afraid there are many others in the same predicament. Ray particularly asked me to ask you to send him out some more money to Poste Restante, Montreux. But I'm afraid you'll have difficulty in doing so."

"I'll see the bank first thing in the morning. They'll manage it somehow. And what opinion did you form of things generally over there, Doctor?"

"I had small chance of hearing anything. I've heard a great deal more since I reached home."

"You were in Italy, you say. Well, what's Italy going to do? She's an important factor in the case."

"Undoubtedly!"—with a sagacious nodding of the ponderous head. "A very important factor.... What she will ultimately decide it is impossible to say. She is not anxious for war, that is pretty certain. She is poor, you see, and somewhat exhausted. If she had been going in of necessity, as a member of the Triplice, she would have declared herself before this. It depends, I should say, on whether the others can force her in."

"Not a volunteer, eh! And maybe at best an unwilling conscript. I should say she'd be well advised to keep out of it."

"If she can.... Ah, here are the young ladies!"—as Honor and Vic came in with looks that demanded tea.

"Goodness!—" gasped Vic.

"Gracious!—" continued Honor, and they both ended on a most emphatic "Me!" and stood staring at him with faces full of amazement.

"The voice is the voice of Jacob but the face is as the face of—who is it, Vic?"

"Mephistopheles.... What on earth are you playing at, Doctor?"

"Playing?" he remonstrated, pulling up the point of his Napoleon and trying to look down at it with melancholy regret. "Playing, indeed!"

"I fathom it," said Vic gleefully. "It's an omen. Germany's going to be beaten so you've transformed yourself into the likeness—such as it is—of Napoléon Trois. Good business!"

"Napoléon Trois has always been my particular detestation, Miss Vic-who-ought-to-have-been-Balaclava,"—which was his usual counter-stroke to her thrust,—"as you very well know. This was imposed upon me by force of circumstance. I had to get home, you see,—for all your sakes. And to get home I had to come across France."

"And you were afraid of being taken for a German spy! I see."

But he had known her since her hair hung down her back and he would not take offence.

"I might very well have been taken for a German, anyway, and Germans are not held in high esteem in France at the moment."

"Nor anywhere else in the world except in Germany. And I hope they'll be blotted out even there before long. Detestable wretches!"

"Ta—ta! There speaks hot youth. But it does not trouble me since I have nothing in common with Germany."

"Except your name, and your birth, and your looks,—when they're normal that is, mein Herr! They'll intern you, for certain, at Dorchester, or Porchester, or wherever it is, and you *will* have a time."

"All that does not concern me, my dear. I am a British subject just as much as you are."

"Not a bit of it, mein Herr! I was born one."

"The more credit to me. You couldn't help yourself. I acquired the right of my own good free-will."

"He has you there, Vic," said the Colonel, who always found huge enjoyment in their sparring. "But he has brought us news of Ray and Lois—Mr and Mrs Ray Luard, I should say—"

"No!" and the two girls flopped down into chairs simultaneously.

"Fact,—at least we have every reason to hope so. When the Doctor saw them—at Hospenthal—they were making their way down to Montreux, with the expressed intention of getting married as soon as they got there."

"Well!... I—am—"

"'Hammered!' as Gregor says," supplied Honor. "What a pair of families we are! Vic, my dear, the atmosphere of war is packed with marriage-germs. We must be careful. I'm sure they're catching. Mother, dear, some tea, please. Quick! I feel faint," and, first carefully taking off her hat, she subsided gracefully against the back of her chair.

"All the same, Nor, it's rather too bad, you know," said Vic resentfully. "That's two weddings we've been done out of. It's really anything but fair."

"It's abominably shameful," said Honor, undergoing a quick revival at thought of their wrongs. "I don't believe they'll have been properly married out there. It ought to be done over again as soon as they get home. How do you know it will be all right?" she put it to the Colonel. "Ten years hence it may come out that they are not really married at all and there'll be a dreadful scandal."

"I'll trust Ray to see himself properly married, my dear," laughed the Colonel. "Don't you worry your pretty head about it," and then with a touch of concern in his voice, to the Doctor,—"I hope they'll not give you any trouble here, Rhenius. Some of the yellow rags are making something of an outcry against foreigners—enemy foreigners, I mean. You see, there undoubtedly is an immense amount of espionage going on, and folks are apt to run to extremes at times and lose all nice sense of discrimination."

The Doctor shrugged his big shoulders. "I was naturalised years before some of you were born. They will not trouble me," he said with confidence. "If they do I'll come to you for a character, Colonel."

CHAPTER XIX

I N course of time and on the principle that Heaven helps them that help themselves, the stranded English in Montreux formed a committee of repatriation, which met in a room placed at their disposal by the authorities of the Kursaal, and, by dint of much writing and wiring and hustling, towards the end of the month their arrangements, such as they were, were, with the assistance of Cooks, who had now returned to business, satisfactorily completed.

The penniless were to be sent off first, then the rest by degrees in inverse ratio to their staying powers.

Anxious as they were, for some reasons, to get home, Lois, at all events,—with the knowledge that getting home might well be but the beginning of sorrows—found herself full of regrets at leaving Montreux. The little inconveniences of their stay there had been gloriously impearled with the glamour of their love. They had been perfectly happy, and perfect happiness comes not often in life nor ever lasts too long.

They had taken leave of their friends, and Ray had duly given the Vice-Consul a draft on Uncle Tony for the money he had advanced them. Monsieur and Madame and all the four demoiselles of the Pension Estèphe, and Anna the maid, had all come to the station to see them off, and were full of regrets at losing them, and now their train was jogging along towards Lausanne bound for Geneva.

They had been instructed to take with them provisions for three days, within which time it was hoped the journey to Paris might—failing accident —be accomplished. And so they had, with the assistance of Madame of the Pension, provided themselves with much bread, and butter, and a tin of tongue, and a cold boiled fowl, and apples and pears and tomatoes, and cheese, and two bottles, one filled with wine and the other with cold tea. And they wondered if they would ever get through such a pile of eatables and felt prepared for a siege.

Hand-baggage alone was to be taken, and theirs consisted entirely of their provisions, as everything else they possessed went into the rucksacs on their backs. Those who attempted to take too much had to leave the excess in the Consigne at the station, to be forwarded later if opportunity permitted.

They had been told to be at the station at 5 a.m. and to form themselves into parties of eight, which would just fill a compartment, and as Lois and Ray had made few acquaintances they had some difficulty in making up their complement. They made hasty quest round, however, and Lois discovered two little elderly maiden ladies, waiting timidly in a corner for someone to take them in hand and tell them what to do, which she immediately did, and they wept gratefully. And Ray picked out two nice-looking boys of about his own age, who were standing watching the confusion in aloof amusement,—found they were not engaged, and secured them on the spot.

The final two in their carriage were thrust upon them at the last moment when the authorities found their numbers short. They were two young men from Lancashire, who did not speak a word of French—or indeed of anything but broad Lancashire—and they rarely opened their mouths. They were decent quiet fellows, however, and made no trouble.

The little ladies had just started on a Swiss trip to which they had been looking forward for years, and the war had made short work of it.

"We came to Switzerland once before, when our father was alive. But since he died—well, we have been keeping a school,"—confided one of them to Lois,—"and we have just disposed of it—"

"You see these newer subsidised schools are making things hard for the private schools," said the other, as the train jogged along the side of the lake, still wreathed with swathes of fleecy mist. "And when the chance offered we were glad to retire."

"And we thought it would he so delightful to renew our old memories of Switzerland. We were at Zermatt—"

"I was trying to remember where we'd seen you," said one of the stranger youths, with just enough of a drawl and intonation to betray a trans-Atlantic origin. "We were at Zermatt too. We came across to climb something and they told us Matterhorn was about as good as anything. So we went to Zermatt and made a start on Matterhorn—"

"You began at the top," said Ray.

"Matterhorn's not a thing you can begin at the top. But we started from the Schwarzsee, and that's 8945 feet up."

"8495," said his brother.

"And you got on all right?" asked Lois, while the little ladies regarded them with silent admiration,—men who had actually been up the Matterhorn, at which they themselves had gazed in fearful rapture from below!

"It was all right. We had guides, four of them, very good fellows, and ropes and axes and all the usual things. And they got us through. The only thing that happened to us was a stone in one of the couloirs that came down on my brother's wrist and smashed his watch, and cut him a bit."

"Had you done any climbing in America?" asked Ray.

"Nary! Never climbed anything—"

"'Cept stairs!" said his brother.

"Plenty stairs, yes, but no mountains to speak of. That's why we came —to see how it felt."

"And it felt good," said his brother.

"Yes, it felt good, and if we could have stopped we'd have climbed some more. But this flare-up's knocked everything sky-high. We couldn't raise a red cent on our letters of credit, and there we were, stony in a strange land, and not even able to tell what was the matter, 'cept when we struck someone that had the good sense to speak English."

They were extremely nice fellows, graduates of Harvard, one studying law in Boston, and the other medicine, and their humorous outlook and comments on life in general did much to palliate the discomforts of the journey.

They had gone in strongly for fruit as provisioning, and had a couple of melons, a large supply of grapes, apples and pears and nuts, and of course tomatoes. The little ladies' ideas had run to sandwiches and chocolates and a few bananas, all of which they confidently asserted were extremely nutritious.

At Geneva they had to change trains for the journey through France. They were all bundled out into the courtyard outside the station, and stood there in the broiling sun till soldiers with bayonets separated them into parties of forty and finally marshalled them to their carriages.

These were a decided come-down,—old non-corridors, five-on-a-side, and some without even racks for their parcels. However, it was all part of the adventure, and our party, all sticking together, were glad to find themselves at last securely locked in and really started on the journey home.

It was slow business, however, and freighted with discomforts, but they made as light of these as they possibly could, and did their best to look upon it all as a joke.

When, in the course of the night, Lois produced a small spirit lamp she had lavishly expended two whole francs on, and, after several times nearly setting them all on fire, managed to produce cups of tea all round—an operation which took time, since her kettle was of the smallest and they had only two aluminium folding-cups—they could none of them find words commensurate with their gratitude. Time, however, was the one thing they did not lack, and their absorbed interest in that precarious tea-making, and

134

the attention they had to give to unexpected conflagrations, and then their exultation and enjoyment over their cups of hot tea, rejoiced her greatly and fully compensated her for her prodigal expenditure on the spirit-lamp and kettle.

Even the new members of their party, a somewhat reserved young Englishman and his wife, returning dolefully from a short-cut honeymoon, thawed by degrees under the influence of hot tea at midnight, and became quite cheerful and friendly, in spite of the fact that no formal introductions had taken place.

They were packed pretty tight in their old-fashioned carriage, and but for the general goodwill the discomforts would have been almost insupportable.

They chatted and ate, and ate and chatted, and made tea at intervals, and now and again dozed with their heads on one another's shoulders quite irrespective of persons. The ladies were accorded the corner seats and the men acted as pillows and buffers between. And so they jogged slowly along through the night, drawing up now and again with a succession of clangorous bumps that ran from end to end of the train and died with lugubrious creakings into startling silence, then starting again with a jerk that shook them all wide awake. It was as though they were cautiously feeling their way through the darkness and unknown dangers ahead.

Of official stops there were almost none. When one did come, and the guard announced 'dix minutes d'arrêt,' everybody poured out of the carriages, to fill their water-bottles at the station pump and stretch their cramped legs gratefully.

In the very early morning they had a stop of nearly an hour and heard that it was because a lady had been taken ill. They blessed her fervently, washed their hands and faces at the pump, and many boldly produced toothbrushes and did their teeth. And all the time afterwards, their American boys kept suggesting that Lois, or one of the little ladies, or the young bride, should go sick and procure them another such happy release from their cages.

Everywhere, as they waited in sidings, there were heavy train-loads of soldiers speeding to the front. They were all obviously in the best of spirits, eager to get to the long-expected red work and to make an end of it for good and all. They leaned out of the windows and cheered the waiting trains, which gave them back cheer for cheer and hearty God-speeds.

Their young Englishman, with more zeal than aptitude for foreign tongues, roused great enthusiasm by leaning as far out as he could get and shouting at the top of his voice, "Vive la Président!"—which was invariably greeted with laughter and heartier cheers than ever. And so, by slow degrees and haltingly, they crept up towards Paris, where one of Cook's people met them, and took them round by the Ceinture railway, and saw them safely off for Dieppe.

CHAPTER XX

MRS DARE was sitting by the fire in the parlour at Oakdene, knitting long deep thoughts into a Balaclava helmet. On the other side of the hearth sat Auntie Mitt, similarly occupied on a body-belt, which, being more straightforward work, suited her better. Both their faces were very grave, and they had not spoken a word for close on half an hour. There was so little to speak about and so much to think about.

The news from the front was not good. It did not bear discussion. The Germans were still pressing furiously on towards Paris. Their losses had been enormous and ours had been terribly heavy though slight in comparison with theirs. But life seemed the very last thing worth their consideration. So long as they won the bloody game nothing else mattered, and they were fouling the game with every tricky manœuvre and abominable brutality their twisted minds could contrive.

It was a time indeed for anxious thought on the part of all who had any stake out there, and Mrs Dare's heart ached with fears for Con. If he were still alive he must be somewhere in the hands of these pitiless savages, and according to the papers they spared none. They even seemed to go out of their way and beyond human nature in the pursuit of that gospel of frightfulness which the Kaiser openly preached.

Her heart had been wrung over Belgium and Northern France. What chance had any man of coming alive out of such a welter of crashing deaths? At times her faith in the goodness of God and the ultimate triumph of Right seemed to her overborne by the high-piled horrors of the morning's news. How—could—God—permit—such—doings?

And when she was in that low state of spiritual health it was always a comfort to her to hear the Colonel's cheerful voice at the door, and to set eyes on his grave but always confident face.

Her husband was so sorely tried in these days that even she—helpless and almost hopeless as she felt herself at times—had to play the part of faithful helpmeet as best she might.

The moratorium had indeed relieved him of the heaviest of the pressure for the time being, but his business was practically killed and the future weighed on him almost beyond bearing.

To both of them the Colonel played cheerful Providence, and did his utmost to dissipate their clouds.

"My dear Mrs Mother," he would adjure her. "Have we not gone through just such times before—"

"Never quite so dark—nor coming so close home to one."

"That has been your happy fortune. But to thousands of others they have come close home in just this same way. Always in the end we pull through;—ay, even when we've had less justification than we have now. If there's a righteous God overlooking this matter—and you're not going to tell me you doubt it—"

"No, I'm not. But I'm sometimes sorely put to it when I think of it all, —the horrors—the hideous—"

"Don't think of them. Think of the way our lads are behaving out there. They're simply grand. And the way they're toeing the line here is just as fine. And the Colonies!—and Ireland! By Gad, ma'am, we're living in no-ble times! And we'll see grander times yet. We're—going—to—win! Tough work first, maybe, but win we shall, as sure as God's God."

And his faith in his country and in the Higher Powers never failed to cheer her into renewed hope.

To John Dare he was equally helpful.

"Cheer up, John," he would exhort. "There's a lot of life and work in you yet—"

"I feel sometimes as if I'd like to go to sleep and never wake up again."

"I know. I've been there, but I'm glad now that I thought better of it and waked up as usual. Things'll pull round all right. Darkest hour before the dawn, you know."

"That's the trouble. It's all dark and I see no dawn."

"It's there all the same, man. Thousands of other men feeling just same, but you'll all come up smiling again in the end."

But he was harder to beguile of his morbidity than his wife. And, in-deed, with a carefully-built business crumbled to nothing at a stroke, and five-and-fifty years behind him, it was not easy to regard the future with much confidence. It was not to be wondered at that he was terribly de-pressed, and at times a little irritable. Life was touching him on the raw, and he found it hard to bear.

"Well, we'll have tea," said Auntie Mitt, breaking the half-hour's si-lence and ringing the bell. "I hoped Sir Anthony would be in by this time. Perhaps he will bring us some good news from town."

"I've almost lost the expectation of hearing good news," said Mrs Dare. "It would be a refreshing novelty to hear something cheerful again."

"We must never lose hope, my dear. While there's life,—you know."

"That's just it. I can't help fearing he's dead all this time—"

"Who, my dear? Sir Anthony?"

"I was thinking of Con. He's in my thoughts all the time."

"Sir Anthony seems to feel certain he will be all right. If—if the worst had happened, he says, we should certainly have heard before this."

But Mrs Dare shook her head. "I don't know. This war seems different from any other war. They do such dreadful things. They seem to respect nobody."

"They are certainly behaving very badly, if one can believe all the papers say. I sometimes think they exaggerate a little, you know,—make the worst of things and the best, just as they think it will please people. The papers are very different from what I remember them."

"They have changed a bit in the last seventy years or so, haven't they, Auntie Mitt?" said the Colonel, who had come quietly in behind the maid with the tea-tray.

"Oh—Sir Anthony! Seventy years! They have changed terribly in the last twenty years."

"Of course they have. When you and I first knew them— Thanks!" as she thrust a cup of tea at him.

"Any good news?" asked Mrs Dare.

"In the papers—none. Confidentially, I hear that the tide is about to turn. They're not to get to Paris anyway."

"I'm glad of that. It would have been hateful. They would have crowed so. And Paris has suffered from them before. What is going to happen?"

"Oh, having drawn them on, now we're going to roll them back."

"Wouldn't it have been better to keep them out?"

"Yes, if we could have done so, but we couldn't. They were too strong for us. But we've been getting stronger every day and now we're going to turn and rend them."

"I'm not blood-thirsty by nature, but truly I've come to the point of longing to see them rent in pieces. It is very horrible, I know, but I can't help it."

"It's very human, Mrs Mother. We'll rend 'em in pieces for you all right, but it'll take time and some doing."

"And terrible loss," she said with a sigh.

"No gain without loss, and their losses have been awful. There never has been anything like it. How long they can stand it, I don't know."

"I've given up caring for their losses in thinking of our own. I'm growing inhuman."

"Not a bit! Couldn't—no matter how hard you tried. Now who's this, I wonder. Some of Auntie Mitt's old tabbies, I expect. I'll bolt."

But the door opened and disclosed the maid's face all alight with excitement as she announced with a jerk, "Please, ma'am,—Sir Anthony,—Mr and Mrs Luard!" and Ray and Lois walked in.

The Colonel rushed at them with a shout. Mrs Dare jumped up. And Auntie Mitt almost upset the tea-table into the fire-place.

"Well, well, well!—Mr and Mrs Luard! My dear,"—as he kissed Lois heartily,—"This is a great day for us! There,—go to your mother. She's been aching for you. Ray, my dear boy, you're a champion. How did you get here? Where have you come from? How are you?"—All which incoherencies testified his feelings better than many set speeches.

"I suppose you never got the wire I sent from Montreux, sir?" asked Ray.

"Never got a thing, my boy. But Rhenius got home and told us you were wanting money and I've been doing my best to get some sent out, but so far it's been impossible. How did you manage?"

So they unfolded the idyl of their great adventure over many cups of tea; each supplementing the other with suddenly remembered intimate little details, the one taking up the running whenever the other ran dry, or out of breath, or stood in need of sustenance.

"We spent the night on the boat," concluded Lois, "with eight hundred others. It was an awful pack and we had to sleep anywhere—"

"She slept on a bench on deck, and I lay under the bench, and every bone of me's sore—"

"So are mine," said Lois, "and it was none too warm—"

"Fortunately it didn't rain, and we managed to get some hot tea early in the morning which bucked us up a bit. But it's not an experience I'd care to repeat—not just that part of it, I mean."

"Now tell us all the news," begged Lois. "We've been in the wilderness for a month and we know practically nothing except that we're at war. How's everybody? And how are things going?"

All that would obviously take much telling, and Auntie Mitt, foreseeing a considerably enlarged party for dinner, disappeared quietly to look after the commissariat.

The wanderers were mightily astonished at the tale of the last month's happenings. They rejoiced at Alma's marriage, but were greatly disturbed at Con's disappearance. Having as yet been told nothing of the savage brutalities in vogue among the Germans, they were, however, hopeful that he would turn up again all right in time.

"It is terrible for Alma, all the same. We must go up and see her, as soon as possible, Ray."

"We'll go to-morrow, and give her a surprise."

A foretouch of future shadows fell on them when they heard of Noel and Gregor MacLean having joined the London Scottish.

"What about the First Battalion, sir?" Ray asked at once.

"Mobilised for Foreign Service, my boy."

"Where are they?—Head-Quarters?"

"Watford."

"There'll be some papers waiting here for me, I suppose."

"You'll find them all in your room."

"I must go up to-morrow first thing. Did you tell them why I hadn't answered, sir?"

"Yes, I called at Head-Quarters and saw Colonel Malcolm. He said it would be all right, and he would keep your place open as long as possible. They'll be glad to see you, even if you're a bit late."

"You really feel you must go, Ray?" asked Mrs Dare anxiously, full of thought for Lois and remembering Con.

"Yes, mother dear. I must go. We have talked it all out, and Lois feels as I do about it. It is evident that we're going to need every man we can put into the field, and if there are any shirkers they ought to be shot."

"It will be hard to part with him," said Lois bravely. "But he cannot stop when all the rest are going."

Mrs Dare picked up her knitting and went quietly on with her work. Her heart was overfull. This monster of War was taking them one by one. What if none of them ever came back? What terrible gaps it would make in their lives! God help them all!

The Colonel's hand dropped gently on Lois's and patted it softly in token of his high approval.

And presently Ray slipped away to look over his equipment and pack his kit. To make sure that everything was in order he put on his uniform, and when he went down to them again it was as First Lieutenant Luard of G Company of the London Scottish, and very fine and large he looked as he came striding into the room.

"I think everything's all right," he said. "If anyone sees anything amissing, kindly mention it."

And Lois looked on him with shining eyes and a flush of pride in her face. But in her heart she was saying, "He is splendid, splendid,—but suppose it only leads to his death."

Such thoughts, however, were for private consumption only, and her face was all in order as she commented with quiet approval on this detail and that, and asked in matronly fashion if he was sure all his buttons were stitched on tight.

She liked him so much in his fine feathers that he consented to keep them on. "For," she said to herself, "to-morrow he will be gone and I would like to think of him like that."

Vic and Honor came in only in time for dinner and could hardly believe their eyes. They loaded Lois with reproaches for her hole-and-corner wedding and commented adversely on her German frock, which they advised her to burn forthwith, or as soon as she could procure something decent enough to be walked with, and she promised to attend to their wishes in town in the morning.

The Colonel had sent word to the Red House for Mr Dare to come over if he came in, and presently he appeared, so worried-looking and dispirited that Lois's heart was touched and troubled about him. But he brightened up at sight of her and Ray, and gave them very hearty greeting. The lack of news concerning them had been an addition to his load. The sight of them now, alive and well, lightened it to that extent.

He brought the cheering news of a heavy defeat of the Austrians by the Russians at Lemberg, but had nothing encouraging to report from France. There we were still falling back and there was talk of the Government removing itself from Paris to Bordeaux, which was not reassuring. It sounded so fatally like 1870.

"Wise, all the same," said the Colonel confidently. "Every additional step the Germans take from their base is a possible added risk for them. But I heard better news than that, Dare. We think they've come far enough and now we're going to call a halt. And maybe we'll even drive them back."

Over dinner, the great adventure had all to be gone through again, and the girls did their best to convince Lois that she was not properly married and certainly ought to go through the ceremony once more to make quite sure, for her own satisfaction and theirs.

"Think how awful it would be," said Vic portentously, "if in ten years' time you found it was invalid, and Ray could just shake you off with a simple 'Good-day, Madam!'"

"Horrible!" laughed Ray. "Don't you worry yourself thin over it, Balaclava. I've seen to it that she can't get rid of me, no matter how she wants to. Everything is quite all right, my child. Trust me for that."

And Lois, smiling confidently, was yet praying in her inmost heart, "God spare him to come back to me! It may be that when he goes I may never see him again."

They were still deep in talk when the boys came swinging in about nine o'clock, and at sight of the uniform they drew themselves up and saluted smartly.

"Three paces in front and three in the rear!" said Noel, and they marched solemnly past Ray before dropping their hands. "And if a simple

142

private may be permitted to address his superior officer,—where the dickens have you two dropped from—a Zeppelin?"

"No, only the Folkestone boat—" and, after a brief outline of their wanderings abroad, they fell into talk of regimental matters.

"Maybe they'll put you back into the Second Battalion," suggested Gregor, and Lois's heart beat hopefully.

"Oh, will they, my boy? Not if I know it. The Colonel knows all about it and he's holding my post for me."

"Lucky beggar!" said Noel enviously. "I wish we were off to the front. Greg and I are as fit as any man in the First, and I'll bet you we'd knock spots off most of them in the shooting line, eh, Greg?"

"And what are you playing at all day?"

"Oh, mouching about Head-Quarters while the Hossifers change their minds as to what we should do. There's a fearful lot of mouching about in this business."

"Worse than Throgmorton Street," said Gregor.

"To-day we did a route march to Richmond Park. Jolly hot it was too, and some of the fellows had about as much as they could stick. Greg and I didn't turn a hair. By the way,"—to the girls,—"you remember us telling you of the old lady who comes out on to her balcony every time we go out Putney way, and waves a black cardboard cat to us for luck? She was there again to-day, waving away like a jolly old windmill, and we gave her a cheer that did her heart good, I bet."

"Dear old thing!" said Honor. "Perhaps she's got someone in the battalion."

"I don't know. But she's undoubtedly gone on us."

"I don't see why," said Vic critically. "Any news of uniforms yet?"

"On the contrary," laughed Gregor, with quiet enjoyment. "Some of the fellows in the First Battalion, who couldn't go abroad for one reason or another and so have been put back into the Second, have had to give up theirs to fellows in the First who were short, and they're as mad as bears at having to tramp in civvies. Dear knows when we'll all get fitted out."

"Oh well," chimed in Noel, "I'd sooner wear my own things than go about like a convict in blue serge, as some of Kitchener's poor beggars have to."

"Yes, they do look rotten."

"Feel rotten, too, you bet. If they put me in convict dress I'd feel like chucking the whole thing."

"Kilt before country!" suggested Vic ironically.

"Not a bit. Kill't for one's country, if you like, so long as it's in a kilt. But I can tell you it makes a difference to your feelings—padding along like an out-of-work procession, with every kind of coat and cap that ever was made. Makes one feel like a rotten old jumble sale."

"You'll get your togs in time," said Ray. "The great thing is to have the man that's to go inside them fit and well."

"Well, we're all that anyway. We've been route-marching ourselves and potting clay-pigeons for a month past."

Mr and Mrs Dare were noticeably quiet. She, because, in spite of herself, her heart was depressed at all this close approximation of the Juggernaut of War. It was impossible to close her mind to the fears that beat blindly at it. Con gone already—possibly gone for good. Ray going,—he might well never come back. Noel and Gregor longing to go,—they would jump at any chance that offered. They too might never come back, and she had fathomed Gregor's feeling for Honor, from the shy anxious glances he cast at her whenever opportunity offered. About Noel and Vic she was not so sure; their manner towards one another puzzled her. But already she forecasted all the boys lying dead and all the girls left broken-hearted.

Mr Dare had his own reasons for withdrawing into his shell. Business, of course, for one thing. And for another,—Noel.

144

CHAPTER XXI

NOEL, embryo warrior, was a very different personage from the Noel of six weeks ago looking forward without enthusiasm to the stool in St Mary Axe.

The sudden enlargement of his horizon to the boundless possibilities of military life and active warfare had, unconsciously, and perhaps unavoidably, wrought changes in him.

From being a boy, dependent on his father for both present and future, he had become suddenly a man, independent, and at times somewhat resentful of either control or advice.

His whole heart and mind were given with his active body to his new duties. He was soldier first, and anything else afterwards. To Honor it was quite understandable. He was jovially patronising to her and she held her own by chaffing him royally when chance offered. To his father and mother it was understandable also, but none the less somewhat of a trial at times.

Their boy was no longer wholly theirs. He had suddenly become a soldier and considered himself a man. They rejoiced in the better points of his manly development, but both felt keenly their deprivation in him; Mr Dare perhaps the most.

They saw very little of him. He was away early and home late. He was making many new acquaintances. Home and its associations counted for less with him. There was a general loosening of the old ties. They felt it, indeed, a beginning of the end that might find its consummation out there in the battle-smoke.

"We are losing him already," said Mr Dare with a sigh, one night when a telegram had come from Noel saying that as he had to be on orderly duty early next morning he would sleep at the Soldiers' Home opposite Head-Quarters. He had hinted at the possibility once or twice, but they had not taken it very seriously.

"We must not lose him," said Mrs Dare quietly. "He is keeping all right, John, I feel sure. He said he might have to stop now and then, you know. He's got to take his turn with the rest."

"I know, I know," said Mr Dare, a trifle irritably. "All the same I feel as if we were losing our hold on him."

"I suppose it's inevitable to some extent. We must do our best to hold on to the little that is left us.... If he ... if he comes through it safely, as we pray that he may, perhaps he will come all back to us.... Perhaps," she said, following up a side thought, "it is nature's way of softening the blow if he should not come back to us. The parting is beginning even now."

"Hmph!" grunted Mr Dare resentfully. "He's getting out of hand, that's certain. I asked him to see to something the other day ... I really forget what it was,—some small thing that he'd have done in a moment two months ago,—and he simply let it slide,—never gave it another thought apparently—"

"Boys are very thoughtless when their minds are full of their own concerns. I expect he just forgot all about it."

"That doesn't make it any easier to bear."

"I know. It only explains it perhaps."

"And I'm beginning to doubt if he'll ever settle down to ordinary work again. He has never been so keen on anything in his life before. I don't understand it. Where does he get it from?"

"It's partly boyish love of adventure, and partly, I don't doubt, real feeling that every man is needed, and when so many are going he wouldn't be one to stop behind. We will give him credit for that. But, indeed, it is the last thing in the world I would have desired for him."

"Or I," said Mr Dare, with a sigh.

The change in their relationship manifested itself in many little ways, —quite trifling some of them, but to Mr Dare's already bruised and sensitive feelings none the less galling.

The frank confidences of boyhood, which kept back nothing, were gone. Beyond the bare statement that they had done a route march to Richmond or Hampstead, or had been mouching about Head-Quarters all day, or playing about in Hyde Park, even his mother's interested attempts to draw him out came to little.

His manner at times seemed to hint that it would be waste of time on his part to enter into the details they would so have enjoyed hearing, since, being mere civilians, they could not possibly understand purely military matters.

When, occasionally, by some lucky chance, his Company was dismissed earlier than usual, if he did not stop in town to go to a theatre or music-hall with some of his fellows, he would rush in for a meal and off again almost before he had swallowed it, to call on this one or that one where he evidently found more congenial company than at home.

If they all happened to meet outside, at Oakdene or elsewhere, they would find him in the highest of spirits, reeling off merry yarns of their doings en route or at Head-Quarters, and they felt a little sore that all this brighter side of him should be kept for foreign consumption when the home market was pining for it.

"Have we failed in any way in our duty to him?" grumbled Mr Dare, after one such evening at Oakdene, as he and Mrs Dare went along together to their own house, which had never felt so lonely since they came to it.

"No, John, we haven't," said Mrs Dare. "It's just that he's very young still though he thinks he's a man, and youth draws to youth. It's always the way, I expect."

"It wasn't so with Con, or Lois."

"They had the younger ones—and they were all younger together. Young birds must quit the nest, you know."

"Youth is apt to run to selfishness, it seems to me. I think we'd better take a smaller house."

"We might well do that, but I would be sorry to leave Willstead and all our friends."

CHAPTER XXII

RAY went off in full rig first thing in the morning, taking his kit with him, in case, as he thought probable, he should be ordered to join his company at once.

Vic and Honor had business in town, so they went with him and Lois to the station, where they found Noel and Gregor marching impatiently about the platform for the train to come in.

"You can't travel with us, you know," said Noel. "We go third. Officers—"

"Thanks, my child! 'Out of the mouths of babes—'"

"The girls will of course follow the uniform," said Noel, while Gregor grinned hopefully.

"Of course," said Honor, and they got in with Ray. He leaned out of the window for a last word with Lois, who was going up later to do some shopping; and then they were gone, and she stood watching the joggling end carriage till it was out of sight, and wondered forlornly if she would ever see him again.

She was still standing watching, with an odd little feeling in her heart that when she turned away it would be like cutting the last link with the happy past and turning to face the anxious future, which stood waiting peremptorily just behind her, when the down-train ran in. She turned with a sigh that was almost a sob, and went out into the road.

Her eyes were misty as she went. It was the beginning of partings, and if he went to the front, as he most assuredly would if the rest went, it might be the beginning of the end.

And life was just at its fullest with them, just opening its fairest white flowers. They were so very happy,—and would have been happier still, if this hideous war had not come.

But she must be brave. Ray was feeling it just as much as she was. But he had gone to his duty with high heart and quiet face, and she must do no less.

But it was hard, hard, hard, to part with him so soon. God help them both! They were in His hands, and she must cling to that with might and main.

"Lois!"—and she turned quickly and found Alma hurrying to come up with her.

But a much-altered Alma. The beautiful face, which used to be all agleam with the joy of life,—the gracious curving mouth, where quick smiles and ready laughter used to hover,—the eloquent eyes which caught your thought in advance of your words,—they were all there but frozen to the semblance of a marble saint. Lois caught her breath at the change in her.

"Am I too late? Has he gone?" panted Alma.

"Just gone. Oh, Alma! My dear! My dear!" and they embraced one another there in the road, oblivious of who might see them at it. For the tragic web of circumstance in which their hearts were caught lifted them above all care for such small mundane considerations.

"Vic wrote me a line last night about you two, and I knew Ray would have to be off at once, so I came as soon as I could possibly get away. I *would* have liked to see the dear old boy once more. How is he feeling and looking?"

"Just as you would expect him to. He looks splendid. He is feeling— well, very much as we are, I suppose."

"Yes, these are sad and sober times for us all, but chiefly for us women. I think it hits us harder than the men. They have all the glamour and the activities. There is not much glamour in it for us who sit at home and wait for things to happen and fear the worst all the time."

"No ... Al, dear, I can't tell you all I feel about you and Con. But, dear, I feel somehow that he will come back. I do not believe he is ... gone for good."

"I don't myself. But the waiting and hearing nothing is hard to bear.... I thank God a dozen times a day that I have my work and that it is hard and taxing. If I hadn't I should break down. You must get some work to do, Lois. It is the only way to bear it.... But when Con and I parted, the evening of the day we were married—it was just outside the big gate at the hospital —I just knelt by my bed half the night. I could not think of sleeping. And I gave him up, there and then, to God and his country, and made up my mind that I might never see him again."

"It was brave and strong of you, dear. I'm afraid I haven't got up to that yet."

"It is best so. We may never see again any of those who go. If we can bring ourselves to really understand that, and say good-bye to them in our hearts, I think the pain of the actual news will be lessened."

"But we can always hope for them."

"Of course. We can, and do, and will. And if the hope is realised, so much the better. But if not, the pain will be less."

"It is all very terrible. Who would have thought it three months ago?"

"Ay, indeed!... I cannot help hoping that those who brought it about may suffer in themselves every bit of the suffering they are causing."

Her unexpected visit was a pleasant surprise to the Colonel and Auntie Mitt. It reminded them of her sudden home-swoops of ante-war-days, but with the unforgettable difference. Auntie Mitt, indeed, kept stealing surreptitious glances at her, as though she were not absolutely certain in her own mind that this really was their own Alma. And the Colonel's voice had a novel inflection in it when he spoke to her.

"No news, Uncle, or you would have let me know," was her first word to him.

"Nothing yet, my dear. I shall hear the moment they have anything definite. But they all seem quite hopeful."

But she had heard that so often that it had come to lose its savour for her.

"I am very sorry to have missed Ray. I got off as early as I could, but we are terribly busy. Have you any further idea as to my going out?"

"My dear, you could go out, I imagine, with any party that is going. But ... I really think your best place is here,—at your own work, I mean. If any news came, and you were away out there somewhere,—think how awkward it might be. We might want you at once and never be able to find you. Can't you bring your mind to stopping at home?"

"I suppose I must if you put it so. But I feel as though I would like to go out and tackle harder work still,—the harder and grimmer and redder, the better."

"I know," said the Colonel understandingly. "And if I thought it best I would say so, and help you there. But I really think you are best at home—for a time at all events. Now I must run, my dear. I promised to be in town at eleven. Stop as long as you can. I'll send you good news as soon as I learn any."

She stayed till close on mid-day, ran in for a short chat with Mrs Dare, had an early lunch, and then Lois walked back to the station with her.

"You will keep me posted as to Ray's doings, Lo," she said, as they stood on the platform. "For your sake, dear, I could almost wish he might not have to go. But I know him, and you know him, and we both know that if the rest went and he was left behind, it would break his heart."

Lois nodded. Her heart was very full. She wished Alma could stop at home. They could have helped one another. Life was all partings at present.

"Remember, dear," said Alma, as the train came round the curve, "we are more than ever sisters now. We must help one another all we can. And

—don't forget!—throw yourself into some good work or other. It is the very best anodyne."

And, the next minute, Lois was watching the joggling end of the train as it carried her away.

She went slowly home to discuss with her mother what work she should set her hand to. But before they had decided anything the matter was settled for them, for the time being, in quite a different way. A telegram was brought over to her from Oakdene, and it was from Ray at Watford.

"Have got rooms for you at Malden Hotel here. Come along."

This meant a quick fly round if she was to do him no discredit. Within an hour she was in town and whirling in a taxi to Regent Street. Inside another hour she had chosen, tried on, and had properly fitted, a costume and hat equal to the occasion, and she reached the Malden at Watford just in time for tea.

Then she waited joyously for Ray to put in an appearance, her clouds for the time being lightened by the certainty of seeing him again, and of having at all events some small share in him for a few days longer.

She knew well enough that it was but a postponement of the evil day, a very temporary lifting of the war-clouds to let the sun of their happiness shine briefly through. But possibly, to one under sentence of death, a respite of even a week may seem a mighty gain,—seven long days and nights snatched from the shadow beyond. Possibly!—for to some it might seem better to have it over and done with rather than to live on in the inevitableness of the ever-approaching menace.

Yet most would be gratified for even the gift of days, and Lois was so. Like Alma, she felt that when the actual parting came it would be wisdom to look on it as possibly—probably final. And so these few unlooked-for extra days were jewels beyond compare, vouchsafed them by the goodness of God,—to be made the very most of, and afterwards to be treasured as long as memory lasted.

Ray came striding in on her just before dinner.

"Well!" he said, when he had kissed her to their hearts' content, and then held her off at arm's length to take her all in,—"We are smart!"

"To be upsides with you, sir."

"However did you manage it? I was half afraid it would bother you to come, but the Colonel gave permission and it was too good a chance to miss."

"I should think so, indeed. I am so glad you managed it."

There was a joyous surface-light on his face though below it was set in firm restraint. Like herself,—but with larger knowledge of the actual facts and so a clearer estimate of the possibilities—he thought it more than likely they might never see one another again when they said their last good-bye. The slaughters out there were terrible. Officers especially were going under at a terrific rate. It seemed, from what they heard, that it was an essential part of the new low German fashion of fighting to make a dead set at every man in officer's uniform.

But not for one moment did he regret what they had done. If the worst was to come, his last breath would be the happier for the knowledge that their lives had been one, and that Lois's future was secure so far as Uncle Tony's generous hands could make it.

His billet was not very far away, but the Colonel, who had known him for years and Uncle Tony still better, and who had heard all about their little romance, permitted him the privileges of the hotel so that he might spend as many of these last precious hours with his new-made wife as possible, and Ray saw to it that love trespassed not on duty by so much as one hair's breadth.

He was up and away each day before she was properly awake, and he came in at night—when he came in at all—tired and hungry, but hungriest of all for another sight of her.

And Lois spent the days intercepting the Battalion on its route marches or exercising itself in cover-taking and trench-digging and manœuvering at Fortune's Farm.

And always, when she managed to catch the long line on the march, the sight of the intent masterful faces under the cocked bonnets, and the rhythmic swing of the kilts and bare knees and hodden-gray stockings and blue flashes, to the spirited skirling of the pipes, brought her heart up into her throat, and, often as not, the tears into her eyes.

They looked so gallant and so gay, so eager to be at it, so gloriously young and full of life, so ready to do, and dare, and die,—and, inevitably, some of them, many of them maybe, would swing away into the war-cloud, just like that—gaily, gallantly, eagerly, and would never come out of it. The glorious young life would gasp itself out on the foreign soil,—those who loved them would know them no more save as happy memories,—and maybe that life that was dearer to her than her own would be among them.

It was a sweet, poignant, uplifting time, and she lived to its utmost every vital moment of it. As in one of those gorgeous death-banquets of old, the ever-pressing knowledge of the inevitable end heightened and deepened and quickened the vitality of the moments that were left. Life—in herself and in these others—had never seemed so wonderful and so desirable. For —for some of them—its hours were numbered.

CHAPTER XXIII

L OIS was present, in a corner, at that last parade at Fortune's Farm when the new rifles were given out. And, later on, with misty eyes and that troublesome choking in the throat, she was watching the long wavering gray line as it swung gallantly away with skirling pipes and eager faces—en route for the front.

Then she turned to go quietly home to her mother and Uncle Tony, and to wait God's will in the matter.

She was to live at Oakdene as became Ray's wife, but her time was to be spent between the old home and the new, and her energies devoted to cheering them both. For both were lonely now and clouded. Of all the merry company that had filled them with such joyousness of youth, she was the only one they could now count upon.

Victoria and Honor were out all day, slaving on Out-of-Work-Girls and Belgian Refugee Committees, organising crowds of willing but in many cases incompetent workers,—arranging accommodation and hostels,— procuring houses, funds, and furniture, and getting them into something like working order.

Noel was only in for supper, bed, and breakfast, and not always that. The Colonel was carrying on a recruiting campaign with a patriotic vehemence much in excess of his years and his bodily powers.

Miss Mitten meekly, and Mrs Dare boldly, did their utmost to keep his exertions within reasonable limits. But to all their expostulations and warnings his invariable reply was,—"We need every man we can get, and since I can't go out, I must do all I can at home. Better to wear out than to rust out or go under to those damned barbarians."

"But you'll do no good by killing yourself," Mrs Dare had remonstrated, one morning when he looked in as usual in passing, and punctuated his paragraphs with muffled sneezes.

"Oh—killing myself! It's not got to that yet. (Att-i-cha!) I'm enjoying it, I assure you, Mrs Mother. We got twenty fine (Att-i-cha!)—boys at

Greendale last night."

"Well, do keep your hat on when you must speak outside, I beg of you. The nights are getting cold and you're not as young as you were, you know."

"It's my one com—att-i-cha!—complaint. And it's only the outer husk that feels it. I'm really wonderfully young inside, you know. I tell you, I was quite put out yesterday when a young fellow insisted on giving me his seat in the train."

"It was very nice of him."

"Hmph! Well, no doubt it was,—att-i-cha!—But, hang it all, I don't look as decrepit as all that, do I? However, I got the better of him by giving it to an old lady—a really old lady—a minute or two later. By the way, Lois had a post-card from Ray this morning."

"What does he say? Where have they got to?" she asked eagerly.

"Says nothing except that he's well and very busy. No word as to where, of course."

"And no postmark?"

"Nothing. They're behind the war-screen now. We shall know nothing more,—unless through the despatches, maybe. Now we've got to live on—att-i-cha!—on faith and hope," he said meaningly.

"And keep our hats on when we speak outside," she retaliated.

"That's all right," he laughed. "I'll begin taking you and Auntie Mitt with me, one on each side, to hold it down. I want to wave it all the time nowadays, at thought of having those infernal Huns on the run at last. More good news again to-day. Russia's smashed Austria into little bits in Galicia. Whurr—att-i-cha!—oo!"

"They were retiring somewhere yesterday."

"In East Prussia. Quick advance there was by way of diversion no doubt, and now they've done their work and are taking up safer positions."

"When any part of our side retires it's always a strategic retreat," smiled Mrs Dare. "But when the Germans retire it's always a rout."

"Well—so 'tis," he laughed, and shook hands and sneezed himself away.

"You'd be very much the better of a couple of days in your bed," was her last piece of advice as he went down the path.

"When the war's over. Did you ever manage to keep John in bed for a couple of days?"

"Yes—once,—for about two weeks—when he had pneumonia."

"Well I'll stop in bed when I get pneumonia," and he waved his hand again and marched away.

At teatime, when Miss Mitten and Mrs Dare, and their respective body-belt and jersey, were keeping one another company in friendly silence in the Oakdene parlour, Lois having gone into town to complete her outfit, the Colonel came in looking no more than a washed-out rag of his usual cheerful self.

"I've decided to take your advice, Mrs Mother, and lie up for half a day," he said depressedly. "I ought to be at Northcote to-night, but Penberthy has taken it on instead. He's a good chap, Penberthy, but unfortunately he can't speak worth a button. However—"

"The sooner you're in your bed the better," said Mrs Dare. "You can't afford to neglect a cold such as that."

"I always obey superior orders, don't I, Auntie Mitt?"

"I'm sure you did, Sir Anthony,"—at which he chuckled, but less heartily than usual.

"Just one cup of tea to cheer me up, and then, if you will be so good, Auntie Mitt, a good big white-wine posset,—one of your very best, and you'll send me up a bit of dinner later. Nothing like one of Auntie Mitt's big white-wine possets for chasing a cold out of the system. Talk about grateful and comforting!"

"I know them. Take my advice and put your feet in mustard and water as well," said Mrs Dare. "You've got a very bad cold on you."

"I shouldn't wonder if it's a touch of influenza," said Miss Mitten, when she returned from compounding the posset. "They say there's a good deal of it about. I don't know that a posset is the best thing for him. He seems hot enough to me. But it's no good arguing with him. He always does just as he pleases."

"I thought you agreed that he always obeyed superior orders," smiled Mrs Dare.

"And so he does, but they're always his own. When he was in the army I have no doubt he did all he was told and sometimes perhaps a bit more. That's how he won his V.C. But since he retired he's been his own master entirely."

"If he seems feverish in the morning I should send for Dr Rhenius, if I were you. He has been grievously overworking himself of late, and, since he won't take care himself, you must be careful for him."

"Yes, I will," said Auntie Mitt, with a very decided nod and pursed lips. "He forgets his age sometimes."

Next morning the Colonel was so limp and full of pains that he raised no objection when Miss Mitten suggested the Doctor.

"A stitch in time sometimes saves nine," quoth she.

"I've got 'em already," grunted the patient.

"Then it's a touch of pleurisy, I expect," and she hastened to get advice on the subject.

Dr Rhenius at once confirmed her speculative diagnosis.

"You're my prisoner, Colonel, till I say the word, or I won't answer for consequences. You've been altogether overdoing it, you know."

"King and Country need you," grunted the Colonel in extenuation.

"Well, you'll be more use to them alive than dead, and you've got to knock off now, or you'll knock out. Besides, they can spare you well enough for a bit. They're getting all the men they can handle, aren't they? In fact they don't seem able to handle properly those they've got, according to the papers."

"Big job, you see, ... machinery hardly in order yet.... Took us unawares, ... but we're going to see it through."

"What have you got up to now?"

"What Kitchener asked for.... Half a million or so.... We'll need lots more before we've done with it.... Get me right again as quick as you can.... I'll go crazy lying here."

"If you follow my instructions, and keep still, and don't talk so much, I'll get you right again. And when I do, just try and remember that you can't stand as much as you could when you were five-and-twenty."

The Colonel grunted, since talking set the pain in his side stabbing again. Dr Rhenius wrote out a prescription, gave Miss Mitten very specific directions as to treatment, shook a warning finger at the obstreperous one, and promised to call back in the evening.

"He'll not be easy to manage," he said to Miss Mitten, as he went downstairs. "Shall I send you in a nurse?"

"Is it as bad as that?" asked Auntie Mitt, to whom an outside nurse suggested extremity. "If you think it necessary, Doctor, we must have one."

"No need to be alarmed—as yet. But I know him, and he'll be a handful. And then there's the night work, you see."

"If you think it necessary then."

But as he went down the path he met Mrs Dare coming up to enquire how things were. And when he told her, she said at once, "Nurse? We don't need any outside nurse. We'll manage him between us all right. Lois will be a great assistance."

"She's home then? And Ray?"

"They've all gone,—to the front, we suppose;—the first Territorials to go. They consider it a great honour. For myself ... it makes me sick to think of it all."

"Very well, then. The three of you ought to be able to manage him among you. We will leave it so."

"We'll manage him all right. Tell us just what you want done and we'll do it. It will be good for us all and keep our minds off other things."

No man could have had three more devoted and indefatigable nurses. They spared themselves nothing and put up with the safety-valve growlings of their patient like angels.

The Colonel had had so little illness in his life—apart from wounds, which were quite a different matter—and felt so keenly his country's need for him to be up and doing, that he took his shelving with anything but a good grace. Auntie Mitt and Lois alone would never have been able to manage him. But to Mrs Dare he submitted—a little grumpily, at times—but still submitted, and exploded all his objurgations on things in general under cover of the bed-clothes.

He insisted on Lois reading all the latest news to him from the morning and evening papers, and forbade her to say a word in her letters to Ray about his illness. "No good worrying him," he said. "He'll have his hands full out there without having me on his mind."

But presently he developed pneumonia in addition to the pleurisy, and the Doctor put a peremptory embargo on all war news, since it invariably sent his temperature up. Absolute lack of news, however, had just as bad an effect, and finally he was permitted to hear from day to day that things were going well, and all the papers were kept for him to read when he got better.

They made much of the fresh loyal offers of help from India, and of the successful aeroplane raid on the Dusseldorf Zeppelin sheds, carefully withheld any hint of the sinking of the Aboukir, Cressy, and Hogue, and the impudent quarter-of-an-hour's bombardment of Madras by the lively Emden, and soothed him with assurances that France and Britain were splendidly holding their own along the Aisne, that Russia was forging ahead in Galicia, and that recruiting was quite up to expectations. In fact they played motherly censor to him with the already over-heavily censored news, and permitted nothing whatever of an upsetting nature to reach him; and of course they overdid it,—just as the other censor did.

He grew suspicious of all this cotton-woolling, and at last insisted on Lois holding the paper before him each morning so that he might scan the head-lines. Then he indicated what he wanted read and there was no getting out of it.

Dr Rhenius, appealed to, did his best to break him off it, but the result was disastrous. The Colonel's temperature went up a degree and a half through suppressed indignation, and he had to be allowed his news.

"Not a da-asht infant," he murmured. "Can stand it—good or bad. Must know."

But the fever sapped his strength to such an extent that at times he lay so listless and apparently careless even of news that Auntie Mitt grew apprehensive.

"I don't like it," she confined to Mrs Dare. "It's so very unlike him. I would really be thankful to hear him swear a little."

"The fever has weakened him. Once the crisis is past he'll begin to pick up again, and then we'll tell him you want to hear him swear again."

"It's not really that I want to hear him swear, you understand, my dear," Auntie Mitt superfluously explained, "but that I wish he were well enough to do so."

"I know. I would like to hear him too."

To keep the house quiet Victoria was stopping with Honor at The Red House, which was quite to Noel and Gregor's taste.

They were still doing heavy route-marching almost every day, and on the off-days and Friday, which was pay-day, they mouched about Head-Quarters or put in a bit of drill in Hyde Park.

The pay of three shillings a day—to cover travelling expenses and daily rations—was to Gregor a negligible matter. But to Noel, who had never earned a farthing in his life, it was uplifting. He was actually keeping himself—in cigarettes and amusements,—and in conjunction with Gregor even took the girls to a theatre now and again. It was a grand thing not to be dependent on anyone for his pocket-money, and it made him feel excessively manly.

He and Gregor—who, like a good chum, did his best to keep his purse to the level of his friend's—made many quaint discoveries in the matter of restaurants where they got a cut off the joint and two vegetables and bread, and choice of cheese or sweets, for the all-round sum of one shilling.

Marching days, however, were lean days with them, when they were dependent on the none-too-filling sandwiches and biscuits, and apples and ginger-beer, of the travelling canteen. And those nights they took home tremendous appetites and were unjovial till they had been satisfied,—a task which they divided about equally between The Red House and the White.

Mrs MacLean rejoiced whenever they went to her, and would have liked them to come every night, and she was never caught short. The girls did their best. But the boys' movements were as a rule so unforeseeable, and at all times subject to such unexpected alteration on the spur of the moment, that providing for them was no easy matter.

Gregor, at all events, showed no sign of complaint, and doubtless the presence of the girls more than made up for any little defects in the commissariat. Noel expressed himself freely on the subject if occasion offered.

"Wait till we go into camp," grinned Gregor. "You'll learn things, my boy. Bully beef and hard potatoes, and mouldy cheese, and jam that's all the same whatever it calls itself!"

"Rotten! They might at all events feed us properly."

"It's a shame," said Honor. "I should strike, or mutiny, or whatever's the proper thing to do in such a case."

"Proper thing is to grin and bear it and buy some extra grub outside to fill up with. If you kicked you'd be taken out and shot at dawn," said Gregor gravely.

"I don't think soldiering's as nice as I thought it was."

"It's not,—not all of it. But it's got to be done since the Kaiser's said so."

"The wretch! I wish he would die."

"Not yet. He'll suffer a lot more if he lives. At least I hope so."

"He can never suffer as he deserves to," said Vic. "I would have all the pain and misery he has brought about visited on his own head, but that's not humanly possible."

"He'll suffer," said Gregor weightily.

"If we lick him all to pieces, as we shall do," said Noel, "he'll surrender to England and be given a palace to live in and a nice little pension. We're altogether too soft-hearted. When a man's down we're always sorry for him, no matter what he's done, and we sentimentalise over him like a lot of silly schoolgirls."

"That all you know?" said Honor.

"What about those kilts?" asked Vic.

"Next week, please the powers! Things are turning up by degrees. A lot of sporrans and spats came in this afternoon. I saw them myself."

"We'll be getting clothed bit by bit," said Gregor. "You'll see us swanking it in one spat and a sporran maybe. There's no kilts come yet, and as for tunics!—you see there's more khaki wanted than they can turn out, though the mills are working night and day, they say."

"And pretty poor stuff it is, from all accounts," said Noel. "You should hear a song the fellows have about the rotten time they're taking to give us our uniforms. How does it go now? They roar it at top of their voice whenever the Colonel comes along,—

> 'There's a matter here to which we call attention,
> Concerning which we feel a trifle warm,—
> The days are getting cold, and we're slowly growing old,
> And here we are without our uniform.'

"Chorus, Greg!"

159

'Sunday we pray we soon may get 'em;
Monday, our spirits rise a bit;
Tuesday is the day they say they're on the way, but not a bit of it!
Wednesday, we grow a shade mistrustful,
Thursday our hopes begin to fall;
On Friday we're despairing,
On Saturday we're swearing,
We'll never get the—er—ruddy things—at all.'"

"Bravo!" cried the girls. "Encore!"

But just at that point Mr Dare came in, with a tired nod to them all, and Noel's high spirits seemed to lower at once by several degrees.

"How is the Colonel to-night?" Mr Dare asked Vic.

"He's just about the same, Mr Dare. The stabbing pain has gone, they say. But he's very limp. Even good news of the war hardly bucks him up. He seems to want just to lie quiet, and I've never in my life known him do that before. It shows how pulled down he is."

"It's the crisis to-night, I think, and it's going to be a wild night,"—as the wind shook the windows as though trying to force its way in. "A bad night for the trenches and a worse on the sea," and he subsided into the evening paper.

"Lois had another post-card from Ray this morning, father," said Honor.

"That's good. He's all right so far then. Doesn't say where, I suppose?"

"Gives no clue. Not allowed. Simply says he's quite all right and awfully busy."

"Well, we must be thankful for that much. The losses all round are terrible to think of. If it goes on much longer at this rate—" but consideration for the boys cut his Cassandra ruminations short.

"Has the City any views as to how long it'll last, sir?" asked Gregor.

"Any amount of views but no knowledge. Some are sure it'll be all over by Christmas—"

"Rotten! I jolly well hope not," jerked Noel.

"—And some say it will last two years or even three."

"There'll be a lot of wastage if it goes on that long," said Gregor. "And all the countries would be bankrupt, I should say."

"It's too ghastly to think of. We'll hope for better things," and he took to his papers again.

160

CHAPTER XXIV

THE big trees clashed and roared all night in the gale. In the morning a huge limb of one of the Oakdene elms lay on the lawn, and Vic, running across, anxious for news of the Colonel, brought back word that he had had a very restless night but was now sleeping quietly, and that Mrs Dare was sure he was no worse,—which in itself was great gain—and was not sure that he was not even a little better.

And so it proved when the Doctor called. He pronounced the crisis passed and had every hope that his patient was now on the road to recovery. Every care was still needed, however, as one could never tell what might happen in the case of such a trying combination as pneumonia and seventy-eight years of age.

Dr Rhenius himself was looking somewhat fagged and overworked. He said there was a great deal of sickness about, and set it down to some extent to the general depression of spirits caused by the war. Every house he went into had some connection with it, and the sense of anxiety was widespread, —not, he admitted, as to the ultimate issue, on which all minds were made up, but as to the fate of relatives at the front. For the descriptions which came home of the fierceness of the fighting and the effects of the huge German shells, which dug holes in the ground big enough to bury an omnibus in, seemed to leave small hope of escape to any who might be exposed to them.

The stories of the atrocious barbarities practised by the German hordes in Belgium and Northern France depressed them all greatly,—Malines, Termonde, Rheims—there seemed no bounds to the inhumanity of these twentieth-century Huns. They had shed off the thin veneer of their civilisation and reverted to savagery, and the whole world stood aghast. That a nation professedly Christian, and calling on God to assist its nefarious enterprises, could not only descend to such depths but could actually exult in them, was a shock to the moral sense of humanity at large.

161

What chance could there be for any who fell into their vengeful hands? What chance even for those who went out to meet them in fair fight? For trickery and treachery and every mean device were the chosen weapons of their dishonourable warfare. Nothing was sacred if it stood in the way of their winning. They played the game like dirty little gutter-snipes whose intention was to win at all costs, and the fouler the means the more they exulted in the success of them.

There were heavy hearts at home in those days, and 'Missing' came to be regarded as almost more hopeless than 'Dead';—certainly more pregnant of sorrows, for the dead were happily done with it all and could suffer no more.

Con was ever in their thoughts. When his mother read the grim accounts of the dastardly ill-treatment meted specially to British prisoners, she was tempted at times to wish his name had been in the fatal list which left no room for further hopes or fears.

And Ray,—any day might bring similar word concerning him. Now and again a brief post-card reached them saying he was well and busy. But even as they read the precious words and rejoiced in them, each one knew full well that since they were written the end might have come. When bullets are flying and shells are bursting it takes so little to end a life. And those venomous Germans made a point of picking off every officer they could crawl within range of.

And presently Noel and Gregor would go. They were as keen for the front as though they bore charmed lives and death and mutilation were not. There were sure to be drafts before long to make good the inevitable wastage in the First Battalion, and these two, splendidly fit and eager for the fray, were certain to be among the chosen.

Mrs Dare and Lois and Alma knelt long of a night, and carried prayers in their hearts all day; Honor and Vic perhaps also, but the matter had not come so poignantly home to them as yet. Their younger eyes were still somewhat misted with the pomp and glamour of war, but from the others' the scales had fallen and only the horror and misery were apparent to them.

Alma had run over to see how Uncle Tony was getting on, and they were all six of them for once sitting over their tea together, working busily, and talking quietly in the shadow of the war-cloud. Lois had been sitting with Uncle Tony till he fell asleep. He slept much of late and was often listless and drowsy and very unlike himself, when awake, especially in the afternoon.

It was Alma who said, out of the fulness of her heart and of much inevitable brooding over the matter,

"You know, if the women of all the world would only say the word, and say it together, and not only say it but mean it with all their souls and

162

lives, there could be no such thing as war in the world."

Mrs Dare suspended work for a minute and regarded her thoughtfully. Auntie Mitt peered at her over her spectacles in wonder. Lois nodded comprehendingly, with a star in each eye. Honor shook her head doubtfully. Victoria said, "If we had the vote—perhaps."

"The vote will come all right in time," said Alma. "But I was thinking larger than that. In all wars the women are the greatest and final sufferers. If they could join hands all over the world and say 'There shall be no more war!'—well ... there would be no more war."

"I don't see why," said Honor. "The men would make war all the same if they wanted to—as they would."

"Not if the women meant what they said, and were prepared to stand by it and all its consequences. Ey!" she said, throwing up her arms in a supplicatory gesture, "I wish I could rouse them to it! It could be done. I'm sure it could be done. And just think what it would mean!"

"It would mean new life and new hope,—a new Heaven and a new Earth," said Mrs Dare impressively. "It would be a Second Advent.... My dear, it is a wonderful idea.... If only it were possible!"

"It is quite possible," said Alma, with a quiet confidence which impressed even Vic, who gazed at her in wondering amazement, "The idea came to me in the night, as I lay thinking of Con and Ray and the boys, and all the other men-folk of all the other women in the world. And I saw how it all might be done if it only could be done."

"How then?" asked Vic, impatiently, as Alma fell silent and sat gazing thoughtfully into the fire.

"Why,—in this way.—All men—except the few in every country who hope to benefit by war—want peace. Peace and happiness are the natural and healthy states of life. War is unnatural and unhealthy. It is a lapse. Women crave peace still more, for they are the greatest sufferers by war. Let them unite all over the world—"

"Women don't unite," snapped Vic.

"Even for such a trifling thing as the Vote they have shown that they can unite. But when this war is over—it has got to be fought out, I quite see that.—But it will leave the heart of womanhood all over the world so sore and bruised that, unless I am mistaken in my sex, the women will be ready to do greater things than we have ever dreamed of to prevent a recurrence of such doings.... I can imagine a World-Wide Women's League for Peace; —membership, every right-thinking woman in the whole world—"

"Phew!" whistled Vic. "How'd you get 'em?"

"Easily, I think. That is a detail. I'll deal with it presently. Such an organisation, pledged to prevent war, would be all-powerful. And, if it could do this greatest thing of all, it would naturally have its say in all the minor matters which, through men's mishandling and easily-roused passions, so often lead to war."

"You're a suffragette, Alma," said Vic.

"I detest them and all their ways, as you very well know. But the greater necessarily includes the less. Let women ensure peace, and they will be accorded their rightful voice in all the smaller matters. Be sure of that."

"And how would they go to work to ensure peace?" asked Mrs Dare.

"Perhaps my vague ideas will seem rather crazy to you. But they are something like this. Imagine the women of the world pledged to keep the peace at risk even of their lives. Two nations verge on war. To the women that means loss in every way—chiefly in the lives that are dearer to them than their own. Very well,—then let them stop it by risking their own lives. It is the smaller risk after all. After exhausting every other means of averting the war, let the women of each such nation rise in their millions and if necessary take their stand between the contending armies and defy their men to fight."

"Through my heart first!" said Vic.

"Exactly. The Germans, they say, fire on Belgian women and children. Do you think they would mow down their own? Not for all the Kaisers ever heard of. War would stop. But I do not think it would ever come to that final test. Certainly it would never come to it more than once. A thousand women shot down by their own men would create such a revulsion of feeling that wars would end. Telemachus ended the fights in the arena by giving just his single life. Here would be a thousand Telemachuses,—a million if need be!!! If their determination was known, and that it would be persisted in to the very uttermost,—to death itself,—the men would understand that war was impossible, and they would find some other way out. But, mind you, if women had their proper share in the councils of the state their voice would always, on both sides, be for reason and righteousness. It only needs reason and righteousness on both sides to arrive at the proper solution of any dispute."

"I wish with all my heart you could bring it about, my dear. It is a grand idea," said Mrs Dare. "But—"

"How were you thinking of roping all the women of the world in, Al? It's a mighty big contract," asked Vic.

"At first it seemed to me that if you could show the militant women how much more likely they were to attain their ends by my ideas than by theirs—they could do it. But I am not sure. They have turned the world against them by their follies. Nobody would trust them. And then, suddenly, I thought of the Salvation Army. I see a good deal of them, you know, round our way. And those gentle-voiced women, with the quiet happy faces and shining eyes—it is just the very work for them. They are in and of every country in the world, and everywhere they are held in esteem. They certainly could do it. Those Salvation Army women could save the world from War."

"Alma," said Mrs Dare, with shining eyes and deep conviction. "You lay awake to some purpose, my dear. It is a noble idea. I wish it could be brought about."

"It could. But whether it can—"

"The Krupps, and all the other war-mongers in every country, would fight you like Death," said Vic.

"Of course. That is their only raison d'être. But the women could beat the war-mongers."

"And all the Kings, Kaisers, Tzars, Emperors, and such like would be dead against you."

"Yes. It would be better for my schemes if they were all done away with. Republics don't as a rule go to war as readily as Kingdoms and Empires."

"South America," suggested Honor.

"They are exceptions because they are not yet educated up to self-government. But where a King is the best man for the post I should let him remain—as president."

"There was one of our stalwarts at the Pension Estèphe," said Lois. "Who used to argue such matters with Ray. And I remember him saying one day,—'You in England are very well-placed. You have practically a Republic with a permanent head.' It struck us both as very sensible."

Then the Colonel's bell, the push of which lay to his hand on the bed, announced peremptorily that he was awake, and Lois ran upstairs to him while Auntie Mitt hastened to prepare his glass of warm milk and cognac, which at the moment did duty with him for afternoon tea.

"He is a very sick man," said Alma, when Auntie Mitt had left the room. "Pneumonia is a serious matter at any age, but at seventy-eight it is almost hopeless. The great thing is to keep him quiet and—"

"And that is no easy job," said Mrs Dare, with a reminiscent smile. "We tried to keep the papers from him by telling him the news and suppressing anything we thought might upset him. But he was too sharp for us and insisted on seeing for himself, and now he sees the paper every day and makes Lois read the bits he wants."

"I can imagine the state he would be in. His heart is wrapped up in England's fortunes. I wish it could all end and give us back our boys."

"Ay, indeed!" said Mrs Dare.

"It can't end till Germany's beaten flat," said Vic, with emphasis. "It's no good half-ending it and simply laying up trouble for the future."

"Of course," nodded Alma. "We are all agreed as to that. Now I must run and look after my sick men."

CHAPTER XXV

JOHN DARE was sitting all alone by the fire one evening in the parlour of The Red House. The boys were at Mrs MacLean's that night, and Honor and Vic were assisting in an entertainment to the Belgian Refugees at a neighbouring hostel.

Desirous as they all were of being of service to the exiles, circumstances had not permitted of their taking any of them into their homes. And so they all subscribed towards one of the many hostels and assisted in such other ways as their many engagements allowed time for.

And Mr Dare took no exception to it all. It was an unavoidable part of the general upsetting, and to tell the truth he was so depressed and uncompanionable these days, that he felt himself better company for himself than for any of the younger folk.

Honor had got for him from the library the two big volumes of Scott's Last Journey to the Pole, and with these and a pipe he was doing his best to forget for a time business troubles and German delinquencies.

With a tap at the door, the maid announced, "A gentleman to see you, sir."

"Who is it, Bertha?" he asked, with a touch of annoyance at the disturbance of his peace.

"I don't know, sir. He said you would not know his name, but it's important."

"Oh well, show him in here," and he closed his book and stood up to meet the intruder.

"You won't know me, Mr Dare," said the newcomer, when the door closed on Bertha. "I am Inspector Gretton from Scotland Yard. I've come to consult you on a certain matter and I want all the information you can give me."

"At your service, Inspector. Won't you sit down? Have a cigar,"—and he got out a box from the cupboard under the bookcase. "Now what's it all about?"

"It's this, Mr Dare. For some time past the wireless stations at New-stead and Crowston have complained of jamming. In other words, unauthorised messages are passing, and by a process of elimination and deduction we are satisfied they emanate from somewhere in this neighbourhood. As an old resident and a Justice of the Peace—"

"A very nominal J.P. of late, I'm afraid,—thanks to the war."

The Inspector nodded. "We felt sure, however, that any assistance in your power you would render us."

"Assuredly. Anything I can do. But I don't at the moment see what."

"From the nature of the messages that have been intercepted,—they are in code of course, but our people have managed to get an inkling of their meaning,—it is evident that someone is sending out information of moment to some enemy station, probably nearer the coast. And we've got to get to the bottom of it. Very powerful instruments are being used and probably from a considerable elevation. Now is there anyone in this neighbourhood, within your knowledge, likely to be up to anything of the kind?"

"I should not have thought so.... In fact it is hard to believe it of any of one's neighbours...."

"Unfortunately, our experience is that the folks who are in this kind of business are just the ones one would least expect. What enemy aliens have you round here?"

"Quite a lot,—or we had. And mostly quite nice people. But a number have left since the war began,—either they thought it safer to get back home, or you are taking care of them elsewhere."

"We've got quite a lot on our hands, but evidently not all. Would you tell me, sir, who there are left about here?"

"Well,—let me see. There are the Jacobsens,—they claim to be Danish, I believe. He's a produce-importer in quite a big way."

"What age of a man, and what family?"

"He'll be somewhere about fifty, I should say. Family,—wife, two daughters and a boy of seventeen."

"Where does he live?"

And so they progressed through such a list as Mr Dare could make out on the spur of the moment. The Inspector making an occasional note and asking many pointed questions.

And when Mr Dare's spring of information had apparently dried up, he asked suddenly,

"Whose is the tall old-fashioned red-brick house up there on top of the hill,—the one with the double-peaked roof and the tall old-fashioned chimney-stacks?"

"That? Oh that's Dr Rhenius's. But he's quite above suspicion. He's lived here for over twenty years."

"What is he? German?"

"It's the one thing he resents—to be called a German," said Mr Dare, with a smile. "His father was a Pole from somewhere near Warsaw. He himself has been naturalised for twenty years at least—"

"Do you know that?"

"Well,"—with a surprised lift of the brows—"if you put it as a legal point,—no! I don't know that anyone has ever questioned it. You see, he is our medico round here, and is greatly esteemed and liked. He's an uncommonly clever doctor and everybody's very good friend."

"I see. Quite above suspicion, you would say, Mr. Dare?"

"Oh quite. He hates Prussian Junkerdom as every Pole must."

The Inspector nodded acquiescingly, and they chatted on about the war and things in general till his cigar was finished and he got up to go.

"I will ask you to keep all this absolutely to yourself, Mr Dare," he said. "Not a word to anyone, if you please, sir."

"Certainly, Inspector. I'm afraid I've not been of much use to you. If you think of anything else—"

"I'll let you know, sir," and Mr Dare saw him out of the front door, and returned to Scott and the South Pole.

As for Inspector Gretton, he wandered off to have a closer look at the old-fashioned red-brick house on top of the hill.

Just a week later he called again on Mr Dare, late one night, and, as before, found him all alone.

The Colonel had suddenly, when apparently getting on well, developed pneumonia in the other lung and was in a very critical condition. Mrs Dare spent all her time at Oakdene in unremitting attendance on him, with every help that Lois and Auntie Mitt and Honor and Vic could render. The boys were sleeping in town that night as they had to be on early fatigue next morning.

"Well, Inspector? Any success?" asked Mr Dare, as Gretton was shown in.

"I've come to end the matter, Mr Dare. I thought perhaps you'd like to see the last act."

"Really? Got him. Who on earth is it?"

"If you care to come with me I'll show you, sir," and Mr Dare got into his hat and coat in record time and went out with him.

At the gate they were met and followed by half-a-dozen stalwarts in flat caps and overcoats, who in some subtle fashion conveyed the impression of law and order, armed not only with right but with other weapons of a more practically coercive nature.

The roads were almost in darkness in accordance with recent orders, lest undue illumination should offer mark or direction for lurking menace up above. They turned into the road up the hill and came to the gate of Dr Rhenius's old-fashioned red-brick house.

"You don't mean to say—" jerked Mr Dare in vast amazement.

"Sh-h-h!" whispered the Inspector, pressing his arm. "See that tree!"— a huge elm towering a hundred feet high just inside the gate. "I've been up there every night since I called on you, with a pair of the strongest glasses made—Zeisses," he said with a chuckle. "Your friend has visitors of a night and later on he gets busy."

Mr Dare was dumb. He could not take it all in. There was some grotesque mistake somewhere.

"We're a bit early yet," said the Inspector. Then, adjusting his field-glasses and peering up at the house, "No, it's all right. He's at work in good time to-night."

He handed the glasses to Mr. Dare, and whispered, "Look at that chimney-stack. Get it against the Milky Way. See anything?"

"I see the chimney.... Yes, and something like a flag-pole projecting above it...."

"Exactly,—a wireless pole. We'll catch them at it."

He said a word to his men. They had had their instructions. They all went noiselessly up to the house, some to the back and sides, the Inspector, Mr Dare and two others to the front door.

"Keep out of sight till I go in," said the Inspector, as he rang, and in the distance inside they heard the thrill of the bell. But no one came. He rang again.

"Good thing no one's dying in a hurry," he growled.

It was not till after the third appeal that they heard steps inside and all braced up for the event. As the door opened Inspector Gretton quietly inserted his foot.

"Is the Doctor in?" he asked.

"He is oudt," said a voice, which Mr Dare recognised as Old Jacob's, the Doctor's factotum.

"Then I'll come in and wait for him. I want him at once," and the Inspector pushed his way in.

As he did so Old Jacob dropped his hand against a spot in the wall, and far away upstairs a tiny bell tinkled briefly.

"Quite so!" said Gretton, and as his men followed him in, with Mr Dare behind them in no small discomfort of mind,—"Secure the old boy, Swift," and to his still greater discomfort Mr Dare heard the click of handcuffs.

"Now quick,—upstairs!" and they followed him at speed.

He seemed to go by instinct. Up two flights and they came on a door which evidently led to a higher storey still. A curious door—of stout oak, without a handle, and for keyhole only the polished disc and tiny slit of a Yale lock.

The Inspector wasted not a moment. He was up to every trick of his profession.

"Barnes," he said quietly, and indicated the lock, and in a trice Barnes inserted a thin stick of something into the slit, and as the Inspector waved them all back there came an explosion and the stout oak about the lock was riven into splinters. Gretton swung open the door and ran up the narrow stairs.

In the top passage they came on a short ladder leading to a skylight through which the night air blew chilly. The others climbed quickly up. Mr Dare stayed below. He regretted having come. He did not quite know why he had come. He had not of course known where he was going when he accepted Inspector Gretton's invitation. Then the matter had developed too rapidly to permit of him backing out.

Exclamations came down to him through the skylight—the sound of a brief struggle, and presently Gretton came down again obviously well-pleased with himself.

"Got him,—red-handed!" he said.

"Not Dr Rhenius?"

"If that's his proper name. The man you've known by that name anyway. And all his tackle. Two minutes more and his poles would have been out of sight. He lowers them down the chimneys."

He kicked open a door in the passage, but the room inside was empty and unfurnished. Two other rooms yielded the same result.

Then the Inspector, searching about, discovered a trap-door, such as might lead to cisterns, high up in one corner of the passage, and shifting the ladder, he ran up, pushed the trap open, and said, "Right—o!"

"Come up and see for yourself, Mr Dare," he said, as he crawled out of sight; and Mr Dare followed him.

It was a long tent-shaped apartment formed by the pitch of the roof, well-lit by electric lights and littered with electric apparatus—a number of powerful accumulators, spark coils, condensers, inductances, a heavily built morse key, and so on,—everything necessary for sending long-distance wireless messages.

Mr Dare gazed about him in amazement.

"There is no doubt about it then?" he jerked uncomfortably.

"Not a doubt. How many lives all this may have cost us, God only knows. However, he's scotched now, and it's one to me."

"Rhenius!" jerked Mr Dare again. "I can hardly credit it even yet. Such a good fellow he always seemed, and we all liked him so! It's amazing—and damnable."

"Damnable it is, sir. And there's too damned much of it going on. We're infants in these matters and altogether too soft and lenient. However, this one won't send out any more news."

"What is the penalty?"

"If it's as bad as I believe, he'll be shot. We shall know better when all these papers and things have been gone into. He's been a centre for spy-news, unless I'm very much mistaken, but this ought to end him, as far as this world's concerned anyway."

They went down the ladder again and Gretton replaced it below the skylight and hailed his men, "Bring him along there."

And presently, preceded by one stalwart and followed by the other the prisoner was brought down.

The actual sight of this man who had been on such friendly terms with him, had been admitted to every house in the neighbourhood on the most intimate footing, had doctored them all in the most skilful way possible, who was even then in attendance on their good friend the Colonel,—and who all the time was playing the spy for Germany, gave John Dare a most gruesome shock. He felt absolutely sick at heart.

"Rhenius!" he gasped. "Is it possible?"

But Dr Rhenius looked at him without a sign of recognition and spoke no word.

He was hurried away down the stairs. Inspector Gretton left two of his men in charge of the house, and with the rest and his prisoners went off in a taxi which he called up by the Doctor's telephone.

Mr Dare went back home feeling bruised and sore. Duplicity and treachery such as this cut at the roots of one's faith in humanity. If he had been told this thing he would not have believed it. Nothing less than what he had seen with his own eyes and heard with his own ears would have convinced him. But he was convinced and saddened.

He went across to Oakdene first thing in the morning. His wife had to be told. The Colonel's welfare had to be seen to—another medical attendant provided,—explanations concocted.

"What is it, John?" asked Mrs Dare, as soon as she set eyes on his face. "Bad news?"

"Yes, Meg,—bad news. But not touching any of ours,"—at which the anxious strain in her face relaxed somewhat.

"Dr Rhenius is in prison as a spy—"

"John!"—and she sank aghast into the nearest chair.

"It is true, Meg. I was there. His house is just one big wireless station. They caught him in the act. It is horrible to think of such treachery. I've hardly slept a wink all night."

"No wonder! But—is it possible? Is there no mistake?... Dr Rhenius?... I would have trusted him with my life."

"Yes. It is beyond me. But there is no possible doubt about it. They have taken him and Old Jacob away, and the police are in charge of the house. They say he will be shot."

"How terrible! Not the shooting. If he has done this he deserves to be shot. But ... our Dr Rhenius! Oh, I cannot take it in yet."

But in time she had to accept it, and they fell to discussion of ways and means.

The Colonel was to be told that Rhenius had been suddenly summoned from home,—which was grimly true, and Mr Dare was to call at once on Dr Sinclair in the village, give him the same explanation, and beg his attendance on their patient.

As he expected, Dr Sinclair received him with a certain amount of professional surprise at the irregularity of his procedure. He hummed and hawed for a time, and put such very pointed questions that Mr Dare was inclined to believe that he must have had suspicions of his own—provoked possibly, he thought, by professional jealousy and Rhenius's German-sounding name; all of which was natural enough.

All he permitted himself was that Dr Rhenius had been suddenly called away, and his return was so very doubtful that they felt it necessary to call in another doctor at once. And Dr Sinclair went. The Colonel was much put out and not easily reconciled to this transfer in which he had had no voice. It was so unlike Rhenius to go off like that without so much as a good-bye. He fumed weakly and fretted over it, and was barely civil to Dr Sinclair, who shook his head doubtfully when he went downstairs with Mrs Dare.

"He is very weak," he said. "Keep on as you are and above all things keep him quiet and free from disturbance of mind."

"It is not easy."

"I see that. But it is absolutely essential. The fever has pulled him down terribly and his heart is in a very ticklish state."

The following day the papers had the matter with bold head-lines —"WELL-KNOWN WILLSTEAD DOCTOR ARRESTED AS SPY, HOUSE FULL OF WIRELESS APPARATUS," and so on.

They did their best to keep the paper from the Colonel. But the very attempt aroused his suspicions and sent his temperature up again.

In despair he was allowed to glance at it—and the mischief was done. He insisted on Lois reading every word, and all the time he lay looking at her with a dazed look on his white face.

"Rhenius!" was all he said, in a strange shocked whisper, when she had finished, and then he lay back among his pillows and turned his face as far away from them as he could.

And—"Rhenius!"—they heard him murmur more than once during the day, as though he were groping painfully among his shadows after some understanding of it all.

About tea-time, when Lois was sitting with him,—just sitting quietly by his bed-side so that he should not feel lonely, for he had declined to be read to, he turned quietly to her and feebly extended his hand.

She took it in her two warm ones throbbing with life and sudden fear. It felt very thin and cold, and, with a great dread at her heart, it seemed to her that his face was changed. It was gray, and very weary.

"I am so glad, dear,—so very glad," he whispered,—"about you and Ray.... Good lad! ... he will come back to you ... and Con—good lad too!... God bless you all!—all!"

Lois had slipped on to her knees beside the bed, and the tears were running down her face in spite of herself.

"No!" he said. "Don't cry!... Very tired.... I shall be glad ... to rest."

Then he suddenly raised himself in the bed, and looked beyond her.

"Last Post!" he said, quite clearly. "Thank God, I have done my duty!" and then he sank back. And Lois released one hand, from the thin cold hand which had no longer any response in it, and beat upon the floor with it to call the others.

CHAPTER XXVI

ALMOST inevitable as it had more than once seemed, in the crises of his illness, the Colonel's death was a great shock to them all.

At the sound of Lois's hasty tattoo on the floor, the others had hastened up to her. They found her still clasping the one thin cold hand with one of hers and still beating the floor with the other.

They thought at first that it might be a fainting fit—which in itself, in the circumstances, would have been ominous enough. But briefest examination showed them that their old friend had answered The Call and was gone.

They were down again in the small sitting-room, discussing it quietly and sadly, when Auntie Mitt, after staring fixedly at Lois for a full minute, as though she had suddenly detected something strange in her appearance, said suddenly,

"My dear, you are Lady Luard now."

And Lois stared back at them both with a startled look, and gasped, "I never thought of that. Oh, I wish Ray were here!"

They all wished that, but no amount of wishing will bring men home from the war.

"We must send Alma word at once," said Mrs Dare. "I will write out a telegram."

"It will be a shock to her," said Auntie Mitt. "Perhaps, my dear, a letter—"

"Alma was prepared for the worst," said Mrs Dare. "Last time she was here she told me it would be a miracle if he got through such an illness at his age. She would like to know at once, I am sure," and she sat down at the writing table to prepare the telegram.

And while they were still in the midst of these agitations, and Lois was wondering how she would ever be able to reconcile herself to the inevitable changes, she happened to glance vaguely through the window and saw Alma coming quickly up the front path.

"Here she is," she cried, and jumped up and ran to meet her.

At sight of Lois at the door, Alma exultingly waved a paper she carried in her hand and quickened her pace almost to a run.

"Good news!" she cried. "Word of Con at last."

"Oh, Al, I *am* so glad," and she burst into tears.

"Why, Lo, dear, what's up? It's good news—"

"Uncle Tony has just died. Mother was just writing a telegram to send to you."

"I am not surprised, dear," said Alma, putting her arm round her. "I had very little hope of his pulling through. He was an old man, you see. I am sure he was not very sorry to go; though he would have liked to see the end of this war, I know. And I do wish he had heard about Con. He would have been so glad. However, he knows more about it all now than any of us, and that will please him mightily," and they went in together.

So the good news and the bad—nay, why call the news of a good man's promotion bad news?—let us say, the other news tended to counteract one another in the hearts of those who were left. Indeed the net result that remained with them all was a sense of thankfulness,—for the peaceful passing of the fine full life, and for the young life spared for further work.

Alma's letter was not from Con himself, which at first sight was disturbing. But the contents explained. Lieutenant Dare had been wounded— in the hand, the writer said,—at Landrecies during the retreat from Mons. He was now a prisoner in Germany—at Torgau, and was being well looked after. He was making good recovery from his wounds which had been severe, and they were all hoping that something might presently be arranged in the way of an exchange of medical-staff prisoners. The writer signed himself Robert Grant, R.A.M.C.

"I can't tell you what a relief it is," said Alma. "I almost danced when I got it. It's worry that kills, and I was beginning to worry about the boy. What about Ray?"

"It's ten days since my last letter," said Lois. "I'm hoping for the next every minute.... Do you know, Al, just at the very last, when Uncle Tony knew the end had come, he said, 'Good lad, Ray! He will come back to you. And Con—good lad too! God bless you all!—all!'—that was almost the last thing he said."

"The dear old man!... We will take it as a good omen.... I think, you know, that just at the last they often have an outlook—a forelook—altogether beyond our understanding. They see with other eyes than ours."

"Undoubtedly!" agreed Mrs. Dare.

Alma's stay, even under the circumstances, could not be a long one. They had had forty-nine wounded officers in, two days before, many of their nurses had gone to the front, and they were very short-handed.

Lois walked down to the station with her, and they talked in quiet sisterly fashion of the past, present, and future.

"It is very curious how things seem to work together at times," said Lois.

"Always, maybe, if we knew more about it all, dear."

"Yes, I suppose so. Here have I been so taken up with nursing Uncle Tony that I really have never had time to get anxious about Ray."

"Ray will be all right, you'll see. I pin my faith to Uncle Tony's vision."

"And yet, when one allows oneself to think about it all, after reading the terrible accounts of the fighting—and he would have me read them all to him—it seems almost impossible that any of them can come back alive."

"We had forty-nine of them the other day, and it's amazing how well they stand it. They're as cheerful as can be, laughing and chaffing and joking. And yet some of them are pretty bad. It's just as well for all of us to take the cheerful view of things."

"And then, just when Uncle Tony goes, and we were feeling it so badly, you come in with your good news of Con. I can't tell you how glad I am, Al."

"I know, dear. And I'll be just as glad for you one of these days. Pin your faith to Uncle Tony."

And through the many dark days when no news came—and in those days no news did not as a rule mean good news—the thought of Uncle Tony's last words held mighty comfort for them all.

They would have liked to bury him quietly, with no great outward show of the esteem and love in which they held him. Their feelings were too deep for any outward expression and the times hardly seemed suitable for making parade of death. There was sorrow enough abroad without emphasising it.

But Colonel Sir Anthony Luard, V.C., C.B., was a person of consequence. He had died for his country as truly as any man killed at the front. The higher powers decreed him a military funeral, and the quieter-thinking ones at home had to give way. And, after all, they believed it would please him.

So, on a gun-carriage, escorted by a detachment from the reserve battalion of his old regiment, with muffled drums and mournful music, and the Last Post and the crackle of guns, he was laid to rest. And the others picked up the threads of life again and kept his memory sweet by constantly missing him and remembering all his sayings and doings.

His lawyer, Mr. Benfleet of Lincoln's Inn, came out immediately after the funeral and explained to all concerned—so far as they were available—the remarkably thoughtful provisions of his will.

It had been made—or remade—immediately after the return of Ray and Lois from abroad, and it aimed at the comfort and security of all his little circle, so far as he could provide for these.

There were many wet eyes and brimming hearts as Mr. Benfleet went quietly through the details.

To Miss Amelia Mitten—"my very dear and trusted friend"—he left four hundred pounds a year for life. And Auntie Mitt, with her little black-bordered handkerchief to her eyes, sobbed gratefully.

To Margaret Dare—wife of John Dare of The Red House, Willstead, —"in token of my very great love and esteem,"—he left the sum of £20,000, settled inalienably on herself, with power to will it at her death to whom she chose.

"To my niece, Victoria Luard—who-might-have-been-Balaclava,"—it was down there in the will in black and white, and they came near to smiling at the very characteristic touch,—the sum of £50,000 on attaining the age of twenty-one.

To Dr Connal Dare—if still alive—the sum of £25,000; and to his wife Alma, formerly Alma Luard, an equal sum. In case of Dr Connal Dare's death the whole £50,000 came at once to Alma.

To Lois Luard, formerly Lois Dare, the sum of £25,000 in her own right.

To Raglan Luard, the residue,—which, said Mr. Benfleet, would amount to probably £100,000 or more when the securities, in which it was all invested, appreciated again after the war.

There were many little minor legacies and gifts to old servants and so on. And Uncle Tony, if he was present in the spirit at the reading of his will, must have been well pleased with the effect of his generous forethought.

CHAPTER XXVII

MRS DARE, wise woman and excellent housekeeper, had for some time past been doing her best to cut down her proverbial coat to suit the exigencies of the shrunken war-time cloth at her disposal.

In other words, she had been curtailing the running expenses of The Red House so as to bear as lightly as possible on the attenuated income from St Mary Axe. Income, indeed, in actual fact, St Mary Axe had none. Mr Dare was, of necessity, living on such remnants of capital as he had been able to save from the stranded ship.

So Mrs Dare found another place for her housemaid, prevailed on her cook, who was a treasure and had been with her over five years, to remain as 'general,' with promise of loss of title and reinstatement of position as soon as times mended, and with Honor's assistance and an occasional helping hand from Mrs Skirrow, managed to get along very well.

Mrs Skirrow had always been a source of amusement at The Red House. She had a point of view of her own and a sense of humour, and an almost unfailing cheerfulness amid circumstances which drove many of her neighbours to drink.

Mrs. Skirrow did not drink. She had too much hard-earned common-sense, and she could not afford it. With three men more or less on her hands, and mostly more, it took every half-crown she could earn at her charing to keep the home together.

But the war had marvellously altered all that. Not only had she no men to keep but the boot was on the other leg. Her men were actually helping to keep her. She woke up of a night now and then and lay blissfully wondering if it was all a dream, or if she had died and gone to heaven. To be kept by her lazy ones! It seemed altogether too good to be true. And yet every Friday, when she drew her money, proved that true it was. No wonder she hoped with all her heart that it might go on for long enough,—so long, of course, as none of them went and got themselves killed. But men were as a rule so contrary that she lived in daily expectation of one or other doing that same.

For the first two months,—due possibly to some default on her part in filling up and sending in the necessary but bewildering papers,—or it might be to the general muddle at Head-Quarters—she received no money at all. So she kept steadily on with her own work, and having only herself to keep, got along very nicely, meanwhile never ceasing to push her claims with all her powers, and few were better equipped in that way. And Mrs Dare was kept fully informed of everything with racy comments on all and sundry.

Then at last, to Mrs. Skirrow's great satisfaction, the matter was arranged, and by some extraordinary method of calculation, promoted without doubt by herself and argued with characteristic vehemence and possibly just a trifle of exaggeration here and there, her money began to come in.

She received nearly ten pounds of arrears in a lump sum, and was to get twenty-three shillings a week.

She had never had ten pounds all at once in her life before, nor an assured income of over a pound a week without needing to lift her hand. And, strange to say—yet not so very strange, seeing that she was Mrs Skirrow,—she did not lose her head and go on the ramp as some she knew had done.

In the first place she bought herself a new dress and coat and hat, such as she had vainly imagined herself in, any time this ten years, and fancied herself exceedingly in them.

The choosing and buying of that dress and coat and hat, the going from shop to shop and from window to window, comparing styles and prices, with the delicious knowledge that the money was in her pocket and she was in a position to pick and choose to her heart's content, was in itself one of the greatest treats she had ever known, and she spread it over quite a considerable period.

And when she turned up one night in her new rig-out, to explain to Mrs Dare that she would not be able to come to her next week as she was going to the seaside, Mrs Dare did not at first recognise her.

When she did she complimented her on her taste and good sense in taking a holiday and hoped she would come back all the better for it.

"I will that. You bet your life, mum! Fust reel holiday I've had for twenty years an' I'm going to enjoy it. Seaside and decently dressed—that's my idee of a reel holiday. It's not some folk's though. There's me neighbour, Mrs Clemmens, now. She had no money for a while, same as meself. Then she got twenty pound all in one lump. She's got a heap o' boys at the war. And what did she do with it? She gathered all her old cronies—an' a fine hot lot some of 'em are, I can tell you, mum!—and she took 'em all up to London, and fed 'em, and drank 'em, and music-halled 'em, till they was all blind and th' hull lot of 'em was run in at last, and in the mornin' she hadn't enough left to pay the fines. A fair scandal, I calls it!"

"Disgraceful!" assented Mrs Dare. "I'm rejoiced to know that your common-sense condemns that kind of thing, and I hope you'll have a real good time and come back all the better for it."

"I will, mum. You bet your boots on that!"

And she did. She journeyed down to Margate in a 'Ladies Only' third-class carriage, and bore herself with such dignity that her fellow-travellers were divided as to whether she kept a stylish public somewhere in the West End or a Superior Servants' Registry Office. She picked out a cheap but adequate lodging, she revelled in all the joys of Margate, ate many winkles, and went to 'the pictures' at least once each day, and the whole grand excursion, fares included, totalled up to no more than thirty shillings,—"an' the best investment ever I made in me life," she told Mrs Dare over her scrubbing brush, the following week, "an' I'm thinkin' I'll run down for th' week end now and again, if so be's this blessed war keeps on a bit."

Mrs Dare found it really refreshing, amid the abounding troubles of the times, to come across someone who had not only no fault to find with them, but was actually, by reason of them, enjoying quite unexpected prosperity.

For her own heart had been heavy enough in those days, what with the Colonel's illness and her husband's very natural depression as to the future outlook.

He had come in one night, some time before, in a state of most justifiable exasperation. And yet the whole thing was so amazingly impudent that in telling his wife of it he could scarce forbear a grim smile. At the same time it was an eye-opener as to the truculent immorality of the firms he had been dealing with for years past in the most perfect good faith, and he vowed he would never forget it.

Two of his best customers, one at Hamburg and the other at Frankfort, owing him between them close on £5000 had coolly sent him word that, as no money could be sent out of the country, they had invested the amounts due to him in the German War Loan and would hold the scrip, and the interest as it accrued, in his name. Both principal and interest would be paid in due course, that is to say—when victory crowned the German arms.

It took Mrs Dare some time to realise that it was not merely a distorted German form of practical joke. But her husband assured her that it was not.

"I had heard of it being done," he said bitterly. "But I never expected either Stein or Rheinberg would play so low a game on me. I've turned over hundreds of thousands of pounds with both of them, and now—this! It's damnable!"

"Perhaps the Government forced them to it."

"It's dirty low business anyway, and it won't make for German credit when things settle down again."

But presently there came to him a bit of good fortune which made him feel almost himself again.

Business men who travel daily to and from town by train fall almost inevitably into sets, who occupy always the same compartment and the same seats in it, and among whom exists a certain good-fellowship and friendliness.

In John Dare's set was a certain John Christianssen, of Norwegian extraction, long established in London in the timber business, which his father had founded sixty years before.

Christianssen was British born, his father having been naturalised. He had two sons with him in the business, and both had got commissions through the Officers' Training Corps, and were heart and soul in their work and eager for the front.

More than once he had lamented to Mr Dare his loss in them just at this juncture. Not that he grudged them to the service of his adopted country but that their going made him feel, as he said, as if he had lost his right hand and one of his feet.

Mr Dare sympathised with him but assured him it was better to have a healthy body even with only one hand and one foot than to have no body left. And Christianssen, knowing the nature of the business in St Mary Axe, understood, and thought the matter out.

And so it came to pass, one morning when they got out at Cannon Street, that he said to Mr Dare, "I will walk your way, if you don't mind. I want to talk to you."

And when they reached the office, where one small office-boy now represented the busy staff of old, he sat down in the second chair and lit a cigar, and said, "I know pretty well, from what I have heard and from what you have told me, Dare, how you are situated here. I have a proposal. I can't go on without help. I want to be across in Norway and I want to be here at the same time. Now that Jack and Eric are away my hands are tied. There is huge business to be done with all this hutting going on, and I'm going to miss my share unless I make proper provision. And that is you! What do you say?"

"It's killing to be out of work, which I never have been before for over thirty years. My business is gone, as you know, and most of my capital. Some of it's invested in the German War Loan—"

"No!"

"Yes! The low-scaled rascals, instead of remitting what they owe me, write to say they have loaned my money to their infernal government and it will be repaid with interest when the war is over—meaning, of course, over in the way they would like it."

"That is low business!"

"Business! I call it simple dirty robbery. But it's not only the fact that they've done this, but—well, I just feel that I would be glad never to have any dealings with any German again as long as I live."

"I do not wonder. But that is all the better for me. We have known one another now, what is it—ten, fifteen years? Come in with me. We can arrange satisfactory terms. You see, my lads may come back, or they may not. My wonder, when I read the papers, is that any man of them all ever comes out of it alive. But even if they are not killed I am doubting much if they will find office-stools agreeable sitting for the rest of their lives. If they do come back it will be the overseas part they will want. So there it is. What do you say?"

"I can't tell you what I feel, Christianssen. The very thought of it makes a new man of me. But—I don't know the first thing about timber."

"If you will relieve me of the office work and financing, it will be good business all round. Details as to woods, etc., you can pick up by degrees. I have a good staff here, but the best staff in the world is the better for being looked after. If I can be free to get across to Norway and feel quite safe in going, it will mean much to me and to the business. You will say yes?"

"I'll say yes with more in my heart than I can put into words," and they shook hands on it.

So John Dare took up a new lease of life and hope, and was himself again and twenty years younger than he had been any time this last three months.

And presently, for his still greater comfort and relief of mind, came Uncle Tony's unexpected legacy to Mrs Dare. It was a veritable Godsend. For the heaviest part of his burden, during these late months of no income and vanishing capital, had been the fear of what might befall his home-folks when the worst came to the worst.

The thought of it had kept him awake of a night and plunged him into the depths. He had racked his tired brain to find some way out of his difficulties. But it was like trying to climb a huge black wall whose top shut out even the sight of heaven. For always the grim fact remained that his business was utterly gone and he saw no prospect of its revival.

By the grace of God and Uncle Tony and John Christianssen he was delivered from torment. The home-folk were safe whatever happened, and he took up his new duties with all the enthusiastic energy of a heart retrieved from despair.

CHAPTER 28

U PON none of them did the burden of these weighty times lie so heavily as on Lois Luard and Alma Dare.

They both received occasional letters indeed, but Ray's, though always
full of cheery hopefulness, were very irregular and subject to lack of conti-
nuity through one and another occasionally getting lost on the way. And,
great as was Lois's joy and thankfulness when one arrived, telling of his
safety and good health eight or ten days before, she could never lose sight
of the terrible fact that five minutes after he had written it the end might
have come.

With what agonising anxiety she scanned each long, fateful casualty
list as it came out, only those who have done that same can know. Sore,
sore on wives and mothers, and on all whose men were at the front, were
those days when the desperate German rush on Calais and the coast was
stayed by the still greater and more desperate valour of our little army,
fighting odds as David fought Goliath of Gath. The mighty deeds done in
those days will never be told in full, for in full by one Eyewitness only were
they seen, and He speaks not.

But doings so Homeric are of necessity costly. Britain and the world at
large were delivered from the Menace, but Sorrow swept through the land.

Alma continued to receive word of Con, but at irregular intervals and
always by the hand of Robert Grant, R.A.M.C., Con himself being still unable to put pen to paper.

Mr. Grant, however, wrote with a clerkly hand, and Alma came to
know it well and to like it. The words were Con's own for the most part, but
the writer occasionally appended as postscript a few remarks of his own, always hopeful and encouraging, but neither of them at any time gave any
clue to the nature of these troublesome wounds which prevented the suf-
ferer using his pen.

And this worried Alma not a little. She enquired as to them more than
once but received no explicit answers, and the matter began to get some-

what on her nerves.

Fortunately they were almost run off their feet at the hospital, and with the certainty that Con was at all events alive she devoted herself heart and soul to her patients, and that left her small time for her own personal anxieties.

Lois missed Uncle Tony dreadfully. Her assiduous care of him had occupied her mind and kept her thoughts off her own troubles. Her eyes were opened to the strange guise in which blessings are sometimes vouchsafed to us.

But now that Uncle Tony was gone her fears for Ray loomed larger and larger. She envied Alma her over-hard work and her knowledge of the worst. For herself—in spite of herself—she lived in constant fear, and cast about for some engrossing work that should constrain her mind in other directions.

She spent much time on her knees these days,—when not bodily, still in heart. And she came to recognise, as never before, the wonderful applicability of the Psalms to all the affairs of human life, especially to those who are in trouble and fearful of the future. She could hardly open her Bible at the Psalms without coming straight on some verse that might have been written for herself and the times. Even the damnatory passages satisfactorily fulfilled her desires, since they obviously applied to the Germans, against whom, as the causers of all the trouble and the imperillers of what she held dearest, her feelings grew ever more bitter.

The terrible waste of humanity's best, this all-superfluous sorrow thrust upon a world which never lacked for sorrows, the inhuman savagery of this new German warfare, the impossibility, as it seemed to her, of any single man coming out alive, from the inferno of shot and shell described by the papers, and those awful casualty lists,—all these lay heavy on her soul in spite of all her utmost efforts after hope and faith.

"Alma was right. I must get to work or I shall go mad," she said to herself.

And after consultation with Auntie Mitt and her mother, they decided, with an eye to Uncle Tony's wishes in the matter, to offer the hospitality of Oakdene to the War Office for any wounded they chose to send, either officers or privates.

In due course an official came down, inspected the premises, indicated the necessary preparations, and presently the house was as busy as a hive with the ordered doings of ten wounded officers and four nurses in charge. And in face of the actual and urgent necessities of these warmly-welcomed guests, neither Lois nor Auntie Mitt nor Mrs Dare had a spare moment to waste on their own anxieties and fears.

CHAPTER XXIX

RAY LUARD was sitting on a barrel in a little station in the north-west of France, watching his men unload railway trucks, when he received the news of Uncle Tony's death.

An escort just returned from Head-Quarters had brought up the belated mail, and glancing quickly at the envelopes, he hurriedly opened the one in Lois's handwriting, with a tightening of the lips at its narrow black edging.

He was not altogether unprepared. In spite of the Colonel's desire that word of his illness should not add to his nephew's already mighty anxieties, they had not judged it right to keep him entirely in the dark.

"Dear old chap!" murmured Ray to himself, as the news broke on him. "Well ... he did his duty and died for his country as surely as any of the rest of us.... (Steady there, boys, or some of you will be getting smashed!)... But they'll miss him terribly.... I wish this cursed business was all over.... Lois is Lady Luard ... I wonder how she feels about it. I'll bet she nearly had a fit when the first person called her that. And I bet that would be Auntie Mitt. She's the one for giving folks their proper titles. ("Knock off for a quarter-of-an-hour, Mac!"—to his Sergeant. "That's heavy work.") Well, well!—Lady Luard!—and a sweeter one there never could be. Damn this business! It *would* be rough luck to be knocked out right on top of this. However, Lois is all right. That's one comfort."

He looked lean and fit. Since Lois watched them swing away to the skirling of the pipes at Watford, they had travelled far, though at the present moment they were nearer home than they had been any time this month or more.

They had had a triumphal passage down the Solent, greeted by cheers and whistles from all the neighbouring boats, which at once blunted the edge of the parting from England and put a still finer point to their patriotic zeal. Some of them, they knew,—perhaps many of them—would never see the green cliffs of Wight again. But they were there on highest service, and their hearts were strong and their spirits above normal. They had gone first to Le Mans, then to Villeneuve St Georges, and finally to Paris—such a different Paris from all Ray's recollections of it!—and yet in some ways a greater Paris than he had ever known it. It was no longer the city of gaiety and light, but the heart of a nation travailing in the birth of a new soul.

France and Britain had had to fall back before the tumultuous rush of the better-prepared German hosts,—from Mons to Le Cateau,—to St Quentin,—to La Fère,—to Compiégne,—to Chantilly,—very near Paris now. But there the quarry turned and hurled itself at its pursuers. The hunters became the hunted and were forced back to the Marne, across the Ourcq, to the Aisne. And it was while this was going on that the Scottish came to Paris for the cheer and satisfaction of its citizens.

Bit by bit, each to prevent the other overlapping and outflanking, the hostile lines had spread further and further towards the coast. From the banks of the Aisne, by way of Soissons and Compiégne and Amiens to St Omer, General French's eagle-eyed prevision had swept the British forces round behind the French lines to that north-west corner of France where Calais lay all open to the invader. From the north came Sir Henry Rawlinson, with the 7th Division and the 3rd Cavalry Division, covering the retreat of the gallant but exhausted Belgian Army from the neighbourhood of Antwerp, and held the wolves at bay till the gap by the coast at Nieuport was closed and the long line locked tight from the sea right round to Belfort in the east.

But, so far, the duties of the London Scottish, onerous and important as they had been, had not taken them into the actual fighting line. They were drawing nearer and nearer to it, however, and were all looking forward with keen anticipation and the very natural desire to be the first Territorials actually in the mêlée alongside their comrades of the regular army.

They had acted as body-guard to Sir John French; they had served as military police and as railway-porters. And they had done everything required of them, no matter how unpleasant or how different from their usual avocations, with the zest of men whose souls had risen to the great occasion.

They had handled mountains of stores, and guns and ammunition, and convoys of wounded and prisoners, and had buried many dead.

They had travelled in cattle-trucks and on loaded coal-waggons. They had slept in stations and barns and caves of the earth. They had left all their kits behind them at Southampton and possessed only what they carried on their backs. They had washed when they could, and shaved whenever opportunity offered.

They had stood-by ready to go anywhere and do anything for anybody at any moment. All of which had always so far petered out many miles to the rear of the fighting, though they had more than once come within sound of the guns. But it had all been to the good. They gained new experiences every day; they grew hard and fit under the taxing work, and each day now was bringing them nearer to that for which they had left home and friends and all that had hitherto made life worth living. And not a man of them but was glad to be there.

Ray had wondered much what it would actually feel like to be in a red-hot fight. It had seemed at first as though modern fighting must always be at long range, with no slightest chance of seeing what killed you, or of hitting back except at a venture, the results of which you could not see, and they were all agreed that this was a most unsatisfactory and unsportsman-like style of business. But, from all they could hear, things were changing in most amazing fashion and there had even been bayonet-work and actual hand-to-hand fighting.

The huge German shells, which dug holes big enough to bury an omnibus in, were diabolical, but apparently they did less mischief than might have been expected, and one even got used to them to the point of giving them sporty nick-names and treating them with contempt.

He wondered how he and the rest would comport themselves when the time came. They were fine fellows all, but new at the actual red game of killing and being killed, and it was bound to be terribly trying—the first time at all events. He hoped they would bear themselves well and come through it with credit.

Any moment they might be ordered to the front. Rumour had it that there was terrific pressure against our long-drawn-out line in places. The Germans wanted to get to Calais and seemed determined to hack their way through at any cost. Well, if it lay with the Old Scottish they would make that cost heavy or they would know the reason why.

He thought constantly, in sub-conscious fashion, while his mind was actually dealing promptly and clearly with the inevitable kinks in the day's work, of them all at home, especially of Lois. "Lady Luard!"—he murmured to himself again, as he sat on his barrel in the station. Yes, it would be a little harder still to leave it all before he had even greeted her in her new estate. But her future was at all events secured. He had made his will before leaving, and old Benfleet had it safely stowed away in his big safe. And, after all, every man in a regiment was not wiped out as a rule, however hot the fighting.

When at last the job on which he was engaged was finished, he knocked his men off, got them bucketsful of hot coffee and dashed it with rum, since it had come on to rain and they were all very damp. Then he saw them safely into the old barracks allotted to them as sleeping quarters, made his way back to the station, and took possession of an empty first-class carriage, scribbled a brief note to Lois,—scrappy little letters they were, in pencil, and the paper at times got soiled, but she valued them more than jewels of price,—and then he lay down and was sound asleep in two minutes.

Their time seemed to have come the next afternoon. Orders came to move forward at three o'clock. Rumour, with a score of tongues, was on the ramp. Kitchener had sent word that they were not to go into the firing-line. Hard-pressed Generals all round were clamouring for them. Half-a-dozen other Territorial Regiments were coming up and they were all to go on together. They were not wanted. They were badly wanted. The So-and-Sos had been practically wiped out. And the Etceteras had had to fall back before three whole army-corps.

At half-past four, motor-buses by the score came rolling up—from Barnes and Putney, from Cricklewood and Highgate,—and the old familiar look of them made them all feel almost at home. There were no conductors, no tickets, no tinkling bell-punches. Everything was free on the road to death. They climbed on board and whirled away between the poplar trees, over roads that were cobbled in the centre only and all the rest mud. Now and again a bus would swerve from dead-centre and skid down into the mud and have to be shoved bodily back into safety. Now and again one would succumb to such unusual experiences, and its occupants would storm the next that came along and crush merrily in on top of its already full load.

But whatever their actual feelings—and when did a Scot ever show his actual feelings?—they treated it all as the best of jokes, and sang and laughed and chaffed as though it were a wedding they were going to. And so indeed it was, the greatest wedding of all—the wedding of Life and Death on the Field of Duty, whose legitimate offspring is Glory and Honour —of this world or the next.

Not one of them there, I suppose, though they bore themselves so cheerfully, had any desire for fighting for fighting's sake. They were men of peace,—lawyers, barristers, students, merchants, clerks. They had come away from comfortable homes and good prospects. They had left parents and wives, lovers and friends, at the highest Call Life's bugles sound for any man. They did well to be merry while they might. It is better to be merry than to mope, though your name be cast for death while the laugh is on your lips. They laughed and joked, but the White Fire burned within them. They were answering The Call.

It was the longest ride any of them had ever had in a Putney bus, and those on top got very wet, as it rained hard all night. They were dumped down, in the raw of the morning just before daybreak, at the pretty little town of Ypres, in Belgium, and rejoiced greatly at the feel of solid earth under their feet once more. They crowded for shelter into the Cathedral, into the station, into cover wherever they could find it, and in time they got something to eat.

In the morning they marched out to a wood, where a British battery was hard at work and German shells came whistling back in reply. And all the way along the road wounded men were passing in an endless stream to the rear, while the shot and shell from other British batteries hurtled over their heads, and not far away was the rattle of heavy musketry firing.

There was less light-hearted laughter now and little joking,—just one jerked out now and again as outlet for over-strain. But most of the clean-shaven faces were tense and hard-set, for this looked like the real thing and Death was in the air.

Then it was found that they were not needed there, and as the German shells seemed to have a quite uncanny tendency in their direction, they were ordered back into the town.

And presently, about nightfall, their motor-buses came rolling up again and carried them off to the little village of St Eloi, and the sounds of heavy fighting drew nearer.

The village seemed deserted, so they took possession and made themselves as comfortable as the big guns and their big thoughts would permit. To-morrow, they knew, must surely see them into it and the thought was sobering.

Rations were issued and tongues were loosed again, but conversation was spasmodic and joking somewhat at a discount. They were all very tired; to-morrow would be a heavy day, and one by one they fell asleep—for some of them the last sleep they were to know. And Ray, finishing a hasty scribble to Lois, lay down also and slept as soundly as any.

They were up with the dawn, and rations and more ammunition were served out. Ray managed to get a rifle and bayonet and found the feel of them comforting. Nothing but a revolver—and a dirk in his stocking—had made him feel very naked and unprotected when bullets would be flying. Now he felt very much more his own man, and ready to repay in kind anything that came his way, except "coal-boxes" and shrapnel which were beyond arguing with.

They moved on to another small village—Messines,—where there was a large convent, and not far away, a pumping-mill. The pumping-mill began to turn as soon as they showed face, and instantly German shells began falling thickly about them.

Then came the final order to fling themselves into a gap between a regiment of Hussars on the right and of Dragoons on the left, to dig themselves in as close to the enemy as possible, and hold them at all costs. There was an unprotected spot there, and the keen-eyed Germans had spied it and were heading for it in a torrential rush.

190

"Forward, boys! And Steady! Scottish!—Strike sure!"—and they were into it up to the neck.

It was a magnificent demonstration of mind over matter. These boys, who had never faced red hell before, went in, keen-faced, tight-lipped, tensely-tuned to Death and Duty. All their long training, all their hardening and hardships, all that mattered in this world and the next centred for every man of them into this mighty moment, this final fiery trying of their faith and courage.

And neither failed them. It might have been Wimbledon Common with the canteen and lunch awaiting them in the hollow behind the old Windmill, so calm and steady was their advance, so admirably calculated their extended order.

For a quarter of a mile or so the shells which were pulverising the village behind passed over their heads. Then came an open field swept by heavy rifle-fire and machine-guns. One of the machine-guns was in a farmhouse on the left. Ray ordered bayonets and they tore across the field to stop it, yelling like wild Highland rievers.

It was hot work and men were falling thick. They got to a hedge and along it to the house, but the Germans had bolted, and shells were raining in.

Back to the cover of the hedge, where a ditch gave them time to breathe. And as they lay there panting, with their hearts going like pumps, they found the bushes thick with blackberries and they were mighty cooling to parched throats.

But, presently, shells and the devilish machine-guns discovered them again, so they crawled along till they saw a haystack and made a rush for it, and lay down flat behind it as tight as sardines in a tin. Then, a short distance ahead, they saw a trench, and took their lives in their hands and dived into it and for the time being were safe.

The trench was being held by regulars—Carabineers—and they gave the kilts most hearty welcome.

"Hot hole, sir," said a Sergeant cheerfully—though he put it very much more picturesquely.

"Bit warmish," Ray agreed. "What's next on the menu?"

"Just sit tight till it's dark, and if they come on biff 'em back and tell 'em to keep to their own side. —— —— —— 'em! They don't seem to care a —— how they get wiped."

"Germans are cheap to-day," grinned another.

"I —— well wish some o' their —— officers would come on. I'm 'bout fed up plugging privates."

So they made themselves comfortable there, while the shells screamed overhead and shrapnel and bullets plugged into their modest earthwork.

And surreptitiously they took stock of one another to see who was left. Many well-known faces were missing. Some they had seen go down in the rush. But there was always the hope that wounds might not be fatal.

They scanned the ground they had covered. It was dotted with little heaps of hodden gray and their hearts went out to them. Some lay quite still. One raised his head slightly.

"That's Gillieson!" jerked Ray, and in a moment had crawled out of the trench and was worming his way to the fallen one.

The others watched breathlessly, for a moment, then began to follow here and there, wherever a pitiful gray heap lay within possible reach.

They dragged in a round dozen in this way, bound up their damages as well as they could with the little rolls of first-aid bandages stitched inside their tunics, gave them rum and water from their bottles, and rejoiced exceedingly over them without showing any slightest sign of it.

All afternoon—and never surely was so long a day since Joshua stayed the sun while he smote the Amorites at Beth-horon—they lay in their trench with Death whistling shrilly overhead. They chatted with their new chums and got points from them, heard what had been doing, and learned what was to be done.

And as soon as it was dark they all crept out over the front and forward, till word came to dig in and hold tight; and they dug for their lives as they had never dug in their lives before, with bullets singing over them in clouds, and the much-shelled village burning furiously on their right.

It was hot work in every sense of the word and their bottles were empty. Someone collected an armful and crept along to a farmhouse in the rear to try for water. He came sprinting back in a moment with word that the place was full of Germans.

A guffaw greeted his news as a number of their own kilties came running out towards them, waving their arms triumphantly. But there was something about them Ray did not like. They did not somehow look London Scottish to him. Perhaps it was their unweathered knees.

"Who are you?" he shouted.

"Scottish Rifles!"—with an accent that any Scot would have died rather than use.

"Down them!" he yelled, and let fly himself, and the 'Scottish Rifles' withered away, some to earth and some into the smoke.

It was when they were well under cover and were congratulating themselves on being fairly safe—as things went!—that a burly figure nearly fell in on top of Ray as he crawled about behind his men.

"Hello there?" he shouted.

"London Scottish? You're to clear out of here and fall back."

"What the deuce—" and then a star-shell blazed out in front, and Ray, raking him with one swift glance from his white knees upwards, plucked his feet from under him and brought him down into the trench in a guttural swearing heap.

"Treacherous devils! There's no end to their tricks."

He fingered the revolver at his belt, but he could not do it so. The fellow deserved it, but it felt too like murder.

He kicked the recumbent one up on to his feet. They prodded him over the parapet in front, and as he started to run a dozen rifles cracked and he went down.

These things, and the incessant rain of heavy shells which blew craters in the earth all about them, began to get on their nerves somewhat, but especially this masquerading of the enemy in their own uniform. It produced a feeling of insecurity all round and a diabolical exasperation.

If for a second the storm, of which they seemed the centre, lulled, they heard the terrific din of battle on either side. Heavy fighting seemed going on all along the line.

And soon after midnight came their hottest time of all. It looked as though the enemy had got word where the new raw troops were, and had decided that that would be the weakest spot, and so hurled his heaviest weight against them.

"Here they come! Thousands of 'em!" shouted someone.

The moon had come out and they could see that it was so. Ray had no time to think of Lois or anyone else. His whole being was concentrated on the dark masses rolling up against them. They had got to be stopped. He had no slightest idea of what depended on it. All he knew was that they had got to be stopped, though every man of themselves died for it.

"Steady, boys, and give it them hot," and they blazed away point blank into the serried ranks.

They fell in heaps. The rest wavered and then came on. Ray saw a furious officer thrashing at them with his sword to urge them forward. He sighted him as though he had been a pheasant and the furious one fell. The rest came on—some of them. But the Scottish fire was excellent. The boys were strung to concert pitch. Flesh and blood could not stand their record rapid. The dark masses melted away.

While they were still congratulating themselves a furious fusillade opened on them from one side,—Maxims, Ray judged,—and almost at the same moment came a volley from the rear. There seemed to be Germans all round them.

"Bayonets! This way, boys!" and he tumbled up out of the trench and led the way against the assault from the rear. Obviously if they were surrounded that must be the way out.

He stumbled on the rough ground and his rifle jerked out of his hand. The others thought he was done. But it was only a trip and he was up and off in a moment, leaving his rifle on the ground behind.

He dashed on unarmed, the others yelling at his heels. In front a row of Germans was blazing away at them, the moonlight and the flash of the discharges playing odd tricks with the bristling line of bayonets.

Ray felt himself horribly naked to assault again. But there was a wild, insensate rage in his heart against these men who were dropping his boys as they leaped and yelled behind him. He wanted to tear and rend, to smash them into the earth, to end them one and all.

The wavering gleam of the bayonets was deadly close. He had tried to haul out his revolver as he ran. It was gone—his stumble had jerked it out of its case and broken the lanyard. But he had not played Rugger for nothing.

At the very edge of the bristling line he hurled himself down and under it along the ground, plucked at the first stolid legs he could grab, and brought two heavy bodies down on top of him in a surprised and cursing heap. It helped to break the line too, and the boys were in on them in a moment, jabbing and stabbing and yelling like fiends out of the pit. They were all mad just then. It was their first actual taste of blood at close quarters, and it was very horrible. None of them cared very much to recall the actual details later on. But it had the desired effect. Such of the enemy as had any powers of locomotion left used them, and the panting Scots were for the moment masters of the field,—but the cost had been heavy. How heavy they did not yet fully know.

The machine-gun on their flank had been rushed and was silent. Their rear seemed clear of the enemy. The Scottish picked up all they could find in the dark of their wounded and returned to their trench, and pounded away again at anything that showed in front. This, after the hot mêlée behind, was child's play and it gave them time to recover themselves.

In the dim light of the dawn they took stock again, grieved silently over their losses, and set their faces harder than ever to avenge them if the chance offered.

And the chance came quickly. All along the front as far as they could see, the Germans came on again in dense gray masses,—hundreds to one, they seemed, and the prospect hopeless. There was only one thing to be done, and that was to make the enemy foot the bill beforehand and to make it as big a bill as possible. And the clips of cartridges snapped in merrily, and the gray ones in front went down in swathes, and Ray's rifle barrel grew so hot that he flung it aside and looked about for another. And as he did so, he discovered with a shock that he and his handful were alone in the trench. The order had come to retire but had never got their length.

"Give them blazes, boys!—then follow me!" he shouted, and they gave them a full minute of extra rapid, and then stooped and scurried along the trench as fast as they could go.

Glancing about for cover in the rear, he saw a haystack a hundred yards away across the open.

"There you are!" he panted, and started them off one after the other across the field, and followed himself last of all.

"Miracles still happen," he panted again, as they lay flat for breath behind the stack. "Never thought we'd manage it."

Further to the rear were farm buildings and a glimpse of hodden gray kilts hovering about. So, with a fresh stock of breath, and an amazing new hope of life, they dashed across one by one, with the bullets hailing past in sheets and ripping white splinters off a gate they had to go through.

How any man got through alive, they never knew. But they did somehow. Only two men got hit. Ray, last man as a matter of duty, saw young MacGillivray just in front stagger suddenly and nearly fall. He slipped his arm through the boy's with a cheery "Keep up!" and raced him into safety, and they bound him up so that he could go on.

The other man got it in the shoulder just as he whirled through the gate. He made light of it, but they tied him up also and prepared for the next move.

For the farm was after all only one stage on the road. There were Germans all round them, they were told, except for one possible opening in the rear. And that they instantly took. First, another minute of rapid-firing by every available man to give the enemy pause, then off through a wood, across a beet-field on which machine-guns were playing for all they were worth, across another field of mixed rifle and machine-gun fire, and so at last to a road up which British troops and guns and Maxims were racing to thrust a stopper into the gap.

The Hodden-Grays just tumbled into the ditch behind the guns and thankfully panted their souls back. They were still alive—some of them! They could hardly realise it.

Ray dropped his humming head into his folded arms as he lay full length on his face. The homely smell of earth and grass was like new life. He chewed some grass with relish. After the smoke and taste of blood it was delicious. To be alive after all that! It was amazing—incredible almost. He thought of Lois and thanked God fervently for them both.

He did not know what they had done. He only knew that it had been a hot time and that somehow, by God's grace, he was still alive. He hoped they had given a good account of themselves. They had certainly had to fall back—but in face of such tremendous odds it had been inevitable and he thought no one could blame them. Anyway they had done their best. But he felt just a trifle despondent about it all. Falling back was not a Scottish custom.

He was sitting by the roadside smoking a cigarette to settle the jumpy feeling inside him and soothe his ruffled feelings, when the Adjutant came along.

"You had a hot time, Luard."

"It was a trifle warm. They were too many for us, but we did the best we could under the circumstances."

"You did magnificently. The General said the Scottish had done what two out of three Regular Battalions would have failed to do. The Staff are saying they saved the situation last night."

"You don't say so!" said Ray, cocking his bonnet, and feeling five times the man he was a minute before. "Well, I'm glad they appreciate us. You can always count on the Scottish doing its level best."

And later on came a telegram from Sir John French himself, conveying his "warmest congratulations and thanks for the fine work you did yesterday at Messines,"—and saying, "You have given a glorious lead and example to all Territorial troops who are going to fight in France."

So from that point of view all was as well as it possibly could be, and proud men were they who answered the roll-call at the edge of the wood. Dishevelled and torn and shaken,—and very sober-faced at the heavy tale of missing,—but uplifted all the same, with the knowledge that the record of the old corps had not suffered at their hands.

They had a few days out of the firing line to let their nerves settle down and within a week were back in the trenches.

CHAPTER XXX

THE news of the London Scottish charge at Messines, and their success in holding back the enemy at that time and point of terrific pressure, was made public by the Censor almost at once. And great was the jubilation at Head-Quarters and throughout the Second Battalion, and grievous the anxiety in many a home over the tardy casualty lists, for it was recognised that the losses must necessarily be heavy.

Lois suffered only one day of acutest mental distress, thanks to Ray's precious bits of pencilled notes, three of which—addressed to "Lady Luard"—arrived all together the day after the news was made known.

But that one long day taught her to the full what long-drawn agonies thousands of other anxious hearts must be suffering until all the details were published.

Ray's latest note, scribbled by the roadside just after his elevating chat with the Adjutant, was very short and very scrawly in its writing. But it told that he was alive and that was all she cared for.

"Can't write much," he said in it, "for my hand's got the jumps yet. We've just come through hell and I haven't a scratch. I live and marvel. God's great mercy. They say we've done well. It was certainly hot. Going to have a bit off-time, I believe, and we need it. Keep your heart up. I can't imagine anything worse than we've come through."

Noel and Gregor MacLean swelled visibly with pride in the prowess of their First Battalion,—so the girls asserted,—and certainly in their at-length-completed uniforms they looked unusually big and brawny and ready for anything.

A draft was preparing for the front to fill up the gaps in the depleted First, and they enthusiastically put in for it. And, as they were about the two fittest men in the regiment, thanks to their own arduous preliminary training, they were accepted, and—again according to the girls—forthwith became so massive in their own estimation that it was as much as one's place was worth for ordinary mortals to venture to address them.

But the keenness of the draft for the front could not prevent a certain heaviness of heart in those at home. The very necessity and the urgency of the call induced forebodings as to the future. The First Battalion had made a record. The draft would be emulous to live up to it. Not one of them, as they helped the happy warriors in their preparations and kept strong and cheerful faces over it all, but felt that they were most likely parting with the boys for good, and that when the good-byes were said they might well be the last ones.

Mrs Dare especially felt bruised to the heart's core. Con gone, and lying wounded somewhere,—and undoubtedly sorely wounded, for they had never had a line from himself yet. Ray out there in the thick of it, and any moment might bring word of his death. And now Noel plunging into the mêlée with a joyous zest such as he had never shown for anything in life before. And Alma and Lois on the tenterhooks of ceaseless anxiety. It was a time that kept the women-folk much upon their knees, and their hearts welled with unuttered prayers as they went about their daily work.

A time, however, that was not without its compensations. If anxieties filled the air, all hearts were opened to one another in amazingly un-English fashion. Men with whom Mr Dare had had no acquaintance, made a point of coming up to him and congratulating him on his son-in-law's safety in that hot night at Messines.

They expressed their sympathy in the matter of Con and hoped he would soon have better news, and spoke admiringly of Noel's pluck in volunteering so speedily for the front.

And everywhere Mrs Dare and Lois and the girls went it was the same. The frigid angularities of the British character were everywhere broken down. The touch of common feeling evoked a new spirit of national kinship. What touched one touched all. But in varying degree. Pleasant and helpful as it was to experience this new feeling of kindliness and sympathy in the air, the hearts most vitally affected alone knew how sorely the war was bruising them.

But, as Alma said, whenever she could rush away from her patients for a breath of home, "Work is the only thing to keep one's thoughts off one's troubles, and it doesn't pay to dwell on them. Here's another letter from Robert Grant. He says Con is progressing and hints that there is a chance of his being exchanged as soon as he can travel. I do wish we could hear from himself, if it was only just a word. I can't help fearing he's more hurt than Mr Grant tells us."

"It's a great comfort to know that he's alive, my dear," said Mrs Dare, "—when so many have gone for good."

"Oh, it is. I assure you I am grateful, Mother. And yet I can't help longing for just that one word from himself. If he only signed his letters even, it would be something."

"We must be thankful for the smallest sparing mercy in these days. It seems incredible that any of them should come back alive when one reads the accounts of the fighting."

"I don't believe it helps one to read about it," said Lois, who had sat listening quietly.

"I'm sure it doesn't," said Alma. "I'm glad to say I have very little time for reading. On the other hand one cannot help hearing our men talk about it, and perhaps that's worse, for they were in the thick of it and know what they're talking about. And, oh, if only the slackers and shirkers at home could hear how the others think of them! Their ears would tingle red for the rest of their lives. You hear pretty regularly from Ray, Lo?"

"Every two or three days. I'll get you his last ones," and she slipped quietly away.

"She is on the rack too," said Mrs Dare with a sigh. "Any day may bring us ill news. I dread the postman's ring. And in a few days Noel will be in it too. It's hard on those who sit at home and wait."

"But the boys are just splendid," said Alma cheerfully. "They're doing their duty nobly. Just think how you, and we all, would have felt if Noel had kept out of it. Why, we couldn't have held our heads up, Mother, and you know it."

"I know," nodded Mrs Dare. "I try to look at it that way, but the other side will insist on being looked at also."

"If any of them never come back,—well, we know that they will be infinitely better off. They will have attained the very highest. No man can do more than give his life for his country, and these boys are giving themselves splendidly. I tell you my heart is in my throat at thought of it all whenever I meet a regiment in the street. I could cheer and cry at the same time. They are splendid!—splendid!—and you can see in their eyes and faces that they understand. War is very terrible, Mother, but I cannot help feeling that as a people we are on a higher level than we were six months ago. There's a new and nobler spirit abroad."

"To think—that it had to come in such a way!"

"That is one of the mysteries."

Lois came quietly in with her precious letters.

"I envy you, dear," said Alma, when she had read them. "Just one little precious scrawl like those would be worth more to me than all Mr Grant's letters, glad as I am to get them."

"But you know Con is safe," said Lois softly.

"I have Mr Grant's word for it, but I don't know him from Adam. All I've been able to learn is that he was an R.A.M.C. man and was taken at the same time as Con. He is not a doctor, just one of the helpers."

"I think I would be glad to have Ray wounded and a prisoner—if it wasn't very bad," said Lois. "Though I'm sure he wouldn't like to know I feel like that."

"And I—" began Mrs Dare. "No, it's no good talking about it," and then almost in spite of herself, she said what was in her mind. "I really cannot help feeling that if—if the worst had to come to any of them, it would be better to be killed outright than shattered and useless for life. Oh, it is terrible to think of. And so many will be—"

"I would sooner have them back in pieces than not at all," said Lois quickly.

"So would I," said Alma. "Half a man is better than no man when he's all you've got. Especially when the other half has been given to his country. No, indeed! Let us get back all we can and be thankful."

They were kept very busy at Oakdene with their wounded. In search of extra help Mrs Dare had sent for Mrs Skirrow. But Mrs Skirrow had risen on the wings of the storm.

She came, indeed, but it was only to explain why she could not come as formerly.

"You see, mum, I got me 'ands as full as they'll 'old at present. When I heard they was goin' to billet some o' the boys in Willstead, I says to myself, 'That's your ticket, Thirza Skirrow. Billeting's your job. You're a born billeter.' So I did up my place a bit, and made it all nice an' tidy and clean as a new pin. An' I got four of 'em. Big lads too an' they eats a goodish lot. But we get on together like a house afire. They calls me 'Mother,' an' I makes thirty bob a week and me keep off 'em, and feeds 'em well too. It's better'n charing an' more to me taste, and it's helping King and Country. An' for me, I don't mind how long it lasts."

"I'm glad you've been so sensible," said Mrs Dare. "Perhaps you know of someone else who could lend us a hand?"

"Know of plenty that's needing it,—spite o' the money they're drawin' from Government. But most o' them that could if they would's too happy boozing in the pubs to do anything else. I'll try and find you someone, mum, an' if I can I'll send her along—or bring her by the scruff."

"I hope you have good news of your own boys and Mr Skirrow."

"Never a blessed word, mum, not since they left. They'll be all right, I reckon, or I'd heard about it. We're not a family that worries much so long as things is goin' right. They'll look after themselves out there, wherever they are. And I'm doin' me little bit at 'ome and quite 'appy, thank ye, mum!" and Mrs Skirrow, looking very solidly contented with life, sailed away to buy in for her boys, and round up some help for Mrs Dare if she could lay hands on it.

Out of that came the idea—already essayed in other parts of the country—of opening rooms where the wives of the men who had gone to the front could meet and talk, and spend their spare time in better surroundings than the public-houses offered. And another channel for helpful ministry, and another distraction from brooding thought, was opened to them.

The boys were waiting in hourly expectation of orders to proceed to the front, in the highest of spirits, and with a gusto not entirely explicable to their womankind. By processes of severe elimination they had reduced their absolutely necessary baggage to official requirements and the restricted proportions of their new stiff green-webbing knapsacks. They were now going up and down each day in full campaigning kit, and looked, as Noel said, like blooming Father Christmases, so slung about were they with bulging impedimenta of all kinds. They looked bigger and burlier than ever,—'absolutely massive,' said Honor.

Then at last the call came. They were to parade at Head-Quarters and remain there ready to go on at a moment's notice.

Farewells to the elders were said at home. Neither Mrs Dare nor Mrs MacLean would venture on them in public. Lois knew what it would be like, having been through it already, and she stayed with them. Auntie Mitt wept unashamedly, though she pretended it was only the beginning of a cold. And when they had gone, all four shut themselves up for a space in their bedrooms and betook themselves to their knees.

Honor and Vic, however, went up with them to Head-Quarters, to see the impression they created in the trains with such loads on their backs, to share in their reflected glory, and to delay the parting by that much.

And the impression was highly satisfactory to all concerned. For all minds were full still of the gallant work of the First Battalion at Messines, and all knew that these young stalwarts were off presently to fill the gaps. Appreciative glances followed their bumping progression in and out of trains and stations, and the girls really felt it an honour to be in such high company.

At Head-Quarters they—being connected with the draft—were admitted to the floor of the house and found themselves in a bewildering maelstrom of circulating Scots.

"I never saw so many bare knees in all my life," whispered Vic.

"Aren't they all splendid?" said Honor, sparkling all over, but not referring entirely to brawny knees.

And splendid they were, though there were many eyes that saw them but mistily—whereby they doubtless looked more splendid still. And obtrusive lumps had to be forcibly choked down many throats, as fathers and mothers, and sisters and other fellows' sisters, tried their best to keep brave and cheerful faces while they watched—knowing only too well that they might be looking for the last time on the clear fresh faces and bright eyes and stalwart forms.

It was dreadful to think that within a day or two these eager upstanding boys, with their swinging kilts and cocked bonnets and cheery looks, might be lying stiff and stark, rent into bloody fragments by German shells. It did not do to think of it.

Honor and Vic went up into the gallery and watched the multifarious crowd below.

"It makes me think of one of those colonies of ants you buy at Gamage's in a glass case at Christmas," murmured Vic. "I had one once, but the glass got broken and they all got out and got lost.... I suppose they all know what they're supposed to be doing, but they're awfully like those ants pushing about every which way—"

"They'll get out soon. But I hope they'll not get lost," said Honor, with a glimpse of the chill foreboding.

"Do you know, Nor, those boys walk quite differently since they got their kilts," said Vic, as they watched their two down below.

"I know. They fling out their toes with a kind of free kick as though the world was at their feet. See that man—he does it beautifully. He's a sergeant or something. He looks as if he'd done it all his life."

"It's rather like the way cats walk on wet grass," said Vic.

And then, suddenly, sharp words of command down below,—the floor cleared as if by magic of all but the draft for the front, and they formed up in two long lines, and a General came along and inspected them and said a few cheery words to them.

The girls thrilled at the general silence, the concentration on the draft. They watched their two absorbedly, and to both it came right home with almost overwhelming force that the parting that was upon them might well be the final one. They would march proudly away with their swinging kilts and skirling pipes, and then—they might never see them again.

"Look at their faces!" whispered Honor. "Are those two really our boys?"

"They're ours right enough. That's their fighting-face. They're splendid."

More words of command, they formed up in fours, the big doors swung open, the pipes shrilled a merry tune, and with heavy tread of ordered feet they passed out into the gray November day.

"Are they going?" gasped Honor, and turned to follow.

"Only to Central Hall," said a Second Battalion man who was leaning on the rail alongside them. "They're to come back here for lunch presently. They'll go on later,—that is if they go on to-day at all. Somebody was saying the transports aren't ready."

"They say there's a German submarine dodging about the Channel waiting for them," said another next to him.

"This place breeds a fresh rumour every five minutes on an average. You're never sure of anything till it's happened."

So the girls waited hopefully, and criticised the setting of the tables down below by obviously 'prentice hands; and in due course they were rewarded by the draft marching in again, without kits this time, and they all sat down at the tables and ate and drank in apparently jovial humour.

But to the girls, subdued in spirit somewhat by the pertinacious intrusion of the future possibilities which took advantage of this long-drawn farewell, the rough-and-ready banquet had in it something of the solemn and portentous,—something indeed of a sacrament, though the apparently jovial ones down below did not seem to regard it so. It was a farewell feast. It was hardly possible that all those stalwart diners would return. And as their eyes wandered over them, returning oftenest to their own two, they wondered who would be taken,—who left to return to them.

"I couldn't eat to save my life," said Vic.

"Nor I. And I don't believe they're eating much either. They're just pretending to."

When the feasting was over the place became a maelstrom again, with much hearty wringing of hands, and good lucks, and good wishes, and parting gifts of plethoric boxes of matches and cigars and cigarettes. And then they were all formed up into two long lines again, and the girls sped down the narrow stone staircases to be near them at the last.

They were just in time to march alongside their own two as far as the Central Hall, but it was only when the hodden-gray mass was slowly making its way down the dark stairway that they had the chance to speak.

"We've got to sleep in this hole to-night, they say," said Noel. "Rotten!"

"When do you think you'll go?" asked Honor.

"Dear knows. We never know anything till we're doing it."

"We shall come up in the morning to see if you're still here."

"That'll be nice. But don't bother!"

"We may be here for days," said Gregor. "We've got used to hanging on and waiting orders. It's the weariest part of the work."

"Well, we'll keep on coming up till you go. We'd like to see the last of them, wouldn't we, Vic?—I mean," with a quick little catch of the breath that nearly choked her, "the last till you come back."

"Rather! You see, we wouldn't be sure you really had gone unless we saw it with our own eyes."

"Think we'd bolt?—Or want to get rid of us?" grinned Noel.

"Oh—neither. Just to know, you know."

And then the boys had to go below, and the girls went away home, and hardly spoke a word all the way.

They went up again next day and found the draft still standing-by in huge disgust at the delay.

And again the next day—and the next,—and the next; and each time found the boys growling louder and deeper.

"Got us out of Head-Quarters and forgotten us, the bally idiots!" was Noel's opinion. "You might just trot round and ask 'em what they jolly well mean by it. Tell 'em we're not going to put up with it much longer."

"All going to desert for a change," said Gregor. "It's a sight harder work than fighting."

Then one morning when the girls arrived at the Hall it was lonely and deserted. The draft had gone.

"Just as well, maybe," said Honor philosophically, when she had got her face quite straight again. "I believe I should have cried at the last, and I hate crying in public."

"Crying's no good," said Vic valiantly. "I'm glad they're away at last. It was beginning to tell on all of us."

CHAPTER XXXI

FOR a week after that hot night at Messines the Hodden-Grays had a fairly easy time, and they deserved and needed it.

They marched back to Bailleul and found billets in the farmhouses round about, and there they had the chance to clean up and refit, to recover themselves generally, and to grieve over their heavy losses,—though you would not have thought it, perhaps, by the look of them.

Simply to be sleeping once more beyond the reach of sudden death was a mental tonic, and its effects showed quickly in a universal bracing up to concert-pitch and anything more that might be required of them.

The pressure on their special front was still heavy and continuous, however, and the end of the week's holiday saw them back in the fighting-line, with their hearts set dourly on paying back some of the heavy score if opportunity offered.

They were moved from point to point, but finally settled down in a wood, the trees of which, so much as was left of them, told their own grim story of fiery flagellations. The German trenches were in the same wood about three hundred yards away but were invisible on account of fallen tree-tops and branches.

There Ray's company remained for five whole days, shelled incessantly and so harassed with attacks between times that rest was impossible, and through sheer strain and weariness their nerves came nigh to snapping. But they held tight and slogged on, and longed for relief and a heavenly night's rest out of the sound and feel of bursting shells.

Even well-seasoned regulars—and they had a very crack battalion on their left—found it overmuch of a bad thing, and some got 'batty in the brain-pan,' as Ray put it in his letters to Lois, and had to be sent back to hospital. It was amazing that men accustomed to experiences so different could stand it. But they did, and held their own with the best, and suffered much.

The weather was horrible. Some days it poured without ceasing. At night the rain turned to hail, and they had fierce gales which brought the remnants of the wood down on their heads, so that between whirling hail and falling branches they could not see five yards ahead. They were soaked to the skin and chilled to the bone all day and all night, and the only thing that kept them alive was the incessant attacks of the German hordes which had to be beaten back at any price,—and were.

But it was bitter hard work and only possible by reason of urgent and final necessity. Never were more grateful men on this earth when at last the reliefs came up, and they trudged off through nine inches of mud to a village in the rear where they got hot tea,—the first hot thing they had had for a week.

Then followed a short spell in the reserve trenches, which were full of water and still subject to shell-fire, but just a degree less racking than the actual fighting-line in as much as the enemy could not get at them without ample warning.

Still, they were 'standing-by' all the time, ready to supplement the front at any moment, so there was little rest and constant strain. They dozed at times, sitting in the mud and more than half frozen with the bitter cold. Their sopping clothing stuck clammily to their chilled skins. They dreamed of beds and hot baths, and now and again they fed on bully beef and bread and jam, washed down with hot tea laced with rum, and blessed the commissariat which did its level best for them under very trying circumstances.

Then at last,—since human nature can stand only a certain considerable amount of affliction without being the worse for it, and they had done their utmost duty and had about reached the limit—they were ordered to the rear for a proper rest, and right gladly they took the muddy road and left the sound of the guns behind them.

There followed a few days of recuperative rest, interrupted only, but more than once, by orders to 'stand-by' to reinforce the front, which was enduring much tribulation from overwhelming odds. The front held firm, however, and their tension relaxed again.

They cleaned themselves up and did some parades and route marches to keep their muscles from cramping, and then, one heavenly day, Ray, hearing that the officers of other battalions were getting short leave for home, put in for the same, and got it, and twelve hours later walked up the drive at Oakdene and Lois rushed out and flung herself into his arms.

CHAPTER XXXII

WHAT a home-coming that was!

They counted him almost as one returned from the dead, and Mrs Dare and Lois could hardly let him out of their sight for a moment. He was gift of the gods and prized accordingly.

And they talked and talked, though of course it was Ray who did most of the talking, and held them spell-bound and shivering with the mere telling of the things he had seen.

Auntie Mitt suspended her work to gaze at him with eyes like little saucers, and finally expressed the opinion that it sounded worse even than the Crimea.

"And you saw nothing of the boys?" asked Honor disappointedly.

"They hadn't arrived when I left. General opinion is that they've got mislaid en route, but they'll probably have turned up by the time I get back. We're needing them badly to make up our strength. Losses were very heavy at Messines, and there's a certain wastage going on all the time, of course."

"Wastage indeed!" sighed Mrs Dare, thinking of her own. "You speak as if they were no more than goods and chattels, Ray. Every wasted one means a sore sore heart at home."

"I know, Mother dear. One gets to speak of it so. War is horribly callousing. If it were not no man could stick it out. But we think of them differently, I assure you, and nothing is left undone that we can do for them. You've heard from the boys, of course."

"We've had several letters, just hasty scraps—"

"That's all one has time for, and we're not allowed to say much, you see."

"How long can it possibly go on, do you think?"

"I can't imagine how it's ever going to come to an end. You see they're dug in and we're dug in, and neither of us can make any advance. Seems to me an absolute stalemate and as if it might go on so for ever."

"How awful to think of!" said Vic. "Can't you get round them somehow and turn them out of their holes?"

"We haven't a quarter enough men. That's why it's been so rough on those that were there. We can beat them at fighting any day, even at three to one odds, but they outnumber us many times more than that. How's Kitchener's new lot getting on?"

"They've come in splendidly, and they're working hard and look very fit —those that have got their uniforms. The rest look like convicts, but they'll be all right when they're decently dressed."

"Well, I tell you,—we want every man of them, and as quickly as possible. Our long thin line is terribly pressed, and our losses are heavier in consequence. It's rough on the nerves, you see. One day in and one day out of the trenches would be all right. But five days and nights on end is a bit tough. Lots have been invalided home almost dotty with the strain."

He had a great time and savoured every second of it. He had hot baths till he felt respectable, and got a cold in the head as a consequence, and went up and had a Turkish bath in town and thought of the icy water of the trenches as he sat in the hottest room.

He went up to Head-Quarters, and saw the new chiefs there and some old chums who had been unable for various good reasons to go out with the rest.

But most of his time he spent with Lois—golden hours which both felt might possibly be the last.

Three days later he was back at Brigade Head-Quarters, and one of the first things he saw was Noel Dare kicking a fine goal in a game of soccer, Draft v. Veterans, and Gregor MacLean, who was better at golf than at footer, cheering him for all he was worth.

They all three forgathered when the game was over and the crowd had finished booing the referee, and Noel, in the pride of his goal and brimful of youthful eagerness, broke out, "I say, Sir Raglan, can't you get them to get a move on? We chaps came out to fight and we've done nothing yet but play footer and route-march. It's almost as bad as being at home."

"You wait till you get five days and nights in the trenches, my son, with water up to your knees and the rest of you nothing but mud, and you'll be wishing you were back here having a holiday."

"Bet you I won't! We're just aching to have a slap at those beastly Boches, aren't we, Greg?"

"Rather!—Sickening, hanging about round here."

"You'll find war's mostly hanging about round somewhere, with an occasional scrap thrown in, and overmany shells all the time. You get used to them, of course, but you'll come to be grateful to get away from the sound of them for a bit."

"Everybody all right at home?" asked Noel. "Suppose you got a sight of them!"

"Yes, I got all the sight of them I could cram into the time. They were all first rate, but full of anxieties for all of us. I suppose you write now and again."

"Oh, occasionally. But you see there's really been nothing to tell them so far."

"You can't write often enough to please your mothers. They're feeling it sorely."

The days dragged on and found them still 'fooling about,' as Noel put it, —footer, route-marches, parades, alarm-parades, church-parades, an occasional sudden order to 'stand-by' in case of need, now and again a bit of musketry-drill, and some educational manœuvering and trench-digging. But it was all very far short of what the fire-eating newcomers had looked forward to, and strung themselves up to, and felt very much let down through the lack of.

Then they heard the King was coming to have a look at them, and they were set to scraping a foot or so of the surface mud off the road so that his motor should be able to get through somehow.

And they did it merrily enough. It was a change anyway and all in the day's work. But, said Noel,

"Hanged if I ever expected to get down to road-scraping. I feel like one of the old duffers that pretend to sweep the roads at home, with W.U.C. in brass letters on their caps, and mouch about most of the time with their brooms over their shoulders."

The King duly came and went, which passed one day, and they had more drills, new double-company drills, more route-marches, more parades, and came at last to doubt if any real fighting was to the fore at all.

The news of Admiral Sturdee's sinking of the German Fleet off the Falklands cheered them up, and later on came word of the bombardment of Scarborough and Whitby, and they were inclined to think that would help Kitchener in his recruiting.

It rained most days and they got accustomed to the constant living in wet clothes. And rumour, as of old, had fine times of it—a fresh 'cert' each day, but the most persistent and long-lived that they were presently to go to Egypt; —at which Master Noel growled, "Rotten luck!"

They were constantly 'standing-by,' hopeful that it meant business at last, but the order was always cancelled and they stayed where they were.

Then, right in the middle of a game of footer, peremptory orders came and they were really off at last, full of fight and jubilant at the prospect of fresh fame for the Battalion in the near future.

And presently Noel and Gregor found themselves in a real fighting-trench, with mud and water almost up to their knees, and the roaring of big guns and the rattle of musketry somewhere on in front.

It was a reserve trench, and between them and the enemy the front line men were doing their best to retake a trench that had been lost, and behind them were several companies in support, so that the new men were as yet in no great danger.

They felt terribly warlike and anxious to get at them. Huge shells came hurtling through the darkness and exploded all too close, with terrific noises and ghastly blasts of lightning.

"Bully!" jerked Noel, with his teeth set tight. "Bit of the real thing at last, old Greg! Wonder when we do anything?"

"It's dam damp to the feet," said Gregor. "I'd jolly well like a run to get warm."

There was no chance of a run just then, but presently they were all ordered out into the open to dig a new trench, and the Germans sent up star-shells and found them out and gave it them hot.

Bullets pinged past them and over them like clouds of venomous insects swept along by a gale. Shrapnel burst with vicious claps over their heads. Life seemed impossible and yet to their surprise they lived, and, whatever their private feelings, the new men stuck valiantly to their work and dug for dear life.

Noel and Gregor were alongside one another delving like navvies, while sweat and shivers chased one another up and down their backs which felt horribly naked to damage.

"Keep as low as you can, boys," was their lieutenant's order, as he paced the line behind, preaching better than he practised.

"Navvies," jerked Noel, through his teeth to Gregor, so strung up with it all that he must speak or burst. "Just jolly old navvies and grave-diggers and road-scrapers! That's what we are, my son."

And then—a gasp alongside him, and a groan, and Gregor was down.

"Greg, old man! What's it?" and he was down on his knees beside him. But Gregor did not speak.

Noel rose and hauled him up into his arms and began to stagger back with his burden towards the rear. A machine-gun somewhere on the flank opened on them. A hail of bullets swept into them. They both went down with a crash.

"Stretchers here!" shouted the lieutenant, and then fell himself in a crumpled heap.

*   *   *   *   *

Let Ray's letter tell the rest.

Lois had rushed to meet the postman, as they used to do at The Red House, but never so eagerly as now.

He handed her the letters with a grin. He wished all the houses he went to had a similar practice. It made him feel himself a universal benefactor.

It was sleeting and the letters were sprinkled with drops—like tears. Lois picked out her own special, tossed the rest—none of which were of the slightest consequence compared with this one—onto the table in the breakfast-room and sped upstairs. She always read Ray's letters first in sanctuary.

She sliced it open very neatly, for even envelopes from the front were precious. And then as she glanced over it, with eyes trained and quickened to the vitalities, her face blanched and her lips tightened, and then the tears streamed down without restraint.

"Lois dearest,

I have bad news for you, but you will bear it bravely and help the mothers. Our two dear lads are gone. They were doing their duty nobly and their end was quick and I believe painless,—a grand death for any man to die.

They were trenching at the front on Tuesday night with the rest. The Germans located them in the dark by star-shells and directed a heavy fire on them. I was sent to order them to withdraw as the enemy had crept up on the flank with machine-guns. I met bearer-parties coming in and they said casualties were pretty heavy. One stretcher I passed as I returned had two bodies on it, and one of the bearers explained that they found them locked together like that. 'This one had been trying to carry the other, I reckon,' he said, and I flicked my torch on them and found to my great grief that it was Noel and Gregor. Gregor had been shot dead and Noel had evidently been trying to get him to the rear.

"We may not mourn overmuch. It is hard to lose the boys but it was a grand death to die. Gregor died for his country. Noel died for his friend as well.

Break it to the mothers. It will be a sad task, but tell them how bravely the boys did their part. They were always cheerful and happy —anxious only to get to the real work for which they had prepared themselves so well.

I am very well and fit and have not had a scratch so far. God be thanked, for both our sakes!..."

*　　*　　*　　*　　*

Break it to the mothers! What a task for any girl!

She fell on her knees by the bed and buried her streaming face in her hands, and prayed for help for them all and especially for the mothers.

Her own mother, she knew, would bear it bravely. She had many left. But poor Mrs MacLean!—her only one!—her all! And she ageing and frail.

And Honor! Oh, Death cut wide swathes in these times. It would be very sad for Honor. She would get over it in time, no doubt. She was young. But now it would darken her life and leave a terrible blank in it.

And Vic! She was not quite sure if there had been anything between Vic and Noel. She had imagined the possibility at times. Oh, Death was cruel, and War was hateful and horrible.

These dear boys, with no ill-feeling for anyone—done to their deaths by the evil machinations of the war-makers! In the depth of her sorrow her anger burned. She prayed God vehemently to requite it in full to those who had brought all these horrors on the world for their own evil ends.

But nothing would bring back their boys. And upon her lay the dreadful task of breaking the news to the rest. She prayed now for strength and guidance, and they were given to her.

She got up and bathed her face and eyes, and went downstairs.

Vic met her expectantly.

"Any news, Lo?... Why—what is it?" at sight of her eyes, which swam in spite of herself.

"Very bad news, dear. Come in here,—to the library," and she closed the door behind them.

"Noel and Gregor," she said, with a break in her voice—"They are both gone—"

"Oh, Lo!"—with a sharp agony which Lois understood. "Not both!"

"Yes, dear, both. It is terrible, but you must help us to bear it."

Vic gave her one woeful glance, which haunted her for months, and then put her arms round her neck and broke into sobs. "Oh, Lo! Lo!" and Lois put her arms round her understandingly and patted her soothingly. No further word was said between them, and presently Vic disengaged herself and bowed her head and ran up to her room.

Lois just told the news to Auntie Mitt, whose old face worked and broke, and then, slipping on her Loden cloak with the hood over her head, she went across to The Red House.

They knew in a moment by the sight of her face that she brought bad news. Mrs Dare had all along, while relaxing nothing of her faith and hope, been prepared for such. Many times a day she had said to herself, "How is it possible that they can come back alive out of such horrors? God's will be done!"

Now she asked quickly, "Who is it, dear?"—as one who was prepared.

"It is the boys, Mother dear."

"Not both?" with a gasp in spite of herself.

"Both," said Lois sadly, and dared not look at Honor, who sat rigid and stricken. "I will read you Ray's letter."

"Ray is safe?"

"Thank God, he is safe—so far," and she read them his letter.

When it was all told, Mrs Dare gave a great sigh as though part of her very life had gone out of her.

"The—poor—dear—lads!" she said softly.

"We must remember that they are infinitely better off, Mother dear," said Lois quietly. "They did their duty and they died nobly."

Mrs Dare sighed again. "I did not think it possible they could all come back. How could we expect it when so many are gone? But—oh, how we shall miss them!—the dear lads!—the dear lads!"

"Who will break it to Mrs MacLean?" said Honor, in a low, strained voice tremulous with tears. "It will be terrible for her!"

"Perhaps I had better go," said Lois. "But it will be very trying—"

"I think I will go, Lo," said Honor, very quietly but very firmly. "He was very dear to me too. We must comfort one another."

"Can you stand it, Nor, dear?"

"Yes, I can stand it. We've all got to stand it. You will lend me Ray's letter? I will be very careful of it," and Lois handed it to her.

"She is very brave," said Lois, when Honor had gone off to put on her things. "I don't think I could bear it so well if Ray were taken from me. Oh, Mother, how terrible it all is! It all seems like a horrible nightmare. I stand and ask myself sometimes—'Is it real? Is this really Christmas of 1914,—or shall I wake presently and find it all an evil dream?'"

"Ah—if it only were!" said Mrs Dare, with the tears running unheeded down her cheeks. "We must try to bear it as bravely as Honor does. It will be a great blow to your father too. But we have forecasted it. It seemed impossible that all of them should come back to us...."

They heard the front door close quietly as Honor let herself out.

"... My heart is very sore for Gregor's mother," she said softly. "He was all she had. I am still rich. She loses all. But if anyone can comfort her it is Honor."

"And to think—that a million, perhaps many million, women are feeling as we are, and suffering as we are—and all because of a little handful of evil ambitious men! Mother,—it is terrible that any men should have such evil power. I cannot help wishing they may suffer in their turn. But they can never suffer enough."

"They will suffer," said Mrs Dare quietly. "Since God is a just God. We may leave them to Him, dear,—and trust the outcome to Him too.... It is sad to think of our dear lad cut off so soon. But—I have thought much in the night, when I could not sleep for thinking of them all,—he is better so, Lois, than growing up like some we know. Oh, far better so."

"Yes, indeed, dear!"—It was good, she felt, for her mother to talk. She would have all the rest of her life for thinking.

"Your father was telling me, a night or two ago, how he came down in the train with young Nemmowe,—you know,—of 'The Hollies.' He had been drinking, but he was not drunk—only assertive. Someone in the carriage asked him when he was going to the front. And he chuckled and said, 'Not me! Not my line at all. I'm a man of peace. Besides we've got too much on. Can't spare me at this end.' They're big army contractors, you know, and are making a huge fortune out of the war, it is said. And the man who had asked him, said, 'If I was as young as you, and as strong as you, I'd sooner die out there ten times over than stop rotting here. If England came to grief you'd wring a profit out of it some way, I presume.' And the Nemmowe boy laughed and said, 'Shouldn't wonder if you'd like some of the pickings yourself.' And since then no one will pass a word with him. Better to be lying dead in French soil than like that, dear."

"Far, far better, Mother dear. It is well with our boys. But—oh, it is sad to have them go! And any day Ray may be with them," and she fell on her knees and laid her head in her mother's lap as she had done when a child.

"It is in God's hands," said her mother, gently stroking her hair. "But, thanks be to Him, our boys are proving themselves men."

CHAPTER XXXIII

HONOR walked quickly, with bent head to keep the sleet out of her eyes. She despised umbrellas and enjoyed braving the weather, when circumstances permitted her, as now, to wear a knitted toque and a rainproof. The bite of the sleet was in accord with her feelings. She would have liked to tramp against it for hours.

Noel gone! Gregor gone! It seemed incredible. Those two dear boys so full of bounding life and energy. Gone!—lying dead and cold under the French mud. She could not quite realise it yet. She felt numbed with the shock of it. Dead! Never to return to them! Never to see them in this life again! Oh, Gregor, Gregor!

But she must be brave, for, just across the Common there, was Gregor's mother in happy unconsciousness of the blow that had befallen them. Oh, it would hurt her. It would bruise her. It might break her. She, Honor, must be brave and strong and help her to bear it.

And as she breasted the wind, and the sleet bit at her face, her mind began to work again with acute clarity of understanding. It carried her above herself. She saw—as though scales had fallen from the eyes of her spirit—that this fearsome Death which seemed so dreadful was not the end but the beginning. Their boys were possibly—probably—nearer to them even than they had been in life. The dear bodies might be lying there in France, but all that had been really *them* was living still and might be—would be, she thought, watching them now, near at hand, nearer than ever before.

So full was her mind of the thought that she actually found herself glancing upwards into the sleety sky as if she might catch sight of them.

There was only gray sky and whirling sleet up there, but the belief was strong in her and she went on comforted.

The maid greeted her with her usual bright smile, and helped her off with her dripping coat. They all knew how things stood between Mr Gregor and her and cordially approved.

"Is Mrs MacLean down yet, Maggie?" she asked.

"Not yet, Miss Honor. She was feeling the cold, so she said she would have her breakfast in bed,"—as she showed her into the morning-room at the back, where a wood fire was burning brightly with cheerful hissings and spittings and puffs of smoke, and everything spoke of comfort and the quiet joy of life.

"Will you please ask her if I can see her at once, Maggie?"

"Yes, Miss Honor. Not bad news, I do hope, Miss," but she knew that it was, for Honor's face was tragic in spite of herself.

"Don't hint it, Maggie. Just tell her I must see her," and Maggie went quietly, as though she savoured the coming news already.

A table with newspapers and books and magazines was drawn up near the fire alongside Mrs MacLean's favourite chair. On it was a photograph of Gregor in his uniform, in a massive silver frame. He looked bravely out at her. Just his own dear look as she knew him best. Quiet, reserved, but with the smiles just below and ready to break through on smallest provocation.

And it was all over. He was gone,—lying under the blood-stained soil across there. No,—she was to remember—he was more alive than ever, nearer to them than ever,—but—ah me!—they would never see him again on this side.

She was still bending over the photograph when Maggie came in, with a quiet, "Will you please to come up, Miss Honor?"

She turned the handle of the bed-room door, with her eyes anxiously seeking the extent of the news in Honor's face. And Honor went into the room.

It was a full hour before she came out again. What had passed was between them and God. We may not trespass.

But her face had lost and gained in that hour inside with Gregor's mother, and her eyes were red with weeping.

Maggie had been dusting within earshot of that door ever since it closed. She came now to meet Honor, and they went into the morning-room together.

"Is he wounded, Miss Honor?" she asked anxiously.

"He is dead, Maggie,—" and there was a sob in her voice as she said it. "And my brother also. They died together," and Maggie burst into tears and nearly choked with the effort to do it quietly.

"Oh, Miss Honor!—Dead!—and him so fine and strong and only just got there! Oh, Miss!—And the mistress? Is she—will it—"

"I am going home now to get some things, and then I am coming back to stay with her for a time. She wishes it, and it will comfort her."

"And your poor mother too—"

"It is very terrible for us all, but worst of all for Mrs MacLean. He was all she had. We must all do what we can to comfort her. They died splendidly, one helping the other. And Ray says it was instantaneous and so they did not suffer. Tell the others, Maggie, and don't any of you give way— more than you can help—before Mrs MacLean."

"We'll do our best, Miss Honor, but it'll no be easy. It's too awful," and Honor passed out into the sleety morning.

Mrs Dare quite understood and fully approved. Her old friend's need was greater than her own. She gave Honor loving words for her right out of her heart, helped her to get ready the things she must take back with her, and promised to come over to see Mrs MacLean very shortly, when the freshness of their wounds should have had a little time to heal.

Mr Dare's grief was great when he came home that night to such news. But, like his wife, he had forecasted the possibility, and as they talked together of their boy, he said again, "Better so, dear, than growing up like some one knows—like that Nemmowe fellow for instance.... He did all he could and no man could do more."

"He would never have turned out like young Nemmowe," said Mrs Dare confidently.

"I don't believe he would, seeing that he was your boy."

Lois came over while they were still quietly talking of it all, and she brought with her a suggestion that made for their comfort all round.

In Honor's absence Mr and Mrs Dare would find The Red House very empty, whereas for want of room at Oakdene they had reluctantly been compelled to refuse several fresh patients lately. So Lois's idea was to transfer herself and Vic and Auntie Mitt, if she would come, to The Red House and so form a more complete family party there. They could then leave Oakdene entirely to their guests and the nursing staff, and could still do their own part in the way of providing and superintendence from next door.

"These trying times make one inclined to draw closer together," she urged, and it seemed to them good, and the matter was decided on.

Vic, usually so light-hearted and full of talk, had become the silent member of the household. She had suffered a sore wound, and it was the harder to bear because it was more or less of a hidden wound and not to be spoken of or sympathised with.

She went for days like a stricken thing, scarcely speaking to any of them and preferring solitude. Then Mrs Dare ventured on her privacy and got her to talk about Noel, and they cried together over their loss and both felt the better for it. And presently she and Mrs Dare went across to see Mrs MacLean and Honor, and in their efforts to cheer and comfort Gregor's mother they found some consolation themselves.

Mrs MacLean begged so anxiously to be allowed to keep Honor with her still that Mrs Dare could not find in her heart to say no. They were like mother and daughter, and Mrs MacLean's only hope for the future was that the relationship which might have been should be realised as nearly as possible—as though Honor and Gregor had been married before he went out.

"I have thought sometimes when I saw in the papers about young people getting married like that that it was not very wise," said the old lady. "But now I see it differently. It is the best thing to do, for it puts everything on a proper and legal footing. But, my dear, I know how very dear you were to him, and you are just as dear to me as if you had been married. Stay with me as long as you can put up with me. My heart would be very empty without you."

And Honor kissed her and promised to stay.

"You see, my dear," said the old lady, another time, to Honor's very great surprise, "I have no one very near to me in kin, and I know just what our boy would have wished me to do. That large blue letter that came this morning was from Mr Worrall, the solicitor to the firm, and it contained a copy of Gregor's will, which he had the good thought to make before he left. The bulk of his father's money came to me, of course, and would have passed on to him when my time came. God has willed that otherwise, but I can still do what I know would have pleased him—which I know will still please him if he is still concerned with us below here, as both you and I rejoice to believe. Mr Worrall tells me he left all he had to you, and it may be somewhere about twenty thousand pounds—"

"Oh—but—"

But the old lady's tremulous white hand constrained her to hear her out.

"And when I go, my dear, there is no one in the world he would have desired the rest—or most of it—to go to but yourself."

But Honor's head was down in the motherly lap and she was sobbing heart-brokenly.

"I know, my dear. Sooner himself than all the money in the world," and she stroked the shaking head tenderly. "But God saw differently, and He knows best. We will treasure our memories together, you and I.... Oh, my boy! my boy!" and the white head bowed upon the brown, and the great burden of their sorrow was easier for the sharing.

CHAPTER XXXIV

IT was on a bleak afternoon in the middle of January that the quiet little circle at The Red House was surprised by the sudden irruption of Alma in a state of intensest excitement.

She had come down at once when their sorrowful news about the boys reached her, but that had had to be a short visit as they were terribly busy at St Barnabas's and shorter-handed than ever.

"He's coming home. He's in England," and she showed them a telegram she had received an hour before, which said—

> "Just landed. Will go straight to Willstead. Hope find you all well. CON."

"It's from Folkestone and he may be here any time," she cried, radiant with hopeful excitement. "Isn't it delightful to see his own name again, even at the end of a telegram. The dear boy! He must be better or he couldn't have come. I wonder how he got released. Anyway it's splendid to have him back," and she looked at her watch every second minute to make the time go quicker.

"I wonder which house he will try first?" said Mrs Dare.

"We'll soon settle that," said Alma. "A sheet of paper, Lo, and a couple of drawing-pins!"—and she hauled out her fountain-pen and printed in big letters—"THIS WAY, CON!" and ran out in the rain and fixed it on The Red House gate-post, and opened the gate wide.

"He's bound to see that, coming from the station," she panted. "I'd go there and wait for him, but it's such a bitterly cold place and I'd hate for his first sight of me to be chiefly red nose and watery eyes. That wouldn't make for a cheerful welcome to the returned exile."

"He would sooner find you here, my dear. The Dares are never very effusive in public, and it has been a very trying time for you both," said Mrs

Dare quietly.

Never did minutes drag so slowly. They could none of them settle down even to soothing knitting, except Auntie Mitt, who went quietly on with a body-belt which was child's play that she could have done in her sleep.

"The trains are very much out of order, you know, with the passage of troops," said Mrs Dare, as Alma prowled restlessly about but turned up at the window at least once each minute.

"If he had wired from Boulogne I'd have been afraid of submarines or mines. But surely nothing could go wrong just between Folkestone and here! That would be too cruel."

"He'll be all right, Al," said Lois. "There's hardly been time for him to get here yet since he sent off the telegram. I wish Ray was coming too, but he says there is no chance of leave again for a good while yet."

"His news is good?"

"Wonderfully good. He seems to be living in mud and water all the time. It makes one shiver to think of it this weather. But he says he's keeping very well so far, in spite of it all."

"It's amazing to me how they stand it. One of our men was telling me — Here he is!"—as the peremptory hoot of a motor was heard in the road, and she dashed out just in time to see a long gray car, driven by a man in khaki, and bearing O.H.M.S. in big red letters on its wind-screen, sweep up the Oakdene drive.

It had come the other way, down the road, and so had missed the notice on the gate. She was just about to rush after it when it came scudding back down the drive, backed up the road towards the station, and then leaped forward, missed the gate-post by half an inch and came whirling up to the door, and she saw Con's face looking out from under the hood.

"Oh, my dear! How thankful I am to see you again!" she cried ecstatically, and wrenched open the door.

A lean-faced young man, with bright eyes and a quiet face, had got out at the other side and come quickly round to assist. He gave his arm to Con and helped him out, and Con put both his arms on Alma's shoulders and kissed her warmly again and again.

His face showed something of what he had gone through. It was thinner and older looking. There were none of the old laughter-creases in it. Instead—a soberness—almost sombreness—as of one still haunted by the shock of untellable things, and in his once-merry eyes memories of honors and a curious almost imperceptible sense of doubt and recoil. It was very slight, but Alma's eager eyes, as she took him all in at a glance, discerned it in a moment as something quite new in him.

And as his arms rested on her shoulders she was conscious of a strange lack in the feel of them. His hands should have clasped her to him. Her whole being should have leaped to the thrilling touch of them as their two beings came into contact once more.

But these things were lacking. His arms indeed lay on her shoulders, and it was good to feel them there again. He had not had time to take off his gloves, but one can clasp one's wife to one's heart even with gloves on, though it was not like Con to do so.

But there was something more than that,—something undefinable, something in the unresponsiveness of the arms on her shoulders akin to that other new something in him, of which her first quick glance had apprised her, and a throb of fear tapped at her heart.

Con lifted his arms from her shoulders and turned to the khaki-clad chauffeur.

"You'll have time for a cup of tea and a bite of something to eat before you go back?" he asked quietly, and the man saluted and intimated his readiness, and then Con and Alma went up to the others who stood waiting in the doorway.

He kissed his mother warmly, and Lois, and Vic, and Auntie Mitt, and introduced the lean-faced young man who was lagging quietly behind.

"This is my very good friend, Robert Grant. If it hadn't been for him I should never have seen any of you again." And they turned on Robert Grant and put him to confusion with the volume and warmth of their welcome, and then they all went on into the parlour.

Grant was for eliminating himself again, but they would not have it. Mrs Dare took him by the arm and led him in, murmuring her gratitude again for his care of their boy. Auntie Mitt went off to see the chauffeur properly provided for.

And when they were inside the room Con turned quietly and said, with a little break in his voice, which was deeper than they had known it, and that new strange look in his eyes, "It's good to be home again, but ... Alma dear, they've sent me back a cripple. They cut off my hands."

And if there had been some lurking fear, born of the long months of suffering and brooding, that that would make any difference in her love for him, it fled on the instant.

She understood it all in a moment,—his doubts as to the wisdom of their hasty marriage,—his fears for the future,—all the black clouds that had weighed on him during these bitter months of pain and exile.

But if there had been in him one smallest doubt as to her love for him, she scattered it and all the rest by the feel of her arms about his neck and the cry that came right out of her heart.

"Oh, my love! My love! You are dearer to me than ever. I thank God for His great goodness in giving you back to me!"

And Con, who had suffered more than most, both in mind and body, without wincing, though he could not hide the effects, hid his face on her breast and shook with sobs that he could not choke down.

Their faces all showed the shock and strain of the distressing news, except Robert Grant's. His shock had come five months before and he had had time to get over it.

"Tell them how it was, Bob," said Con, in a muffled voice, as he lifted himself again. "You know more about it than I do. And give me a cigarette before you begin."

Grant pulled out a cigarette-case and put a cigarette into his lips and lit it, and started on his story.

"Well, it was like this. We were up near Landrecies—in the retirement from Mons, you know,"—his north-country speech, with its sympathetic inflections and ringing r's, admitted him right into Mrs Dare's heart.—"It was bad times for our men and our hands were overfull, trying to pick up the wounded, for the Germans were rolling along after us ten to our one. It was said they were behaving very badly to any who fell into their hands. But, you must remember, things were moving so quickly that they really hadn't much time for anything but the fighting. It was life and death all round, and a man who went down was out of it and not of much account.

"We were at the corner of a wood and our men were fighting splendidly and seemed to be holding them for a bit. But casualties were very heavy and we could not pick them up fast enough. Then, on a sudden, there came a great rush of Germans in close formation. It was like a bore going up a river. They simply swept over our men and rolled them back, and we were left in a kind of backwater.

"Dr Dare told us to stick to business, and we went on with our work. Then an officer who was running past caught sight of us. I cannot say he knew what we were. There was great confusion. Anyway, he saw the Doctor's uniform and levelled a revolver at him and shouted in English, 'Hands up!' and we put our hands up above our heads.

"And just then, as evil luck would have it, a squadron of cavalry—hussars—came galloping round the wood to take our men in flank. And one of them, on our near side, as he passed behind us, just slashed at the Doctor's lifted hands with his sword, as he would have done at a turnip on a pole in the practice field. It was sheer devilment and without reason. And when he saw the Doctor's hands fall to the ground he turned up his face and laughed, and they all laughed. The wicked devils!—if you'll pardon me."

The faces of all his hearers were pale as they pictured the horror in their own minds.

"What utter fiends!" jerked Alma, white with anger at thought of the ruthless savagery of it.

"It is just the German war-spirit at its worst," said Con quietly. His lips had puckered on the cigarette as Grant told the story. But he had recovered himself. "The spirit of absolute selfishness and indifference to others. I really felt very little at the moment. Just the sharp cut, then a numbness, and I saw my hands lying on the ground. They looked awfully queer. I just remember thinking, 'Good God! Those are my hands!' Then everything began to go round and I fell. Proceed, Robert!"

"The officer who had actually caused the mischief by holding us up had been staring very hard at Dr Dare. When he saw what happened he went white in the face and swore hard in German at the hussars. Then he turned to me and said, in English, 'Bind him up quickly! Will he die?' I told him I did not know. But with another fellow's help I bound the Doctor's wrists very tightly to stop the bleeding, and put on tourniquets above each elbow and twisted them as tight as I could. Then he handed us over to a sergeant and half-a-dozen men,—there were eight of us altogether;—he gave him some very particular orders and then went on after the battle. The sergeant presently collared a stretcher and bearers, and marched us to the rear of their advance, and the numbers of men we saw there, pressing on to the pursuit, was an eye-opener. They seemed endless,—moving torrents of gray. I never saw so many men in my life. The sergeant found a doctor, and the doctor looked very grave over the matter. But he was clever. Dr Dare was coming round. He anæsthetised him and sent him off again and made a very good job of the wrists. If he'd been a bungler we would not be here. We were sent off to the rear and eventually into Germany."

"The man who held us up, and so was the real cause of the trouble, was Von Helse—" said Con.

"Ludwig?—Oh, Con!" gasped Lois, horrified.

"He was not to blame for the rest. In fact he was dreadfully cut up about it, and took to himself blame which did not really lie. He has done all he could to make amends. He got permission for me to keep Bob with me all the time, and most of the time we have been on parole at Frau von Helse's house in Leipsic, and she and Luise have done everything they could for me. And it is von Helse who arranged for our release;—how, I cannot imagine, but here we are and it's thanks to him. That's the whole story. As to what I've felt about it all—well, perhaps the less said the better. At first, the only thing I wanted was to die and have done with it all. The thought of going through life handless was too awful. But Bob here won me back to a braver mind. It's really due to him, in a dozen different ways, that I pulled through. And now—"

"We can never thank you properly, Mr Grant," said Alma, reaching for his hand and shaking it warmly in both hers.

"We'll do our best, however," said Mrs Dare, patting him on the shoulder in motherly fashion.

"He's been just absolutely everything to me," said Con, "and he's going to stop on with me and continue his good work. He was studying for a medical, you see, up in Edinburgh, so we get on fine together. But it would be a queer sort that couldn't get on with Bob Grant. He's a white man all through."

Robert Grant's lean cheek responded briefly to the genial warmth of the atmosphere which enveloped him.

"That is very good hearing, Mr Grant," said Mrs Dare heartily. "We could wish nothing better. It will be a joy to have you among us."

The maid came to the door with word that the chauffeur was ready to go.

"Give him half a sovereign, Bob, and my best thanks.—No, I'll thank him myself. He brought us up from Folkestone in fine style. He was driving a motor-bus before the war and he's having the time of his life now with no speed limit," and he and Grant went out together to start their jovial Jehu back to Folkestone in the highest of spirits.

CHAPTER XXXV

ALMA managed to make an exchange with one of the nurses at Oakdene, so that she herself could be with Con and be doing duty at the same time and yet not leave St Barnabas's any shorter-handed than it was.

It was a bit irregular, perhaps, but it was either that or giving up nursing altogether, which she had no wish to do till the war was over.

But be with Con, now that she had got him back from the dead, so to speak, she vowed she would, cost what it might.

"If anyone needs me it is my husband," she told Mrs Matron, "and I'm going to stick to him no matter who else suffers." At which the Matron smiled indulgently and arranged matters as she wished.

"It is dreadful for Dr Dare," she said. "And we must do all we can to help. I saw about it in the papers."

"He was very much put out about that. He can't imagine where they got hold of it."

"He's to have the D.S.O. too, I see. And I'm sure he deserves it. What is he going to do?"

"He's going on with his own work. Young Grant, who saved his life, and stuck to him all through, and brought him home, is just splendid. He's a medical, you know, though he hadn't quite finished his courses. He's to stop and be Con's hands, but I imagine his head will do good service as well. They did a certain amount of study while they were in Germany, to keep their minds off other matters, and they're setting to work again at once."

"That's fine—for both of them."

But before that week was out they had another surprise in a visit from Sir James Jamieson, the Harley Street brain-specialist.

He was a tall, white-haired man, with a forehead like the dome of St Paul's, only much whiter. He knew more about brains than any man in Great Britain, and, in spite of a life devoted to other people's aberrations, was of a most genial and jovial disposition, and of a very tender heart.

"Well?"—was his surprising greeting to Con. "When are you going to be ready to start work with me?"

And Con gazed at him in incredulous amazement, behind which sprang up and fluttered a wild incredible hope.

Sir James, he knew, loved a joke. But he was the last man in the world to spin a joke against a man left handless against the world.

"Do you mean it, sir?" gasped Con, shaken out of his natural politeness by so stupendous an instant levelling of all the barriers he had seen in front of him.

"Mean it, my dear boy?—of course I mean it. Do you suppose I've wasted precious hours coming down into the wilds of Willstead to say things I don't mean? I wanted you before and I want you more than ever now. Those miserable devils didn't chop off any of your brain, did they? Well, it's your good, sound, searching brain I want. We'll find hands for you all right. There is no lack of hands in the world, but brains are sadly lacking, I'm sorry to say, and what there are are not all what they might be."

He had talked on, like the perfect gentleman he was, to give Con time to recover himself.

And now Con looked at him with shining eyes,—eyes in which the light of a new great hope in life shone mistily through the excitation of his feelings, like stars shining up out of the sea,—and he said, "You make a new man of me, Sir James.... I feared ... and now—" and Sir James, being a Scotchman himself, understood better than all the words in the world could have told him.

"Now I want a cup of tea," said the great man jauntily, "and if the two Mrs Dares are available it would be a pleasure to me to make their acquaintance."

Con, without moving, touched a button under the carpet with his foot and Robert Grant, who had fixed it up for him only that morning, came in.

"This is my good friend, Robert Grant, Sir James," and the old man and the young one, in acknowledging the introduction, glanced keenly at one another for a moment and appeared mutually satisfied. "Would you beg my mother to join us, Robert, and tell them to send in tea at once. And then if you'd slip across and ask my wife to come over for a few minutes I'd be much obliged."

"Who's he?" asked Sir James, as Grant vanished.

"He saved my life out there and has been everything to me these last five months. He's a medical, and the best fellow alive. He's consented to be my hands."

"Good! I like the looks of him."

"He's better even than he looks and his brain is quite all right. He's one of the exceptions. We've drawn very close together these months out there. He's consented to stop with me, but he's got ambitions of his own—"

"Of course,—being a Scotchman."

"And I'm hoping that he won't really be sacrificing himself entirely by devoting himself to me. We did a certain amount of study out there and he's getting quite keen on the brain."

"We'll find him his place all right. Keen men are none too plentiful—especially on the brain."

Mrs Dare came in, and Alma a few minutes after her, and when they had been made to understand the wonderful news, while Sir James drank his tea, they were almost as much overcome as Con himself had been.

When they tried to express a little of what they felt about it, Sir James genially stopped them with, "You see, I want him. I don't know any other youngster whose ideas chime with my own as his do. And I like that Grant boy. And I like you two. I'm inclined to think we shall all get along uncommonly well together. You have lost a son out there, Mrs Dare."

"Our youngest. He was just nineteen."

"I saw about it. It is sad for us to lose them so young and in such a way. But the gain is all theirs when they die as your boy did, and we may not mourn unduly. My dear lad died in South Africa and in very much the same way—trying to save a friend. After all—it's a noble death to die. And you are nursing, my dear?"—to Alma.

"Wounded officers at Oakdene, next door. I was at St Barnabas's but I made an exchange. You see, I hadn't seen my husband since the morning we were married."

"Quite right! Your experience will at all events bring sympathy to his work."

"That's why I took up nursing, four years ago."

"Good girl! You're the right kind for a doctor's wife," and then he shook hands with them, patted Con on the shoulder and bade him get ready for the move into town, shook hands cordially also with Robert Grant and told him they would know one another better before long, and then hurried into his impatient motor and whirled away back to town.

"Now isn't that wonderful?" said Con, with a happier face than he had worn since Landrecies.

"He's splendid," said Alma. "I love him already."

"For your sake I am very thankful, my dear boy," said his mother. "God is very gracious to us. If He takes, He also gives, and His ways are very wonderful."

CHAPTER XXXVI

RAY LUARD was having the time of his life out there, in the sodden fields and soggy mud-holes which did duty for trenches in north-west France.—The time of his life, but not in most respects as the term is usually applied.

It was a perpetual amazement to him that anything human and non-amphibious could stand it. That boys, brought up to the comforts and amenities of life, could not only stand it but could and did maintain exceeding cheerfulness under it, provoked his profoundest admiration. And regarding himself aloofly, and from the outside as it were, he shared in his own amazement at his own share in it, and took no little credit to himself, for he certainly never would have believed himself capable of it.

But they all kept in mind, and constantly chuckled over, the vehement exhortation of a certain well-known General, who had inspected them shortly after that ghastly-glorious night at Messines.

"Keep your billets clean! Keep your bodies clean! Cock your bonnets! And, for God's sake, smile!"—was what he asked of them; and there had been no more-smiling faces or perkier fighters along that sorely-pressed Western front than the boys with the bare knees and swinging kilts since he said it.

They splashed and floundered along roads a foot deep in slime to get to their advance trenches, where the mud and water were at times up to their waists.

They sank and stuck bodily in affectionately glutinous mixtures which would not let them go till at times they paid toll of shoes and almost of the feet inside them.

For ten days at a time, on occasion, they never had their boots off—unless the mud took them by force,—nor their sodden clothes.

They were plastered with mud from head to foot. Their kilts, water-logged and frozen and tagged with mud, scored their bare legs. They ate in mud, they slept in mud. And when their off-time came, if they could find a

228

blanket to wrap round their muddy bodies before depositing them on a stony floor in the rear, they thanked God for it and accounted themselves rich, and slept like troopers.

Circumstances rendered full compliance with the vehement General's exhortations impossible, but what they could they did,—they cocked their bonnets, and for God's sake and their country's, they smiled.

It was the most wonderful and soul-bracing exhibition of the power of mind over matter that Ray Luard had ever seen, and he would not have missed his share in it for any money.

At times they had a few days' rest in the rear,—for the time being no longer actual targets for shells though an occasional one came closer than was necessary to their comfort, but the sound of the guns was never out of their ears, and at all times they were liable to sudden urgent summons to stiffen the front against unexpected assault.

It snowed, and it sleeted, and it rained and froze, and the trampled mud of the highways and byways got deeper and deeper and ever more tenacious in its grip on them.

At the rear they slept off their first dog-tiredness and had hot baths and an occasional impromptu concert. They ate and drank in peace and comparative comfort, and always, for God's sake and their country's, they smiled. And now and again,—impressive under such circumstances even to the most frivolous,—they had Church Parade and Communion. Then, rest-time over, away back to the water-logged trenches and all the stress and strain, and the ever-present chance of sudden death.

Ray's great time came about the end of January, when the Hodden-Grays were sent to hold some trenches in a brickfield, and they had barely taken possession when, in the early morning, the enemy made a dead set all along that portion of the line and succeeded in denting it in places. They had quietly sapped up close to the advance trench and mined it. They fired their mines, threw in smoky bombs, and in the confusion got in under cover of the smoke with the bayonet.

The Scots gave them a warm welcome, and there was some very pretty fighting in the dark, and many a fine deed done of which none but the doers and the done ever heard a word.

But, as it chanced, Ray's doings stood out somewhat prominently.

When he raced with his company into the brickfield, floundering all of them in the dark over piles of bricks and into shell-craters full of water, they found the late occupants of the trench holding a brick-kiln as a defensive work against the irrupting Huns who seemed all over the place.

A Sergeant was in charge and gave Ray hasty word of what had happened. Their officers were down, and the enemy's onrush had been so sudden and overwhelming that it had been impossible to bring in either them or the machine-gun which was on a small platform at this end of the trench.

Ray saw his obvious work. He mustered his men behind the kiln, ordered bayonets, explained in two words what was required of them, and then with a cheery, "Strike sure, boys!"—they were off, with a Scottish yell that told the Huns their time was up and their presence there no longer desired.

A volley as they ran, and then quick work with the bayonet, and they were at the trench and across it, and that section was momentarily cleared.

Hasty search with electric torches—the wounded, including two officers, picked up and sent back,—the machine-gun and ammunition-boxes lifted and carried to the kiln, and as supports for the enemy came piling up and massed in front for another assault, they raced back to cover to prepare his welcome.

Ray, strung to concert pitch, flung his orders sharply.

"Wounded, down under!—Take those other kilns some of you,—lie flat,—make cover with the bricks! Don't fire till they're at the trench. Some of you up here! The rest where you can, and lie low! Up with that Maxim, Mac, and build a bit of a screen! Hand up those boxes, there!"

They toiled desperately, piling up little heaps of bricks on top of the kiln, and on the ground bricks, clay, mud, anything for cover, and then they lay flat, with their eyes glued to the parapet of the trench beyond.

"Here they come! Now, boys, give them blazes!" and rapider fire than the Hodden-Grays had ever produced in their lives before poured point-blank into the solid dark masses in front.

They went down in heaps before the pitiless hail. The rest came floundering over them and went down in turn.

On top of the kiln, Ray, with Mac's good help, kept the Maxim going full blast. He pressed hard on the double button so that the trigger was held back out of the tumbler, and while Mac fed in the feed-belts for dear life, he slowly turned the muzzle from side to side so that the ceaseless stream of bullets met the stumbling line in front like a fiery fan. Nothing human could possibly stand so deadly a flailing. The floundering line yelled and cursed and withered away. That little fight was won.

Some of the boys, overstrung and mad with the blood-thirst, were for leaping out after them with the bayonet. But Ray sternly called them back.

They had won and he would take no risks.

Stretcher-bearers came hurrying up from the rear. The wounded were picked up and carried back, and Ray and Mac set the rest to work to strengthen their kiln-forts in case any further attempt should be made. Later, if the enemy's guns found them out they would have to take to their trench again, but, for the time being, fairly dry bricks were better than eighteen inches of mud and water.

Before dawn a field kitchen came up to the rear within reach, and they got hot coffee and bread and bully beef, and ate with the gusto of men who have fought a good fight and won.

As soon as they could distinguish anything in the glimmering light, they crept out to pick up any of their wounded who might have been overlooked in the mêlée. And then they turned their attention to their fallen foes.

They lay in heaps, piled two and three on top of one another,—grim enough by reason of their numbers but, shot mostly in the body, not so ghastly as if they had been ripped to fragments by shell-fire.

Ray and his trusty Sergeant were prowling about when they came on an officer, buried all but his head under a pile of bodies. His eyes, straining and bloodshot with impotent fury, showed still plenty of life and ill-feeling in him, however sore his wounding.

Ray called up a couple of bearers and they all set to work to free him from his lugubrious load, and all the while he scowled at them like a vicious dog and said no word of thanks.

As they lifted off the last body, and bent to raise him, he drew his hand out of the breast of his unbuttoned greatcoat, and, before they knew what he was at, let fly with a large automatic pistol full at Ray. One bullet took off the lobe of his ear, the rest went crashing into his left shoulder. Before the vicious wretch could do any more mischief, Sergeant Mac brained him with a rifle-butt and hissed as requiem, "Ye dirrrty snake!" and then turned his attention to Ray.

"I'll have to get back, Mac," he said quietly, and started off at a quick walk.

"Ye'll no!" and caught him as he reeled, and laid him gently on the stretcher.

"Look to things, Mac," as he felt suddenly very tired and inclined to sleep.

"Go quick, boys!" ordered Mac. "His shoulder's in rags and he'll bleed out unless you get him tied up."

One of them pulled out bandages and hastily padded and bound the ragged shoulder, and then they set off as fast as the broken ground would let them.

"During the night the enemy made a violent assault on our advanced trenches. It was repulsed with loss. Our positions are maintained,"—said the despatches.

CHAPTER 36

LOIS had had no letter from the front for four days, which was a day longer than the longest between-time for a long while now, and she was feeling somewhat anxious.

"But," she reassured herself, "delays must happen at times, and letters may even get lost. I have been wonderfully fortunate so far, and I will not be over-anxious or upset. If I have any belief at all in the efficacy of prayer I must keep my heart up and keep on hoping."

And she prayed as she had never prayed before, but found herself bewildered at times when she thought that millions of other women were praying just as earnestly for their own dear ones, and it was impossible that all those prayers should be answered by the safe return of those they prayed for. Women in millions were praying and men in thousands were falling. Still she would go on praying and hoping. For there was nothing else she could do.

She prayed straight for Ray's safe deliverance. She wondered at times if it were quite right to do so. But she went on praying for it, and as the days passed letterless spent much time upon her knees in great agony of mind, in spite of all her efforts after equanimity.

Why should he be spared when so many were taken? Yet, "Oh, deliver him from danger and send him back to me!" was the burden of her prayers, and at times she caught herself remonstrating with God against any smaller answer.

But by degrees she came to higher thought and sobbed, "I do not know what to ask for, Lord. Have him in Thy Care and do what is best for us."

And it was while she was on her knees so praying one day, that there came a hasty tap on her door, and her mother's voice—like the voice of an angel,—"Lois—a letter—from Ray," and she thanked God fervently and ran to open the door.

There was no mistaking the handwriting. She kissed it delightedly, tore it open, and savoured its news almost at a glance.

"He is wounded," she jerked, as she skimmed it rapidly for her mother's benefit. "Getting over it all right.... Will be sent home shortly ... may be out of

232

it for the rest of the war.... Oh, I can't help wishing he might! Surely we have done our share, Mother!"

"Thank God, he is safe!" said Mrs Dare fervently.

"Now suppose you come downstairs and tell us all about it. Auntie Mitt is in a fever to know, and Vic is like a ghost."

"I'll follow you in one minute, dear,"—and on her knees she read her precious letter carefully through once more, then bowed her head in gratitude for its good news, and ran downstairs like herself again.

"I am glad, my dear," said Auntie Mitt, with watery sparkles in her eyes, as Lois kissed her exuberantly, "—very glad indeed. Now we would like to hear all about it."

"Sorry to have missed a mail or two, as I know it will have made you anxious," Ray wrote, "but there was no help for it. We had a rather rough scrap with the Boches, the other night, and I got it at last in the arm,—the left fortunately, as you see. They attacked in force and we held them with the help of some brick-kilns and finally drove them off. One line in the papers, I expect,—if that!—but it was tolerably hot work. It was afterwards that I got my little jag. We were picking up wounded and came on an officer—a Prussian captain. He was under a pile of his own dead, and as we released him he pulled out an automatic and gave it me in the shoulder. Took off a bit of my ear also, but that's a trifle—"

"The horrid brute!" raged Lois.

"—He didn't get much satisfaction out of it, however,"—said the letter—"for Sergeant Mac who was with me picked up a rifle and brained him on the spot."

"Served him right!" said Lois, and then remembered that two minutes ago she was on her knees thanking God for Ray's safety. "It's horrible. It makes one blood-thirsty to think of it."

"It must be awful to be in it," said Mrs Dare. "No wonder they do dreadful things at times, when simply hearing of a treachery like this makes our blood boil because it happens to come so close home to us."

"It seems to me things are getting worse in war instead of better," said Auntie Mitt plaintively.

"—They got me to the dressing station and tied me up, and eventually sent me down on the ambulance train to Boulogne, where I now am,—being very nicely attended to and as comfortable as can be. It is heavenly to be clean again and between clean sheets. It is not easy to know how we stood the trenches so well;—now that I'm out of them the conditions seem perfectly horrible. And yet we lived—and 'for God's sake smiled!' They are saying that our stand that night saved a critical position. Several top-notties have called to congratulate me, and it's said both Mac and I are to have the V.C. You see, we were lucky enough to bring in quite a respectable bag of wounded from the trench,—and so if I come back with only one arm *and* the V.C., you'll have to try and put up with me as best you can."

"Won't I?" said Lois rapturously.

"—Don't think of coming out, dear. I know that would be your first thought—"

"Of course it was!"

"—Everything is being done for me excellently well, and as soon as I am fit again, and properly rested, I shall be sent over. Your minds may be quite easy on my account."

"Thank God, it is no worse!" said Mrs Dare fervently.
"Amen!" said Lois.

*   *   *   *   *

And there this brief glimpse into the home-side of the war-clouds may very well stop for the time being.

In this six short months, Life and Death have been busier among us all than ever before in the history of the world.

Old and young have lived mightily and died nobly. They have died like men and fallen like princes. Not one of the lives so freely given for The Great Idea has been wasted—not one. The life of the community at large, brought so closely into touch with death, has been quickened and raised to higher levels.

But the earth is full of mourning, for War is an evil evil thing, and its fiery trail is strewn with broken lives and broken hopes and broken hearts.

www.ingramcontent.com/pod-product-compliance
Lightning Source LLC
Chambersburg PA
CBHW011031260626
47153CB00019B/2892